Praise for Andrea Penrose's *USA Tod*…
Sloane Myster…

"Compelling . . . an intricately plotted mystery set in Regency England. Its complex story line and authentic historical details bring the early days of the Industrial Revolution vividly to life. Bound to fascinate readers of C. S. Harris and even fans of Victorian mysteries."
—*Library Journal* **STARRED REVIEW**

"A charming, action-packed mix of historical mystery and Regency romance." —***Kirkus Reviews***

"The author captures the Regency era's complexities in vivid settings, contrasting milieus, and a wealth of fascinating details . . . This thoughtful blend of derring-do and intellectual discussion should win Penrose new fans." —***Publishers Weekly***

"This book is very suspenseful and takes many turns, as the clues point first to one person, then another. Penrose is excellent at conveying the details of early nineteenth-century science and experiments with electricity. This was the era of Frankenstein, after all. The relationship between Wrexford and Charlotte is further developed in this book, and I am looking forward to seeing where it leads next."
—***Historical Novel Society***

"A masterfully plotted story that combines engaging protagonists with rich historical detail, international intrigue, and a touch of romance. . . . Another ingenious historical mystery from Andrea Penrose." —***Criminal Element***

"Thoroughly enjoyable . . . with sharp, engaging characters, rich period detail, and a compellingly twisty plot, Andrea Penrose delivers a winner . . . fans of C. S. Harris and Kate Ross will be rooting for Charlotte Sloane and the Earl of Wrexford. Devilishly good fun!"
—**Deanna Raybourn, *New York Times* bestselling author**

"Charlotte Sloane and the Earl of Wrexford are a perfect crime-solving duo as headstrong and intelligent sleuths bucking the conventions of society." —***RT Book Reviews***

"The relationship and banter between the two stars of this series is incredible. Readers will look forward to seeing Charlotte and Wrex again (and, hopefully, very soon)." —***Suspense Magazine***

Books by Andrea Penrose

The Diamond of London

The Wrexford and Sloane Mystery Series

Murder on Black Swan Lane

Murder at Half Moon Gate

Murder at Kensington Palace

Murder at Queen's Landing

Murder at the Royal Botanic Gardens

Murder at the Serpentine Bridge

Murder at the Merton Library

Murder at King's Crossing

MURDER *at the* MERTON LIBRARY

ANDREA PENROSE

www.kensingtonbooks.com

KENSINGTON BOOKS are published by
Kensington Publishing Corp.
900 Third Avenue
New York, NY 10022

All Kensington titles, imprints, and distributed lines are available at special quantity discounts for bulk purchases for sales promotion, premiums, fund-raising, educational, or institutional use.

This book is a work of fiction. Names, characters, businesses, organizations, places, events, and incidents either are the product of the author's imagination or are used fictitiously. Any resemblance to actual persons, living or dead, events, or locales is entirely coincidental.

To the extent that the image or images on the cover of this book depict a person or persons, such person or persons are merely models, and are not intended to portray any character or characters featured in the book.

Special book excerpts or customized printings can also be created to fit specific needs. For details, write or phone the office of the Kensington Sales Manager: Kensington Publishing Corp., 900 Third Avenue, New York, NY 10022. Attn. Sales Department. Phone: 1-800-221-2647.

ISBN: 978-1-4967-3995-7 (ebook)

ISBN: 978-1-4967-3994-0

First Kensington Hardcover Printing: October 2023
First Kensington Trade Paperback Printing: August 2024

10 9 8 7 6 5 4 3 2 1

Printed in the United States of America

For Dr. Patricia Gorman

Not everyone is lucky enough to have a brilliant PhD, professor of English, and lover of libraries as a sister-in-law.

PROLOGUE

Dust motes danced in the air, flickering like tiny sparks of fire as a blade of sunlight cut through the grisaille glass of the medieval window. The head librarian flinched, his eyes involuntarily squeezing shut as the harmless little flashes ignited the crackle of gunfire inside his head.

Smoke, screams, the glint of steel, the stench of blood . . .

Bile rose in his throat. Panting for breath, he shook his head, trying to clear his mind of the visceral horrors.

And then, mercifully, the episode passed, and the hammering of his heart softened to a steadier pulse. He raised a hand and traced his fingers along a row of books on the age-dark oak shelves of the study alcove in which he stood, the smooth calfskin and corded spines a calming caress against his flesh.

"It's peaceful here," whispered the librarian as he inhaled the parchment and leather scent of the Merton College Library. *An oasis of tranquility within Oxford University, a world away from the brutalities of the battlefields.* The wars were over, he reminded himself. Napoleon had been exiled to the island of Elba, and the ravaging armies no longer fomented death and destruction.

And yet . . .

And yet the horrors refused to retreat from his head. The army surgeons had told him it was a temporary trauma brought on by his body's struggle to recover from his grievous war wounds. They had said that the shock would soon fade.

But it hadn't.

Things had improved since he had arrived here and taken up the position of head librarian. However, over the last fortnight, one memory—a quieter one, but no less disturbing—had been coming back with increasing frequency.

He feared that it had been sparked by his recent conversations with a visiting researcher from the Continent—an erudite scholar who served as personal librarian to King Frederick of Württemberg.

Damn the fellow for wanting to discuss the Peninsular War.

Though he had not meant any harm, of course. Indeed, the two of them had formed a pleasant friendship over the past month. But the scholar's talk of military strategy and the disastrous British retreat that led to the Battle of Corunna had stirred old demons.

And now, the whisper of hazy words and a flickering image were becoming sharper, and more insistent. . . .

The sound of approaching steps drew the librarian back to the present.

"Mr. Greeley?" His assistant, a tall, gangly fellow with unruly chestnut hair, spoke softly. An observant young man, he had noticed that the librarian did not like loud noises. "The next batch of scientific books have arrived for us to sort through and catalogue for Mr. Williams."

Under the aegis of its head librarian, George Williams, the Radcliffe Library at Oxford had been reorganized into the university's main repository for scientific books and manuscripts. But the herculean task of collecting the requisite material from all the self-governing colleges that made up Oxford University—Merton was one of the oldest and most prestigious of them—was not finished, and Greeley had offered to help with cataloguing the collections.

"I've looked through them," added Greeley's assistant, shifting the small crate cradled in his arms. "It's a small consignment of rare old manuscripts from the library of Balliol College. I would be happy to stay late and finish it."

"Thank you, Mr. Quincy, but you've done more than your fair share today." The library was due to close in an hour, but Greeley welcomed the excuse to stay late, hoping that the task would help calm his unsettled mind. "I enjoy looking at old manuscripts. Give them to me."

Greeley took the crate from Quincy and headed to his private office, a small space crammed into the far corner of the West Wing. His desk, as usual, was in a state of cheerful disarray. It drew a rare smile as he took a seat and placed the crate on his blotter. *Scholarly ideas*—they were far more comfortable companions than people.

Wads of balled-up paper had been wedged around the manuscripts to keep them from shifting and damaging the fragile covers. He pulled them out and tossed them into a scrap pail—only to pause on recalling what he had discovered the previous week among the crumpled paper of another consignment.

Greeley glanced at the pile of documents on his desk, then reluctantly pulled a colorful print out from among them and unfolded it.

It was a commentary from several months ago by the infamous A. J. Quill, London's most popular satirical artist. Greeley paid little attention to current events, preferring to keep himself cloistered within the ivory tower of academia, but he was aware of the man's work and appreciated his clever drawings and scathing humor.

Everyone knew that the moniker was only a pen name, and speculation as to A. J. Quill's real identity was a parlor game throughout the beau monde. *Senior government official, high-ranking military officer, a titan of the Bank of England or the East India Company*—given all the intimate information that A. J. Quill knew, the assumption was that he had to be someone within the highest echelons of power.

A man who knew how to ferret out every secret in London, no matter how well hidden.

Greeley studied the print for a moment longer, then made himself push it away, feeling a little foolish for letting it upset him. It meant nothing. The earlier recurrence of the disturbing memory had put him on edge, that was all.

Opening the ledger that came with the crate, Greeley drew in a calming breath and began the meticulous task of cataloguing the manuscripts.

He worked in peaceful contemplation as the familiar sounds of the library quieted after the closing hour. But then, without warning, the bedeviling memory once again exploded inside his head. And all of a sudden, a long-ago moment—two men huddled together, their whispers teasing through the night breeze—flickered free of the muddled haze. The words were no longer just an amorphous buzz. They sharpened to a startling clarity.

Oh, surely not.

And yet, as he shot a glance at the print he had put aside, a chill ran through him, as if cold steel had kissed up against his spine.

What if the scene that I am remembering is true?

He sat for a moment longer, the question bedeviling him, and then rose abruptly.

Several hours later, after studying the recent newspapers in the reading room and doing some research in the West Wing's archives, he had uncovered enough unsettling information to send him rushing back to his office to dash off a letter. A glance at his pocket watch showed that there was still time to hand it off to the late-night Royal Mail coach heading to London.

After returning to the library, he resumed his work. Shadows flitted over the books and papers on his desk. A breeze tickled against the ancient leaded window. Looking up, he released a sigh. "Perhaps I have let my imagination run wild." At the moment, evil seemed very far away.

Still, as Greeley put down his pen and shuffled through the hastily scribbled notes he had made concerning his suspicions, he was glad he had sent the letter. *Truth—I must know the truth*. And if anyone was capable of discerning truth from lies, it was the man to whom he had sent the letter.

He paused and once again picked up the print by A. J. Quill, the candlelight flickering over the colors as he re-read the captions. *Damnation*. He folded it up and shoved it back into the jumbled pile of papers on his desk, willing himself to put the matter aside for now.

But on suddenly recalling another book in the West Wing that might help confirm his hunches, he got to his feet. The challenge of fitting the pieces of a puzzle together—especially this one—had his blood thrumming. Taking up the glass-globed candle on his desk, he went to fetch it.

As he retraced his steps, a flutter of light caught his eye. It was coming from his office.

Moving quietly, Greeley crossed the corridor and slipped into the room. A man was riffling through the crate of rare manuscripts. A grunt of satisfaction sounded as he grabbed one of them—

"Stop!" commanded Greeley.

The intruder whirled around.

No—this cannot be. Greeley blinked. And then blinked again. "Y-You!"

"Yes, me." A smile. "How nice to see you, Neville. It's been what . . . six years?"

Greeley didn't reply. He had forgotten how the man's slate-dark eyes always seemed to hold a touch of malice.

"What are you doing here?" he demanded. "And why are you stealing—"

"Oh, my dear Neville, you completely misunderstand my intentions," interjected Slate Eyes. "I learned earlier today that this manuscript had been delivered to you, and I am merely borrowing it for a bit." He sighed. "I would have asked, of course, but I have heard that you are so easily distressed these days."

A smile, sheened with an oily gleam in the flickering candlelight, touched his lips as he held up the manuscript. "Be assured it will be used for the Higher Good—and I know how much you value such altruistic ideals."

Dropping his voice, Slate Eyes added, "But a caveat—for now it's best to be hush-hush about your loan of it to me. It needs to remain a secret for reasons too complex to explain. But as I said, it's all for the good." A pause. "And of course, I will pay you handsomely for your discretion."

"How dare you suggest such a thing!" retorted Greeley. "My silence—and my honor—isn't for sale."

"Honor? Oh, yes—one of your precious principles." Slate Eyes gave a mocking smile. "Only look where they have gotten you."

That sneer. It was then, in a flash of recognition, that Greeley knew for sure his suspicions were correct. And he suddenly realized how Slate Eyes was the key to how the pieces of a horribly perfidious puzzle from the past fit together.

"Go to the devil! Whatever you have planned, I am sure it is nothing good." He grabbed the manuscript from Slate Eyes and put it back on his desk. "Evil," he whispered. "You reek of evil."

"Good heavens, I—" Slate Eyes assumed a look of injured innocence. "I have no idea what you mean by that."

"No?" Greeley then said a name.

Slate-Eyes contrived to look even more baffled. "I'm afraid

you're not making sense." A pause, and then he made a sympathetic *tsk-tsk* sound. "But then, I've heard that you are troubled by demons."

"I remember now . . . I smelled a rat back then," said Greeley slowly. "And the odor is growing even more foul as we speak."

"What are you insinuating?" Slate Eyes shifted. "If I'm being accused of some scurrilous deed, it seems only fair that I have a chance to defend myself."

"How dare you speak of fairness?" Greeley clenched his jaw, the other man's look of amusement sparking an unholy rush of anger. "You wish to have it spelled out? Very well—here's exactly what I think . . ."

It all came out in a rush. The past, and how it connected with the present.

A moment of silence hovered between them once Greeley finished his lengthy exposition. And then came a mournful sigh.

"My dear Neville, I fear your terrible wartime experiences have confused your wits." Slate Eyes closed his hand around Greeley's arm with surprising force. "Come now, sit down and calm yourself."

The unexpected move threw Greeley off balance. A shove forced him to fall back into his chair. He looked up—the slate eyes were now a reptilian black—and realized that he had made a terrible mistake.

Steel flashed, but he was an instant too late in seeing the deadly strike coming.

The knife cut through wool and linen, angling upward to slice between two ribs and lodge its point deep in Greeley's heart.

A whoosh of breath, a spurt of blood . . .

And then a sepulchral silence.

"A pity you made me do that. But I couldn't risk having you

repeat what you just said to anyone else." After calmly cleaning his blade, Slate Eyes picked up the manuscript and tucked it inside his coat.

Two quick breaths blew out the candle flame as well as his own lantern. Slate Eyes watched the plumes of smoke curl upward, ghostly pale against the ancient oak ceiling, before turning and slipping away into the darkness.

CHAPTER 1

A rumbled roar shattered the night, as if the deepest pit of Hell was tearing free from the underworld. Flames shot up, red-gold against the black velvet sky, and in the next instant a section of the building's roof collapsed in a cacophony of splintering wood and brick. A joist snapped, throwing up a shower of sparks that shimmered with a terrifying beauty as they floated back to earth.

So delicate. And so deadly . . .

Charlotte, Countess of Wrexford—though hardly a soul on earth would recognize her dressed as she was in rags rather than fancy silks—winced as a bank of windows exploded in a blinding flash of light. The blast forced her back into the shadows of an alleyway bordering Cockpit Yard, a cluster of brick buildings just south of the Foundling Hospital in Bloomsbury.

Shouts collided with screams as the onlookers shied away from the conflagration. A wagon filled with sloshing buckets rumbled past her, its wheels bouncing over the cobblestones. Slipping and sliding over the smoking debris, the band of men pulling at the ropes managed another few steps and stopped to heave a wave of water over the flames before retreating for another load.

Gasping for air, Charlotte swiped a hand over her face, adding another layer of gritty soot to her brow. She had received word just an hour ago about the fire and had immediately resolved to see it for herself after changing into her second—or was it third?—skin. *Raggle-taggle urchin... high-and-mighty countess... London's most popular satirical artist....*

She turned her gaze from the shadows, forcing herself to focus on her reason for being here. Working under the *nom de plume* A. J. Quill, she kept the public informed of the current scandals, politics, and serious social issues of the day with her colorful satirical drawings.

Fires ravaged through London every day. But this was no ordinary one. The burning building housed the laboratory of—

A flicker of movement caught Charlotte's eye. A group of men with wet rags wrapped around the lower part of their faces was fast approaching the flames. A *whoosh* of smoke suddenly knocked the hat off one of the leaders, revealing a flash of guinea-gold hair.

Her breath caught for an instant in her throat.

Ye gods—why is Kit here?

Christopher Sheffield had been her husband's closest friend since their days at Oxford, and Charlotte had formed an equally strong bond with him over the course of a half dozen dangerous investigations.

A friendship forged by fire, thought Charlotte with a wry smile.

Sheffield suddenly looked her way. He hesitated for just a heartbeat as she moved in the shadows. Smoke hazed the air, but he had seen her enough times dressed as a ragged urchin to recognize her silhouette. A subtle gesture—a tiny flick of his hand—acknowledged her presence, and then he kept moving. Glass crunched underfoot as the men rushed for the far end of the building, which had not yet burst into flames, and hurriedly kicked their way through the side door.

Hell's teeth—are there poor souls trapped inside?

Fear rose in her throat as she watched them disappear into the black maw. Charlotte spun around and darted out of her refuge, intent on edging around to where Sheffield and his companions had disappeared. The thunder of snapping timbers and crashing walls was growing louder—the very air crackled with warning.

Damnation, Kit—it's too dangerous to be caught within such a raging inferno.

The smoke thickened, slowing her steps. She paused to pick out a path through the swirling embers and started forward—

Only to be stopped short by the clatter of iron-shod hooves on stone and the screech of another water wagon skidding around the corner of the street.

Drawing a steadying breath, Charlotte retreated and chose a more roundabout route that skirted the worst of the falling debris and frantic flailings to douse the flames. In the past she might have ignored the blatant danger, but her recent marriage had brought not only profound joy but a heightened awareness of her responsibilities to her loved ones. Not that she would ever give up her passions—

She ducked low and took cover in the opening of an alleyway as a jumble of crisscrossing lantern beams swept over the yard.

"Oiy! Oiy! Move off, ye little gutter rats," bellowed a group of night watchmen, trying to make themselves heard above all the noise and confusion. Waving their truncheons, they began to herd back the street urchins who had crowded the cobbled carriageway to gawk at the fire.

Charlotte crept into the shadows snaking along the edge of the carriageway and under the cover of darkness stealthily made her way to the far end of the building.

A conventional wife I am not, she thought, pausing to make a swift assessment of the surroundings. A fact that on occasion drove her husband to distraction.

Her lips twitched. *So be it*. Wrexford might not always agree with her passions, but she knew that he admired them, heart and soul. Which was why, despite the outward differences—reason versus intuition—they made a perfect pair.

For an instant, Charlotte wished that Wrexford was here by her side. If Sheffield—

A shuddering *crack* pulled her thoughts back down to earth.

She moved closer to the smashed doors. Framed by the splintered moldings and creaking hinges, the opening seemed to glower with menace through the ghostly flutters of smoke. It was black as Hades. . . .

Charlotte thought she saw a tiny flicker of light, but it was gone in an instant.

Hell's bells. Sheffield was family—perhaps not in a traditional sense, but in every way that mattered. Be damned with the dangers—she couldn't simply walk away.

She was about to start forward when the light winked again, then grew stronger. As the wind gusted, setting off a chorus of moans through the buckling roof slates, she squinted through the clouds of choking vapor and whirling ash. A jumble of dark-on-dark shapes materialized into a group of men, tripping and stumbling as they wrestled with a load of crates.

Craning her neck, Charlotte spotted a gleam of golden hair. "Thank God," she whispered.

Harried shouts broke out to her right. Tongues of red-gold fire suddenly licked up from a gap in the outer wall.

"Make way, Make way!" A bucket brigade trundled closer, and a wave of water doused the threat.

She retreated to the alleyways just as Sheffield and his companions stumbled free of the building and started across the carriageway with their loads.

"More water!" cried the man next to Sheffield, waving desperately at the fire wagons. "If we work fast, I think we can keep the blaze from spreading to this part of the building."

Charlotte recognized him despite the whirling light and shadows—it was Henry Maudslay, the brilliant inventor whose engineering wizardry had made him famous throughout Britain's scientific community.

And these days, his name was becoming more familiar to the public—thanks to her series of drawings on Progress.

Maudslay set down the crate he was carrying and rushed off to help the bucket brigade. The others followed his lead.

Save for Sheffield, who hesitated and glanced around the yard.

Keeping well back in the shadows, Charlotte let out a low whistle.

He walked across the cobbles to her side of the yard and turned, as if intent on assessing the scope of the damage. "There's no reason for you to linger. All that's left to do is get the remaining flames under control," he said, just loud enough for her to hear. "Go home. I'll join you there as soon as possible and explain what I know about what's happened here."

"Oiy," acknowledged Charlotte, then added, "Be careful," before slipping off into the gloom. Sheffield was right. She had seen what she needed to see for any potential artwork. There was nothing left for her to do. . . .

Save to wonder whether it was merely an unfortunate accident that Henry Maudslay's new research laboratory was going up in smoke.

"Here I go out for a quiet evening of scholarly discussion over port and brandy, and . . ." Expelling a martyred sigh, the

Earl of Wrexford cast a baleful look at Charlotte, who despite having changed into more conventional attire still had a streak of soot on her face and ashes in her hair.

"And all hell breaks loose," he finished as Sheffield entered the earl's workroom.

Tactfully ignoring her husband's grumbling, Charlotte hurried to help their friend out of his sodden overcoat. She gave it a shake, sending up an acrid fug of burnt wool and stale smoke, then draped it over one of the work stools.

"Shall I pour you a whisky or a brandy?" she asked, offering Sheffield a wet cloth soaked in lavender-scented hot water.

He took it and gave her a grateful look before wiping the filth from his face. "I'm happy to quaff anything as long as it's liquid," he mumbled through cracked lips. The bright lamplight showed that his face was raw and red from the heat of the fire.

As their friend brushed a tangle of hair off his brow, Wrexford saw it was singed in several spots.

"Sit down, Kit," said the earl, reaching out to steady Sheffield's stumble. After settling him in one of the armchairs by the hearth, he added, "You look like bloody hell."

Charlotte hurried to bring Sheffield a glass.

A good choice, noted Wrexford. Scottish malt was stronger than French brandy.

"How did you know about the fire?" she asked.

Sheffield closed his eyes for an instant and took a long swallow of the amber spirits before replying. "One of our clerks was drinking with friends at a nearby tavern when it started." Sheffield and his fiancée, Lady Cordelia Mansfield, were partners in a very profitable shipping company—secretly, of course, as the strictures of the ton didn't permit aristocrats to sully their hands in trade. "He sent word to me right away, knowing of my interest in Maudslay's work."

Wrexford frowned. Maudslay's expertise in engineering didn't seem to align with the practical demands of moving goods from here to there as swiftly as possible.

"What, precisely, is your interest?" he asked.

Henry Maudslay was famous throughout the scientific world for creating innovative lathes that had greatly improved both the speed and accuracy of mass-producing interchangeable parts for steam engines, looms, and a myriad of other important mechanical devices. It might sound mundane to most people, mused the earl, but in truth it was revolutionizing a great many industries.

"He's been working on a special project involving an innovative new design for a steam engine," replied Sheffield.

Wrexford was still puzzled. "What does that have to do with your business?"

Sheffield pressed his fingertips to his temples. "A great deal, actually. He's working on a radical idea that would revolutionize the transportation of goods and people around the globe—a *marine* propulsion system utilizing a steam engine."

The answer took Wrexford aback. "But that's hardly new or revolutionary. Lord Stanhope, a talented man of science despite his other eccentricities, was tinkering with steam-powered boats at the end of the last century. And I seem to recall that a Scottish engineer launched a commercial steamboat—I believe it was called *Charlotte Dundas*—in 1803. To my knowledge, it's proved very successful in hauling barges along the canals of Scotland."

"And the American, Robert Fulton, launched the first successful river steamboat seven years ago in New York City," offered Charlotte. "Granted, the Americans appear to be far more advanced in their marine steam engine technology than we are, but I also remember hearing of another steamboat innovation in Scotland. Henry Bell launched the *PS Comet* two years ago, and it's been running regular passenger service on the River Clyde—"

"Maudslay's marine propulsion system isn't meant for canals and rivers," said their friend.

Charlotte blinked in surprise. "You mean it's for . . ."

"For crossing oceans," confirmed Sheffield.

"That would be revolutionary, indeed." Wrexford did some quick mental calculations. "The size, the weight, the amount of fuel needed for such a long journey . . ." He pursed his lips. "Surely the practical limitations make such a dream impossible . . ."

Sheffield coughed, which made him wince. "New technological ideas always seem impossible—until someone figures out a way to do them."

"Fair enough," conceded the earl.

"As you pointed out, we have boats powered by steam, but the current technology isn't capable of conquering the rigors of ocean travel," continued Sheffield. "So there is, in effect, a great race going on to see who will figure out a way to overcome the challenges—and the winner will possess unfathomable power."

He tapped his fingertips together, his expression turning very solemn. "Think about it. The ramifications are profound—economically, politically, militarily—so it's no surprise that a number of groups are working on developing a successful model. It's not just the steam engine that needs redesigning. The current mode of propulsion is paddle wheels, and they simply can't stand up to the storms and waves of the oceans."

"What's the alternative?" asked Wrexford.

Sheffield made a face. "If I knew the answer to that, I would be a *very* rich man."

He let out a long breath. "The competition is fierce. First and foremost are the Americans, who have the most experience and expertise in marine engines and propulsion systems. Cordelia and I have heard from our business agent in New York that there are several steamboat companies competing with each other to come up with a viable oceangoing ship."

"I would imagine that our government, which believes that our powerful navy and our trade with the East are the lifeblood of our nation, is also engaged in the race," said Wrexford.

"That would make sense," mused Charlotte. "Though I vaguely recall hearing a talk given by some of the Royal Navy's top engineers . . ." She frowned in thought. "And the fact that while they expect great innovations to be made in nautical technology, they feel that those discoveries still lie over the horizon."

"The Royal Navy is not the only entity in Britain working on the challenge," replied Sheffield. "Eight months ago, a consortium led by the Earl of Taviot announced its involvement in marine propulsion. Word is they have a leading luminary in the field as their technical director, a fellow who has been working for some years in America with the leading steamboat designers."

He paused to take a long sip of his whisky. "In addition, Taviot and his partners are beginning to approach some very prominent names about investing in their company. Money is key, as innovation doesn't come cheaply."

"Given his genius for innovation and his experience in engineering, surely Maudslay holds the advantage in this country," said Wrexford.

"Tonight's fire is a huge setback. A number of his precision lathes and milling machines were damaged by the extreme heat. Given how long it will take to retool them, he might fall too far behind the others to catch up." Sheffield frowned. "Maudslay had, in fact, been talking to me about investing in his project. But of late, he has been expressing some reservations about the prospect of success. He is quite sure someone will come up with a theoretical design that works. However, he worries that at this point in time we simply don't have the capability to fabricate the sophisticated machinery needed to make an actual working model."

Sheffield ran a hand through his disheveled hair. "That said, Maudslay seemed upset at not finding his latest set of technical drawings with the crates we salvaged. He was quite sure that he had placed them in that section of the laboratory, which wasn't touched by the flames."

"Paper is awfully fragile," pointed out Charlotte. "An errant spark might have blown in and set them ablaze."

"Perhaps," said their friend. But his expression remained troubled.

Wrexford said nothing.

"In any case, it's likely there are others at work on the challenge," mused Sheffield after a lengthy silence. "I've heard rumors that Tsar Alexander of Russia is desperate to become a naval power and expand his ability to establish trade routes around the world."

"The Russians have only one major port on the island of Kotlin, just west of St. Petersburg," said Charlotte. "It seems wishful thinking for them to aspire to be a naval power, especially as the Baltic Sea has such unpredictable weather."

"All the more reason for wanting oceangoing steamships. It's said that the tsar has offered Robert Fulton a monopoly on all commercial river routes in Russia if he will come to St. Petersburg and develop steamboat technology," growled Sheffield.

Charlotte frowned in thought.

"But that said, you are right," he added. "I don't see the Russians being a factor in the race. My money is on the Americans."

Wrexford noted that his friend's voice had taken on a brittle edge.

"In their country a man is free—indeed, he is encouraged—to develop his skills and talents, unconstrained by the strictures of social standing. While we remain in thrall to traditions of the past and forbid our aristocracy to take advantage of a changing world and profit from building the future. It makes absolutely no sense!"

"I couldn't agree more, Kit—" began Wrexford.

Sheffield was too agitated to pay him any attention. His voice rose as he forged on. "The Industrial Revolution has created so many innovations, which in turn have opened up so many new business opportunities. New companies are starting up all over the country. Investment opportunities abound. And a new type of men is emerging to take advantage of it all. The French have a word for them—*entrepreneurs*, deriving from *entreprendre*, which means *to undertake*. We need to have that spirit here in Britain."

"You've made yourself into that sort of man, Kit. And it's something of which you should be very proud," pointed out Wrexford. "An entrepreneur, whose aspirations to start up a business and investment acumen are a perfect example of what you have described."

"Yes, but I'm still so bloody limited in what I can do. I must hide the fact that I'm involved in running a business and pretend to be naught but an indolent wastrel. It's . . ." He muttered an oath. "It's damnably frustrating."

"I sympathize with your sentiments," responded Charlotte.

"Ye gods, I'm very aware that intelligent and capable women like you and Cordelia must feel even more angry." Sheffield fixed her with an apologetic grimace. "The rules that corset what you can and cannot do are impossibly restrictive." A sigh. "It makes no sense to assume that half the populace are naught but featherbrained widgeons."

"Perhaps with intellectuals like Mary Wollstonecraft writing manifestos about the rights of women, their arguments will eventually bring about change," she replied. "But I won't hold my breath waiting for it to happen."

Wrexford leaned back in his chair. "It's true. If we don't alter our attitudes, we shall find ourselves left in the dust by progressive-thinking countries like America."

"As I said, the world is changing." Sheffield drank the rest of his whisky in one swallow. "And by God, we had better change with it."

The earl rose and moved to the sideboard. "Let me pour you another drink."

Sheffield waved him off. "Steam engines may be forged out of iron, but I am made of flesh and bone." A grunt. "Every particle of which is aching like the devil right now. So I think I shall bid you goodnight and toddle off to my bed."

"Let us summon the carriage for you, Kit," said Charlotte.

"No, no." He waved off the offer. "It's only a short walk to my lodgings, and I need some fresh air to clear my lungs."

Wrexford walked with him to the front door and then, lost in thought, slowly made his way back to Charlotte.

"Why the black face?" he asked as she looked up from straightening the books on his desk. "Aside from the smudges of soot on your chin."

She forced a smile, but her gaze remained troubled. "I'm not quite sure." A hesitation. "It's just that . . . I had a bad feeling about the fire from the moment I set foot in Cockpit Yard."

"Are you speaking from facts?" he asked. "Or intuition?"

The two of them had often argued over whether reason should overrule emotion. They still disagreed—often sharply—but Wrexford had come to respect her belief that logic didn't always have an answer for the complexities of human nature.

"Let's just say that I sensed an unseen specter of Trouble lurking in the shadows. And I fear that we haven't seen the last of it."

* * *

Taking the steps of the back stairwell two at a time, Raven—the older of the two former street urchins who were now officially the wards of Charlotte and Wrexford—reached the top landing and headed for the schoolroom, where his brother Hawk and their friend Peregrine were waiting.

"I think m'lady and Wrex are hiding something from us," he announced, after quietly shutting the door.

The large iron-grey hound who lay sprawled on the rug beside the two boys pricked up his ears and let out a low *woof.*

"What?" asked Hawk, Raven's younger brother.

"Dunno," muttered Raven as he placed a book on one of the desks and joined them on the floor. "M'lady told me the fire was nothing to fret about when she returned home . . ."

It was Raven who had learned about the blaze while visiting with one of his urchin friends who swept a street corner near Cockpit Yard. He had quickly brought the news back to Berkeley Square, but Charlotte had forbidden him to come along with her when she went to see it for herself.

"But from what I heard just now, I have a feeling that something havey-cavey might be afoot." Raven scowled. "She's trying to protect us from the sordid things in life," he went on. "As if we haven't seen the worst of human nature."

He and his younger brother had once been homeless orphans, fending for themselves in the squalid stews of London. But after a chance encounter with Charlotte, she had taken them under her wing.

"Oiy," agreed Hawk. "She and Wrex ought to know that we've no intention of turning into proper little aristocrats." As for their first meeting with Wrexford, it hadn't gone well—he had dubbed them the Weasels because Raven had stabbed him in the leg and Hawk had thrown a broken bottle at his head. He had long since forgiven them because they had thought he was threatening Charlotte. But to everyone's amusement, the moniker had stuck. It was now a source of mirth and, for the Weasels, a badge of honor.

"By the by, how do you know there's trouble lurking?" inquired Hawk. "Were you eavesdropping?"

"No . . . not precisely," answered Raven. "As I was looking for a certain book on mathematics in Wrex's library, I couldn't help but overhear Mr. Sheffield mention something suspicious about the fire."

"Why does this particular fire concern m'lady and Lord Wrexford?" asked their friend Peregrine—or rather, Lord Lampson. Raven and Hawk had taken the orphaned heir under their wing when Wrexford and Charlotte had been drawn into a harrowing murder investigation involving Peregrine's uncle and a devastating family betrayal.

Their bond forged—quite literally—by fire, the three boys had become the best of friends, and with things fraught among his own relatives, Peregrine had become an honorary member of their family, a situation that suited everyone. He was spending the month of August with them before it was time for him to return to his schooling at Eton.

"Because," answered Raven, "the building that burned down was Henry Maudslay's laboratory."

"Maudslay?" Peregrine's eyes widened. "The brilliant inventor and engineer?"

"Oiy. Mr. Sheffield found it odd that some technical drawings seemed to have disappeared from a part of the building that was untouched by the fire. And we all know . . ." Raven made a sympathetic sound before continuing. "We all know that inventors can be a tempting target because of jealousy or greed."

Peregrine's late uncle, who had specialized in designing advanced mechanical devices, had been murdered by someone who wished to steal his revolutionary innovation and sell it for a fortune.

Hawk gave a solemn nod and glanced at Peregrine before responding.

"So what are we going to do about it?"

"I think," answered Raven, "that tomorrow night we should do a little sleuthing on our own around Cockpit Yard and see whether we can discover any helpful information."

CHAPTER 2

Despite the long night, Charlotte awoke early, only to find that Wrexford had already risen. Perhaps he, too, had been plagued by unsettling dreams.

She dressed in a rush, unsure why a feeling of misgiving still plagued her thoughts. The fire, however unfortunate, didn't spark a reason for A. J. Quill to bring it to the attention of the public. As for the so-called race to discover an oceangoing marine propulsion system, she didn't know nearly enough about the subject to make an informed commentary.

Not yet. She had already done a series of prints on steam engines and their momentous effect on society. But if this new development was as revolutionary as Sheffield had implied, perhaps it merited a closer look.

The ambrosial scent of fresh-brewed coffee drew her to the breakfast room. Wrexford wasn't there, so after pouring herself a cup, Charlotte headed to the rear of their townhouse.

She paused in the doorway of his main workroom. He was sitting at his desk, head bent, his face half in shadow. She guessed that he hadn't heard the whisper of her slippers in the corridor, for he didn't look up.

Charlotte took a moment to study his profile. Even hazed in the half-light of early morning, she could recognize all the little subtle shades of his expression, all the tiny fissures and angles of his face that had become so inexpressibly dear to her. . . .

"What's wrong?" she asked softly. "Have you learned something more about the fire?"

"No, no." He gave a wry grimace. "I doubt Kit will rouse himself from sleep until suppertime."

Yet there was an undertone of agitation in his voice that stirred a frisson of alarm. "Then what's troubling you?"

"I'm not entirely sure," confessed Wrexford, still staring at his desktop.

Spotting what looked to be a letter lying on the blotter, Charlotte moved to his chair and placed a hand on his shoulder. "Would you care to explain?"

In answer he handed her the single sheet of paper. "This arrived in the early morning post."

It was a short missive, written in a neat hand and punctuated with a looping signature. "*Lord Wrexford, I beg you to come visit me in Oxford at your earliest convenience*," she read aloud. "*I have something of the utmost importance that I wish to discuss with you—and given its momentous significance, I dare not commit it to paper.*"

Charlotte looked up. "Who is Neville Greeley?"

"A fellow I knew only slightly at Oxford, when we were both students at Merton College, and later encountered briefly in Portugal during the war."

He paused, but Charlotte refrained from asking the obvious question. She sensed there was something more complicated lurking beneath the earl's simple explanation. And so she waited, leaving it up to him to decide whether to tell her what it was.

"However, he was—" Wrexford looked away, but not before Charlotte saw a darkness ripple beneath his lashes. "—my brother's closest friend."

Ah.

Her heart clenched in sympathy. The earl's younger brother, Thomas, had been killed during a reconnaissance mission in Portugal when his cavalry detachment had been caught in an ambush set up by the French. The two of them had been very close, and she knew that Wrexford, however unreasonably, blamed himself for not being able to keep Thomas safe.

"In fact," added the earl, "Greeley was part of the detachment that rode into the French ambush. He was badly wounded but survived—the only man who did so, I might add." Wrexford paused to draw a breath. "However, from what I've heard, he's never fully recovered from the horrors of seeing his comrades slaughtered."

"How awful." She pulled over a chair so she could sit beside him.

"I helped arrange—privately, of course—for him to be appointed head librarian of the Merton College Library. He was an excellent scholar at Oxford, and I've been hoping the tranquility of the academic world would help quiet his inner demons."

Charlotte leaned in to feather a kiss to his cheek.

"Poor fellow. He's had a dauntingly difficult path to tread." Wrexford took her hand and pressed it to his lips. "And here I am—a lucky devil blessed with all the good fortune in life that a man could wish for." A sigh. "Though I've done nothing to deserve it."

She said nothing. *We both know that Life is unfair* would sound like a platitude, which both of them despised.

They sat in companionable silence, and Charlotte knew her husband well enough to sense that her closeness was providing more solace than any words could give.

"I feel beholden to go see him, of course," he finally said. "As soon as possible."

"Of course," she agreed. "Let us summon Tyler."

"He's probably still sleeping. One would think *he* is the indolent aristocrat, not me."

"Ha! I heard that." The earl's valet, who also served as his laboratory assistant, stepped out of the adjoining storage area with a load of freshly polished glass beakers cradled in his arms. "Most men would take that to mean that their services weren't properly appreciated."

"But not you, Tyler," said Charlotte. "You know quite well that Wrexford couldn't survive without you."

The earl made a rude noise.

"True," said the valet. "Who else would put up with having to remove all sorts of noxious chemical stains from his clothing?"

"Speaking of clothing," she added, "His Lordship needs a travel case packed for a visit to Oxford."

Tyler came instantly alert. "Do you wish for me to accompany you?" The valet was also an excellent sleuth and had played a part in their previous investigations.

"That really isn't necessary," replied Wrexford. "It's a social call, nothing more."

"Oh?" said Tyler, his brows tweaking up. "Since when have you become sociable?"

Repressing a smile, Charlotte quickly rose and gathered her skirts. Theirs was, admittedly, an exceedingly eccentric household. "Come, the sooner we pack, the sooner Wrex— "

She stopped abruptly. "Drat—I just recalled that as a favor to the hostess, I accepted an invitation for us to attend Lord and Lady Marquand's soiree tomorrow evening in honor of the visiting diplomatic delegation from Saxe-Coburg and Gotha."

But her expression suddenly brightened. "However, it is of no matter. Kit and Cordelia are also invited. I shall go along with them so as not to disappoint Her Ladyship."

Wrexford, she noted, looked a little relieved. He didn't enjoy the superficial swirl of Polite Society.

"You are sure?" he asked.

"Quite sure," answered Charlotte. To Tyler, she added, "Let us make haste. If Wrex catches the next Royal Mail coach, he can be in Oxford by early evening."

"Back so soon, milord?" The head porter came out of his lodge in the gatehouse to greet Wrexford as he passed from the street into the entrance archway of Merton College.

The earl smiled. He and Charlotte had lodged at the college during the recent gala banquet and award ceremonies held for the visiting monarchs of Europe. "So it would seem."

"Perhaps you have come to realize that the life of an academic is an idyllic one." The porter added a mournful sigh. "You were a brilliant student during your days as an undergraduate here at Merton, sir. A pity that is no longer an option for you."

Dons of the college were not permitted to be married. The male camaraderie of High Table, with its nightly ritual of elegant dinners and fine wines, was considered the only relationship that really mattered in life.

"Despite the undeniable charms of Merton, I'm not regretting my choice," replied the earl.

The porter looked unconvinced. "The Warden has been saying that as one of the leading luminaries of the scientific world in Britain, you would have added great luster to our beloved college had you not . . ."

"Been caught in the parson's mousetrap?" finished the earl.

A sniff. "Your words, not mine, milord."

"Are you married, Jenkins?"

The porter's eyes widened in horror. "Heaven forfend."

"Yes, well, aside from the fact that our views on the pleasures of matrimony differ, I would find monastic academic life far too quiet for my temperament."

Wrexford looked around at the ancient-as-Methuselah stone buildings and caught the glimmers of colored light flickering off the magnificent stained-glass window gracing the chapel. The college had stood in scholarly splendor since 1264, when Walter de Merton, chancellor of England and later bishop of Rochester, had first established a self-governing "house of scholars" on this hallowed spot.

Though part of Oxford University, Merton, like all the individual colleges, administered its own affairs, led by its Warden, the titular head of the college. Merton's high outer walls now surrounded a cluster of courtyards and gardens that had grown over the centuries, creating an oasis of tranquility.

A world unto itself.

An important one, reflected the earl. *But I prefer the messy chaos of the real world, where ideas collide and ignite controversy, sparking frightening new ideas that knock old traditions arse over tea kettle—*

"Oh, aye, milord." The porter's gravelly voice interrupted his thoughts. "We all know your penchant for solving murders." A brusque cough. "I imagine that's why you're here."

Wrenched from his reveries, it took the earl an instant to react. "What the devil do you mean?" As far as he could recall, the only thing to suffer a violent death within these hallowed walls was the hope of getting the students to spend their hours studying instead of drinking and wenching.

"Terrible it was, sir. So much blood." Jenkins made a pained face. "Some of it spattered on several valuable books."

The mention of books stirred a sharp foreboding. "Who was the victim?" he demanded.

"Our head librarian, Mr. Greeley," answered the porter. "The poor fellow was—"

But Wrexford was already rushing across the sloping stones of the main courtyard and heading for the archway that led to Mob Quadrangle.

CHAPTER 3

The wheels of the carriage clattered to a halt in front of a handsome stone building on Bond Street. Raven threw open the door and scrambled out, with Hawk and Peregrine right on his heels.

"Mind your manners," called Charlotte as she and McClellan climbed down to the pavement.

The stalwart Scot—a plain-faced woman with greying hair and perceptive eyes—served as Charlotte's personal maid. But she was far more than that. Trusted confidante, occasional sleuth, firm-handed taskmaster of the Weasels, baker of ambrosial ginger biscuits—McClellan was, in a word, the glue that helped bind their household together.

"And remember, no hijinks," added Charlotte. The boys had recently begun taking fencing lessons at Angelo's Academy and were being taught by the illustrious Harry Angelo himself. The famous fencing master had confided to Wrexford that he much preferred teaching such clever pupils rather than his usual clientele of overfed aristocrats.

"Peregrine is far too well-behaved to make any mischief. But let us pray that the Weasels don't think it a funny jest to prick some starchy lord in the arse with their blades," said McClellan after watching the boys race helter-pelter through the front door.

"That's *not* amusing, Mac." Though in fact it was. Charlotte began to imagine a drawing of half-clad aristocrats fleeing in terror from a sword-wielding imp . . . then reluctantly forced her attention back to the long list of errands in her hand.

"Lud, we have a lot of shopping to do. There are a myriad things that Peregrine needs for the upcoming school term."

They started walking.

"A half dozen new shirts, several books on Roman history from Hatchards, a cricket bat," intoned Charlotte as she read over the items. "By the by, where do you think we should look for—" She turned, just in time to see McClellan's eyes widen and the color drain from her face.

"Mac!" Charlotte stopped short for an instant, then rushed forward as the maid staggered and slumped against the storefront two doors down from Angelo's Academy.

"Sorry, sorry!" McClellan steadied herself and gave an apologetic grimace. "I—I don't know what came over me. I felt a sudden rush of—of nausea." The maid drew a shuddering breath. "I must have eaten a bad kipper for breakfast."

Charlotte gave a hurried look up and down the street but saw only the backs of three gentlemen walking leisurely toward Conduit Street. "Don't move. I'll summon a hackney so we may return home—"

"No, please! I'm perfectly fine now . . ."

To Charlotte's eyes, McClellan still looked awfully green around the gills.

"As you said, we have a great deal to do, so we ought not lollygag," added the maid.

"Good heavens, don't be ridiculous—"

"Please! Let us not make a mountain out of a molehill. I'm quite recovered now and prefer to continue with our errands."

Something in the maid's voice made Charlotte swallow her

objections. "Very well. If you are sure, we'll go on to Hatchards." The bookstore was quite close. "From there, we'll decide how to proceed."

On reaching the shop, Charlotte insisted that McClellan sit quietly in one of the reading nooks while she and the head clerk moved through the bookshelves collecting the titles on her list. The task done, she sent the fellow to find a hackney before rejoining the maid.

"Come, we are returning to Berkeley Square," announced Charlotte in a voice that brooked no argument.

McClellan rose—a little unsteadily—and followed without a word. The short ride home also passed in silence. It wasn't until the two of them were settled in one of the parlors and a pot of strong tea had been served that Charlotte spoke again.

"Mac . . ." She put her cup down untasted. "Now that a touch of color has finally returned to your face, why don't you tell me what's *really* wrong."

Cutting across the historic swath of grass—Mob Quadrangle was the oldest university courtyard in all of Britain—Wrexford approached the small group of silver-haired gentlemen in academic robes who were milling around the entrance to the library. Up close, their expressions were just as black as the somber-colored wool.

"Milord!" The Reverend Mr. Peter Vaughan, who was the Warden of Merton College, looked around in surprise. "Good heavens, the body was just discovered several hours ago. H-How did you know—"

"I didn't," Wrexford cut in. "Greeley sent a note asking me to pay him a visit. I left London early this morning."

"You must have pushed hard to make such good time," commented the rector, a big, beefy man whose ruddy complexion hinted at an overfondness for port. As part of his official college duties, he served as an advisor to the Warden.

The earl ignored the remark. Until he knew more about the crime, he had no intention of revealing anything about the contents of Greeley's missive and why he had chosen to come so quickly.

"Well, I'm very grateful that you are here, sir." The Warden blew out his cheeks. "What a terrible tragedy. Greeley was well respected by all who worked with him. I—I can't imagine what provoked such a heinous crime."

Another shaky sigh. "The murder at Magdalen College last month, and now this . . ." The Warden swallowed hard. "Ye heavens, do you think there is some madman on the loose with a grudge against academics?"

Wrexford had investigated the Magdalen murder for the government but wasn't at liberty to reveal the details. "I think it best for me to have a look at the body before we let our imaginations run wild."

"Yes, quite right, milord." The Warden cleared his throat. "Greeley—that is, his mortal remains—are in his office, which is—"

"I do know where the librarian's office is," said Wrexford as he took a step toward the door. "Unlike many students, I actually read a great many of the books in our collections during my time here."

The Warden and his group of advisors hastily shuffled aside, allowing him to throw it open and enter the Lower Library.

Without pausing, he headed to the narrow stairs and took them two at a time to the Upper Library, which held the bulk of the library's treasures. The librarian's office lay to the right, down the South Wing's central walkway. Sunlight flooded through the lovely oriel window at its end, filling the small foyer that connected the two wings with an ethereal light.

But as soon as he made the turn into the West Wing, Wrexford found himself shrouded in shadows. *A fitting metaphor*, he reflected, *of the task that lay ahead.*

The door to the librarian's office was closed. He lifted the latch and stepped inside.

Greeley's corpse was still in the chair but had been covered with a sheet of white linen. A young man with a shock of unruly hair was kneeling beside the body, gently smoothing the rumples from the length of cloth lying over the outstretched legs. He looked up at the earl, his eyes pooled with sorrow.

"M-Mr. Greeley was a very nice man," he stammered. "Why would anyone want to hurt him?"

"A good question."

The young man blinked in confusion as he took in the earl's elegant clothing and polished boots. "The mortuary men have been summoned. B-But you can't be . . ."

"No. I'm an old friend." Wrexford glanced at the desk, hoping that the scene hadn't been disturbed. "And you are?"

"Robert Quincy, sir. Mr. Greeley's assistant." Quincy's look of sorrow pinched to one of guilt. "If only I hadn't left him alone last night—"

"Don't torture yourself with recriminations, Mr. Quincy." The earl took a moment to survey the rest of the small office. It was crammed with books and papers, messy perhaps, but with an underlying sense of order. Nothing seemed amiss. "As of yet, we have no idea why Greeley was murdered. Rather than sink into self-loathing, help me ascertain whether there are any clues that might shed light on what happened here last night."

To his credit, Quincy rose and squared his shoulders. "Yes, sir." A pause. "H-How do we start?"

"By you telling me what time you left Greeley here."

"It was an hour before closing time, sir. I offered to remain and finish cataloguing a crate of manuscripts for the Radcliffe Library, but he said that he wished to do it himself."

"Was there a reason?" asked the earl.

"I—I didn't ask."

"There is no reason that you would," said Wrexford gruffly.

"But in a murder investigation, it's always best never to ignore any clue." His attention returned to Greeley's desk. "Tell me, did you shift or remove anything—anything at all? And it is imperative to be absolutely honest. The slightest detail might prove vital."

"No, sir, I did not," answered Quincy without hesitation. He swallowed hard. "Y-You sound as if you have done this before."

"Alas, yes," muttered Wrexford. Clasping his hands behind his back, he leaned in to make a closer scrutiny. "You must have been in and out of here frequently, and so are familiar with Greeley's habits. Does anything look odd to you, or is anything missing?"

Quincy approached and, mimicking the earl, he clasped his hands behind his back before beginning his scrutiny.

Wrexford liked that the young man was taking his time to look carefully before answering.

"None of Mr. Greeley's things are gone," said the young man. His brows furrowed. "But . . ."

"But what?" urged the earl.

"I'm not certain, but it looks like one of the manuscripts might be missing from the crate." Quincy leaned closer. "Mr. Greeley is—I mean, he was—meticulous about making sure nothing went astray when we were moving materials back and forth between the colleges and the Radcliffe Library, so I was careful to count them."

"When did you give him the crate?"

"A little before four o'clock."

So, likely that was before Greeley wrote the urgent note requesting a meeting, decided Wrexford. *Otherwise, it would have been posted with an earlier Royal Mail coach.*

"Would you like me to check through them, sir?" asked Quincy.

Wrexford nodded.

The young man made quick work of the task. "Yes, there is definitely one missing. In fact, I remember it quite clearly because its cover was an interesting shade of burgundy, rather than mud brown."

"Can you tell me the title?" Wrexford asked.

Quincy made a face. "I'm afraid not, sir. As you can see, most of these ancient manuscripts are bound in plain leather, with no titles stamped on them."

The earl muttered an oath. Knowing the specifics might be meaningless, but it was at least some sort of clue.

"However," added Quincy, "if I take the crate back to the Balliol College Library, and cross-check the contents with one of the librarians, I should be able to get you an answer."

"Off you go then." Wrexford heard the bump and shuffle of the mortuary men entering the building, punctuated by the Warden's pleas not to damage the library's ancient woodwork. He wished to have a look at the body without anyone else present.

As Quincy hurried away, the earl closed the door and returned to the shrouded corpse. Taking hold of the linen, he eased it down and let it fall over the dead man's lap. After gently closing Greeley's unseeing eyes, he crouched down for a closer look at the man's bloody chest.

"Sorry, my friend," he murmured, then took up the pen knife and enlarged the tear in the librarian's shirt so that he could subject the wound to a thorough scrutiny.

It was harder than most people thought to stab someone in the heart. But after wiping away the blood with the tail end of the shroud, Wrexford was able to probe around enough to discern that the mortal knife thrust had cut upward between two ribs, perfectly angled to strike the heart. Which meant, he reflected, that the killer had been extraordinarily lucky . . .

Or had experience in wielding a lethal blade.

He frowned in thought. The fact that Greeley was seated and

there was no sign of a struggle seemed to indicate that the librarian had known his attacker. So, the first line of inquiry must be whether the poor fellow had any enemies in town.

Sitting back on his haunches, Wrexford absently cleaned his fingers. "However, if it's a personal grudge, why is the manuscript missing?" he whispered. Before he could formulate an answer, the door latch rattled and clicked open.

The earl rose and pulled the shroud back in place just as the lead mortuary man stuck his head into the room. He was a big, brawny fellow and clearly the one in charge.

"It's a bloody wonder that there's a single book left in the rest of England," muttered the mortuary man on regarding the overstuffed shelves. "And why would anyone voluntarily read them?" Shrugging off the thought, the fellow returned to a more familiar subject and assessed the shrouded corpse with a professional eye.

"Hmmph. At least it looks like the first stiffness of death has passed and we'll be able te get the corpse on our plank wivout doing too much damage."

The Warden, who along with the rector had followed the mortuary men to the office, turned pale as a ghost.

Anxious to get rid of the college officials so that he could search the office without their hovering, Wrexford forced a solicitous smile. "Reverend Vaughan, you and the rector have suffered quite a shock. There's really nothing you can do here, so why don't you retire to your lodge for a restorative sherry while I take care of managing what needs to be done."

"I . . ." The Warden pulled a silk handkerchief from his pocket and blotted his brow. "I would be most grateful, milord." Inclining a small bow, he and his companion retreated and disappeared around the corner.

The earl lost no time in moving to help the mortuary man and his assistant maneuver their plank into the cramped office and clear a space for it on the floor.

"Carefully, if you please," he said as they moved to the chair and took hold of the librarian's corpse. That all humanity was eventually reduced to a lifeless jumble of flesh and bones was a fact Wrexford accepted with scientific detachment. However, watching his foully murdered friend being lifted like a sack of stones stirred a sudden wave of sadness.

His hands clenched as the body thumped down against the well-worn wooden plank, and in that instant Wrexford made a silent pledge to Greeley to find the killer and bring him to justice.

Working with practiced skill, the two mortuary men roped the corpse in place for the descent down the narrow stairs.

"I realize it's a change in the usual routine," said the earl as the men finished the last knots. "However, I wish for the body to be taken to London rather than the local mortuary." He took a leather purse from his pocket and gave it a shake, setting off the sonorous chink of gold against gold. "I will make it very worth your while . . ."

An agreement was quickly negotiated.

Wrexford picked up a pen from the dead man's desk and wrote out the directions to the lodgings of his good friend Basil Henning, a former military surgeon who was part of his and Charlotte's inner circle. Baz would no doubt grouse about having another uninvited body show up on his mortuary slab. But his expertise in the infinite varieties of violent death had proved instrumental in solving a number of other puzzling murders.

"A pleasure doing business with you," said the mortuary man as Wrexford handed him the note.

He and his assistant then hefted their load and moved with surprising grace through the doorway. The footsteps faded as soon as they turned the corner into the South Wing. Wrexford decided to leave the door slightly ajar in case Quincy returned and turned back to the desk.

Where to start?

A jumble of ledgers peeked out from beneath the helter-pelter piles of books and periodicals. Frowning in frustration, Wrexford grabbed the papers lying on the edge of the blotter and began to skim through them. Given their position on the desk, they appeared to be whatever Greeley had been writing when interrupted by his killer. And yet they made no sense—*cryptic half sentences, strings of seemingly random numbers, odd little doodles in the margins. . . .*

"Bloody hell." Wrexford looked around and spotted a document case wedged between two stacks of books. He gathered up the rest of the sheets and stuffed them inside it. Charlotte always noticed things that escaped his own eyes. Perhaps she could help decipher what Greeley had been thinking.

Turning his attention to the desk drawers, he opened the top one and commenced a methodical search—

"Stop at once!" A bespectacled gentleman dressed in a dark frock coat and buff-colored breeches pushed the door all the way open. "What are you doing in here, sir?" Behind the round lenses, his eyes were narrowed in suspicion. "This is Mr. Greeley's private office, and I was told that nobody was permitted to enter it before the local magistrate arrived to take charge."

So, word of Greeley's murder had spread.

Wrexford shoved the drawer closed and opened the one below it. He wasn't in the mood to argue with some stiff-rumped university administrator. "Consider me a higher authority."

The gentleman appeared confused. "Is not 'magistrate' a high authority here in England?"

"It is," agreed Wrexford. The gentleman spoke flawless English, so at first he hadn't noticed the slight but now unmistakable Germanic accent. Rather than try to explain his sarcastic comment to a foreigner, he merely said, "However, I'm here at the personal behest of the Reverend Mr. Vaughan, Warden of Merton College, to investigate the crime."

The Warden's name elicited a grim smile. "For the sake of justice—which the good soul of Mr. Greeley richly deserves—I am glad to hear that the Reverend decided to take what I told him seriously."

Wrexford went very still. "What do you mean?"

"I mean, sir, that he seemed hesitant to believe me when I told him what I had seen and heard last night."

"You were here in the library last night?"

"Yes."

"At what time?" pressed Wrexford.

A guilty flush colored the gentleman's cheekbones. "After working all day in the archives downstairs, I left for supper. But I suddenly had an idea on where to look for several books that might confirm a surmise I had for the historical paper I am writing." He made a wry face. "I'm afraid that we scholars sometimes find ourselves caught up in the passions of the hunt . . ."

Wrexford had spent too many late nights hunkered over his microscope to disagree. "So you returned."

"I did," answered the gentleman. "Mr. Greeley had said that I was welcome to work at night if he was staying late. I saw the light in his window . . . and found the side door of the West Wing open."

His mouth thinned for an instant. "I fetched my candle lantern from the Lower Library archives—I had permission from Greeley to possess a light for nighttime study—and came up to the South Wing, which contained the items I wished to consult."

Permission to carry a flame was not given lightly, reflected the earl. An errant spark among all the dry-as-tinder paper and vellum was a librarian's worst fear. Which meant that the gentleman was someone Greeley considered trustworthy . . .

"Go on," said Wrexford, deciding not to press the gentleman for his identity just yet.

"After arriving, I worked for perhaps an hour, and then had a question for Mr. Greeley. I left my lantern in the stall—the moonlight coming through the windows was enough to illuminate the way—and made my way to his office. But as I approached, I heard raised voices coming from within. Mr. Greeley sounded agitated—"

"Did you perchance get a look at the person who was with him?" interrupted the earl.

The gentleman shook his head. "The door was shut, and I did not think it my place to intrude on a private altercation. However, I—I couldn't help but hear what Mr. Greeley was saying before I withdrew."

A pause. "It was a name. As I told you, he seemed upset and angry—"

"Bloody hell, just tell me the name!" demanded the earl, his patience dangerously close to snapping.

Startled, the gentleman flinched. "W-Wrexford," he stammered. "Greeley was shouting about someone called Wrexford."

CHAPTER 4

"I would rather not," replied McClellan. "Tell you, that is."

Charlotte waited, giving the maid time to compose her thoughts. But no further explanation was forthcoming.

Outside in the entrance hall, she heard the noisy clatter of the boys returning from their fencing lesson. *Hoots of laughter, good-natured chatter*—the sounds of everyday friendship in play. While a sidelong glance at McClellan showed her features—always stoic to begin with—now looked as if they had been chiseled out of Highland granite.

"Why?" she finally asked.

In answer came a loud slurp of tea.

Sitting back in her chair, Charlotte folded her hands in her lap and drew in a measured breath. The refusal hurt, but she tried not to show it. She had thought their bond of trust went far deeper than a mere casual friendship between mistress and servant.

Have I somehow assumed the airs and graces of a pompous aristocrat and Mac no longer trusts my moral compass?

The thought made Charlotte's stomach churn. "I'm grateful

that you at least felt I merited an honest reply," she said, striving for a light note, "rather than being fobbed off with a tarradiddle about rotten fish."

McClellan's expression turned even more stony, though for an instant a hint of emotion seemed to ripple beneath her lashes.

Unable to bear another moment of the stilted silence, Charlotte rose and forced a brittle smile. "Well, I had better go and have a word with the boys. I need to tell Peregrine that I've purchased his books for school and remind Raven that Cordelia is coming this afternoon for his mathematics lesson."

"And I should head to the sewing room," replied the maid as she began gathering up the tea things. "I should check that Nancy is making the necessary repairs to several of Peregrine's jackets so they will be ready for him to take to Eton."

Mac withdrawing, Peregrine leaving . . . it felt to Charlotte like her close-knit family was suddenly unraveling before her very eyes.

Tears prickled against her lids. And for a mutinous moment, her thoughts strayed back to her old life, where the fears were at least simpler . . .

Charlotte stopped short in the corridor, shadows flitting around her as if trying to swallow her in darkness. Squeezing her eyes shut, she summoned up a flash of images—*Wrexford's smile, Hawk's gap-toothed grin, Raven's fierce scowl of concentration as he puzzled out a mathematical problem.*

"As if I would *ever* want my life to be any different," she whispered, and then to her infinite relief began to feel her heart swell with light and love. "Family, friends . . ."

Ashamed of her mental whinging, Charlotte headed for the stairs, determined to set aside her worries over McClellan, at least for now. She and Wrexford had solved far more daunting conundrums. They would do the same with this one.

A sigh slipped from her lips. Though she couldn't help hoping that the earl would deal with Greeley's problem swiftly and return from Oxford soon to help smooth the waters here at home.

"Wrexford," repeated the earl.

"Yes, I'm quite sure of the name," said the gentleman without hesitation. "Greeley said it several times."

"Bloody, *bloody* hell."

"Do you know him?" Eyes suddenly widening, the gentleman let out a gasp. "*Ach du lieber*—are you thinking that he may be the killer? Shouldn't we summon the authorities to—"

"*I* am Wrexford," growled the earl. Seeing the other man shrink back, he hastily added, "And no, I didn't kill Greeley."

Which raised the question . . .

He rose abruptly. "Who the devil are you? And why shouldn't I consider *you* a suspect, since you've just admitted to sneaking back into the library late at night?"

To the gentleman's credit, he stiffened, looking more affronted than frightened. "I, sir, am a respected scholar, not a cutthroat barbarian who would foully take the life of a worthy man like Neville Greeley." He blinked, and belatedly added, "As for my identity, I am Ernst von Münch, librarian to King Frederick of Württemberg."

Wrexford raised his brows. "You work for Fickle Freddie? That's hardly a mark in your favor."

Von Münch maintained a dignified silence.

The earl felt a grudging respect for the librarian's reticence. King Frederick was a highly controversial fellow. A larger-than-life monarch—quite literally, as he stood nearly seven feet tall and had a prodigious girth that made him the butt of satirical drawings—he was loathed by a great many people for the self-serving switching of alliances he had made during the Napoleonic Wars. For a time he had sided with the French, despite his close ties to the British royal family.

"I take it that your king came to London to help celebrate

the centennial of his father-in-law's family serving as the rulers of Britain," he continued. After the death of his first wife, King Frederick had married King George III's eldest daughter, Charlotte, and his first wife's sister was Caroline of Brunswick, the Prince Regent's estranged wife.

"Yes," replied von Münch tersely. "I have accompanied King Frederick to England, but not as part of his entourage for the celebrations. I'm here to do research at Oxford and Cambridge." He glanced at the bookshelves, his expression softening. "I am a historian as well as a librarian, and as part of my official duties I am writing a detailed history of King Frederick's life and ties to the British monarchy."

"It will require a very clever pen to cast your subject in a favorable light," drawled the earl.

Von Münch finally allowed a twitch of his lips. "It is the victorious who usually get to write history, so yes, I understand that I may feel compelled to use some artistic license."

A pause. "Allow me to say that I rebuffed the attempts of King Frederick to hire me until he ended his alliance with Napoleon and switched sides to join with Britain and its allies. I have no love for tyrannical despots."

Wrexford was liking the librarian even more. But he quickly turned his thoughts back to the murder.

"Our political philosophies align, Herr von Münch. However, at the moment, I'm more interested in solving a crime than meditating on abstract ideals," he replied. "Think hard—can you recall any other detail about Greeley and his routine, no matter how small, that might help shed light on why he was killed?"

The librarian's brow furrowed in thought, and Wrexford moved to the leaded glass window so as not to distract him. Down below in the courtyard, the shadows were beginning to deepen with the hues of twilight. Robes flapping like the wings of a raven—a traditional harbinger of ill omen—the Warden was hurrying across the grass toward the library's main entrance, accompanied by a dour-looking man who was likely the local magistrate.

"I'm sorry, milord, but most of my time was spent in solitary study," responded von Münch.

Wrexford turned. But before he could reply, the sound of footsteps came to life in the corridor.

"Wrexford!" The Warden paused in the doorway, looking flustered. "The magistrate is—"

"Is not pleased with your decision to have the body taken to London," sputtered the magistrate, a dour-looking man whose face was bristling with indignation. "Highly irregular—"

"As Lord Grentham's office may wish to be involved in the investigation, I thought it best to do so," interrupted Wrexford, mouthing the lie without batting an eye.

He had recently done a rather large favor for Britain's minister of state security. And though the two of them were not on friendly terms—in fact, if forced to choose between trusting Grentham or a cobra, the earl would not hesitate to pick the snake—he felt entitled to exploit the minister's much-feared name for his own purposes.

The magistrate paled. Given Grentham's reputation for ruthlessness, few people chose to cross paths with him. "I-In that case, I—I shall, of course, defer to the minister's authority."

He backed off and scuttled away, anxious to distance himself from even a shadow of danger.

The Warden turned to Wrexford with an anguished look. "Of course justice must be served, milord. B-But I pray that you will be able to keep Merton's august reputation from being tainted by any whispers of skullduggery going on within these walls."

"I shall do my best." After gathering up the document case filled with Greeley's notes, he added, "I will spend tomorrow in Oxford visiting Greeley's rooms and seeking further clues as to who might have wished him ill before returning to London. However, I may need to come back, so please keep this office undisturbed until you hear from me."

The Warden nodded.

After a last look around, Wrexford headed for the West Wing stairs. Von Münch hesitated, then followed.

As they cut around the college chapel's sacristy, a breathless hail echoed off the ancient stones, which were now shadowed in twilight.

"Lord Wrexford!"

The earl paused and waited for Quincy to catch up. Someone was playing the chapel's organ, the heartbreakingly beautiful notes of Mozart's *Requiem* floating out through an open side door.

"I've discovered the title of the manuscript, sir!" The young man's face was flushed with excitement. "The under-librarian and I cross-checked through the ledgers, and we found it." He offered the earl a slip of paper.

"Well done, Mr. Quincy," said Wrexford as he unfolded it and read what was written.

Nihil Est Quod Hominum Efficere Non Possit.

Dredging up his schoolboy Latin, he translated the words—*There is nothing that man can't accomplish*. It meant nothing to him, but perhaps one of his fellow members at the Royal Institution would have some idea of what sort of information the manuscript contained.

"Ummm . . ." Quincy shuffled his feet. "Since Balliol's copy is now missing, I pressed the under-librarian on what other collections might also possess one. He suggested checking the King's Library, which is currently located at Buckingham House."

"Thank you." The young man had the instincts of a good sleuth. "That was excellent thinking."

"D-Do you think it will help us catch the cold-blooded fiend who murdered Mr. Greeley, sir?"

Von Münch went very still and regarded the earl with an expectant look.

A good question. Wrexford pocketed the slip. "As to that, perhaps you should go to the Radcliffe Library and search through the alchemy collection for instructions on how to brew a potion for good luck."

For I have a feeling that we are going to need all the luck we can muster to solve this crime.

Raven put down the platter of ginger biscuits that he had filched from the kitchen, and after gobbling two of them, he began to strip off his shirt. "It's dark enough for us to move unseen through the streets, and m'lady is working on a drawing, so let us head off to make some inquiries among our friends near Maudslay's ruined laboratory."

Peregrine watched Hawk hurry from the schoolroom into one of the adjoining rooms and begin rooting around under his bed for his sack of ragged clothing.

"I'm coming with you," he said.

"Absolutely not." Raven kicked off his moleskin breeches and wriggled into a pair of foul-smelling canvas pants.

"Fawwgh." Peregrine held his nose. The odor also woke Harper, who gave a canine sneeze. It was truly disgusting.

"Why not?" demanded Peregrine.

"Because of the new house rule," replied Hawk as he adjusted the brim of his filthy hat. "After your new guardian gave his permission for you to stay with us this month, m'lady gave strict orders that you aren't to accompany us into the stews. She feels a responsibility to your family to keep you safe from scandal."

"Your lordly reputation would be in tatters if you're recognized dressed as a filthy gutter rat," pointed out Raven, "and Eton might give you the boot."

"I *hate* being a lord," retorted Peregrine, eyeing their rags with longing.

"Life isn't always fair," observed Raven. He looked at his brother. "Ready?"

A nod.

"Actually, there's something very important that you can do here," said Hawk after scrambling out to the window ledge. The night breeze rustled through the twines of ivy.

Peregrine squared his shoulders. "Just name it."

"Keep Harper from eating the rest of the ginger biscuits."

A short while later, the Weasels had made their first discovery. After asking around among their urchin friends, they had learned that Billy Bones and Carrot-Top, two lookouts for a gambling ring from Seven Dials, had been keeping watch on a dice game behind Maudslay's laboratory on the night of the fire.

Another inquiry allowed them to track down the two boys in an alleyway near Cockpit Yard.

"Oiy, I saw da fella wot smashed a window and tossed the firebomb into the building," said Billy Bones in answer to Raven's question.

"Can you describe him?" asked Raven,

A shrug. "Naw—wuzn't lookin' at him."

"Wot I can tell ye is that wuddever was in the bottles that he lit wiv da fuses, it weren't no ordinary lamp oil," piped up Carrot-Top. "When he tossed dem through da broken window, the place exploded in a holy hell o' flames."

Raven and Hawk exchanged a sharp look.

"Which window of the building did the man break?" inquired Hawk.

"Not sure," said Carrot-Top.

"Perhaps this will help you remember." Raven held up a gold guinea.

Eyes widening, the urchins put their heads together and began a fierce exchange of whispers.

"If yer facing the back o' the building from Cesspool Alley, it's the second one in from the left," said Billy Bones.

"You know that you'll never get another farthing from us if you ain't telling us the truth," cautioned Raven.

"Oiy, we know," said Carrot-Top. He held out his hand.

Raven tossed him the coin and then nudged his brother. "Let's be off."

They gained entrance to the ruins of Maudslay's laboratory by crawling through a tiny gap beneath a shutter that had come loose on the undamaged back office.

"Sshhh," warned Raven as Hawk took a step and a shard of burnt wood crunched under his boot. "I'll light the candle for just a moment, so we can pick a path through the rubble," he whispered, opening the small folding metal lantern he had brought with him. "It's best we don't keep it lit in case a night watchman walks by."

Steel struck flint, and a tiny flame flared to life. Raven studied the jumble of collapsed beams and tumbled brick, then blew it out. "Follow me."

The half-collapsed roof let in a dribble of moonglow. Jagged shadows gave the interior a menacing look. Wraithlike shadows loomed in the vaporous murk, setting off ripples of dark and light. Moving stealthily, they made their way to the charred hellhole where the fire had started.

"Careful," said Hawk as Raven sidled closer to the back wall. A glance up showed that the beam above them was tilted at a precarious angle. "What are we looking for?"

"You heard Carrot-Top. Whatever flammable substance was used to start the blaze, it was far more powerful than lamp oil. If we can find the bits of bottle glass, Wrex and Tyler may be able to identify the chemical residue on them. And that might give us a clue as to who is behind the arson."

Hawk crept around a slew of broken bricks and crouched down beside his brother. They both began poking through the debris.

"We should hurry," added Raven. A gust shivered through the dangling shingles, dislodging a crumbling of ashes and burnt bits of tar. From deep in the gloom came the groan of iron hinges swinging in the wind.

"Before what's left of the building comes crashing down around our ears."

CHAPTER 5

Charlotte awoke the next morning, her eyes gritty from lack of sleep as she squinted at the flickers of sunlight playing over the tangled bedcovers. Once again, an unsettling nightmare had plagued her fitful slumber, but unlike her reveries on the fire, this one had been on a far more personal level. . . . *Mac fleeing into a dark forest, and when she tried to follow, she had become tangled in a maze of vaporous shadows and thorny vines, the spiky points tearing at her flesh—*

"It was just a bad dream." She sat up in bed and chafed at her chilled arms, acutely aware of the empty space on the bed beside her. Strange how Wrexford's absence felt like an integral part of her was missing. Fiercely independent, even as a child, she had always imagined that letting someone take hold of her heart would make her weaker, not stronger.

And that, Charlotte decided, was the magic of Love. It was a beautifully inexplicable contradiction.

She smiled. Not even Wrexford, with his incisive logic and scientific genius, could offer a rational explanation for how it defied all the clockwork laws of the universe.

Buoyed by that thought, she rose and dressed, determined to keep her blue devils at bay.

After a simple repast of coffee and fresh-baked sultana muffins in the breakfast room—McClellan had bustled in and out, acting as if nothing was amiss between them—Charlotte retreated to her workroom.

Decisions, decisions.

She sat down at her desk and pondered her next piece of art for Fores's printshop.

"My pen has power," Charlotte reminded herself. She knew that her drawings influenced public opinion. To her that was a solemn responsibility, one that weighed heavily on her conscience. "And I have promised myself that I will never wield it recklessly."

Her gaze moved to the rough sketch for a drawing that lay on her blotter from the previous day—the first in a series that she planned to do on the plight of soldiers returning from the wars and unable to find employment. It was an important subject. Now that peace reigned and the army was reducing its ranks, the streets of London were filling with ragged men—many of them with injuries to both body and mind from serving their country on the brutal battlefields of Europe—who had nowhere to go. The cost of bread was rising, begging was rampant . . . and the government seemed stubbornly determined to ignore the growing crisis.

Even though they were sitting atop a powder keg, and a single spark could ignite a conflagration.

Charlotte paused. The idea of an innovative marine propulsion system and how it would change the world still tickled at her consciousness. From what Sheffield had said, it was a hugely important topic. However, she reminded herself that to do it justice, she needed to know far more about it. Not just the technical complexities but also the conflicts and ramifications of who would ultimately control such a revolutionary invention.

It was just the sort of challenge that quickened her pulse. The elemental reason for taking up the pen of her late husband, who had created A. J. Quill, was to bring such important issues to the attention of the public.

Pursing her lips, Charlotte began to think about how to begin her investigation. But the ticking of the mantel clock soon drew her back to the present moment. She had a drawing due today, so for now . . .

Charlotte picked up her pencil. "The public needs to care about our discharged soldiers and the fact that they need help and support in returning to their former lives," she murmured as she set to work, refining the visual elements of the drawing and carefully composing the captions.

Tired and frustrated by a day spent searching for any clues that might shed light on Greeley's murder, Wrexford returned to his rooms at Merton College and poured a glass of brandy from the decanter that the porter had supplied. Its fire, however, did nothing to warm his inner chill.

The visit to Greeley's spartan abode had been dispiriting. He had discovered nothing to shed light on why the poor fellow had been murdered. Indeed, aside from his books and academic journals, Greeley's life seemed depressingly empty. No sign of hobbies or hidden vices, no sign of romance or friends . . .

Save for ghosts from the past.

Wrexford took another mouthful of brandy, letting its burn trickle down his throat before reaching into his coat pocket for the miniature portrait he had found propped up on Greeley's desk. It was painted on an oval of ivory and fitted into a silver case that closed like a pocket watch to protect the delicate brushwork.

He drew a shaky breath and willed himself to flick open the clasp.

And felt his heart clench.

The artist had captured the three young officers in a light-hearted moment. It was an excellent likeness of his brother, who was flanked by Greeley and an Oxford friend from the King's Regiment of Dragoons. The artist had caught the gleam of good-natured humor that always seemed alight in his brother's sky-blue eyes . . . and the curl of his lips, where a smile looked about to burst into bloom at any moment.

"You were always the Sun, Tommy." Feeling a salty sharpness prickle against his eyelids, Wrexford looked away. "While I was the Moon."

He rubbed at his brow. "Dark. Moody. Irascible. In contrast to the light you brought to all of our lives." The silver case closed with a muted click. "God, I miss you."

After sliding the portrait back into his pocket, he rose and refilled his glass, though he knew that no amount of brandy would dull the ache in his heart. He could remember his brother and Greeley—the best of friends—as always so full of life. Confident, cheerful young men. Brave and honorable.

And then in a cruel twist of Fate, they were both destroyed. One in the space of a heartbeat while the other had suffered a slow, painful loss of his true self.

Wrexford closed his eyes, welcoming the blackness. "I promise you, Tommy," he whispered. "I will find whoever robbed your friend of what little he had left of life and see that the miscreant is brought to justice."

Heaving a silent sigh, Charlotte forced a smile as Sheffield handed her down from the carriage and turned to assist Cordelia. She was heartily tired of the endless parties—the pomp and pageantry of the Peace Celebrations and the Royal Centennial had kept Mayfair aswirl in glitter and gaiety throughout the summer. Polite Society had feasted on an excess of sumptuous splendors. . . .

Money that would have been far better spent feeding the poor.

However, Charlotte pushed such thoughts away for now. She had accepted Lady Marquand's invitation to attend tonight's festivities, and it was only right to do so with good grace.

A glance at Cordelia showed that she, too, appeared less than enthusiastic about the evening. But then, her friend—a brilliant mathematician and noted Bluestocking—had little taste for beau monde frivolities either.

Sheffield smiled. "Shall we go in?" he suggested, offering each of them an arm.

The drawing room was ablaze with candles, the crystalline light from the chandeliers fluttering over the colorful silks, sparkling jewels, and peacock splendor of the military medals and diplomatic sashes.

A footman appeared and offered them champagne.

"Quite a crush, especially for August," observed Sheffield. At this time of year, the aristocracy usually left the city for their country estates and the start of the shooting season.

"With so many prominent people still gathered here in London from all over the Continent and beyond, nobody wishes to miss out on all the intrigue and gossip swirling through the drawing rooms," said Charlotte dryly.

Indeed, the side salons off the drawing room were also filled with guests and the convivial sounds of clinking crystal and conversation. Following Sheffield's lead, the three of them began to circulate through the crowd, exchanging pleasantries with various acquaintances.

"Ah, Lady Wrexford!"

Charlotte turned as she and her friends entered one of the side salons.

A gentleman approached and bobbed a friendly bow. "Is His Lordship here tonight?" he asked.

"Alas, no, Lord Mulgrave," she answered. The Earl of Mulgrave had served as First Lord of the Admiralty until several years ago and was currently Master-General of the Ordnance. He had recently consulted with Wrexford over a metallurgy problem with a certain type of mortar shell.

"He was planning to attend," added Charlotte, "but an urgent request from an old friend called him away to Oxford."

"In that case, please pass on my thanks for his help in solving our artillery issue. I'm very grateful," answered Mulgrave, who had a keen interest in scientific subjects. "He also suggested that I attend the recent lecture by his friend Hedley on the latest developments in his steam locomotives, which I enjoyed very much."

"As did I," said Sheffield.

The comment made her smile. William Hedley was a brilliant engineer and had helped her and Wrexford on several of their previous investigations. During one of them, Sheffield had been captivated by Hedley's "Puffing Billy," a prototype steam locomotive, and invested in the project—which had proved to be a very lucrative decision.

Charlotte had also attended the recent lecture and responded with enthusiasm. "Wasn't it fascinating! The idea that we will soon travel with astounding speed over rails . . ."

A spirited conversation began among the four of them. Mulgrave was both knowledgeable and thoughtful, and Charlotte found herself enjoying the party more than she had expected.

"Indeed, Mr. Sheffield," said Mulgrave. "Hedley mentioned to me that you were an early investor in "Puffing Billy." What a prescient choice on your part— "

"Ah, there you are, Lord Mulgrave." A dulcet voice interrupted the Master-General of the Ordnance.

It was followed by a *swoosh* of silk as a lady—Charlotte didn't recognize her—glided through the archway, her hand on the arm of General Aldrich, a senior member of the military command at Horse Guards.

As the lady and her escort came closer, Charlotte noted that the newcomer was one of those women who would be called handsome rather than beautiful—her face was a little too long, her cheekbones a little too sharp. But she held her head as if she were wearing a crown—chin slightly lifted, spine ramrod straight, eyes glittering with a regal hauteur and a shimmering intelligence.

The effect was magnetic. Like a lodestone inexorably attracting iron filings, the lady drew the attention of the men in the room, their eyes subtly shifting to follow her progress.

"Lady Kirkwall—what a pleasure to see you here tonight," replied Mulgrave. He then introduced his companions.

Lady Kirkwall's gaze lingered on Charlotte. "Your reputation precedes you, Lady Wrexford." Their eyes met. "Word in the drawing rooms of Mayfair is that you and your husband are a formidable pair."

"I can't imagine why my name would be mentioned," responded Charlotte. "I rarely participate in the social swirl of Polite Society."

"Perhaps that's what makes you so intriguing." Without waiting for a reply, Lady Kirkwall turned to Mulgrave and tapped his arm with her folded fan. "Might the general and I steal you away for a moment to discuss the matter we mentioned at yesterday's reception?"

Mulgrave hesitated. It was clear that he had been enjoying the conversation with Charlotte and her friends and felt awkward about leaving in the middle of it.

"Ahhh . . . I very much wish to speak with you, milady," he replied. "But might we do so a little later in the evening? Or perhaps tomorrow at the Foreign Office reception?"

For a fraction of a second, a flare of emotion—annoyance? anger?—seemed to spark in the lady's eyes. But it was gone so quickly that Charlotte put it down to a quirk of the flickering sconces.

"But of course, milord," replied Lady Kirkwall with a gracious smile. "We certainly wouldn't want to take you away from your present companions." She glanced around. "I see that Lord Haverwood looks a bit bored at the moment, and he has been most anxious to speak with us. We will go rescue him and chat with you another time." A pause. "If the matter remains relevant."

As she turned her attention to Haverwood, General Aldrich gave a small cough and moved a little closer to Mulgrave. "I would much rather give you the opportunity before we broach it with Haverwood," he said softly, though Charlotte caught his words. "But timing is of the essence, as it won't be available for long."

Mulgrave drew in a breath and regarded her and her friends with an apologetic look. "Would you mind?"

"Not at all, sir," assured Charlotte. "We mustn't monopolize your company."

He gave her a grateful look before moving off.

Sheffield watched the threesome retreat to one of the alcoves at the far end of the room. "I imagine they are discussing business related to Lord Taviot's consortium," he said.

Charlotte thought she detected a note of envy in his voice.

"What makes you say that?" asked Cordelia a little sharply.

"Because Lady Kirkwall is Lord Taviot's sister and is involved in the project," he answered.

"Involved?" Charlotte's brows shot up in surprise. An aristocratic lady allowed to be part of running a business? That would be remarkable. But then, Lady Kirkwall appeared to be no ordinary female. "Are you implying that she's actually part of the consortium?"

"Not officially," said Sheffield. "The lady is a widow and serves as her brother's social hostess. But I've also heard that she's been very active in approaching prominent members of Society to discuss possible investment opportunities." He watched the tiny bubbles spark and fizz in his wine. "She apparently possesses great savoir-faire and uses her charms to great advantage. I've heard that the consortium has already raised a great deal of money."

From her brief interaction with Lord Taviot's sister, Charlotte could well understand how gentlemen would find the lady alluring.

"Well, I fail to see Lady Kirkwall's charm," muttered Cordelia. "If you ask me, she was quite rude in the way she interrupted us."

Sheffield said nothing, his gaze still lingering on the alcove.

"And furthermore, what is she selling? For all the rumors floating around about its innovative research, Lord Taviot's consortium has revealed nothing about the details of its work."

"Its head of technology, the mechanical genius who is in charge of the project, is giving a lecture at the Royal Institution later in the week, so I daresay we shall all learn more about their efforts," countered Sheffield. "And secondly, I don't blame them for being secretive. The company that succeeds in inventing an oceangoing marine propulsion system will be worth unimaginable riches. So it's quite understandable that the consortium is being closemouthed about the specifics of its work to avoid any risk of having the idea stolen."

Charlotte was about to reply when out of the corner of her eye she caught a glimpse of a face within the milling crowd. She quickly turned, but the gentleman had disappeared.

"What is it?" asked Cordelia, who hadn't missed her reaction.

"I thought I saw . . ." Charlotte shook her head. "But that's not possible," she added, more to herself than to her friends. "He's in Vienna."

A string quartet struck up a sonata in one of the side salons, adding its lilting notes to the gaiety of the party.

Cordelia set aside her empty glass. "Shall we return to the drawing room and fetch another round of champagne?"

It was clear that she was unsettled, but Charlotte was puzzled as to why. Her friend was fascinated by technology and its potentials—indeed, she had played a role in helping a brilliant inventor design a revolutionary computing engine—so talk of a new type of marine propulsion system should be of great interest to her.

And yet . . .

On spotting a friend of her great-aunt Alison, the dowager Countess of Peake, Charlotte felt compelled to stop and exchange pleasantries before following Sheffield and Cordelia.

Her own glass still half full, she paused as she entered the drawing room and, after slipping into the shadows of a large floral display, took a moment to watch the interactions of the crowd.

The crème de la crème of London Society was here, she mused. One could almost see the silvery strands spinning through the guests, weaving a web of power and influence. *Alliances being made, deals being sealed, secrets being revealed . . .*

"A penny for your thoughts, Lady Wrexford?"

The voice from behind her sent a prickling down her spine.

Charlotte slowly turned and met the gentleman's gaze with a cool smile. "I doubt you would find them worth a farthing, Mr. Kurlansky."

She had crossed paths with the Russian diplomat during their last investigation. He had been introduced to her as the private secretary to Prince Rubalov, Russia's top military attaché stationed in London—though Kurlansky had later admitted that was a lie.

He was far more important—and far more dangerous—than that.

"Oh, you might be surprised at how much I value the way your mind works," replied Kurlansky.

She ignored his flummery. "I thought you had left England and were headed to the Peace Conference in Vienna."

"I tarried in Paris for several weeks. But then Tsar Alexander sent word for me to return to London and resolve a small matter before journeying to Austria."

"What matter would that be?" asked Charlotte.

He chuckled. "Nothing that concerns you. Or your husband."

She hadn't expected a real answer. "I devoutly hope not." A pause. "For both our sakes."

Kurlansky laughed again and cocked his glass in salute. "Please give my regards to Lord Wrexford." Without waiting for a reply, he turned and, in the blink of an eye, disappeared in the crowd.

"Was that—" began Sheffield as he and Cordelia squeezed their way past a group of French diplomats and came over to join her.

"Yes," she said through gritted teeth.

"What's Kurlansky up to now?" asked Cordelia.

"I have no idea," replied Charlotte. "But we can be sure that it's nothing good."

CHAPTER 6

A dark, churning sea, fraught with peril and uncertainty . . .

Charlotte gave a wry grimace as she took up her cup of fresh-poured coffee and went to stand by the breakfast room windows. She wasn't usually plagued by bad dreams, but the past night had brought yet another troubled reverie—one that felt like a metaphor for her current state of mind.

A silvery mist still clung to the plantings and ornamental trees in the gardens, blurring the textures and colors to an amorphous grey as she fretted over her various worries.

The stony silence of McClellan, the air of tension between Sheffield and Cordelia, the Russian's mysterious appearance . . .

Her mood was further dampened by Wrexford's continued absence. Charlotte had been disappointed to find no missive from the earl in the early morning post. As she took another sip of coffee, she couldn't help but wonder what was keeping him in Oxford.

A sigh misted the glass panes. Oddly enough, the only letter on the silver salver had been addressed to Peregrine. She hoped it wasn't bad news. The boy had suffered enough losses for someone of his tender years.

The sudden patter of footsteps caused her to turn away from the window. Half-hidden in the shadows, Peregrine was standing in the doorway, with Raven and Hawk just behind him.

"I'm sorry to disturb you, m'lady—" began the boy.

"But Falcon has just received a special invitation!" blurted out Hawk. "And we are all included—"

"Sshhh!" Raven elbowed his brother to silence. "Let *him* do the talking."

Charlotte smiled on seeing their expectant faces. "Do go on, Falcon," she urged. "This sounds very intriguing."

"Mr. Samuel Tilden, a good friend of Uncle Jeremiah, has invited us to visit him," said Peregrine.

"Mr. Tilden is an inventor, too," offered Hawk.

The name sounded familiar, but Charlotte couldn't remember why.

"I met him a number of times at the Royal Armory, and he wrote me a very kind letter after my uncle's death," continued Peregrine. "We've kept up a correspondence since then—he knows I'm interested in mechanical devices—and a note just arrived this morning asking if we would like to visit the laboratories at the King's Dockyard in Greenwich this afternoon."

The King's Dockyard? The boy now had her full attention.

"The Royal Navy does its experimental work on weaponry at the Royal Armory at Woolwich," explained Peregrine, who had good reason to know that because his late uncle had been one of its top engineers. "But the laboratories at the King's Dockyard are home to all its research on nautical innovations."

Charlotte was well aware of that. And given her thoughts of the previous day about learning more about marine propulsion systems—as well as Wrexford's observation on why the government had a vested interest in being the first to create the new technology—the invitation provided a perfect opportunity to begin her investigation.

Raven and Hawk fixed her with pleading looks. They, too, had become fascinated by mechanical devices.

"Why, that sounds like a splendid idea!" she announced.

There were advantages to the fact that Society thought women's intellectual abilities couldn't hold a candle to that of men, she added to herself with an inward smile. A lady, especially one married to a gentleman known for his interest and expertise in science, could ask a great many questions without stirring any suspicions.

"I'll have the carriage readied," she added, "and ask Mac to pack a hamper of food and blankets so that we can picnic by the river."

She set aside her cup. "You three should change into heavier jackets, as it can turn chilly down by the water. Then let us be off without delay."

As the boys raced off to ready themselves for the trip, Charlotte went to find McClellan in the kitchen. The news of the planned trip brought the first real smile to the maid's lips since their uncomfortable tête-à-tête.

"Aye, the lads will love mucking about in such an interesting place," replied McClellan. "It will be a long day, so I had better pack enough food to feed a regiment of Hussars."

Charlotte chuckled at the quip—and then reached out to take hold of the maid's arm as she started to turn. "Mac, I can't bear the tension between us. Please, if you feel that I have somehow changed . . ." She swallowed hard. "And have taken on the airs and graces of a pompous aristocrat, you must be honest and tell me—"

"Ye gods—no!" McClellan's eyes widened in surprise, and then she quickly looked away. "It has nothing—*nothing!*—to do with you, m'lady. I simply need some time to . . ." The maid hesitated. "To sort out some things. I fear—"

"Surely you know that Wrexford and I would do anything to help you."

That drew a mirthless laugh. "Aye, that's what I'm afraid of." McClellan caught Charlotte's hand and gave it a squeeze.

"Please, allow me to work this out on my own. I promise that I will explain. I—I just can't say when."

"I shall, of course, respect your wishes." She felt a measure of relief at the maid's explanation. "But please consider what I said."

The arrangements were soon completed, and once the carriage broke free of Mayfair's streets and the tangle of market traffic near Covent Garden, they passed over London Bridge to the south bank of the river. From there, the miles rolled by, and the boys soon had their noses pressed up against the window glass as the masts of the Royal Navy frigates at anchor came into view.

The wind turned gusty as the carriage rolled through the main entrance of the King's Dockyard, rattling the rigging of ships moored at the docks and raising foam-flecked whitecaps on the river. A pair of marine sentries met them and led the coachman through a series of archways to a cobbled square down by the wharves. The horses came to a halt in front of a heavy-set stone building that stretched the full width of the square and faced out at the water.

From the hum and clatter resonating from its walls, Charlotte guessed it housed the naval laboratories.

As one of the marines opened the carriage door and the boys scrambled out, she saw a tall, rail-thin man dressed in a long canvas smock emerge from the entrance portal and hurry to meet them.

"Halloo!" he called, giving a friendly wave to Peregrine as he rushed to offer a hand to Charlotte as she started to descend.

"Welcome, Lady Wrexford." He glanced into the shadows behind her and looked a bit disappointed at spotting only McClellan. "I'm delighted that you were amenable to making the journey here with the boys on such short notice. Allow me to introduce myself—"

"It is a pleasure to meet you, Mr. Tilden," interjected Charlotte before he could go on. Again, she had a niggling sense that she had seen him before. But clearly he had no memory of an encounter. "Peregrine has told us so much about you during the journey here," she added, fixing him with an admiring smile. "I am very grateful for your kindness to him. It has helped soften the pain of his uncle's loss."

The tips of Tilden's ears turned bright red, and not just because of the biting wind. "I, too, miss Willis terribly. He was a lovely man and a brilliant colleague. I think he would be very excited about our latest project—"

Tilden caught himself and gave a brusque cough. "But I won't bore you with technicalities. The reason I asked you to come today is because we are running some tests on our new precision lathes, and as Peregrine has told me that your two wards are also very interested in mechanical devices, I thought the boys would enjoy touring the workshops and seeing how we make our engineering ideas come to life."

"That sounds magical," replied Charlotte as McClellan climbed down to join them. The air was sharp with the tang of salt, and another brisk gust tugged at her bonnet.

"Not magic, milady, science!" Seeing the ribbons flap around her face, Tilden hurriedly added, "How rag-mannered of me for making you stand in the cold!" He offered his arm and called for the boys to come away from admiring the thirty-two-gun war frigate that was tied up at the near wharf. "If you and your maid will please follow me, milady."

The noise grew even more pronounced as they passed from the entrance foyer into the central corridor. Tilden led them through a set of thick oak doors. The machinery sounds were muffled as they swung closed behind them.

"This section of the building holds the offices of our inventors." His lips quirked. "We need a modicum of quiet in which to think." He continued on to a closed door halfway down the corridor and opened it with a key that he pulled from his pocket.

"The work we do here is—"

"Secret," intoned Peregrine.

Tilden nodded. "Well, yes, we must protect our innovations, as they contribute to keeping our nation safe." He offered Charlotte a seat in the chair facing his large and cluttered desk. "But there is no need to worry. We are very careful to maintain a high level of security to thwart spies from other countries."

He paused and smiled, as if seeking to lighten the mood. "And closer to home, heaven forfend if a fellow like A. J. Quill managed to poke around in our restricted areas and see what we are doing."

"Dear heavens," exclaimed Charlotte, exchanging a furtive glance with McClellan.

"Oh, I didn't mean to alarm you." A nervous laugh. "I assure you, our defenses are more than a match for foreign agents, as well as the likes of A. J. Quill."

Charlotte inclined a polite nod and changed the subject. "What magnificent pictures of our stalwart fighting ships!" she said.

"They represent some of our most fabled naval victories—the Battle of the Nile, Trafalgar, Copenhagen . . ." Tilden's eyes lit with patriotic pride. "They remind all of us of the importance of what we do here."

"Indeed," she said softly.

McClellan whispered a warning to the Weasels to stop fidgeting.

"Ho, the boys are rightly impatient to see the machinery," exclaimed Tilden with a friendly wink in their direction. "Though I hope the noise will not be an unpleasant experience for you, milady." A pause. "Er, what with all the metal shavings and drops of oil that are inevitably spit off by the machines, it can also get a little . . . messy."

Charlotte chuckled as she slipped off her heavy cloak. "With three lively boys in our house, I assure you, I am not the least bothered by noise or less-than-pristine surroundings."

"Excellent!" Tilden looked relieved. "Though I also must warn you that it's a bit cramped in the aisles between the machinery."

"Why don't I stay here with our outer wraps and reticules?" suggested McClellan. She lifted the bag looped over her arm. "I have brought along some knitting."

"Does that meet with your approval, Mr. Tilden?" asked Charlotte.

"Yes, that works out very nicely," he replied.

After offering his arm to Charlotte, Tilden turned to the Weasels and Peregrine. "Come along, lads. I hope you are not afraid of getting your hands a bit grimy."

McClellan choked back a snort.

Raven glanced at her with an evil grin before scampering off.

"Lead the way, sir," said Charlotte. "Though I daresay I won't comprehend much, I am very much looking forward to seeing what it is you do here."

The chatter of moving steel, the whir of spinning gears, the chuff of steam-engine pistons rising and falling—the laboratory was alive with a symphony of industrial sounds as Tilden led them into a long, narrow room with three lathes spaced along its length. All were humming along at full speed.

Peregrine's eyes widened in wonder as the man in charge of running the nearest one clamped a small block of iron into a central worm screw and flicked a lever, sending it through lines of different milling blades that cut it into an intricate shape.

"I-Is it really possible that every piece that the lathe operator makes is identical?" demanded the boy.

"Thanks to the genius of Henry Maudslay, the answer is yes. He's invented a whole new range of innovative machines that are key to making improved versions of other machines!"

"What do you mean?" asked Hawk, venturing closer to the whirling levers.

"Careful—any closer and you might lose your nose!" Tilden caught him by his collar and drew him back. "What I mean is . . ." He straightened and signaled the man running the lathe to shut it down.

Once the blades had spun to a stop, Tilden allowed the boys to move right up to the behemoth machine. Charlotte, too, inched closer, fascinated by the opportunity to see how a lathe worked.

"You see, the lathe operator can set the milling blades to any number of precise configurations," explained Tilden. "And once the blades are locked in place, he can make hundreds—or thousands—of identical parts."

"Mass production," said Raven with a glance at Charlotte. "A. J. Quill did a series of drawings on the subject."

"Yes, and the artist was actually quite thoughtful and accurate in explaining to the public why that has changed our world," mused Tilden. "With mass production, we can produce parts far faster and in greater quantities than by hand. Which means we can make a wide range of machinery far more efficiently and at a lower cost."

"Very impressive," replied Charlotte.

The inventor gave the lathe a fond pat. "It may not sound very exciting, but it truly is. As costs drop, the public will be able to afford more goods that will make their lives more comfortable."

Turning to Peregrine, he smiled. "Your uncle Willis loved scientific innovation. I wished that he had lived to see the remarkable progress we are making in precision engineering. The lathes are now allowing us to create smaller and smaller tolerances."

Seeing the questioning looks from the boys, he hastened to explain. "Quite simply, what that means is pieces of a machine fit together more snugly." He paused to let his words sink in. "That is especially important for steam engines. You see, if the steam can't leak out, the engine will be more powerful."

And, thought Charlotte, *a powerful engine is key to moving a ship through the rough waters of the oceans.*

"Good heavens! More powerful machines?" She widened her eyes. "I have heard my husband and his scientific colleagues discussing Mr. Hedley's Puffing Billy, a steam-powered carriage which they said will soon carry people around the country at unimaginable speeds! I confess, it sounds rather . . . unbelievable."

"Not at all, Lady Wrexford! Progress is moving at lightning speed, and transportation is leading the way," replied Tilden. "Things will radically change—but one should think of that as exciting rather than frightening."

Charlotte nodded. "That is exactly what Wrexford says." Her brows drew together. "Come to think of it, he also mentioned an American—a man named Fulton, I believe—who has created boats powered by steam that can travel up and down rivers." A pause. "But because of the, er, thingamabobs that push them through the water, Wrexford thinks they will never be able to navigate the oceans."

"Not at the moment, but there is a great deal of interesting experimentation going on with the thingamabobs." A spark lit in Tilden's eyes. "As well as work on— " His voice faltered for an instant.

"On some other ideas," he finished in a rush.

The whirring of the other lathes filled the momentary silence. Tilden then cleared his throat and, after turning and instructing the lathe operator to restart his massive machine, led the way through an archway to another section of the laboratory.

"We do some very interesting experiments with smelting iron in our foundry," he explained. The temperature grew noticeably warmer as they walked down the corridor. To Charlotte, he added, "Being a chemist, Lord Wrexford would appreciate how we tinker with our formulas to test the different strengths we can create in the finished metal. For steam engines, we are looking to— "

From within a recessed foyer, a door—an imposing iron-banded slab of oak that would have looked at home guarding a medieval castle—was suddenly flung open.

"Tilden!" a harried-looking man sporting a grease-stained leather apron skidded to a halt as he spotted the inventor. "Thank goodness I've found you. We need to have a conference with the head of the foundry over . . ."

He fell silent on spotting Tilden's companions. "It will only take a few minutes."

Tilden nodded. "Yes, of course." He gave Charlotte an apologetic look. "I shall return shortly."

"Please don't hurry on our account," she replied. She retreated several steps, allowing the two men to hurry off down one of the side corridors.

She had only looked away for a moment, but the boys had already moved close to the half-open door and were peering inside.

Charlotte heard a low whooshing and gurgling, as if a dragon were slumbering in the depths of its lair.

"Maybe we shouldn't— " began Peregrine.

"Mr. Tilden didn't tell us not to go inside," pointed out Raven. He looked to Charlotte in mute appeal.

It was true. He hadn't. And besides . . .

Charlotte joined them by the door. She, too, was eager to see what work was going on inside.

"I don't see the harm in having a look," she decided.

A mammoth trestle table was set in the center of a well-equipped laboratory room. Behind it, a work counter ran the length of the far wall. It was bristling with an array of tools and bottles of pungent chemicals.

Peregrine approached the complex construction sitting atop the table and let out a low hiss of air.

"What is it?" asked Raven.

"Some sort of steam engine . . ." Peregrine tilted his head and leaned over to give it a sideways look. Puffs of vapor rose from its iron belly. "But unlike any other one I've ever seen."

Raven started to circle around the table, followed by his brother.

Spotting a work area tucked into an alcove by the door, Charlotte left the boys to inspect the engine and moved into the shadows to have a look at the sheets of papers spread out on its counters.

The engine continued its snuffling huffs and puffs. Intrigued by the complex diagrams drawn on the papers—they looked to be technical plans—she leaned in for a closer study. There were also some drawings that looked to be exploring design ideas for the thingamabobs—she of course knew they were called paddle wheels—that would allow them to withstand the rigors of ocean travel. Her gaze moved to the margins of the paper, which were filled with very strange sketches, all appearing to experiment with an oddly shaped object with undulating curves.

Intrigued, Charlotte withdrew a small sketchbook and pencil from the hidden pocket in her gown. . . .

The monstrous machine continued its chuffing and gurgling.

In the main room, Peregrine leaned in to touch one of the pistons—

"Avast there!" bellowed a voice from the doorway.

Peregrine spun around as a naval officer—a young midshipman who looked to be no older than he was—rushed into the room.

"You filthy little gutter rat!" cried the midshipman. "This is a restricted military area. How did you crawl in here?"

"I was invited," answered Peregrine.

"You—a Blackamoor?" said the midshipman, eying Peregrine's dusky skin. "Don't make me laugh."

Charlotte was about to intervene when Raven appeared from behind the table, with Hawk right on his heels.

"Oiy, oiy! Keep a civil tongue in your head when you speak

to Lord Lampson!" Raven flexed a warning fist. "Or you'll be digging your teeth out of your gullet."

"Lord Lampson?" The midshipman allowed a momentary flicker of confusion before squaring his shoulders. "And who are *you*? The Duke of Dirt?" he retorted, wrinkling his nose at the streak of sludge now running down the front of Raven's jacket.

"No, he's just the gutter rat who is going to make your fancy little uniform look like it's been to the devil and back," chirped Hawk as Raven took a challenging step closer to the midshipman.

The two of them were now nearly nose to nose. Charlotte moved to the alcove's opening—

"Mr. Porter, is there something amiss?"

The midshipman stepped back and snapped a salute to Tilden, who was standing in the doorway.

"Intruders, sir!" he bellowed, trying to make his voice sound deeper than it really was.

Tilden smiled. "I fear there has been a misunderstanding. Lord Lampson and his friends are here by my invitation."

Porter turned beet red. "I-I'm very sorry, sir," he stammered. "I didn't know—"

"No apologies necessary. Of course you didn't, and your vigilance is to be commended." A pause. "And Master Sloane, I applaud your loyalty to Peregrine. Friendship is a bond of honor that every gentleman should take seriously."

Tilden entered the room. "So shake hands, lads, and cry *pax*. There is no reason to be at odds with one another."

Raven and Porter glowered at each other but reluctantly did as they were told.

"And now, we must all take our leave from this room. The engineers are about to come and turn up the boiler to full power for a test of our . . ." Tilden hesitated. " . . of our prototype, and it is, alas, restricted to only the senior staff."

Raven and Hawk dutifully moved for the door. Porter did the same.

And then came to a halt.

"Tilden! What the devil . . ." A military officer—this one an adult—was suddenly blocking the doorway. "Good God! How *dare* you allow any unauthorized visitors into this building! You of all people know that strangers are strictly forbidden."

"I was merely giving the lads a tour of the lathes, Colonel Jarvis," replied Tilden. "Lord Lampson's late uncle was one of our most brilliant engineers at Royal Woolwich." His brows gave a tiny waggle. "I hardly think their presence represents a threat."

"That is for *me* to decide," snapped Jarvis.

As Tilden drew the officer toward the alcove, Charlotte held herself very still, hoping not to be noticed.

"I regret the door was left open, Colonel," said Tilden in a low voice. "But there is no harm done. They are mere children—they have no idea what they are seeing."

Holding her breath, Charlotte carefully slipped her sketchbook back into her pocket.

Jarvis didn't appear mollified. "You naval men run a damnably loose ship here. It's a good thing Horse Guards sent me to be part of this project—

"Your expertise in engineering has been very welcome, sir," said Tilden, "But I assure you, we have all the proper precautions in place."

"Apparently you don't, for I've just received a report of a possible breach in our security," he growled. "Get your visitors out of here immediately. After I've checked the south doors, the guards and I will be making a thorough inspection of the entire building."

As the colonel and Tilden continued to converse, Charlotte seized the opportunity to slip out of the alcove and into the shadows of the steam engine. A furtive glance showed that Tilden hadn't noticed. But for an instant, she locked eyes with Jarvis.

And a chill ran down her spine.

The colonel, however, made no acknowledgment of her presence. He turned on his heel and marched off without further comment.

Tilden looked around and on spotting her lifted his shoulders in apology. "Jarvis is an awfully strict disciplinarian, but he is only doing his duty." A sigh. "Come, we must do as he says."

Suddenly aware that one of the boys was missing, he froze in mid-step. "Peregrine?"

"Here, sir!" The muffled voice rose up from behind the steam engine. "I—I think you should come look at this."

Tilden hurried into the vaporous gloom. Charlotte signaled for the Weasels to stay where they were and followed.

"Two large bolts are lying here in the drip pan." Peregrine then pointed to a large reinforcing plate on the boiler. "And it looks like they may have been removed from there."

Crouching down, Tilden examined that section of machinery. "Ye gods," he muttered. Charlotte watched as he ducked his head and felt around inside the array of levers and cylinders. "The piston rod . . ."

Tilden suddenly shot up to his feet. "Everybody out—and quickly. My men and I need to shut the engine down."

As Charlotte whirled around to shepherd the boys out to the corridor, she heard what he added under his breath.

"Before the first full blast of steam blows it to smithereens."

Once they were all out of the laboratory, Tilden's call for assistance brought several men running to his aid. He drew them into a huddle and gave a series of orders that sent them rushing to tend to the engine.

After mopping his brow, he turned to her. "Forgive me, Lady Wrexford, but I'm afraid that we must defer the rest of our tour to a later date. Our head engineer had not quite finished replacing several parts, and the laboratory assistant mistakenly started the boiler."

Tilden forced a smile. "No harm done thanks to Peregrine's sharp eyes, but I wish to check that everything else in in order. So if you don't mind . . ."

He beckoned to a man who had taken up a position by the laboratory's closed door. "I'll have our project manager escort you back to my office and then to your carriage."

"Of course," responded Charlotte, pretending to believe his explanation. "We mustn't keep you from your work."

However, she hadn't missed the look on Tilden's face as he bent down to examine the steam engine.

And she was quite certain that whatever was wrong, it was no mere accident.

CHAPTER 7

Wrexford shook the travel dust off his hat before setting it down on the entrance table. Anxious to return to Town as swiftly as possible, he had risen very early and taken a seat in the Royal Mail coach that passed through Oxford just before dawn.

However, the journey had been delayed by a cracked wheel spoke and then a damaged bridge, which required a bone-jarring detour to an alternate crossing. It was now well past dark. . . .

He sighed. A wee dram of malt would soon soothe all the niggling little aches and pains—

"Wrex!" Charlotte suddenly appeared in the foyer and rushed across the black and white checkered tiles to seize him in a fierce hug. "Thank heavens you are finally home," she said, burying her face in the folds of his coat.

"It was just Oxford, sweeting, not the ends of the Earth," he replied lightly. And yet it felt like he had been to Hell and back. However, the feel of her heart thudding against his chest sent a surge of warmth through him. He put his arms around her and tightened his hold.

Life is unbearably fragile, he thought, torn between the joy of holding her close and the piercing fear of ever losing her.

Greeley's death and the poignant reminders of his late brother had affected him more than he cared to admit.

Charlotte leaned back and tucked a lock of hair behind his ear.

"What's wrong?" he asked, seeing a shadow flutter beneath her lashes. "The Weasels and—"

"The Weasels and Peregrine have managed not to inflict any bodily harm on each other with their swords," she assured him. "It's just that—"

She paused, reading the nuances of his expression as quickly as he had read hers. "But first, tell me about Greeley. What did he wish to discuss with you?"

Wrexford expelled a harried breath. "I never had a chance to find out. He was murdered during the night before I arrived."

"Merciful heavens, how dreadful!" Her expression pinched to a mingling of deeply felt shock and sadness. "Was it because of—"

"Of what he wished to tell me?" Wrexford closed his eyes for an instant. "I don't know. But it seems a possible explanation. It was no random robbery." He hurriedly explained about the circumstances of Greeley's murder and the mysterious missing manuscript.

"No one saw or heard anything?" Charlotte asked, once he had finished.

"I was just getting to that." The earl told her about von Münch and what the visiting librarian had overheard.

He felt her muscles tighten. "Greeley sounded agitated?" she demanded. "And then said your name?"

"Apparently several times," he confirmed. "Though I can't imagine why." A sigh. "If only von Münch had heard more of the conversation."

Charlotte's puzzled frown mirrored his own consternation.

"So," he went on, "there is damnably little to go on concerning the murder or its motive. My search of Greeley's desk turned up nothing, though I collected his notes and scribblings for you to examine, in case you see something that has eluded me."

Wrexford made a face. "I also had the poor fellow's corpse sent to Henning, but I don't hold high hopes that he'll find anything." A pause. "The fact is, there is no apparent clue to the crime, save for the missing manuscript."

"Greeley said your name to whoever murdered him. There *must* be a reason," responded Charlotte after a moment of thought. "We need to discover why."

"I have been pondering that elemental question since yesterday evening. And I can't for the life of me muster an answer." Wrexford closed his eyes for an instant. "Perhaps a glass of Scottish malt will help lubricate the gears inside my brainbox."

She took his arm. "Come, Kit is here in the parlor with the boys. I sent a note asking him to come by because of what the boys and I witnessed this afternoon."

"What—" he began.

"We'll get to that after you've had the whisky."

As he approached the parlor, the everyday sounds of the house—the chatter of the boys, the furry thump of the hound's tail—were a more potent balm for his spirits than any Scottish malt. He had always considered himself a man who preferred quiet and solitude. It was strange how he now couldn't imagine his life without . . .

Without his family.

No doubt his brother Thomas would be teasing him unmercifully about his change of heart.

And I would give anything in the world to hear his needling.

"Wrex!" Hawk looked up from feeding Harper a scrap of ham from his pocket. "Something evil is afoot!"

"But not for long, now that Wrex is back," said Raven. "He will soon have the miscreants brought to justice."

The boy's faith in him only made Wrexford more achingly aware of his own frailties. Rather than reply, he marched to the sideboard and picked up one of the bottles from the tray.

To his dismay, he found that his hand was shaking.

"Refill my glass while you're at it," said Sheffield. The earl noted that his friend was looking awfully grave and brought the whisky with him as he moved to the group of armchairs by the hearth.

"So," he said, once he had seated himself and taken a long draught of his drink. "What is the trouble?"

"Let me start at the beginning," answered Charlotte. "Peregrine has been corresponding with Samuel Tilden, a friend of his uncle Willis and a fellow inventor. This morning, he received an invitation to visit Tilden at the King's Dockyard and have a tour of the Royal Navy's nautical research laboratories . . ."

Helped along by numerous interjections from Raven and Hawk—and a few hesitant comments from Peregrine—she recounted what she and the boys had seen.

"Hmmph." Wrexford read in her eyes that there was more to the story, so he refrained from any further reaction.

The Weasels looked about to badger him with further questions, but Charlotte intervened. "Off you fly, fledglings," she said. "Wrex is tired from traveling, and there are some things that we need to discuss with Kit."

"In private," added Wrexford. He eyed the jumble of fencing foils lying on the carpet. "Be forewarned that any eavesdropping, and I may have to lop off a few ears."

Charlotte sweetened the dismissal by adding, "You may take the platter of ginger biscuits with you."

Raven's scowl softened as he scooped up the plate. Harper added a canine grin before rising and padding after the boys.

"You could have asked them to leave some biscuits behind," grumbled Sheffield as the pelter of steps in the corridor died away.

"I think we have more meaty things on which to chew," said Charlotte. "I've yet to tell either of you about the papers I saw in the work area by the prototype steam engine—"

"Before you begin, His Lordship would likely welcome some real sustenance after his journey." McClellan appeared in the doorway with a platter of sliced beefsteak, along with a slab of cheddar and a loaf of bread.

"Thank you, Mac." A soft splash sounded as Wrexford refilled his glass. "Why is it that I have a sneaking suspicion I'm not going to like what I'm about to hear?"

"Because you are developing very good primal instincts to go along with your incisive logic," replied Charlotte, after gesturing for McClellan to remain and be part of the discussion.

A mirthless laugh rumbled in his throat. "It seems that I've just been damned with faint praise." He sat down and began to fix himself a plate of food. "Perhaps some sustenance will make it more palatable."

Charlotte took that as a signal to proceed. "I am no expert on steam engines, but as Peregrine mentioned, it looked distinctly different from any other one I've ever seen."

"How so?" asked Sheffield.

"It was very . . ." Her brow furrowed. "I suppose the best way to describe it is to say it was horizontal rather than vertical, with very unusual condensers and flywheels. But even more curious were the set of technical drawings spread out in the work alcove. There were some exceedingly strange diagrams in the margins." A puzzled shrug. "They made no sense to me, so I can't really describe them. In addition, there also were a number of rough sketches of odd-looking paddle wheels."

She reached into her pocket. "I had a chance to make copies of some of them in my sketchbook." Her lips gave a wry twitch. "Though Colonel Jarvis might have put me in front of a firing squad had he known."

Charlotte passed the book to Wrexford, who merely shook his head and handed it to Sheffield.

Their friend took several long moments to study the sketches and then set down his glass rather heavily. "Damnation." His voice was barely more than a whisper.

"You think this proves that the government is working on an oceangoing marine propulsion system?" asked Wrexford.

"I've been making some discreet inquiries and have heard rumors to that effect," answered their friend. "And these drawings certainly look to confirm them. I've also heard that the Americans are experimenting with some new innovative paddle wheel designs that are more flexible, along with some experimental models that are placed in the interior of the ship on either side of the keel, rather than on the outside of the hull."

Sheffield slowly expelled his breath. "These drawings seem to show that the Royal Navy is experimenting with the same ideas. As for the curved object, I confess I have no idea what it shows."

"But what we *do* know," pointed out Charlotte, "is that two groups involved in the race have recently suffered clandestine attacks on their laboratories."

She fixed each of them with a troubled glance. "The question is, who is to blame?"

Sheffield took another sip of whisky while she twisted the fringe of her shawl between her fingers. "Actually, I think that's fairly obvious," he said after several fraught moments had slid by. "Whoever wins the race to build a workable oceangoing propulsion system will hold unfathomable power. So I imagine that the groups involved here in Britain—the Royal Navy, the Taviot consortium, the Soho Foundry, and even Maudslay—won't hesitate to employ dirty measures to prevent their competitors from taking the lead."

He put down his glass. "And then, of course, there are the foreign governments."

Charlotte saw Wrexford nod in agreement.

"The Americans are probably the overall leader in the race,

as they have been the innovators in river steamboats," continued their friend. "One would imagine that their government might be just as ruthless as ours to preserve their advantage."

"Are you merely speculating?" demanded Wrexford.

"Yes," conceded their friend. "However, it seems a logical scenario to consider." He tapped his fingertips together. "And we also know that Tsar Alexander yearns to make Russia a naval power."

"Again, mere speculation," muttered the earl.

Charlotte slanted a look at Sheffield. "I happened to encounter Kurlansky at last night's soiree."

"I thought he had left for Vienna," said Wrexford

"So did I. But he said the tsar asked him to return to London," she replied. "Of course, he was coy about the reason why."

The earl ran a hand through his hair and let out an exasperated sigh. "Even if it is true that foreign powers are intent on entering the fray, I don't see that there is any reason for us to get involved in the skullduggery surrounding the competition to create a marine propulsion system. It's none of our concern."

His eyes narrowed. "Our government will have its operatives in the thick of things, and they are far more willing to get their hands dirty than we are."

Charlotte drew in a measured breath. "I'm sorry, Wrex, but you can't expect A. J. Quill to stay silent on the subject. The Royal Naval laboratory has suffered a clandestine attack, and there's a question of whether the fire at Maudslay's laboratory was deliberately set. So the skullduggery could have serious ramifications for our country in regards to both its economic and military stability."

She fisted her hands in her lap. "I can't in good conscience ignore those possibilities. So I feel compelled to look more closely into what is going on between the competitors."

* * *

An uncomfortable silence settled over the room. McClellan, who had remained uncharacteristically quiet throughout the discussion, rose and refilled the earl's plate.

"I respect that, my love," said Wrexford, after breaking off a morsel of bread and swallowing it. "I understand, and agree that you must do what you feel is right."

He rose. "As must I."

After moving to the hearth, he picked up the poker and stirred the banked coals. A few weak glimmers of red-gold flickered, only to be swallowed by the ashes. "We have two very different investigations facing us. Yours involves fundamental political, military, and economic issues with international ramifications. While mine is of a far more personal nature."

Wrexford shifted his stance. "But for me it is no less important. The concept of right and wrong applies with equal force, no matter whether it touches an individual or an entire nation."

Charlotte looked up through her lashes and nodded in sympathy. "You need to tell Kit about Greeley."

Sheffield sat up a little straighter. "Yes, Charlotte mentioned that you had been summoned to Oxford by Neville Greeley," he said. "Poor fellow—is he in trouble?"

"He's dead," answered Wrexford bluntly. "Stabbed to death in the Merton College Library before I had a chance to speak with him."

Sheffield listened in shocked silence as he repeated the story he had recounted to Charlotte.

"Good God," he intoned once the earl had finished. "Greeley, of all people. His murder makes no sense."

"It makes even less sense after hearing it a second time," opined Charlotte. "Does nobody at the college have an idea as to who might have wished Greeley ill?"

"No. By all accounts, he lived a very quiet life and kept to himself," replied Wrexford. "However, the position of his corpse suggested that he knew his assailant."

Charlotte frowned in thought. "And nobody saw an intruder or heard an argument save for the visiting librarian from Württemberg?"

"No," he repeated.

"I take it that you are confident that this von Münch fellow is trustworthy and telling the truth?" asked Sheffield.

Wrexford wished that he could snap back with his usual sarcasm. But his self-confidence had been shaken by the murder, in ways that he couldn't explain, not even to himself.

"I'm not sure of anything right now," he answered. "Save for one simple fact . . ."

His gaze moved to the cold ashes in the hearth.

"I've made a promise to myself—and to the memory of my late brother—that I will not rest easy until I solve this murder and see that the killer is brought to justice. Greeley deserves no less."

CHAPTER 8

"Bloody hell, Wrex!" An oath suddenly echoed off the wainscoting of the corridor, followed by the familiar gravelly growl of their good friend, Basil Henning. "Why is it that every time you stumble over a dead body, you have it sent to me?"

"I send the bodies to you, Baz," answered Wrexford as the surgeon entered the parlor, "because you have an ungodly knack for coaxing secrets from the dead."

"Be that as it may . . ." Henning ran a hand over his bristly jaw. "I'm not overly fond of having such an intimate conversation with a man who was a good friend and comrade."

The admission took Charlotte by surprise. Basil Henning—a crusty Scottish surgeon whose sarcasm was as sharp-edged as Highland granite—was not one for betraying any flicker of sentimentality. But as he had served in the military with Wrexford during the Peninsular War, she realized that he must have known Greeley.

"I'm so sorry, Baz. It must have been . . ." *Shocking? Upsetting?* She hesitated, searching for a word that wouldn't reduce a flesh-and-blood individual to a trite condolence.

Unable to summon any lofty sentiments, she simply said, "It must have been heartbreaking."

Henning moved to the side table by Wrexford, leaving a trail of mud on the carpet, and splashed a generous measure of whisky into a glass. "As you know, lassie, I don't have a heart," he muttered after taking a noisy slurp.

His gruff demeanor didn't quite hide the sadness shading his scowl.

"But you definitely have a stomach," she replied, forcing a show of humor. Henning wouldn't thank her for dwelling on emotions. She glanced at McClellan, who had already risen from her chair.

"I'll fetch another tray of food from the kitchen," said the maid.

"Sustenance would be very welcome, Mac," said the surgeon as he slouched down into the chair facing the earl.

"So," said Wrexford, after allowing Henning to take several long swallows of his whisky. "Did Greeley's mortal remains have anything to say about the person who killed him?"

"Just that whoever wielded the weapon knew how to use it," answered the surgeon. "The thrust was perfectly aimed—it didn't even nick a rib—and death was instantaneous."

"My impression was the same," said Wrexford.

"The killer may have just been lucky," pointed out Sheffield.

"Perhaps," conceded the earl. His brows knitted together. "But what I cannot fathom is why anyone would murder Greeley. He was a quiet recluse, a threat to nobody."

Charlotte fisted her hands in her lap. "And yet," she said softly, "someone wanted him dead."

McClellan returned with a fresh platter of meat and bread and set it down on the table beside Henning's chair.

"Bless you." The surgeon sliced off a morsel of roast beef and wolfed it down before heaving a sigh. "We may never know the reason. The Grim Reaper feels no compunction to explain himself to us mere mortals."

An uneasy silence settled over them. The talk of death—a topic that touched her husband and Henning in a very visceral way—seemed to squeeze all the air from the room.

It was Sheffield who ventured to break the tension. "The only clues seem to be the missing manuscript and the fact that Greeley mentioned Wrex shortly before he was killed. So the question is . . ." He frowned. "How the devil do they tie together?"

Try as she might, Charlotte couldn't muster even a ghost of an answer.

Sheffield waited, but when nobody ventured to speak, his gaze moved to Wrexford. "I understand your desire for justice. But how the devil do you intend to solve the murder if you also intend to help Charlotte gather information about the mysterious fire at Maudslay's laboratory?"

"Griffin," said Charlotte. "You must hire Griffin to help you."

She and Wrexford had first met the Bow Street Runner when the earl was the prime suspect in a grisly murder. Their initial antagonism had turned to respect—and then to friendship. Griffin's taciturn demeanor and plodding movements fooled many people into thinking he was slow-witted, though in truth he possessed a clever, methodical mind. He had proved to be a valuable ally in their subsequent investigations.

"Yes," confirmed Wrexford. "I plan to meet with him first thing in the morning." Bow Street Runners were permitted to take on private commissions. "I shall, of course, sweeten the offer by footing the bill for a sinfully expensive breakfast."

Griffin was very fond of hearty meals—especially when the earl was paying for them.

"A wise move," responded Sheffield. "If anyone can help you sniff out the truth, it's Griffin."

The earl blew out his breath. "I am under no illusion that it will be easy," said Wrexford. "One place to start is with the missing manuscript. Greeley's assistant librarian did some research on it. Only five copies were made, and there is documentation that three have been destroyed over the centuries. However, he was told by the under-librarian at the Balliol College Library that the fifth copy, though rumored to have been lost in a shipwreck in the Tyrrhenian Sea, may in fact be in the King's Library at Buckingham House."

His eyes flicked to Charlotte. "By the by, the manuscript is a copy of a late fifteenth-century Renaissance workbook, and its title is *Nihil Est Quod Hominum Efficere Non Possit*."

"There is nothing that man can't accomplish," she translated. "What sort of workbook? Is it considered an important scholarly work?"

"I've no idea," replied Wrexford. "The catalogue notes at the Balliol College Library had no information on its contents."

"Mysteries wrapped in mysteries," muttered Sheffield.

Charlotte felt a cold-as-ice pebbling of gooseflesh skate down her arms. That she and her loved ones had been drawn into not one but *two* difficult—and possibly dangerous—investigations stirred a frisson of fear.

The earl said nothing.

"Too damn many of them," added their friend. "You both need to be careful."

"That goes for you, too, Kit, if you intend to help Charlotte gather information about the race to build an oceangoing steamship," said Wrexford. "Asking questions about the government and its research could stir up a nest of vipers."

He turned to Charlotte. "And you, my dear—be damnably sure that you don't deliberately poke your pen into Grentham's eyeball just as a personal challenge."

She understood his fears. Britain's shadowy spymaster was not a man with whom to trifle. But she had promised herself never to let fear or expediency nudge the needle of her moral compass away from the Truth.

"You know that I take my responsibilities to the public very seriously, Wrex," responded Charlotte. "I have sworn an oath to myself never to be petty or reckless."

"Yes, it's one of the myriad reasons I admire you." He released a grudging sigh. "It's also one of the myriad reasons you terrify me."

"Bah!" Henning refilled his glass. "I still say Grentham wouldn't dare reveal A. J. Quill's identity, even if he knew it. The government would be the laughingstock of the country if it were known that a woman has been bedeviling the high and mighty for years without them knowing it."

Sheffield bit back a laugh. "I have to say, I agree with Baz." But after a glance at Wrexford he hastily added, "However, it would be best not to put the assumption to the test."

The lamplight flickered, accentuating the sallow hue of her husband's face and the lines of fatigue etching out from the corners of his eyes.

"I think we've had enough shocking revelations for one night," said Charlotte. "I suggest we . . ."

She looked around on hearing footsteps in the corridor. A moment later, Tyler came through the doorway. The look on his face didn't bode well.

"I learned some unsettling news this evening while out with a few acquaintances." The valet had a wide range of contacts all around Town, including in less salubrious places where angels feared to tread. She and Wrexford had never inquired as to why, but it had proved very useful in their previous investigations.

"And?"

Tyler looked away, but not before she saw a spasm of guilt. "The authorities have arrested a man and charged him with setting the blaze that destroyed Maudslay's laboratory."

Recalling Sheffield's uneasiness about Maudslay's missing technical drawings and her own bad feelings about the incident, Charlotte drew in a deep breath. "So, it seems I was right to suspect that the fire *wasn't* simply an unfortunate accident."

"Yes, m'lady." Tyler closed his eyes for an instant and released a sigh. "Indeed, I happen to know for sure that it was arson."

"How—" began Wrexford.

"I was waiting for your return, milord, to explain how the truth came to light," interjected the valet. He looked to Charlotte with an apologetic grimace. "I'm sorry, m'lady. You seemed troubled by other concerns . . ." His gaze slid to McClellan for an instant. "So I thought it might be best to hold off until His Lordship came home."

"That bad?" she asked.

The valet had the grace to flush. "You're not going to like it."

"Nonetheless," replied Charlotte, "we need to hear it."

Tyler cleared his throat. "The Weasels overheard you and His Lordship and Mr. Sheffield discussing the situation on the night of the fire and decided that they wanted to help . . ."

Charlotte listened with growing dismay as he recounted what the boys had done.

"Peregrine was not involved in the foray," the valet hastened to add. "And though I know I shouldn't say such a thing, it was quite clever of the Weasels to think of gathering the glass fragments and bringing them to me for examination under the microscope."

A pause. "Given that a violent crime had been committed—one that could have killed innocent workers—I did take the liberty of telling Griffin that the fire had been an act of arson."

Tyler paused. "It seems he assigned some of his junior Runners to investigate, and they found a witness—a tailor's apprentice who was returning home late at night—who had seen the man running away. Based on his description of the man and his clothing, several suspects were rounded up, and the witness was able to identify the arsonist."

"Who is the accused man?" asked Charlotte. "And why did he commit the crime?"

"I'm sorry, m'lady, but I don't know the answers to those questions," replied the valet.

"You did, however, make an analysis of the substance used to start the fire?" inquired Wrexford.

"Yes. The accelerant was a sophisticated chemical compound, not simply lamp oil."

"Which would mean," intoned the earl, "that it needed to be made in a laboratory."

"That is my surmise, milord," said Tyler.

Charlotte understood what that meant. And a glance at the others showed that they did as well.

"I wonder who hired the fellow?" muttered Sheffield.

"That is for the authorities to discover." Wrexford shifted, throwing his face into shadow. "Bloody hell, it's clear that the competition to create a marine propulsion system is fraught with hidden dangers." He waited for a moment, allowing his words to sink in before adding, "And the villains aren't the only ones playing with fire."

His voice had taken on a grim edge. "I will say it again, my love. You and Kit must be very careful in how you go about investigating the race to build an oceangoing steamship. Otherwise, you both run the risk of getting burned."

For a moment the room was deathly still.

Then Henning cleared his throat with a rusty cough. "Bloody hell, this group is always setting off sparks, laddie." Candlelight glinted off his glass as he drank down the last of his whisky.

"And we haven't yet gone up in flames."

CHAPTER 9

"As always, it's a pleasure to see you, milord." The Bow Street Runner looked up from perusing the pages of his pocket notebook and signaled for the tavern's serving wench to come take their order. "I confess, reading makes me hungry."

"*Everything* makes you hungry, Griffin." Wrexford took a seat opposite his friend at the none-too-pristine table tucked into a corner alcove. "Most especially a proximity to me and my purse."

"Indeed, this is an unexpected pleasure," replied Griffin after requesting enough food to fell an ox. "I thought you and your family were planning to rusticate in the country, now that shooting season for you fancy toffs is about to begin."

The earl ordered nothing but a pot of coffee. "I've had my fill of things that go *bang*," he said as the woman hurried away.

That drew a chuckle. Their most recent investigation together had involved recovering the plans and prototype for a revolutionary pistol. The hunt had set off a number of fireworks.

"Understandably so, milord. May you and Lady Wrexford

feast on some peace and quiet . . ." Griffin hesitated, his lidded eyes intent on the earl's expression. "Or is this not a purely social visit?"

"Alas, no," replied Wrexford. "Much as I enjoy watching you stuff your gullet, this meeting is for professional reasons."

The serving wench returned with a monstrous tray and placed several large platters on the table along with the earl's pot of coffee.

"There's been a murder," he continued, once they were alone. "And I wish to engage your services to help me track down the killer."

Griffin forked up a bite of shirred eggs. "If you need my assistance, then I take it the case is a complicated one."

"Actually, it may be an impossible one. There is no discernable motive, and precious few clues." The smoke-hazed air swirled as a gust rattled against the nearby window. "But I know how much you enjoy working miracles."

Griffin carefully sliced off a morsel of ham. "Miracles will cost you extra, milord."

"I expect no less." Wrexford put an end to their banter by drawing a measured breath and recounting the details of Greeley's murder.

"You say the man is naught but an acquaintance?" mused the Runner after taking several long moments to digest what he had just heard. "And yet your interest in the crime is far more than casual."

He buttered a piece of toast. "I ask, milord, not to pry into your personal affairs but because the more I understand about the case, the better my chances are of helping you solve it."

Wrexford watched the flitting shadows in the gloom behind the Runner. "Greeley was my late brother's best friend. He survived a French ambush during the Peninsular War." The earl looked down at his untouched mug of coffee. "My brother did not."

Griffin quietly put down his fork and knife.

"The wounds left grievous scars, both physical and mental, on Greeley," said Wrexford softly. "That some miscreant has robbed him of what little he had left of life—and thinks that the crime will go unpunished—sits ill on my conscience. I feel that I owe it to both their memories to make sure that the murderer answers for his crime."

Their gazes locked. "I want justice, whatever the cost."

"Where would you like me to start, milord?" said Griffin without hesitation.

"In Oxford," answered Wrexford. "I spent a day looking into Greeley's life, but there is far more sleuthing to be done there." He explained the specifics of the murder and the fact that a manuscript was missing.

"There's a possibility that someone saw the killer entering or leaving Merton College," added the earl. "Or that some small details of Greeley's everyday life will provide a clue to follow."

"I shall leave this afternoon, milord." The Runner cracked his knuckles. "We will find the murderer, milord. No matter how well hidden, there is always a clue that will lead to the truth."

"Hmmph." The dowager Countess of Peake took a moment to polish her quizzing glass before raising it and subjecting Charlotte to a greatly magnified one-eyed stare. "Good heavens, I thought we were taking a respite from solving crimes."

Charlotte gave an inward wince at her great-aunt's use of the word *we*. Granted, Alison had proved both clever and resourceful in several of their previous investigations. However, sleuthing was far too dangerous for a lady of her advanced years.

But heaven forfend that she voice such a thought aloud.

"*We* are," responded Charlotte. "Taking a respite, that is."

As a treat for the boys before Peregrine went back to Eton

for the Michaelmas term, the dowager had stopped by to invite them for ices at Gunter's Tea Shop and then to view the cavalry maneuvers on the parade ground behind Horse Guards and the Admiralty. And so Charlotte had reluctantly explained about the fire and the murder in Oxford, deciding it was better for Alison to hear the details from her rather than from Raven and Hawk, who would no doubt add their own lurid embellishments.

As for the unsettling incident at the King's Dockyard, the boys didn't know about the sketches she had copied, and Charlotte thought it best to keep it that way.

"We have resolved to leave both crimes for the proper authorities to handle," she clarified. That wasn't precisely a lie, simply a little bending of the truth. "I've merely informed you of certain recent events so that you aren't alarmed by any exaggerations that Raven and Hawk might make to the actual facts. But as I said, we are *not* becoming involved in any investigations."

"I see." Alison regarded her with a critical squint, light winking off the lenses of her spectacles.

Charlotte maintained an air of innocence, hoping her cheeks weren't turning a telltale red.

"Well, then." The dowager gathered up her reticule. "If there is nothing else to add . . ."

She shook her head.

"Let us call the Weasels and Peregrine down from their eyrie and see if they have a hankering for some sweets."

The boys were duly summoned, but only Raven and Hawk appeared. "Peregrine went to see Mr. Hedley at his laboratory in the Royal Institution," said Raven. The inventor had given the boys an open invitation to stop by any time with their scientific questions. "He—"

"He wanted to show Mr. Hedley a sketch of his mechanical hound and see if it could be made to move by inserting a gear-

and-spring mechanism," finished Hawk. "If we walk there first, we can fetch him and then all go for ices at Gunter's."

"That's very thoughtful of you, sweeting," said Charlotte. To Alison, she added, "Though that means a rather long stroll to Albemarle Street and back."

Raven immediately moved to offer the dowager his arm. "We will go slowly, and Aunt Alison can lean on me for support."

"And me," piped up Hawk.

"Well, with two such stalwart escorts, I shall have no trouble navigating the distance." The dowager gave them a fond grin. "Besides, I shall be the envy of all the ladies we pass for having not just one but two handsome young gentlemen attending me."

Raven made a rude sound. "Ha! You know very well that we're not gentlemen."

"Yes," said the dowager, a wink of mischief lighting her sapphirine eyes. "But Polite Society doesn't know that, which makes it all the more amusing to cock a snoot at them."

She placed a hand on Raven's sleeve. "Come, let's be off."

"Wrex—" Sheffield stopped short at the entrance of White's on seeing Wrexford come out of the exclusive gentlemen's club and start down the marble stairs. "Are you headed off on some errand?"

"Yes," he answered. "I wish to pay a visit to the British Museum and see if the scholarly staff there has ever heard of the manuscript that was stolen from the Merton College Library."

"That makes some sense," responded Sheffield. "But . . ." He hesitated. "But might you put that mission off for an hour or two? I'm hoping you can accompany me to a lecture at the Royal Institution, which begins shortly."

"Kit, much as I enjoy scientific—"

"It's important, Wrex," interrupted his friend. "I'll explain why, but first you need to hear the lecture."

The earl hesitated. A small delay in talking with the museum's scholars wouldn't make a difference. . . .

And the look on Sheffield's face told him it was no idle request. "Very well. I'll come with you."

It was only a short stroll to Albemarle Street and the imposing classical facade of the Royal Institution, one of Britain's leading scientific societies. Sheffield quickened his steps, leading the way down to the main auditorium, where the featured speaker was just coming to the podium.

A rhythmic *whoosh-clang* suddenly began to sound from behind the crimson velvet curtain hanging on one side of the stage.

"That's the Honorable Reginald Maitland. He's giving the presentation," explained Sheffield as they settled into their seats.

"Reginald Maitland," repeated Wrexford. "Why does that name strike a bell?"

"He was at Oxford with us. A very scientifically minded fellow. In fact, many people thought him nearly as brilliant as you. But your interests didn't overlap."

The earl studied the man's face as he set his folder of notes down and began to shuffle through the pages. He looked vaguely familiar.

"As I recall," observed Wrexford, as a few hazy details came floating back to mind, "Maitland had a very high opinion of himself." A pause. "One that was unmerited on the cricket field."

"A great many fellows don't show well during their university days." His friend smiled. "I seem to recall that there were more than few people who thought your social graces left much to be desired."

The earl ignored the barb.

"At that age, we are young and foolish—and full of hubris. But people can change," said Sheffield dryly. "Just look at me."

The earl gave a rude grunt.

"Word is, Maitland has become quite an innovative thinker and a wizard at engineering," continued his friend. "He's spent the last five years in America, working with some of their boldest men of science in the field of nautical innovations."

Maitland cleared his throat with a cough, quieting the auditorium. And then with a theatrical gesture, he signaled for the curtain to be opened.

A flutter of crimson velvet . . . revealing a machine belching a cloud of silvery vapor.

"Behold!" announced Maitland. "An ordinary steam engine, which as we all know can perform a multitude of supremely useful tasks that were once unimaginable, from pumping water to powering looms and propelling an iron carriage along a set of rails."

He paused, and the audience stirred in anticipation.

There was, acknowledged Wrexford, an element of showmanship necessary in science. One needed to excite people about new discoveries. He waited, curious as to how Maitland would continue.

"But today I come to talk to you about a revolutionary new twist to this machine," announced Maitland. "One that will change our perception of time and distance!"

He paused again and smiled, clearly aware of the unseen electricity that was now thrumming through the auditorium.

"Since ancient times, great minds have strived to understand the clockwork order of the universe. Men like Newton with his laws of motion, and Galileo with his studies of velocity." His voice rose, every word smoothly confident. "Mathematics is one of the keys to unlocking the mysteries of our physical world, and today I shall focus particularly on the renowned Swiss mathematicians Daniel Bernoulli and Leonhard Euler."

Maitland was an excellent speaker, conceded Wrexford.

"As many of you here know, Bernoulli was renowned for his scientific insights regarding fluid mechanics. His book *Hydrodynamica*, published in 1738, contained the famous Bernoulli's Principle, which states that when the flow speed of a fluid increases, its pressure decreases."

Maitland raised a finger. "Keep that in mind, gentlemen."

Wrexford angled a sidelong glance at Sheffield and saw that his friend was as captivated as the rest of the audience.

"It was Bernoulli's close friend Euler who derived Bernoulli's Equation in 1752, which set out Bernoulli's Principle in mathematical form," continued Maitland. "Another important development. But now let us move on to another momentous discovery in the annals of science . . ."

"This is excellent thinking, Peregrine." Hedley looked up from the boy's diagrams. "You have a very creative mind when it comes to engineering." He went back to studying the details. "You're essentially right about how a gear-and-spring mechanism could be added to make your hound walk."

He picked up a pen and drew a series of sketches on a fresh sheet of paper. "Here are some simple ways it can be done. Bring along your prototype next week, and we'll take a closer look."

"Thank you, sir," replied Peregrine. He carefully folded the inventor's sketches and put them in his jacket pocket. "Umm, might I ask another question, sir?"

"Ask as many as you like!" Hedley smiled. "Inquisitiveness is a trait to be much encouraged—especially in lads of your age."

"Well . . ." Peregrine cleared his throat. "The Weasels and I were thinking the other day about steam-powered ships . . ." He hesitated. "Do you believe that a marine propulsion system can be made that is powerful enough to cross the oceans?"

"I like to believe that nothing is impossible in the future," answered Hedley. "But as for now . . ." He rubbed meditatively at his jaw. "It's an excellent question. It would be a revolutionary breakthrough . . ."

The *clack* and *hum* of several mechanical devices running in the laboratory filled the silence as the inventor considered the possibilities.

"Mr. Samuel Tilden, who works for Royal Navy at the King's Dockyard, invited me and the Weasels to visit their laboratories yesterday," ventured Peregrine. "I think . . ." He lowered his voice. "I think that he is working on making an oceangoing steamship."

"Well, it doesn't surprise me that the navy would be in the forefront of such research," replied the inventor. "And Mr. Tilden is a very talented engineer . . ."

Hedley's face was suddenly wreathed in a smile. "Speaking of marine steam power, I've just remembered that I recently received a new illustrated book from America on nautical steam power, including a special section on Robert Fulton's famous riverboat, the *Clermont*. There are some marvelous diagrams and colored engravings of its engine and paddle wheels. You are most welcome to stay and peruse the pages."

After batting at a swirl of steam that floated over his desk, the inventor added, "But it's awfully damp and noisy in here. Why don't you take it to the reading room at the end of the corridor? There is no one else working up here today, so you should have the place to yourself."

Peregrine accepted the book and hurried out the door, eager to study the pictures. As Hedley had surmised, the room was empty. The wood paneling and carved bookcases gave the place a dark formality, and with the lamps unlit and the draperies half drawn, the leather armchairs by the hearth were wreathed in shadows.

The boy moved to the bank of windows and found a cozy spot behind a leather sofa that allowed him to sit cross-legged on the carpet and brace his back against the age-soft calfskin. After opening the book and settling it in his lap to catch the sunlight, he was soon lost in studying the engravings and accompanying technical diagrams.

"I told you this was the perfect place for privacy." The door closed with a muted *click*. "You may be sure that nobody will overhear us in here."

Taken by surprise, Peregrine held his breath.

The sound of steps was muffled to a discreet whisper by the thick Axminster carpet. At first, he thought they were coming toward him, but at the last minute they veered away to a round table set in the center of the room.

A flint struck steel, and a moment later a plume of smoke curled up, filling the air with the scent of tobacco.

"So." A long exhale from The Smoker. "Have you brought the documents?"

"Yes, we finished drawing them up last night," answered a baritone voice. "I think you'll find them to your satisfaction."

A pause. "Take special note of our Advisory Board. As I promised you, the Earl of Mulgrave, the previous First Lord of the Admiralty and currently Master-General of the Ordnance, has agreed to lend his name to the project. As has the royal Duke of Sussex and several very influential members of Parliament. Their show of support will give our endeavor even more gravitas with potential investors."

"Hmmph." Papers rustled as The Smoker set them on the table and began to read through them.

Holding himself very still, Peregrine willed them to finish their business quickly and leave. A sneeze was tickling at his nostrils.

"And of course we expect to add several more distinguished

names to the Advisory Board after Maitland finishes regaling the audience here today with his scientific genius."

"Hmmph." The Smoker inhaled and blew out a perfect ring before continuing. "I've heard that Henry Maudslay is also working on a marine steam engine. Given his astounding successes in technical innovation, I would think he would be a serious competitor to your consortium. So tell me why I should invest with you."

"Maudslay has suffered a serious setback," answered Baritone Voice. "Word is, the unfortunate attack on his laboratory damaged his lathes and a number of milled pieces for his prototype engine." A pause. "Even more importantly, it also seems that his technical drawings, which recorded all the precision specifications, went up in smoke. Which essentially means he will have to start over."

More rustling, and then a moment of silence. "You think Maitland has invented a system that will actually conquer the oceans?" asked The Smoker.

"He has been working for the last five years in New York, where the American geniuses in engineering are far ahead of the rest of the world in this area of innovation," answered Baritone Voice. "Indeed, Maitland was part of Robert Fulton's team that launched the first successful steamboat service on the North River. Then he moved to work with Stephen Vail in the state of New Jersey, where his Speedwell Ironworks was doing experimental work with creating stronger iron for steam engines. With the help of Samuel Carson, who had trained at the legendary Boulton & Watt steam engine factory, they also developed new designs for condensers, boilers, pistons, rods, and pumps, all of which allowed them to design a far more powerful type of steam engine."

His boots shifted on the soft carpet. "He then moved on to work with the leaders in paddle wheel and hull design."

"Impressive credentials," said The Smoker. He paused to exhale another silvery ring of smoke. "But— "

"But the truth is, as a businessman you're asking the wrong question," interjected Baritone Voice in a silky tone.

Peregrine inched a little closer to the end of the sofa, straining to catch the gentleman's next words.

"Let us look at the potential for making money that this initial offering gives to our small circle of charter investors. We are buying our shares at a very favorable price—an insider deal, if you will. Once the company succeeds, the value of our shares shall shoot up in value."

Baritone Voice paused. "And even before then, as word spreads of the company's potential, there will be an immediate clamoring among the beau monde to buy into the consortium. We will issue a set number of new shares to help meet the demand, but so as not to dilute the value of the company, we will also allow charter investors to sell some of their shares at the new, higher prices—resulting in immediate profit before the company is a proven venture."

"But these supposedly innovative ventures are still very risky," pointed out The Smoker. "If this one fails, we as shareholders are liable for all the debts of the bankrupt company."

"Ah, but that is where it gets even more interesting," replied Baritone Voice. "You are familiar with the Bubble Act?"

"I'm somewhat aware of the basics," said The Smoker. "It's the Act that Parliament passed in reaction to the South Seas fiasco some years ago, when the highly speculative venture collapsed, leaving the company penniless and the stockholders liable for its huge debts."

"Yes," agreed Baritone Voice. "They passed that Act in 1720. Now, as gentlemen, you and I need not fuss with all the boring legalities, but the point is that the Act prohibited companies from being formed in such a way as to limit the liability of shareholders to *only* their original investment and protected them from any responsibility for the company's full debts."

"Which is exactly why I am concerned—" began The Smoker.

"Hear me out," interrupted Baritone Voice. "I happen to know that Lady Kirkwall has been having some very substantive private talks with prominent members of Parliament, and she assures me that the Bubble Act will soon be repealed. Our company will thus be organized with that limited liability for shareholders as soon as the repeal is in place."

He lowered his voice. "We charter investors will have all the potential of great profit as well as protection from any debts accrued by the company should it fail."

"That's very useful to know," murmured The Smoker.

"But of course," Baritone Voice added, "I am supremely confident that we are on the cusp of conquering the oceans. Furthermore, Maitland will soon be making an announcement on a remarkable new development, one that will have people clamoring to be part of the consortium."

The papers crackled.

"So if I were you, I would make up my mind quickly. The chance to be one of the chosen few will soon be sold out."

"You're very persuasive." The Smoker exhaled one last puff and stubbed out his cigar. "I'll let you know my decision by nightfall."

They moved to the door. The latch opened and shut with a muted click.

Peregrine slowly counted to one hundred before creeping out from his hiding place and hurrying to quit the reading room. But to his dismay, as he approached Hedley's laboratory he saw that the inventor was standing in the corridor chatting with two gentlemen.

Flattening himself against the dark wood wainscoting, he froze and held his breath.

"... innovative engineering and bold new bold thinking are the catalyst for Progress!" It was Hedley speaking. "By Jove, we live in exciting times, Lord Taviot."

"Indeed, we do." It was Baritone Voice.

"I've heard that you are soon to make a grand announcement," continued Hedley. "I am very much looking forward to it."

Baritone Voice acknowledged the words with a courtly nod. "I'm quite confident that you and General Aldrich won't be disappointed."

CHAPTER 10

"So, what do you think, Wrex?" asked Sheffield.

The lecture had ended, and while most of the audience had crowded around the stage, eager to ask Maitland more questions about his work, Wrexford and Sheffield had exited the auditorium and found an empty study room at the rear of the building.

"I think," replied the earl, "that Maitland displayed an impressive knowledge of scientific developments in his field of expertise. In addition, he clearly possesses an advanced skill of mathematics and an understanding of the physical laws governing speed and motion."

Sheffield nodded enthusiastically. "Yes, yes—I thought the same thing—"

"But I haven't quite finished, Kit," interrupted Wrexford. He then hesitated, wishing to choose his next words with care. "Engineering is not my specialty, so it would be foolish of me to opine on whether his abstract concept of a marine propulsion system powerful enough to tame the world's oceans is possible. However, one would think the fellow would offer a modicum of empirical evidence to back up the assertions that he and Taviot's consortium have made a momentous scientific breakthrough."

"I daresay he's being extremely careful not to reveal proprietary knowledge," replied Sheffield. "We both know the monetary value of patents on mechanical innovations. And given what recently happened at Maudslay's laboratory, one can't blame him for not saying too much about the specifics."

"Those are fair points." The earl hesitated. "Be that as it may, why did you ask me to come hear Maitland spout on about a new wave of progress that is about to change the world?"

In answer, his friend opened the portfolio case he was carrying and took out a sheaf of documents. "Because Lord Taviot came to see me this morning. He overheard Lord Mulgrave mention that I was an early investor in Hedley's Puffing Billy and offered me the opportunity to become a charter investor in his consortium's venture."

Sheffield spread out the papers. "He also asked me to join the Advisory Board, which he says will make me a very rich man if the company is successful."

Wrexford knew how sensitive Sheffield was about money—or the lack of it. A younger son with no assets of his own, his friend had chafed for years under the iron-fisted grip of his parsimonious father, receiving naught but a pittance as an allowance. In retaliation, he had indulged in rakehell excesses, which did neither himself nor his father any good.

"You are already quite prosperous, Kit," pointed out the earl. "You and Cordelia, along with your two partners, have built a solid, reputable company that returns a handsome profit."

"Yes." Sheffield slowly let out a sigh. "But I'm not yet able to afford any meaningful tangible assets. Like land and a manor house—a place where one can set down roots, raise a family, and pass property on to future generations."

He looked up, a martial light in his eyes. "I want to offer that possibility to Cordelia as a wedding present. It will take years before I can do that with my share of our profits from our shipping company."

The earl blinked. Sheffield's yearning made him damnably aware of how fickle life was. Through a mere accident of birth, he had never wanted for anything. As the eldest son, he had inherited a fortune and an earldom on his father's death, along with a number of estates scattered across England and Scotland.

While my brother, the better man of us, was cruelly cut down before his life had really begun.

Ignoring the sudden stab of pain within his chest, Wrexford forced his attention back to the present moment.

"Far be it for me to insult your intelligence or your business acumen, which is far sharper than mine, Kit," he finally said. "After all, *I* wasn't smart enough to invest in Hedley's Puffing Billy."

Hedley's prototype had not yet been developed into a viable commercial endeavor, but Sheffield had seen the potential and had purchased a number of shares in the company—and then had sold them at a great profit.

"However," Wrexford continued, "I feel beholden to remind you that an investment in a new venture is not guaranteed to yield riches. The offer of great reward goes hand in hand with great risk. You could lose your entire investment."

"I'm aware of that." After glancing at the door to confirm that it was firmly shut, Sheffield stepped closer and lowered his voice. "But if it works . . ."

"*If*," repeated Wrexford. "As I've pointed out, for all his impressive eloquence, Maitland has offered no actual scientific details to support his grandiose claims. And to my knowledge, Taviot has no scientific acumen." Indeed, the Scottish earl was said to be very skilled in the art of diplomacy, but a silvery tongue was no substitute for actual knowledge.

"So that would make me leery . . ."

Wrexford had already glanced at the papers on the table and seen the names listed on the preliminary Advisory Board. "But then again, this proposal clearly shows that they have convinced some very prominent people that Maitland and the consortium have the ability to do what they say they can do."

Sheffield's expression brightened. "Precisely! So doesn't that say something about it being a reasonable risk?"

The earl released a slow breath. He didn't wish to throw cold water on his friend's dreams. But there were enough unanswered questions about the endeavor to make him uneasy.

"Not exactly," he replied. "Do keep in mind that your friend Maudslay is considered a genius at engineering. And if he hasn't yet discovered the secret to crafting a successful engine, then perhaps it is prudent to ask how Maitland has triumphed where a leading luminary in the field has failed."

"Even a visionary like Maudslay can be wrong on occasion," retorted Sheffield. "As I recall, everyone thought the American Robert Fulton was a madman when he suggested that steam could power a boat. All the so-called experts insisted that the concept was not only dangerous but impossible. And yet Fulton proved all the naysayers wrong. His steamboat runs on a regular schedule up and down the North River from New York City to Albany, undaunted by wind and currents. And as it has proved faster and more dependable than a sailing vessel, it's proving a financial success."

Wrexford conceded the point with a nod.

"You are the one who is always telling me that innovation rarely follows a straight line," pressed his friend. "So perhaps Maitland is right in implying that he's a greater genius than Maudslay."

"What does Cordelia think?" asked the earl. "You are about to be married, which is an even more important partnership than your business relationship."

"She is dead set against the idea," muttered Sheffield. "But if she doesn't trust my judgment . . ." His jaw tightened. "What sort of way is that to begin a life together?"

How to answer? Sheffield and Cordelia's relationship had been fraught with challenges. They each had vulnerabilities that stirred inner doubts. All their friends could see that they were perfect for each other. But the only thing that mattered was how they saw themselves.

"Disagreement doesn't mean she doesn't trust your judgment. Quite the contrary, in fact. She trusts that you will listen to her objections and that the two of you will come to a decision together."

Sheffield's expression turned mulish.

"I'm simply suggesting that you ask yourself hard questions before making a financial commitment, Kit. It's an important decision for you and your future." Acutely aware of not wanting to push his friend one way or the other, he added, "The fact that you are asking my opinion says to me that you are clearly uncertain of whether this feels right to you. Why not gather more empirical information on the subject? For a start, we can go upstairs and have a chat with Hedley, who understands the concept of steam power as well as anyone."

A breeze wafted through the half-open window, and a shadow cast by the fluttering draperies hid his friend's expression.

"All I'm saying is that it's always best not to rush into a momentous decision," he added. "So that it doesn't blow up in your face."

"Don't wipe those sticky fingers on your breeches," warned the dowager as she offered Hawk a napkin. "We don't wish for the ladies and gentlemen strolling down Bond Street to think that you boys are wild savages."

"We don't?" sniggered Raven, which earned a chortle from Peregrine.

Alison arched her brows. "Would you like for me to purchase a bag of Pontefract cakes before we head to the parade grounds?"

"Yes!" Hawk, who was very fond of the sweetened licorice disks, nudged his brother. "Of course we would."

"Well, then, I'm sure you'll agree it's important to both look *and* behave like proper gentlemen when we take our places to watch the military maneuvers."

"Wrex says that being a proper gentleman is vastly overrated," responded Raven, a saucy grin playing at the corners of his mouth.

"When you are his age, you may say the same thing." Alison waggled her cane. "But until then—"

"Until then," intoned Raven, "we must behave like boring little nitwits."

The dowager stifled an unladylike snort. "I would be happy if you refrain from any unholy mischief—like throwing a stink bomb into the formation of cavalry horses and causing a stampede."

Raven and Hawk exchanged guilty looks.

"Perhaps you should empty your pockets and have the serving maid dispose of any questionable items while I stop for the sweets," ordered Alison.

The cakes duly purchased—with Raven volunteering to take charge of the bag—the four of them climbed into the dowager's carriage, which was waiting outside the tea shop, and made the short journey to Whitehall Street. As they started to walk through the imposing entrance to the Admiralty buildings and the adjoining parade ground, Alison stopped short on spotting a young midshipman coming from the opposite direction.

"*Horatio*?"

The midshipman—it was Mr. Porter from the King's Dockyard—looked up, his eyes widening in surprise.

"My dear boy—it *is* you!" exclaimed Alison. "Come give your Auntie Peake a hug!"

Raven and Hawk exchanged astonished looks as Horatio gave them a sheepish grimace and then hurried to embrace the dowager.

"How is your mother?" inquired Alison, adding a fond pat to the boy's cheek. "And your little sister?"

"Quite well, according to their last letter, Auntie Peake," he replied.

"Horatio's mother is my late husband's grandniece by marriage," explained the dowager to the boys. "Which makes us . . ." She gave an airy wave. "Oh, pish—it makes us family." Another caress. "I didn't realize you were here in London."

"I only arrived a fortnight ago," explained Horatio. "I was transferred from my ship to the King's Dockyard in order to take advanced lessons in navigation and mathematics at the Royal Observatory. I am hoping to join one of the scientific expeditions that the navy undertakes to explore the fauna and flora in remote parts of the globe."

Hawk's eyes widened.

"An interest in science—why, how marvelous!" Alison beamed. "You and my dear nephews and their friend will get along swimmingly!"

"We've met," said Horatio, taking care not to look at the Weasels and Peregrine.

Alison gave Raven a searching look.

The boy averted his eyes. "Would you like a Pontefract cake?" he asked stiffly, holding out the bag to the midshipman.

Horatio hesitated.

"It doesn't mean we have to be friends," said Raven. "Go ahead, have one."

"They're very good," encouraged Hawk.

Releasing a sigh, Horatio gingerly took a piece of licorice.

Hawk ventured a tentative smile. "Have two."

The dowager rapped her cane to command their attention. "I take it there is some bad blood between the four of you?"

"Umm, well . . . Mr. Porter came upon us in the naval laboratory at the King's Dockyard and didn't realize we had been invited by Mr. Tilden—" began Peregrine.

"He called Peregrine a nasty name because of the color of his skin," blurted out Raven. "So I threatened to punch him in the nose."

"I—I am very sorry about that," said Horatio, his cheeks flaming in embarrassment. "And I am ashamed of myself. It's just . . ." He stared down at the tips of his boots. "I—I am aware that someone my age looks absurd in an officer's uniform, and so I feel that I must try to sound . . . tough and manly."

"Hmmph!" said Alison, breaking the long moment of taut silence that followed. "Well, if you ask me, I would say the Royal Navy is lucky to have such a fine officer in its ranks." She regarded Raven with a challenging look. "It takes courage and integrity to admit when one is wrong."

It was Peregrine who responded first. "Apologies accepted, Mr. Porter. I understand what you are saying." He made a wry face. "I don't look like an English lord, and it makes me feel very uncomfortable at times."

Horatio hesitated for an instant before offering his hand. "Mr. Porter sounds so pompous. I would rather you call me Horatio."

Raven made a sound in the back of his throat. "Sorry, I can't say that with a straight face, Admiral."

The dowager narrowed her eyes at the jest about Britain's late legendary hero, Admiral Horatio Nelson, who had perished at the Battle of Trafalgar.

"We all go by avian monikers," he added. "I'm Raven, and that's Hawk." A nod indicated his brother. "And our lordly friend is Falcon." After a moment of thought, Raven grinned. "You're a sea bird—how about we dub you Osprey?"

Horatio grinned back at him. "At least you didn't suggest Albatross."

A handshake sealed the friendship, and suddenly the boys were chattering like magpies with each other.

Alison listened with fond approval for an interlude before reluctantly interrupting. "There will be time for jabbering at some later time, but for now, perhaps Horatio—that is, Osprey—would care to join us in watching the Household Cavalry perform its maneuvers. It's quite impressive, and I wouldn't want you boys to miss it."

Horatio gave a longing look at the parade ground. "Alas, I am on duty, Auntie Peake, and must deliver a packet of documents from the Navy Board to Mr. Tilden at the King's Dockyard without further delay."

"What a pity," responded the dowager. "You must send me a note, my dear boy . . ." She gave Horatio her address. "And let me know the first day you have free. I shall take you all for ices at Gunter's."

Horatio appeared awestruck. "I-I've never had ices before."

"They are very good," confided Hawk. "My favorites are strawberry and pineapple."

Alison smiled. "But of course Osprey must try them all and decide for himself."

"Wait," said Raven as the midshipman turned. "Take these." He held out the bag of Pontefract cakes. "We have plenty of sweets at home."

"T-Thank you." With that, Horatio gave a salute and hurried away to the waiting naval carriage.

"What a lovely surprise," said the dowager as she watched him go. "I do hope you boys will become friends."

CHAPTER 11

Charlotte leaned back against the squabs as the carriage rolled through Mayfair and entered the slightly raffish environs of Bloomsbury. Wrexford had sent word that he would not be home until late, as his meeting at the British Museum had led to one of the curators arranging an evening meeting at White's with an expert on rare books and manuscripts.

Having finished her latest drawing for Fores's printshop—another commentary on the plight of soldiers returning home from the wars to find no way of supporting themselves or their families—Charlotte had not been looking forward to an evening alone brooding about the two daunting challenges that she and Wrexford were facing.

Greeley's death, which had her normally unflappable husband off balance . . . the potential threat to Britain's economic and military power, an issue that A. J. Quill could not in good conscience ignore . . . The afternoon visit from the dowager and the need to explain about the new set of crimes—even though she had been careful to deny that they were pulling her and Wrexford into a web of intrigue—had only exacerbated her worries.

And so she had been grateful for Cordelia's last-minute invitation to join her in attending Lady Thirkell's biweekly gathering for intellectually minded ladies. Or rather, the Bluestockings, which was the less complimentary term used by many gentlemen of Polite Society.

One would assume such name-calling was provoked by fear, she mused. No doubt they felt threatened by females who possessed a brain and the courage to use it.

A smile touched her lips. "With good reason," she murmured, thinking of herself and Cordelia. The high-and-mighty gentlemen of the beau monde would likely be quaking in their boots if they had any inkling of what power ladies were already secretly wielding in Society, their iron fists daintily disguised in velvet gloves.

However, Charlotte's humor quickly gave way to puzzlement over why Cordelia was so insistent that she attend this evening's meeting. It so happened that Lady Kirkwall had been invited to appear as a special guest speaker, and given that Cordelia had clearly taken a strong initial dislike to her, it seemed an odd request.

While I, on the other hand, see Lady Kirkwall in a more positive light despite her steely self-confidence.

Or perhaps because of it. Charlotte understood only too well how difficult it was for a woman to forge an independent life for herself in a man's world. It took courage and cleverness, for a lady who wished to test her mettle was always dancing on a razor's edge. The slightest slip could bring disgrace and censure from Society. And so she couldn't help but admire Lady Kirkwall's obvious intelligence and was not averse to deepening the acquaintance.

As the carriage turned down a side street, Charlotte leaned back against the squabs and conceded that the opportunity to learn more about the players and ramifications of the race to build an oceangoing steamship was an added reason that she had accepted the invitation.

As for why Cordelia was attending . . .

But perhaps that mystery would become clearer once she had a chance to speak privately with her friend at Lady Thirkell's residence.

Which was, as Charlotte recalled, an exceedingly eccentric abode.

Her memory was confirmed as the carriage came to a stop in front of a brick townhouse faced with Cotswold limestone that glowed a mellow gold in the setting sun. The main entrance was flanked by ornate Corinthian columns carved from white marble . . . and the front door was painted a shocking shade of fuchsia pink.

Lady Thirkell was just as colorful. Tonight she was wearing an Indian caftan made of shimmering green silk embroidered with tigers and elephants. Atop her silvery curls was a velvet turban festooned with peacock feathers and chunks of unpolished turquoise.

"Welcome, my dear!" Her hostess bustled around the footman who had opened the door. She grabbed one of Charlotte's hands and gave it a masculine shake in greeting. "It's lovely to see you here tonight. We've all missed your company of late."

"I've been a bit busy," apologized Charlotte.

"Yes, I imagine that marriage makes a great many demands on a lady's time." A mischievous twinkle lit in Lady Thirkell's eyes. "That's why I've taken pains to avoid it."

"Understandably so," replied Charlotte. "I doubt that Horus and Sethos would tolerate another male presence in the house."

Her hostess let out a peal of delighted laughter. "And given the choice between my Egyptian cats and a Tulip of the ton—"

"Ha, the gentleman wouldn't stand a chance," said one of Lady Thirkell's elderly friends who hurried over to join them. She, too, was attired in an exotic confection of silk and feathers.

"That goes without saying, Hortense," replied Lady Thirkell.

To Charlotte she added, "Come, there's champagne as well as ratafia punch being served at the refreshment table."

Charlotte followed the colorful swirls of fabric down the central corridor and into the main salon, whose entrance was guarded by a towering ancient statue of Athena, the goddess of wisdom . . . and of war.

An acknowledgment, she mused, *that the ancient Greeks were wise enough to know women understood the complexities and contradictions of human nature better than men.*

The room itself was a study in contrasts. The wallpaper and draperies featured muted tones of taupe and cream, a quiet counterpoint to the eclectic jumble of decorative objects. Antiquities from Italy rubbed shoulders with exotic painted sculptures from India and Cathay; formal Meissen china sat next to ancient Aztec gourds; two ornate Louis XIV clocks flanked a simple pinecone from the wilds of America. The effect should have been horrifying.

And yet it wasn't.

Charlotte vowed that next time she would bring her sketchbook and travel paint box, and try to do the scene justice—

"Ah, there you are." Cordelia appeared from behind a cluster of potted palms. The trill of laughter and buzz of feminine voices raised in conversation mingled with the clink of crystal. "Shall we go somewhere quieter?" she suggested, indicating the archway that led to the side salons.

They found an empty room and sat on the sofa facing a fireplace whose banked coals gave off a cheery glow.

"Kit has told me about the murder of Wrexford's friend," began Cordelia before broaching her own business. "Have you and Wrex any further ideas on who might have wished Greeley dead?"

"Alas, no. The only clues—a missing manuscript and the fact that Greeley was overheard mentioning Wrexford's name—are baffling." Charlotte explained the details of the murder and how there was no rational explanation as to why anyone would want to kill the reclusive librarian.

"You're right," muttered Cordelia after taking a moment to mull over the facts. "I don't see how it adds up."

Cordelia was a brilliant mathematician. Like Wrexford, she saw the world through a lens of logic.

"I suppose we must accept that Life doesn't always conform to orderly expectations," said Charlotte. "Perhaps Wrexford will learn something useful this evening." She mentioned his meeting with an expert on rare books and manuscripts. "And Griffin has gone to Oxford to begin searching for more clues."

"If anyone can help Wrex find a trail and follow it to the Truth, it's Griffin," said Cordelia. After a small hesitation, she added, "Kit also told me that you and the boys discovered disturbing information at the King's Dockyard—something to do with the current competition to create a marine propulsion system for ocean travel."

"Yes." Charlotte lowered her voice, even though they were alone. "And coupled with the fact that the fire at Maudslay's laboratory was arson, it compels me—or rather, A. J. Quill—to look more closely at the groups involved in creating the new technology." A pause. "And to discern whether any of them might be willing to employ illegal methods to beat their competitors."

"Good," muttered Cordelia.

The curt reply gave Charlotte an opening to probe into what was clearly a fraught subject for her friend. "Given your appreciation of innovative ideas, you seem surprisingly opposed to the idea of oceangoing steamships."

Coals crackled in the hearth, releasing a tiny hiss of smoke.

Eyes narrowing, Cordelia watched the vapor shiver and dissolve into thin air before responding. "I'm not at all opposed to the concept."

Then what, she wondered, was the thorn in her friend's derriere? Charlotte thought for a moment. "It was clear that you took umbrage at Lady Kirkwall's manners, but—"

"I couldn't care less about Lady Kirkwall's manners."

She frowned in frustration. "Then why don't you stop shilly-shallying and tell me what's bothering you?"

Silence—and for a moment she feared that her friend wasn't going to reply. But after fisting her hands in her lap, Cordelia surrendered a sigh.

"Lord Taviot arranged a meeting with Kit this morning." The initial coolness in her voice had now turned to ice. "He had heard of Kit's early investment in Hedley's steam locomotive and decided that Kit would make an excellent addition to the consortium's Advisory Board. And so Lord Taviot offered him shares at a very special charter investor price if he would agree to promote the new company among his friends in both Polite Society and the scientific world."

"And I take it that you don't approve of the idea?" asked Charlotte.

Cordelia smoothed her skirts, taking some time to marshal her thoughts. "As you know, there are a number of players in the game. I was aware of Maudslay's experiments, and it doesn't surprise me to hear that the government is also working on a new type of marine propulsion system," she answered. "And given the success that the Americans are having with commercial steamboats on their rivers, it stands to reason that their inventors are also seeking to conquer the oceans."

A pause, which lasted several heartbeats. "But Taviot told Kit that his consortium is about to make a momentous announcement, one that will virtually guarantee their success."

Charlotte was trying to follow her friend's line of thought. "Are you saying that you don't think it is true?"

"No, that's not precisely what I'm saying," answered Cordelia, which only served to make the conversation even more confusing.

She fixed her friend with a searching stare, waiting for her to explain.

"Kit and I agree that an oceangoing marine propulsion system will be invented. It's simply a matter of time," continued her friend. "A brilliant mind, with access to the latest advances in science and technology, will eventually see the solution to the challenges . . ."

Cordelia blew out her cheeks. "It's also true that Reginald Maitland, the engineering wizard who is Taviot's head of technology and a partner in the consortium, has been working in America with the leading steam engine innovators for the last five years. So it's possible that he has made some momentous breakthrough in technology. But . . ."

Her friend took a moment to smooth a wrinkle from her skirts. "But while Kit seems to think Taviot and his consortium are worthy of investment, I have a very bad feeling about the venture. I have . . ."

She drew in a ragged breath. "I have heard some very unsettling things about Taviot's family history."

Charlotte sat back in surprise. It wasn't at all like Cordelia to let nasty rumors and innuendo cloud her judgment. Her own father's disreputable behavior had cast her brother in a dark light and nearly gotten him convicted of a very serious crime.

"I think most families have members who don't reflect well on them," she replied. "Look at me. I was considered a black sheep among a flock of pristine white reputations." She allowed a small pause. "And look at Kit. His father was convinced that he was a bad seed."

"I concede that my reaction is illogical," said Cordelia, though disapproval remained writ plain on her face. "I'm well aware that a tale may be colored by a purely personal reason, like jealousy or spite."

"Now you have piqued my curiosity," responded Charlotte. "What rattling of skeletons has caught your ear?"

"I would rather not say, so as to avoid further poisoning your thinking." Her friend rose abruptly. "Why don't we go listen to Lady Kirkwall's presentation and then see what your opinion is?"

"Now that we are finally alone, I need to tell you about my visit to Mr. Hedley's laboratory," announced Peregrine as he took a seat on the schoolroom rug and beckoned for Raven and Hawk to join him. After watching the military maneuvers at the Horse Guards parade ground, they had joined the dowager for supper at her townhouse and had just returned to the privacy of their eyrie.

"Let me guess—you learned how to add a gear-and-spring movement to your mechanical hound." Raven flopped down beside him. "So that it can outrace Harper to the platter of ginger biscuits, ha, ha, ha!"

"No, it's something far more important than my hound." Peregrine glanced around to make sure the door was firmly shut. "It has to do with building an oceangoing steamship." Seeing that he now had their full attention, he hurriedly added, "What with the arson at Maudslay's laboratory and the incident at the King's Dockyard, we suspect that Lord Wrexford and m'lady think some dark mischief is going on among the inventors trying to make the first workable prototype, right?"

Raven and Hawk nodded.

"Well, I happened to hear something suspicious—"

"Were you eavesdropping?" demanded Raven.

"Well, um, yes," admitted Peregrine. "Though not deliberately," he added hastily, "And *not* on Lord Wrexford or m'lady."

"Good," said Hawk solemnly. "That's only allowed in the most dire of circumstances—"

"Let's leave parsing through the moral implications for later," cut in Raven. "Tell us what you heard, Falcon."

"I asked Mr. Hedley some questions about marine propulsion systems, and he gave me a book to look at . . ." Peregrine then recounted what he had inadvertently overheard in the reading room.

Hawk scrunched his face in thought. "There's something I still don't understand. There are steam-powered boats navigating the waters here in Britain . . . so why is the idea of ocean travel considered so revolutionary?"

Raven, who was much more interested in the nuances of mechanical devices than his brother, made a rude sound. "Steamboats can travel up and down rivers and canals, but the open sea is too demanding on the current paddle wheel designs. They are vulnerable to breaking apart in storms and high waves."

"Then if it's not possible— " began Hawk.

"We didn't say it wasn't possible," corrected Peregrine. "It's just that as Mr. Hedley pointed out, nobody has yet figured out a workable design."

"However, you think the gentlemen you overheard are claiming to have done so, but that it's a lie— "

They all started at a sudden sound outside the door. However, it was followed by a low *woof*, which made them all relax.

"Don't startle us like that when we are having a Fledgling council of war," chided Hawk as he rose and let Harper into the room.

The hound circled a spot on the rug and flopped down with a canine sigh after seeing no platter of biscuits on the floor.

"I don't know if it's a lie," said Peregrine in answer to Hawk's question. "I just had a bad feeling about the conversation." He frowned. "The man with the baritone voice had a very oily laugh."

"M'lady believes that you should listen to your intuition," pointed out Hawk.

"Oiy, but Wrex says it's also important to have facts, not just feelings," countered Raven.

"Well, the fact is, as I left the reading room, I saw the two gentlemen talking with Mr. Hedley in the corridor, and it turns out that Baritone Voice is Lord Taviot!" said Peregrine. "And he's the head of one of the groups that is involved in the race to building an oceangoing steamship."

"You're getting very good at sleuthing, Falcon." Fixing his brother with an expectant look, Hawk asked, "You think that Lord Taviot is behind all the dark mischief?"

"It's possible." Raven made a face. "But rather than keep chewing over this ourselves . . ."

Harper pricked up his ears at the word *chewing*.

Raven looked at Peregrine. "I say that come morning, we go and tell Wrex and m'lady exactly what you overheard and let them decide what to do about it."

Hawk looked a little surprised. "So we do nothing?"

"Though it pains me to say it, yes, we do nothing." Raven let out a low huff. "For now." He hesitated. "Wrex seems awfully unsettled about Mr. Greeley's murder, and I get the feeling that m'lady is holding something back from us about the visit to the King's Dockyard. So until we learn more, we need to be very careful."

Peregrine scrunched his face in thought. "But how will we learn more if we're being very careful?"

"As to that, I have a few ideas. But until I'm ready to share them, what we need to do is keep our eyes open," answered Raven. "*And* our ears."

CHAPTER 12

Charlotte dutifully accompanied Cordelia back to the main salon. More guests had arrived, and the room had grown a bit warm despite the open windows. The scent of feminine perfumes wafted through the air, twining with the fragrances of the colorful cut flowers on display in an ancient terra-cotta urn.

As she glanced around, she suddenly spotted Alison, who waggled her cane and came over to join them.

"You didn't mention earlier that you were planning on attending tonight's soiree," said Charlotte.

"It was a last-minute decision. The boys told me a little more about the trip to the King's Dockyard, and it piqued my curiosity," answered the dowager and then went on to tell Charlotte about the coincidence of encountering her young relative, Horatio Porter.

After adding a few humorous comments about the boys, Alison raised her quizzing glass and looked around. "Is Lady Kirkwall here yet?"

"She's over there," murmured Cordelia with a nod toward the regal-looking woman standing with Lady Thirkell by the far wall. But just as they started forward, their hostess rang a silver bell.

The voices fluttered into silence.

"It isn't often that I interrupt our evenings of convivial conversations and connections to make a special presentation to the group," announced Lady Thirkell. "However, knowing how much we all appreciate intellectual achievements and innovations that will change the world for the better, I thought you would enjoy hearing from one of our guests, who has accompanied her brother, the Earl of Taviot, to London on a matter of great import to our nation."

An anticipatory rustling greeted the announcement as the ladies crowded in a little closer.

Lady Thirkell waited for the whispering to cease before continuing. "Rather than prose on any longer, I shall let Lady Kirkwall speak for herself and tell us about a most remarkable discovery." A smile. "And a most remarkable opportunity for us to be part of it."

The statement was punctuated by the pop of champagne corks as several footmen began to circulate with the freshly opened bottles to refill any empty glasses.

"Do you think our hostess is being paid for this entrée into Bluestocking Society?" whispered Charlotte.

"Entertaining is not cheap," replied Cordelia. "And Lady Thirkell isn't as plump in the pocket as she wishes to appear. So, yes, I think she occasionally sells her services—in a very discreet and genteel way, of course." Her friend's eyes remained riveted on Lady Kirkwall, who had leaned over to whisper something to their hostess. "I admire her for being smart enough to recognize a business opportunity and take advantage of it."

And clearly our hostess admires the same quality in Lady Kirkwall, mused Charlotte.

A round of applause drew her back to the present moment as

Lady Kirkwall stepped forward and acknowledged the welcome with a graceful flourish of her hand. "Thank you for inviting me tonight, Lady Thirkell. I am humbled to be in such erudite company."

Cordelia made a small sound in the back of her throat.

Charlotte repressed a sardonic smile. True, there was nothing remotely humble about the widow's demeanor.

It was easy to understand why her friend didn't like Lady Kirkwall. There was an aura of supreme self-confidence—and perhaps a sense of entitlement—about the widow, who looked to be around Charlotte's own age. But in truth, Charlotte rather admired the fact that she didn't try to hide her strength of character or her intelligence.

"I have come here to share with you an exciting new advance in science," continued Lady Kirkwall. "Not merely a theoretical one that adds to our abstract understanding of the world but a practical one that will improve the quality of life for people all over the world."

The widow paused, a beatific smile lighting up her face. "Imagine an invention that would allow vital goods—food for the hungry, raw materials for our factories—to travel by ship over the oceans with astounding speed and on a set schedule, rather than being beholden to the vagaries of wind and weather."

A murmur rippled through the crowd. Charlotte looked around at the mesmerized audience.

Lady Kirkwall had them enthralled.

The widow continued, and with the touch of a consummate performer kept her presentation short, extolling the virtues of a new world of marine steam power without giving any sort of technical details. The mention of the investment opportunity was also done deftly, added as an understated aside—which, of course, made it sound all the more special.

Even more impressive was the way Lady Kirkwall ended her

speech, saying that she was especially excited about presenting the opportunity to the group because it was time to change the antiquated thinking that only gentlemen could profit from investments in commercial ventures. Ladies with money of their own should seize the chance to be more modern and take the initiative to learn about business.

"And of course," she added slyly, "we all know that wives also exercise a far greater influence over their husbands than they wish to admit."

A titter of laughter ruffled through the gathering of ladies.

"So, feel free to share what you've learned here with them." A smile. "My guess is that they will thank you for it."

As Lady Kirkwall finished and stepped back, the crowd burst into applause and surged forward, the ladies jostling with each other to gain the widow's attention and ask more about the project.

"That was quite a performance," admitted Cordelia. "I have to admit that she has a certain presence."

"Her message about ladies learning to manage their own affairs is one that certainly appeals to my way of thinking," said Charlotte.

"Indeed," agreed Alison. "In fact, I'm curious to hear more of what she's proposing to the group. Would you two care to join me?"

"You go on. Cordelia and I have a matter to finish discussing." Charlotte observed the scene a moment longer, and then drew her friend into an alcove by the bookshelves. "Now that I've heard Lady Kirkwall for myself, tell me the reasons for your bad feelings about her and her family."

"I know you'll think me mad." Cordelia blew out her breath. "Ye heavens, after hearing that presentation, *I* think me mad!" Her friend gave a harried shrug before continuing. "Lady Kirkwall is articulate, her points are well-reasoned . . ."

"But?" urged Charlotte when her friend hesitated.

"But I just can't help seeing dark shadows lurking beneath that polished shine."

"What are the family skeletons?"

"To begin with, her younger brother died in a fall from his bedchamber window at the family's castle in Scotland—supposedly an unfortunate slip while he was inebriated," said Cordelia. "But rumor has it that he was a thoroughly despicable wastrel, whose legion of evil habits included preying on the servant girls who worked at the castle."

She grimaced. "So there is a question of whether he was pushed."

Alas, the aristocracy was rife with such stories. "You know as well as I do that this is a far more common tale than we would wish," replied Charlotte. "I confess, I'm a little baffled as to why you are taking this particular one so much to heart. Are we to damn every family who has such a crooked branch sprouting from its tree?"

A flush crept up to color Cordelia's cheeks. "There is more. Lady Kirkwall's husband—she married a much older man—perished from a gunshot wound. The story put out by the family was that it was a tragic accident which occurred while he was cleaning his pistols. However, he was on the board of governors overseeing a network of important canals, and there were rumors that he was embezzling money from the other investors."

"Ye heavens, you know how easily such nasty stories are started," said Charlotte, growing a little frustrated over why Cordelia was so intent on disliking the widow. "You keep using the word *rumor*. Have you heard any reputable reports as to whether the rumors about Lady Kirkwall's late husband are true?"

Her friend shook her head and looked away.

But not quite swiftly enough to hide the glimmer of tears beneath her lashes.

"Cordelia!" Shifting her stance, Charlotte took her friend's arm and moved them deeper into the alcove. "This isn't really about Lady Kirkwall and her family, is it?"

Her friend choked back a sob and shook her head. "You're right, I've seized on scurrilous rumors to—to convince myself that I'm right in disliking them."

"Why don't you tell me what's *really* wrong?"

A sniff. "I—" Cordelia's voice wobbled. "I don't want Kit to invest in their company! I know why he's doing it, and—and . . ."

"And what?" asked Charlotte gently.

"And I want for us to earn the money *together*, from our own company, to purchase his dream," blurted out her friend.

Kit's dream? Charlotte hesitated, not wishing to probe too deeply into personal matters. But Cordelia and Sheffield were her dearest friends. . . .

"What is it that he wants to buy?"

"Land . . . a manor house . . . a place for us to put down roots," answered Cordelia. "I happened to catch him studying a list of properties for sale, although he tried to hide it." She blinked back more tears. "When I asked him about it, he insisted that he wished to invest in Taviot's consortium and present me with the fact that a house and lands will soon be within our means as a wedding gift." Another sniff. "But I think it is far too risky! I would much rather that we plan and save and ultimately earn it ourselves."

"Have you discussed it with him?" she pressed. "You make a very compelling argument for doing it your way."

"Yes." A sniff. "He's so bloody sensitive about money. We argued—quite fiercely." A watery rumble of misery welled up in her throat. "And the only agreement we reached was to—to defer setting a date for our wedding."

Charlotte drew Cordelia into a hug. "Marriage is complicated." After a few moments, she leaned back. "Ye heavens, both Wrex and I wrestled with the consequences of taking such a leap of faith. It isn't easy, but don't lose heart."

Her friend's eyes remained pooled with doubt.

"For now, perhaps it's best for both of you to allow your emotions to cool. And in the meantime, why don't the two of us take a very careful look at Taviot's consortium? If we discover that something unsavory is going on, Kit will listen to reason."

Cordelia managed a crooked smile. "Thank you for not thinking me a peagoose to worry over such things."

"You are one of the most sensible people I know." Charlotte emphasized her words with a reassuring squeeze to her friend's shoulder. "Now come, let us go back and listen to what Lady Kirkwall is saying in answer to queries from her potential investors. Indeed, I have a few questions of my own to ask of her."

"Milord . . ."

Wrexford turned, hat and gloves still in hand, as Tyler entered his workroom.

"A letter arrived while you were out, and I thought you would want to see it right away." The valet held out a gilt-edged rectangle of folded paper festooned with a large ornate seal. "It was delivered by a servant whose gaudy livery was an affront to anyone who possesses a grain of taste or refinement," he added with a sniff.

"Not everyone is blessed with your discerning eye for fashion," drawled the earl. He took a moment to study the scarlet wax wafer and then pursed his lips. "Hmmph."

"What is it?"

A discreet crack, followed by the whisper of paper. "An invitation," answered Wrexford. He looked up. "To attend a gala outdoor soiree in St. James's Park tomorrow evening—including a fireworks display and midnight supper—in honor of the Prince Regent's brother-in-law, King Frederick of Württemberg."

Tyler made a pained face. "That explains why the servant

looked like a street fiddler's pet monkey. Prinny is a man of thoroughly vulgar tastes."

Another sniff. "Surely you're not going to accept?"

"On the contrary. Our future sovereign's tastes and temperament may leave much to be desired, but King Frederick's librarian is a very sharp and observant gentleman."

Wrexford re-read the note. "It is Herr von Münch who is inviting me to attend the festivities. He says that he has discovered some important information which may have relevance to Greeley's murder."

CHAPTER 13

St. James's Palace, the king and queen's official residence in London, sat just a stone's throw from Piccadilly Street and looked like a fading spinster in the deepening twilight, its age-dark brick walls and austere lines overshadowed by the flash and glitter of the colorful silk pavilions rising up from a screen of trees bordering the park behind it.

"As if the royal family hasn't frittered away enough money this summer on extravagant entertainments," muttered Wrexford as he and Charlotte descended from their carriage. "This mindless pomp and pageantry are an egregious waste of funds that would be better spent on the common people rather than a gaggle of overfed aristocrats."

"I couldn't agree more." Charlotte had accepted the invitation in order to have a close look at the details of the party and who was attending. If ever there was a perfect event for her to skewer with her pen . . .

A line was already forming to pass through the gated entrance of St. James's Park. As they joined it, the quartet of gentlemen just ahead of them began grousing about the fact that no footmen had yet appeared with trays of champagne. But their ire rapidly turned to the latest drawings of A. J. Quill.

"How dare that scurrilous scribbler imply that the government isn't doing enough for the soldiers returning from the wars," ranted one of them, a jowly fellow with a sheen of Macassar oil highlighting his silver curls. "It only stirs the masses to feel discontent and question the powers-that-be."

His three friends all nodded in agreement.

"The fellow is devilishly dangerous," muttered one of them. "The government ought to hunt him down and put his head on a pikestaff at Traitors' Gate as a warning to those who question their betters."

Charlotte waited for them to march through the entrance. "Pompous popinjays," she said softly. "But it's good to know that I'm ruffling their feathers. It means I'm doing my job."

Wrexford smiled. And yet she noted that it didn't quite reach his eyes.

"Come," he said, "let us join the festivities."

A myriad of flickering torchieres lined the footpaths, their fire-gold flames accentuating the jewel-tone hues of the dinner pavilions and refreshment tents that dotted the lawns.

She squeezed her eyes shut for an instant, the surfeit of decorative gilding, crimson silk, and countless candle flames glittering in the twilight an assault on her senses. Prinny did everything to excess. *Rich food, lascivious friends, extravagant parties, profligate spending on his personal pleasures while the poor are starving . . .*

Charlotte forced her attention back to the moment. "Ah, I see that Alison is chatting with her friend, Sir Robert," she observed, indicating one of the park benches by the main walkway. "I'll go join them and leave you free to find Herr von Münch."

The earl nodded and moved off to join a group of German diplomats gathered around a pair of liveried servants who were serving champagne.

The dowager waggled her cane in greeting. "Sir Robert and I were just discussing A. J. Quill's latest drawing."

Her friend popped to his feet and inclined a courtly bow. "Indeed we were, Lady Wrexford. I admit that I sometimes find the fellow's sentiments a little too radical for my liking—"

Alison made a rude sound, which made Sir Robert chuckle.

"However, one can't argue that asking uncomfortable questions is not always a bad thing," he hastily added. "It makes us think about what is going on around us."

They conversed for a short while on the present state of politics in London—Sir Robert knew Alison well enough not to dare suggest such topics were beyond the understanding of the female intellect—and then the dowager shooed him away with an imperious wave.

"Go have a chin-wag with your friends from the Botanical Society," commanded Alison after rising and hooking Charlotte's arm with her free hand. "I have some private matters to discuss with my niece." To Charlotte, she said, "Come, let us stroll down to the lake. Word is that they have decorated the Chinese pagoda on the bridge with colorful paper lanterns."

Charlotte allowed herself to be led away.

"Should I be alarmed?" she asked dryly, once they turned down one of the quieter footpaths.

Alison's brows shot up in surprise. "Alarmed over what?"

"The fact that you have a suspicious gleam in your eye," responded Charlotte.

"Oh, pffft, what nonsense." The dowager walked on for several steps. "I simply wanted to tell you about an invitation I received. It occurred to me that it might prove useful for our current investigation."

An invitation? That sounded harmless enough. Charlotte smiled, though the niggling little tickle at the base of her neck didn't entirely disappear. "As I told you the other day—"

"My dear Charlotte, kindly drop that charade that no investigation is going on," cut in the dowager. "I wasn't born yesterday." A rueful grimace. "Or the day before."

"I—" began Charlotte.

"Ye heavens, do you really think I'm woolly-headed enough to believe that Wrexford would simply delegate to someone else the task of bringing the murderer of his brother's best friend to justice?"

Charlotte felt herself flush.

"Or that A. J. Quill would not be taking a closer look at the race to build an oceangoing steamship, especially given the fire at Maudslay's laboratory?"

"I'm sorry, Aunt Alison. I was only trying—"

The dowager stopped short and waggled her cane. "If you're about to say 'protect me,' I just might swat you with my stick!"

Taking the ensuing silence as surrender, the dowager resumed walking. "Getting back to my invitation, it's for a gala reception given by the Taviot consortium. The event is being held next week."

A gala reception? That was news to Charlotte. And as to why Alison had been invited—

"Would you care to come along with me?"

She took a moment to think. Wrexford had told her about the conversation that Peregrine had overheard in the reading room of the Royal Institution. Granted, the boy might have misunderstood the nuances of what had been said. But given Cordelia's concerns over the Taviot family—which was at odds with her own more positive reaction to Lady Kirkwall—the chance to spend some further time with Lord Taviot and his sister would give her a chance to form a more accurate opinion.

"Yes, I would very much like to attend," answered Charlotte. "However, I can't help but wonder as to how you came to be invited."

"While you were off talking with Cordelia in private at Lady Thirkell's soiree, I had a chat with Lady Kirkwall . . ." Alison gave an airy wave. "And I may have slightly exaggerated my interest in investing." A small cough. "As well as the size of my fortune."

Before Charlotte could reply, the two of them were hailed by Cordelia and Sheffield. Though they were together, the tension radiating between them was thick enough to cut with a knife.

"What scheming are you two doing out here in the shadows?" asked Sheffield, which earned him a warning whack from the dowager's cane.

"*Ouch!*"

"I don't scheme," said Alison primly. "I plot."

"Speaking of which, what brings you two here?" asked Charlotte. "You don't usually attend Prinny's parties."

Sheffield looked around to make sure no other guests were within earshot. "Wrex mentioned that he was meeting with the librarian who overheard Greeley's argument with his killer." He then hesitated as his glance slid back to the dowager.

"You may go ahead and speak freely, Kit," murmured Charlotte. "Alison has already guessed that we've once again become caught up in the crosscurrents of intrigue."

"Thank God. That cane has a *very* sharp point." Just to be safe, he edged back a step before picking up where he had left off.

"Apparently, the librarian has some new information that may have a bearing on the murder. I wished to be here just in case Wrex needs any assistance."

The answer stirred up Charlotte's worries over her husband's quest. "Herr von Münch gave no hint as to what that information might be. I fear . . ." She looked up for a moment, watching the moon scud in and out of the clouds. "Wrex has taken this murder very much to heart. But with so few clues, I fear he may be terribly disappointed if all his efforts to find the killer come to naught."

Sheffield nodded in understanding. "I'll go join the diplomats gathered by the gardens and keep an eye out for any trouble."

Cordelia waited until the crunch of gravel faded away. "What of the missing manuscript? I take it that Wrex hasn't located a copy of it?"

"Not yet," replied Charlotte.

"What we need is to find a thread that pulls all the disparate pieces of the puzzle together," observed Cordelia.

Charlotte lifted her shoulders in a baffled shrug. "If there is one, I'm not clever enough to see it."

"Lord Wrexford!"

The earl turned as von Münch broke away from a very spirited discussion—in several different languages—on the Peace Conference taking place in Vienna and joined him on the walkway.

"I confess, I much prefer the calm and quiet of a reading room," said the librarian, "where conflicting opinions express themselves on ink and paper rather than in stentorian shouting."

"I, too, find solitude and silence more conducive to serious thinking," agreed Wrexford. "But throwing volatile elements into a cauldron and lighting a fire beneath it can also create worthwhile discoveries."

The observation made von Münch chuckle, but the sound was quickly carried away by the evening breeze. Lowering his voice to a whisper, he said, "Please follow me. I have something very important to tell you."

Gravel crunched beneath their shoes as the librarian abruptly indicated that they should take one of the side footpaths that led through a copse of trees down to the lake.

"As you know, I am working on writing a history of King Frederick's reign, including his complex relationship with Napoleon during the constant wars that plagued the Continent for over a decade." The shadows from the overhanging leaves masked the librarian's face as he spoke.

Just as hard to discern, decided the earl, was where the conversation was leading.

"'Complex' is a polite way of putting it," he interjected. "There are many who would call your sovereign an amoral, opportunistic toady who sold his loyalty to the highest bidder."

"*Ja*, that is true," acknowledged von Münch.

"However, as interesting as the subject may be for you," continued Wrexford, "I don't see how Fickle Freddie's treachery has any connection to my concerns."

The skitter of stones had given way to the rustling of fallen leaves as the path wound closer to the lake. The noises of the gala party sounded very far away.

"I am about to get to that." The librarian came to halt. "It is a terrible but undeniable fact that treachery is rampant in times of war, stretching from the glittering throne rooms to the muck and gore of battlefields too obscure to have a name."

The earl's throat went dry. "What are you saying?"

"The Kingdom of Württemberg supplied troops to the French army when it invaded Spain, deposed its king, and put Napoleon's brother Joseph on the throne," continued von Münch. "Greeley's obvious mental distress when we discussed the military campaign that led to his grievous injuries got me to thinking . . ."

He hesitated for a heartbeat. "And so for the history I am writing for King Frederick, I made a point of arranging to interview one of the senior Württemberg officers who served as liaison with Napoleon's staff at the end of '08."

1808. Wrexford drew in a sharp breath.

"As you know, the British landed an army in Portugal, and under General Moore's command it entered Spain to help fight the French," continued von Münch. "The officer I interviewed mentioned that part of the French success in surrounding the

British army and forcing the disastrous retreat that led to the battle at Corunna came about because of information passed on by a British traitor."

"Who?" rasped Wrexford.

"My officer was never given the traitor's name. But he told me who on the French general staff might have known it."

A pause. "And it so happens that the French officer in question left the military earlier this year and is now an attaché with the French diplomatic service," added von Münch in a rush. "And he's currently here in London."

"You think Greeley may have been murdered because of something he knew about a military betrayal?" asked the earl. "But why now, six years later?"

"I don't know, milord. All I can say is that our conversations about the war in Portugal and Spain appeared to upset Mr. Greeley. He seemed to . . . I am not sure how to describe it other than to say he seemed to be having private conversations with himself. As if his mind was recalling some unsettling memories."

The librarian lifted his shoulders in uncertainty. "I'm sorry. Does that make any sense?"

Wrexford thought about what he had just heard. "Perhaps." The horrors of war did strange things to the mind. "Where is this Frenchman now? Can we arrange to meet with him?"

The librarian pointed down to the lake, where pearls of moonlight glimmered over the placid water. "He agreed to meet with us tonight but wished to do so discreetly. We must circle around to the eastern end of the lake, where a narrow spit of land allows us access to Duck Island." He pulled out his pocket watch and thumbed open the case. "He should already be there."

"I have to confess that I am puzzled by certain aspects of our investigation—or rather, our *two* investigations," mused the dowager after the three of them had resumed strolling along the winding walkways. "I understand why Wrex feels honor-bound by the memory of his late brother to solve Greeley's murder. And I can see that a radical new technology like ocean-going steamships would be a subject for A. J. Quill's pen."

Alison fell silent as she slowed and carefully rounded a rough patch of ground. "But what I don't comprehend is why you seem to have a specific interest in Lord Taviot's consortium. If there is any unholy skullduggery going on between the groups seeking to invent an oceangoing steamship, isn't it a matter best left for the government?"

Light winked off her spectacles as they passed one of the torchieres. "After our last adventure, you and Wrexford made it quite clear that you had no intention of dirtying your hands with any more twisted intrigues involving the lust for money and power."

"A fair question," allowed Charlotte. "I wish I had a simple answer."

"I suggest we have a seat," said Cordelia. She glanced at a nearby bench. "This might require some time—"

"And some champagne," drawled the dowager. Spotting a footman refilling his tray at one of the refreshment tents, she waggled her cane to catch his attention. "I think better with a glass of wine in hand."

Charlotte waited for them to be served before beginning. "The first thing that drew me—that is, A. J. Quill—into the fray was the fire at Henry Maudslay's laboratory—"

"Yes, that's another thing that is confusing," said Alison. "I thought Maudslay only made . . . thingamabobs that make other . . . thingamabobs."

"You're right—he's famous for his lathes," said Cordelia, "which make the parts for many types of machinery, including the latest models of steam engines. However, given the momentous impact oceangoing steamships would have on the world, Maudslay decided to put his skills to working on the technical challenge of designing a whole new type of marine propulsion system."

"Propulsion system?" The dowager looked perplexed. "What, exactly, does that mean?"

"At first, that puzzled me, too," answered Charlotte. "For a ship to be able to navigate the oceans, it requires *two* new innovations. A more powerful steam engine, which uses fuel with enough efficiency so that the ship can carry what it needs to travel great distances. But even more importantly, it also needs a revolutionary new means of propulsion. Right now, river steamboats use paddle wheels, but the current designs would never survive the storms and waves at sea."

"Ah." Alison nodded in understanding. "So what is the alternative?"

"As Kit says," answered Cordelia, "if we knew the answer to that question, we would soon be richer than King Croesus."

"Hmmm." The dowager looked thoughtful.

"Let us put aside the question about the actual innovation needed to propel a ship through the ocean," continued Cordelia. "Given the impact oceangoing steamships would have on our shipping business, Kit became intrigued by the concept and was interested in Maudslay's work."

"Because of Kit's interest, Wrex and I—or rather, the Weasels—looked a little more closely at the fire," added Charlotte, "and discovered that it was arson."

"I see," murmured the dowager.

"And when the boys and I inadvertently discovered some suspicious tinkering in the naval laboratory at the King's Dockyard, I realized the race to conquer the oceans has great implications for our country," she went on. "And thus it is a subject that A. J. Quill can't ignore."

"It's clear from the recent incidents that there is some dark mischief afoot," said Cordelia. "Each of the groups working to create an oceangoing steamship has a powerful incentive for preventing anyone else from succeeding . . ."

Alison listened in rapt attention as Cordelia went on to explain the political and economic—as well as the military—ramifications.

"At present," she finished, "it appears that Lord Taviot's consortium has the lead in the race."

"Taviot . . . and his sister Lady Kirkwall." The dowager contemplated the tiny bubbles fizzing up in her glass. "Ah, now things are coming into sharper focus," she mused. "You think they are behind the attacks on their rivals?"

"It's possible. However, we also have a very personal concern about them," said Charlotte. "Kit has been invited to join their Advisory Board and become one of their charter investors. But Cordelia is adamantly opposed to it for several reasons—"

"One of them being that I've heard some very unsavory rumors about the family," interjected Cordelia.

"Yes." Alison gave a grim nod. "I've heard those rumors, too."

Charlotte waited. The dowager's knowledge of aristocratic families—and what skeletons were hidden in the darkest nooks and crannies of their stately manor houses—was encyclopedic. If there was any truth to the whispers of scandal, she would know about it.

Alison took a small swallow of champagne. "There's no question that Lord Taviot's younger brother—a half-brother from the old earl's second marriage—was rotten to the core." She brushed away an errant drop as it slid down the glass. "Though over the years I have come to believe that it's unfair to condemn a whole family for the actions of one member. Even the best of trees occasionally produces a bad apple."

Cordelia remained silent.

"As for the whispers about Lady Kirkwall's husband . . ."

The dowager paused for a moment of thought. "Lord Kirkwall denied any wrongdoing, and if memory serves me correctly . . ."

Charlotte was sure that it did.

"He announced that he was going to prove his innocence by showing evidence that someone else was responsible." Alison blew out her breath. "But then he apparently shot himself—or was terribly clumsy when cleaning his pistol—and whatever the truth, it went to the grave with him."

"So, it's a family shadowed by lurid speculation," mused Charlotte.

"Where there is smoke, there is often fire," interjected Cordelia. "But then, I confess that I simply don't like them."

"Now you've piqued my curiosity," said Alison. "I shall make some inquiries and see whether I uncover any further details or additional scandals."

"Please do it with all haste." Cordelia set aside her wine. "They have already raised a great of deal of money. If there are any skeletons buried in the family cupboard, it would be best to unearth them now."

Her eyes narrowed. "To ensure that a great many people don't get burned if the devil's hellfire is lurking behind their patrician smiles."

"Let us be careful to keep an open mind on the Taviot family," counseled Charlotte, intent on not letting her friend's raw emotion color their judgment. "We are looking to learn the truth, whether or not it conforms to our preconceptions."

Cordelia bit her lip and looked away for a moment. "Getting back to facts, rather than mere conjecture, Lady Kirkwall has just announced that she and her brother will hold a gala reception for potential investors next week, during which they will be making a momentous announcement."

"Yes—I've been invited," said Alison.

Cordelia's brows shot up in surprise.

"Alison chatted with Lady Kirkwall at the Bluestocking

soiree," explained Charlotte. "And is now considered a potential investor. I shall be going with her." She watched the festive lanterns in the distance, their red-gold flames dancing over the dark stone terrace of Carlton House. "Let us hope the consortium's revelations will shed more light on their objectives."

"Kit has been invited as well," said Cordelia tightly. "He did not ask me—"

A small sound behind their bench suddenly caused her to twist around and peer into the shadows.

"Good evening, ladies." Kurlansky stepped into the aureole of light cast by the pathway torchieres and inclined a polite bow. "What a splendid night for fireworks."

Charlotte clenched her teeth on seeing the spark of unholy amusement in the Russian's eyes. She was beginning to think of him as a thorn in her arse.

"Though," he added with a sly smile, I would have thought that your Prince Regent had had enough *Sturm und Drang* during the Peace Celebrations."

Charlotte regarded him with a cool stare. "As an island nation we are quite used to storm and stress and are experienced in dealing with it." She paused. "You see, we know it always blows over, so we think of it as naught but entertainment."

His smile stretched a touch wider. "Your perspective on things is always illuminating, Lady Wrexford."

"And how is your task for the tsar going?" she countered.

"Oh, I won't bore you with trifling diplomatic matters," replied Kurlansky. "Especially as you ladies look to be having an interesting tête-à-tête. I merely wanted to pay my respects, so I'll let you get back to your conversation."

Another bow. "Enjoy the rest of the evening."

The dowager scowled as she watched him turn toward the lake and slip away into the darkness. "He reminds me of a stalking panther. All deadly grace and elegance when he's not hungry, but heaven forfend if you stand between him and his prey."

Cordelia narrowed her eyes. "Should we be worried about him?"

"Yes," answered Charlotte without hesitation. "We know better than to underestimate Kurlansky as an adversary." The evening breeze ruffled through the nearby trees, setting off a waggle of leafy whispers. "I'm not sure that his objectives will lead him to cross paths with us, but we must stay alert to the possibility." A sigh. "However, a more immediate challenge looms. While Wrex works on solving Greeley's murder, we must try to discern whether there are any treacherous shoals and eddies hidden beneath the Taviot consortium's glittering promises."

Cordelia leaned back, throwing her face into shadow. "And let us hope we spot them," she muttered darkly, "before we're caught in dangerous crosscurrents."

"*Hmmph.*" The dowager waggled her cane. "If any enemies seek to sink our mission, they will find themselves in for a rude surprise."

CHAPTER 14

Seeing von Münch come to a halt, Wrexford quickened his steps over the tangled grasses and brambles. "Why don't you let me go first from here?"

They had left the well-tended footpath to make their way to the rounded jut of land that stuck out into the lake. Though it was called Duck Island, it was really a peninsula, as a narrow finger of overgrown earth and unpruned trees kept it connected to the rest of the park.

The isolated place was, however, not an area that attracted gentlemen of the ton. Dark and uninviting, it had an aura of wildness about it. As a breeze swirled, thorns scraped at their shoes, and gnarled branches clawed at their coats.

The librarian ceded his place with a grateful nod. "A perfect place for privacy," he whispered, his face hidden in the shadows. The dancing lights of the party looked very far away as they started forward.

Raising his voice slightly, von Münch gave a tentative hail. "Monsieur Dalambert?"

The only answer was a rustling of leaves.

Wrexford looked around, feeling a niggling of unease. "Stay behind me," he cautioned, then slowly pushed his way through the tangle of bushes.

"Monsieur Dalambert?" This time the call from von Münch was louder and more urgent.

"I'm here," came the answer. Twigs snapped as a figure stepped out from the leafy shadows into a tiny clearing bordered by a cluster of low bushes that sloped down to the water's edge.

The Frenchman, noted Wrexford, was dressed in the height of fashion—a snugly tailored coat of claret-colored wool, high shirt points, an elaborate cravat trimmed in lace. His face looked to have turned a bit fleshy, but his eyes appeared sharp.

"Thank you for coming—" began von Münch.

"This is not a social visit," said Dalambert curtly. "We need not go through the motions of polite pleasantries." The Frenchman's gaze was on the earl, not the librarian. "Herr von Münch explained the circumstances of your request, and I agreed to see you because as a former soldier I can't help but feel a disgust for any man who would betray his comrades for money. And I sympathize with your quest for justice. But I would prefer to finish with our business as quickly as possible."

"As would I, monsieur," replied Wrexford.

"I make no apologies for my actions during the war. One makes use of any opportunity to gain an advantage over one's enemy," continued Dalambert. "However, now that our countries are at peace, I feel that in good conscience I may tell you what I know."

Catching a flutter of movement in the darkness just across the narrow stretch of water separating Duck Island from the edge of the park and Horse Guards Road, Wrexford suddenly shifted and took a moment to survey the area.

"I was told that this part of the park is deserted at night," said the Frenchman as he noticed the earl's reaction.

The earl saw nothing. And yet his time serving in military intelligence had taught him that survival often depended on trusting one's sixth sense for trouble.

"Yes, it usually is," he replied. "But it's always prudent to err on the side of caution."

"Perhaps we are both on edge," muttered Dalambert. "As I was leaving the festivities to make my way down here, I thought someone was following me." A shrug. "But it was just a drunken reveler who stumbled off toward Pall Mall."

"Just give me the name of the traitor, sir." The earl kept an eye on the edge of the park as he spoke. "And we can both be on our way."

As Dalambert slipped a hand into his coat pocket, a dull boom suddenly shivered through the air, and a burst of fireworks momentarily lit the sky. At the same instant, Wrexford saw a spark of light on the far side of the water. He reacted in an instant, lunging forward and knocking both Dalambert and von Münch to the ground.

The Frenchman lay still for a moment—and then began to chuckle as he levered to his hands and knees. "It's simply the fireworks, milord. Though I understand how a civilian would react to the unexpected sound of gunpowder exploding."

Wrexford rose and reached down to help Dalambert up, noting that von Münch was already on his feet. "As I said," responded the earl, "it's prudent to err on the side of caution." He drew the Frenchman into the trees and motioned for the librarian to follow. "I trust you're unharmed."

"My cravat's knot may have suffered a mortal injury," replied the Frenchman dryly. "But aside from that I am perfectly fine." He brushed away the bits of leaves clinging to his sleeve. "You have excellent reflexes, milord."

The librarian said nothing but glanced back across the water.

"Getting back to business . . ." Dalambert once again reached into his pocket. "I oversaw intelligence operations from general headquarters, and our operations were run so that only the officer in the field knew his informant's actual identity. So I can't tell you a name."

The earl clenched his teeth in frustration.

"But I can give you a few samples of the traitor's handwriting."

Wrexford accepted the packet of papers with a curt thanks. "Is there any chance that I could contact the field officer?"

Dalambert's expression hardened. "As to that, sir, I feel that I've done enough—"

"I hadn't mentioned every detail, monsieur," interjected von Münch. "Lord Wrexford's brother died in the same ambush that caused Mr. Greeley's horrific injuries."

The Frenchman let out a reluctant sigh. "Give me a day or two. I make no promises, but if the man is willing to reveal the information, I'll send word to you."

"Thank you, monsieur," replied the earl.

Dalambert gave a stiff nod. "I have done what my conscience says is right. However, I'm not comfortable answering further questions on French military matters, so please understand that I prefer not to meet again in person."

"I think that is for the best." Wrexford turned abruptly to the tree just behind him and pulled a knife from his boot. "I would also suggest that you make your inquiry very discreetly."

He cut out the misshapen bullet that was buried chest-high in the wood and held it up to his companions. "And it would be wise of you to take precautions for your own safety until I am able to have the traitor apprehended."

"*Ach du lieber Gott*," rasped von Münch. "Had you not knocked us down, milord . . ."

Yes, one of you would be dead.

The Frenchman's eyes widened in shock, but his only acknowledgment of the earl's warning was a curt nod.

"Lastly, I would advise you to return to the festivities by circling back around the lake," added the earl, "rather than taking the shorter way bordering Horse Guards Road."

Dalambert turned on his heel and hurried away.

"Should I also return to the party, milord?" asked von Münch, once the sound of the Frenchman's steps had died away.

Dark on dark, the shadows fluttered in the breeze. "I'd rather you stay with me. I'll escort you to Carlton House, where you can summon a carriage to take you back to your lodgings." Wrexford hesitated. "I would also suggest that you don't go out alone at night from now on." A pause. "In fact, it might be wise for you to return to the king's palace in Württemberg."

"You think *me* in danger?"

"Clearly, someone is willing to commit murder to prevent an old secret from coming to light. And it stands to reason that he knows of your involvement. So it's safer—"

"Safety be damned!"

The librarian's reaction took the earl by surprise.

"I may not have your military experience, milord. But I am not a craven coward who would crawl away just to save his own skin. I am part of this investigation, and I mean to help you see that justice is done." Squaring his shoulders, von Münch added, "No matter the threat."

"Your sentiments—and your courage—do you credit, Herr von Münch. But I'm not sure you truly comprehend the danger."

The librarian gave a pointed look at the gash in the tree. "I think I do, Lord Wrexford. Besides, you could use my help in finding the missing manuscript."

The librarian, Wrexford conceded, had shown himself to be highly intelligent and observant. . . .

"Very well." He expelled a sigh. "We need to fetch Lady Wrexford from the party and head to my townhouse on Berkeley Square. If you are going to be part of this investigation, you need to become acquainted with her."

"S-Surely a countess is too . . ." A cough. "That is, a lady's sensibilities tend to be rather, er, delicate for such dangerous endeavors."

A smile touched Wrexford's lips. "I suggest you refrain from forming any notions on feminine sensibilities until you meet my wife."

CHAPTER 15

The ominous grey clouds of early morning were fast giving way to patches of cerulean blue sky. . . .

"The day looks to be clearing," said Charlotte as she turned away from the window overlooking the back gardens.

"The rain squall that blew through early this morning will likely have washed away any footprints that the shooter may have left at the edge of the park," said Wrexford, not looking up from writing down some notes on the previous evening. "Though I doubt they would have provided any real clues. However, Tyler is going to examine the bullet that I recovered with our microscope to see if it yields any information on what type of firearm was used."

"Do you think Kurlansky could have been the assailant?" Charlotte had told him about the encounter with the Russian. "I saw him heading down to the lake . . ." She made a face. "But why would he have done such a thing?"

"Kurlansky is both very capable and very clever. If he wanted the Frenchman dead, he wouldn't have made a hash of it," Wrexford answered dryly. He jotted a few more thoughts down on paper. "But more importantly, as you pointed out, he has no motive. Whatever byzantine intrigue has brought him back to London, I don't see that it can have any connection to a British traitor from a bygone war."

"I suppose not," conceded Charlotte, though she didn't sound entirely convinced. Her brow furrowed in thought. "But what if there *is* a connection between Greeley's death and the race to create an oceangoing propulsion system? As Kit pointed out, there is reason to believe that the tsar of Russia would dearly love to get his hands on the plans for that technology."

He put his pen down. "The only connection is a purely personal one involving our family. *I* am investigating Greeley's death, and *you* are investigating the skullduggery surrounding the propulsion system."

"Perhaps Kurlansky is targeting you because he knows that I am poking around in the matter and is trying to distract me." Her expression betrayed a very un-Charlotte-like flicker of fear. "Or scare me into giving up."

Wrexford wasn't sure why she was being so stubborn, though he sensed that the Russian had somehow gotten under her skin. "I fear you are allowing emotion to overrule logic and color your judgment." As he said the words, he realized the irony of the accusation.

Charlotte did as well. "You, me, Kit, Cordelia—it seems we all are finding it hard to separate feelings from facts as we try to deal with all the conundrums."

"True. But we must try," he replied. "As for Kurlansky, let us not create specters out of thin air. We have enough flesh-and-blood villains to track down and bring to justice."

Charlotte moved to the hearth, where she took a long moment to run a hand along the carved marble of the mantel. "I confess that I dislike Kurlansky. He is both arrogant and unfeeling. For him, international intrigue is a game that the high and mighty play. Innocent lives are merely pawns on a chessboard, to be sacrificed without batting an eye if it serves his purpose."

Her mouth quivered in outrage. "Ye gods, he threatened our friends and our family during the last investigation, and then had the gall to come to us and suggest that we all chuckle and let bygones be bygones." She watched a shadow play over her fingers before adding, "I'm quite sure that the real reason he came was to boast about his cleverness."

"I daresay he's no worse than our own intelligence operatives," observed Wrexford. "The job of keeping the balance of power from tipping too far in any one direction requires getting one's hands dirty."

Silence. And then a sigh. "Much as I hate to admit it, you're right. I concede that I am overreacting," Charlotte muttered. "I shall heed your advice to put Kurlansky out of my thoughts." A pause. "But that leaves unanswered the key question of who fired the shot at you."

She fixed him with a searching stare. "Do you think it could possibly be the same man who murdered Greeley?"

"That's a more logical surmise." Not that logic was proving any real help in the investigation. "And yet . . ." Griffin had been meticulous in examining Greeley's personal and professional life and had yet to find any thread that might tie him to his killer.

"The damnable truth is," he continued, "I still can't begin to guess as to who might be responsible for either act of violence."

If Greeley's murder had something to do with treachery from six years ago, he asked himself, why had the killer waited so long to act?

Why now?

The most obvious answer was that Greeley had remembered something and summoned the killer for a confrontation. But that didn't explain . . .

Pushing aside the unanswered mysteries, Wrexford rose from his chair. "Forgive me, but I must be off. A fellow member of military intelligence with whom I worked during my time in Portugal has agreed to meet with me. I want to ask him if he ever heard rumors about a British traitor—just in case Dalambert's friend doesn't choose to reveal what he knows."

"Good luck," said Charlotte.

"Luck seems to be playing a pernicious game of hide-and-seek with us. But perhaps it will turn in our favor." He put one of the samples of the traitor's handwriting into a portfolio case. "Speaking of luck, let us hope that you and von Münch will be permitted access to the King's Library at Buckingham House to search for a copy of *Nihil Est Quod Hominum Efficere Non Possit*."

"I like von Münch." Charlotte tucked a loose lock of hair behind her ear. During their nighttime meeting with the librarian, it had been decided that she would accompany him to the King's Library, as her sharp eyes and skill in Latin would be helpful in scouring the shelves for the missing manuscript. "He's not only extremely intelligent and observant, but he seems to possess a deeply felt sense of humanity, which makes him care about Right and Wrong."

"I don't disagree." The earl checked the priming of the pocket pistol on his desk and then tucked it inside his coat. "However, let us bear in mind that whatever forces of evil we are facing possess a cunning cleverness—and ruthlessness. So it's best not to trust anyone fully, save for our inner circle of family and friends."

"Hmmph." The head of the King's Library at Buckingham House handed back von Münch's credentials—which were, Charlotte noted, an impressive confection of flowery script, heraldic crests, and ornate wax seals dangling from scarlet ribbons.

"All looks in order," he said in Latin. "We are, of course, happy to welcome a representative of our king's son-in-law."

After a disapproving look at Charlotte, he nodded politely to von Münch. "Please follow me into the connecting wing, which houses the book and manuscript rooms. I'm sure the lady won't mind waiting here . . ." He gestured to a small sitting room off the main entrance hall. "While we search through the shelves for the manuscript you seek."

"Actually the lady would prefer to come with you," announced Charlotte in equally flawless Latin. She batted her lashes. "Surely three sets of eyes will accomplish the task faster than two."

"Why, that's an excellent suggestion, milady," agreed von Münch. To the head librarian, he added, "I'm sure you have no objection to the Countess of Wrexford joining the hunt."

The man looked scandalized over the idea of a female setting foot in his *sanctum sanctorum*, but on hearing von Münch's mention of her title, he swallowed any protest. Few people went out of their way to provoke the earl's ire.

"I have checked a master compendium of European manuscripts in our reference room, which was compiled by scholars at the Sorbonne at the beginning of the last century." The head librarian had left off his earlier pretensions and was now speaking in English. "It says that the manuscript entitled *Nihil Est Quod Hominum Efficere Non Possit* was a copy of a secret workbook of drawings made for Grand Duke Ferdinando I de' Medici of Tuscany, who ruled from 1587 to 1609."

They passed through a set of double doors and into a long corridor.

"The notation also says that five copies of the manuscript were made," he continued. "Three are known to have been destroyed in the late 1500s. One is in the collection of Balliol College at Oxford—"

"That is the one which has gone missing," said von Münch.

"Which leaves one for which there is no information as to its whereabouts." The head librarian came to a halt and made a face. "As I told you, we have no record of having it here in our collection."

"But from what I have read about the King's Library, all the books and archival materials were first kept in the Old Palace at Kew before being moved here to Buckingham House," said Charlotte. "So it's possible that records may have been lost."

A curt nod acknowledged the truth of the statement. As the head librarian resumed walking, he turned to the question of where to begin their search. "Given the date of the manuscript in question, we are looking at a transition period from Renaissance to Baroque. Which means the manuscript in question could be housed in either of those two sections of our library."

He glanced at von Münch. "You have no further details that might help us decide where to look first?"

"I'm sorry. I know nothing about it, save for the title."

"A thought occurred to me," ventured Charlotte. "The title itself seems to embody the very essence of Renaissance humanism. Unlike his immediate predecessors, Grand Duke Ferdinando was an enlightened ruler, harkening back to the likes of Cosimo the Great, the celebrated patron of the arts in Florence."

Ignoring the head librarian's startled reaction to her knowledge of history, she thought for a moment and then added, "The grand duke was interested in the arts and scientific learning, so my guess is he might have commissioned a number of works reflecting those interests in the first years of his rule."

"*Ja*," said von Münch, "that makes sense, milady."

The head librarian gave a grudging nod. "Then let us start in the Renaissance section." He took the next turn and led them through a passageway that connected the main section of the palatial house with the East Wing.

On entering the second of a suite of cavernous rooms—this

one was shaped like an octagon and topped by a massive dome with arched windows set in its base—the head librarian gestured at the towering shelves that filled all eight of the walls.

"I suggest we each start at a different wall and move on from there." He gestured at the rolling ladders affixed to a set of brass rails on each side of the cases. "Assuming the rigors of research aren't too demanding for Her Ladyship?"

"I shall manage," she replied.

"Then let us get to work."

Charlotte rolled her ladder to the left edge of the nearest wall and climbed up for a clear view of the top shelf. Not all the spines had a title, so many of the items would have to be pulled out and the title page checked. She flexed her shoulders and gave a grim smile. It was going to be a long afternoon. . . .

But the first one to tire won't be me, she vowed.

They toiled in scholarly silence, the only sounds the flutter of paper, the creak of wooden ladders, and the ticking of the tall case clock near the entranceway. After having no luck with her first wall of books and manuscripts, she moved on to another one.

She eventually developed a comfortable rhythm for checking the shelves, though on several occasions she inwardly cursed her skirts, as they snagged her shoes and nearly sent her tumbling to the floor.

A mishap that likely would have greatly pleased the head librarian for reinforcing his prejudices concerning the weaker sex . . .

Distracted by such musing, Charlotte nearly snapped shut the leatherbound manuscript that she was checking with only a cursory look. But the last two words of the handwritten title caught her eye.

Non Possit—

Bracing herself for balance, she carefully raised the cover to reveal the full page.

Nihil Est Quod Hominum Efficere Non Possit.

A smile touched her lips as Charlotte ran a fingertip over the inked lettering.

"*Eureka!*" she called to the others.

No luck.

Wrexford muttered an oath as he shut the door to his workroom, frustration rising bitter as bile in his throat. His former comrade had heard naught but vague rumors about a British traitor, and though he promised to make some inquiries, he held out little hope that they would lead to an actual name.

After closing his eyes for an instant, he crossed the carpet and took a seat at his desk. Every little contour of the padded leather seat fit him perfectly, every item on his desk—the piles of paper, the notebooks crammed with scientific observations, the books and periodicals, the pens and pencils—was intimately familiar.

And yet he felt as if his world was all askew.

The townhouse's unnatural silence was also affecting his equilibrium. Charlotte was with von Münch. McClellan had escorted the boys to their fencing lesson and then was taking them for an afternoon visit and supper with the dowager. As for Tyler, he was attending a chemistry lecture at the Royal Institution. Even the age-old beams and woodwork had ceased their usual little symphony of creaks and groans.

Which only amplified the unnerving whispers that were coming to life inside his head. Wrexford pressed his fingertips to his temples, as if trying to hold himself together. He had never felt so lost.

Grief and guilt over his brother's death had come back to haunt him. But this cursed investigation was also forcing him to face a more elemental mix of emotions. Ones that he had tried to keep locked away in the deepest crevices of his consciousness.

Fathers and sons.

He had always suspected that his father had loved Thomas best.

"And in all honesty, I can't blame him," whispered Wrexford. His own prickly, introspective nature did not match up well with the affable, outdoor-loving late earl. The two of them were like flint and steel, constantly rubbing up against each other and setting off sparks.

After Thomas's death, Wrexford knew that he should have made an effort to comfort his father. Instead, he had avoided ever paying a visit to the Yorkshire estate that was his father's chosen home. At the time, he had told himself it was done as a kindness, so as not to remind the late earl of his loss.

But that, admitted Wrexford, was a self-serving lie. He hadn't visited his father because he had been afraid of reading regret in the late earl's eyes—regret that the wrong son had survived. And so, for two years after his brother's death, he had seen his father only on the rare occasions when the late earl had felt compelled to visit London. A few days of stilted dinners and uncomfortable conversation over port and cigars.

And then, without warning, his father had dropped dead one morning after riding to hounds.

His chest tightened, and it was suddenly hard to breathe.

In a fit of pique, he had once accused his father of loving Thomas best. The late earl had appeared flabbergasted and vehemently protested that he loved his sons equally. At the time, Wrexford had thought it a polite platitude.

But now that he was guardian to two boys—boys who were like sons to him despite having no ties of blood—Wrexford understood what his father had meant.

That knowledge, however, had come too late to change the past.

Suddenly desperate to escape his maudlin thoughts, Wrexford rose and hurried to exit the townhouse through the French doors of the music room. Hyde Park, with its vast stretch of meadows, glades, and footpaths, was just a few streets away. Once there, perhaps he could outrace his demons.

At least for now.

A winged flying machine . . . a war machine bristling with weapons . . . a revolving bridge . . . Charlotte turned back to the beginning of the manuscript. "I can't make any sense of this," she said to von Münch.

After much discussion—and von Münch's veiled threat to have King Frederick of Württemberg intercede with his father-in-law, who owned the King's Library—they had been permitted to borrow the manuscript and take it back to Berkeley Square.

Charlotte had been disappointed to find that Wrexford was still out—Tyler knew not where—but she and von Münch were now ensconced in the earl's workroom, sitting side by side at one of the work counters so as to be able to study the pages of the manuscript together.

"Shall we take a second look?" she added.

"Here, allow me." The librarian took over the duty of turning the sheets of illustrated parchment. "Many of the illustrations seem like mere flights of fancy. But others appear grounded in science." His voice trailed off as he studied the details. "Oddly enough, their style looks very familiar."

After turning back and forth between the pages for closer study, he suddenly announced, "*Ach du lieber!* I know why I recognize them." Looking up, he added, "The title page says the manuscript is a copy of a secret Renaissance notebook. I am now quite sure that the original was made by Leonardo da Vinci!"

"Da Vinci?" repeated Charlotte. "He was a great Renaissance artist. But this?" She shook her head in confusion.

"He was far more than an artist, milady," said von Münch. "Da Vinci was a genius in a great many fields—and excelled in technological and engineering ingenuity. For example, he was hired as a military architect and engineer by the city of Venice to design its defenses against naval attack. He also created war machines for sieges and a series of movable barricades to protect the city of Milan from rival armies."

After pausing for a moment, von Münch added, "As I recall, da Vinci was also a visionary far ahead of his times, creating mechanical inventions like hydraulic pumps, reversible cranks, and steam cannons."

Charlotte's gaze moved to a drawing at the bottom of the page. "This appears to be some sort of—of aerial screw." She shook her head in disbelief. "Good heavens, I think it is supposed to fly a man up into the skies."

"There's some writing in the margin," observed von Münch, who adjusted his spectacles as she shifted to let him lean in for a closer look. "It says '*If this instrument made with a screw be well made—that is to say, made of linen of which the pores are stopped up with starch and be turned swiftly, the said screw will make its spiral in the air, and it will rise high.*'"

"Hmmph." The librarian looked puzzled as he pondered over what he had just read. "I confess, I have no idea as to why it would rise."

Charlotte made a face. "Nor do I." She resumed leafing through the manuscript. "Interestingly enough, there are a number of sketches of swirling water and currents on these pages. But what he sees in them is beyond me. Perhaps Wrexford will comprehend what secrets lie within the sketches." She pressed her palms to her eyes. "However, I find that it's all becoming an incomprehensible blur."

"*Ja*. I, too, make no claim to understand the scientific mind." Heaving a sigh, von Münch rose. "We have at least accomplished something today in finding the manuscript. Though I can't see how it helps us discern who might have wished to kill Mr. Greeley."

Charlotte closed the covers. "Nor can I."

"As you said, perhaps your husband will have some ideas." He took an appreciative sip from his glass and smiled. "By the by, Lord Wrexford possesses a very fine selection of German wines. Few Englishmen appreciate our Württemberg varietals . . ."

He stopped in mid-sentence, a furrow forming between his brows. "Forgive me—a sudden thought has just occurred to me, and I need to leave now if I am to pursue it."

CHAPTER 16

After seeing von Münch out, Charlotte resolved to set aside the mysteries of the manuscript until Wrexford returned. However, the house was quiet—too quiet to offer the usual familial distractions. The Weasels and Peregrine had retreated to their eyrie looking a little green around the gills after having eaten too many sweets during their supper with Alison. McClellan had gone out—she had not said to where—and Tyler was ensconced in the earl's laboratory preparing chemicals for a new experiment.

And so she found herself drawn back to the manuscript's cryptic pages.

"Damnation," she muttered after carrying it up to her workroom. "This *has* to hold a clue as to why Greeley was killed." One by one, she turned through the pages yet again, trying to keep an open mind on which of the bizarre images might be a key piece to the puzzle.

And once again, she felt utterly flummoxed.

Disappointed in herself, Charlotte looked up to give her eyes a rest. The lamplight flickered across her worktable, illuminating all the familiar elements of her daily life—her paints and brushes, the stack of watercolor paper, the sketchbooks. She could make them do her bidding with ease, creating words and images to provoke the public to think about complex ideas. . . .

Her gaze suddenly came to rest on the portfolio case that Wrexford had brought back from the Merton College Library.

The pile of papers and scribbled notes from Greeley's desk.

What with all the other distractions, she had yet to have a look at them.

Charlotte hesitated, half afraid of taking on another challenge that would defeat her. The trepidation wasn't out of mere hubris. Wrexford was a man of tightly controlled emotions, and yet she had never seen him appear so rattled.

So vulnerable.

Greeley's death had opened up an old wound, one that had never fully healed.

"And perhaps it never will," Charlotte whispered. No amount of logic seemed able to banish the unreasonable sense of guilt her husband felt at not being able to keep his brother safe. She also sensed that there were deeper, darker conflicts troubling him.

But for now, solving the murder must take precedence.

"Perhaps finding justice for Greeley will expiate some of the pain."

Grabbing a handful of the papers, she spread them out on her blotter. After opening a notebook and taking up her magnifying glass, she set to work trying to coax some meaning out of the scribbles.

The next time Charlotte looked up, she saw that the shadows of early evening had turned to a more impenetrable darkness. After flexing her shoulders, she put down her pencil and made a face. She had precious little to show for her hours of effort. Greeley's cryptic jottings and notations had defied her efforts to decipher what he had been thinking. One symbol—a strange squiggle with two finlike appendages—appeared with maddening frequency. But she couldn't begin to fathom what it meant.

"Perhaps in the morning, things will look clearer," Charlotte murmured, trying to boost her flagging spirits. Her muscles were cramping, her eyes were burning, but it was the ache in her heart that hurt the most. She wanted so badly to help Wrexford—

"What are you working on, m'lady?" Clad in a nightshirt, his sleep-tousled hair sticking up in spiky tufts, Hawk padded into the room.

"A puzzle," she answered. "It's very late. You should be in bed."

"I was," he replied. "I woke up and was thirsty, so I went to the kitchen for a mug of milk . . . and one or two ginger biscuits." He took a tentative step closer. "May I have a look?"

"Yes, by all means, sweeting." She sighed. "A fresh set of eyes may see whatever it is that I am missing."

Hawk came and stood close to her chair—close enough that the sugary heat from his skinny body warmed some of the uncertainty from her bones. She put her arms around him and brushed a kiss to his tangled curls.

Brow furrowed in concentration, he studied the scraps of paper spread out across her blotter for several long moments. "Why does an eel appear so often?"

"An eel?" said Charlotte blankly.

"Yes, an eel," said Hawk. A budding naturalist, he was particularly interested in creatures that crawled or wiggled through the muck. "You can tell by these two pectoral fins just behind the head and gills." He tapped a finger to one of the sketches. "And the way the body looks taller toward its tail because of the long fluttery fin that wraps its top and bottom."

Charlotte shook her head in confusion. "I can't for the life of me think of how an eel relates to a compendium of technological inventions from the Italian Renaissance."

"Perhaps it's a symbol," suggested Hawk. His expression sharpened. "Or a name. Our friend Smoke, who works down at the dockyards, knows several sailors called "Eel." He made a wry face. "Though it's not meant very nicely."

Charlotte considered the suggestion. There was something to be said for the suggestion.

Or was she simply grasping at straws?

"It's a very interesting idea," she said. "I shall ask whether Mr. Greeley knew anyone called Eel."

Seeing Hawk stifle a yawn, Charlotte ruffled his hair. "But for now, I think we both ought to get some rest."

However, once the boy had padded off to the stairs, she made no move to retire. Wrexford had left no word as to his evening activities, and the fact that he had not yet returned was making her jumpy. She was impatient to tell him about the discovery of the manuscript and show him the arcane drawings.

Picking up her pen, she tried to force her attention back to Greeley's cryptic notes. After several useless minutes, she conceded defeat. Sleep was out of the question, and so she decided to wait in her husband's workroom, where the familiar scents of leather, paper, ink, and Wrexford's bay rum shaving soap might help settle her nerves.

The night's chill hung heavy in the deserted space. After taking a moment to light an oil lamp, Charlotte chose a random book from the shelves and took a seat in one of the leather armchairs.

Where she soon slipped into a fitful doze.

It was way past dark before Wrexford was too weary in both body and spirit to continue his aimless wandering through the park and the adjoining Kensington Gardens. Turning his steps for home, he exited through the Grosvenor Gate and made his way to Berkeley Square.

"Milord."

He whirled around to see a familiar figure step out from the shadows of the wrought-iron fence surrounding the center garden.

"Griffin!" The earl's pulse kicked up a notch. "What are you doing back in London? Have you discovered something?"

"Let us go somewhere where we can talk more comfortably," said Griffin. He hesitated and shot a glance at the earl's nearby townhouse before adding, "I know a tavern near here, by the burying ground off South Audley Street."

"Where I will have the privilege of buying you a midnight supper?" replied Wrexford, using the retort to compose himself. "Or is it time for breakfast?"

"Actually, I'm not hungry, milord."

"Ye gods, are you ill?"

Griffin didn't smile. Shifting uncomfortably from foot to foot, he stood in silence, waiting for the earl to make a decision.

From the look on the Runner's face, Wrexford guessed that the news was bad. Indeed, a sense of foreboding had gripped his heart from the moment he had first touched Greeley's letter begging him to come to Oxford. Still, he couldn't begin to imagine what sort of revelations he was about to hear.

But if he was about to receive an emotional punch to the gut, perhaps it was best to do so away from Charlotte and the rest of his household. His self-control was already a little shaky, and he would rather have some time in which to compose himself.

"Well, then it seems I shall get off cheaply tonight." He gestured for Griffin to lead the way, then fell in step beside him as the Runner picked a path through a tangle of alleyways that led away from Berkeley Square. "How did you know where to find me?"

"I stopped at your townhouse earlier, and Tyler told me you were out. So I decided to wait."

Another sign that the news was not good.

As they emerged onto a narrow side street, Griffin headed for a stucco and timber building squeezed in between two brick warehouses. A gleam of mellow lamplight lit the night as he tugged open the door to the tavern and led the way to a table nestled in a far corner of the room.

Griffin signaled for the barmaid to bring over two tankards of ale and then clasped his hands together and placed them on the tabletop.

"Whatever you have to say," muttered Wrexford, "you might as well spit it out."

A shadow suddenly fell over the table as the barmaid returned. Two tankards thumped down, foam sliding down the dark pewter to pool on the sticky wood.

Griffin took a swallow of his ale before clearing his throat. "I've made no progress on identifying a suspect in Mr. Greeley's murder. Your brother's friend lived a very quiet and solitary life."

"I doubt you traveled here from Oxford just to tell me that."

"Correct, milord," responded the Runner. "I received an urgent note from one of my fellow Runners that convinced me to return to Town." A pause. "I'm aware that coincidences make you highly suspicious. They have the same effect on me."

"Stop talking in circles," growled Wrexford, perplexed as to where the Runner was headed. "Just give me the facts."

"A man has been arrested for starting the fire that burned down Henry Maudslay's laboratory."

The reply caught him completely off-guard. "I'm aware of that, but what the devil does it have to do with Greeley?"

"I'm about to explain, milord," said Griffin, looking as though he would rather eat nails than go on.

Wrexford sat back and folded his arms across his chest.

"It turns out that the arsonist is a former soldier . . ." Griffin looked down into his ale. "And served in an infantry company attached to the same brigade as Greeley's cavalry regiment."

A chill slithered down the earl's spine, but he shook it off. "In this case, a coincidence is likely just that. Foot soldiers and cavalry officers come from different circles of Society. They don't fraternize with each other."

"I haven't finished my explanation," said the Runner. "When he was arrested, the former soldier claimed he had been offered a large sum of money to start the fire by a fancy gentleman, and desperate to survive, he accepted it. He also claimed that he had recognized the man from his time on the Peninsula and could identify him—

"Who?" demanded Wrexford.

Griffin blew out his breath. "The former soldier refused to reveal it to my fellow Runner. He said that he would only speak to me, as apparently word in the stews is that my integrity can't be bought."

"Damnation!" The earl started to rise. "What are we waiting for? Let us go talk to the man now!"

"I had my fellow Runner set up a time for me to interview him at Newgate Prison for earlier today," replied Griffin. "However, when I arrived, I was informed that the fellow had been knifed to death last night in a scuffle between prisoners."

The earl slumped back in his chair. No wonder Griffin was finding the idea of random coincidence hard to swallow.

"As you know, I am like a mastiff—when I get a bone between my teeth, I am loath to let it go." Griffin pressed his palms together. "There are rumors that a number of former soldiers—including officers—have joined with the radical Luddites who see all technology as evil because it's taken away jobs that men need in order to survive. It won't be easy, but I intend to keep delving into this situation and see what connections I can uncover."

He paused. "Or would you prefer that I drop it?"

The earl considered the implications of the question. The Runner was obliquely warning that the truth might reflect badly on Greeley. Wrexford could well imagine that his brother's friend might have sympathized with the returning veterans who now were struggling to find work and joined a radical group.

And von Münch's revelations stirred an even darker thought, though he didn't feel at liberty to mention it to Griffin. Was it possible that Greeley might in some way be connected to the British traitor? Money was a powerful temptation, and Greeley's family had not been plump in the pocket.

But Truth is Truth, no matter how ugly, he reflected. *If I begin to pick and choose when it matters, then I'm lost. I will no longer possess a moral compass.*

"Of course I want you to follow the trail," he replied, thinking of his own pursuit to uncover the truth.

Their eyes met.

"Wherever it may lead, milord?"

"Yes," answered Wrexford without hesitation. "Wherever it may lead."

Roused by the sound of familiar footsteps in the corridor, Charlotte met her husband as he came through the doorway and slipped her arms around him. His body was taut as a tightly wound watch spring but softened as she drew him closer, all his muscled contours and chiseled angles somehow molding to her gentler shape.

She never ceased to feel a spark of joy at how perfectly they fit together.

"Wrex," Charlotte whispered, after feathering a gossamer kiss to his cheek.

He tightened his hold on her, which said far more than words.

"Bad news?" she guessed.

"It seems that one terrible event in the past—a damnable French ambush that killed my brother and scarred Greeley for life—has triggered a number of unforeseen consequences," he replied. "Though in what pernicious way they tie together is still unclear."

"You know from your scientific studies that there are clockwork laws of the universe. Drop a stone in water, and the waves inexorably ripple out." She felt him shift. "You could not have prevented the regiment from riding out on its mission, nor the terrible aftermath that followed, including Greeley's mental trauma and his murder. So it does no earthly good to put the weight of that guilt on your beautiful shoulders."

Wrexford took her face between his palms. "My head may know that what you say is true, but my heart . . ."

She clenched a hand and gave a sharp thump to his left breast. "Then your heart had better listen to *me*. Otherwise, I may cut it out with a penknife and feed it to the Tower ravens—and then draw you a new one."

"Thank you." His lips quirked. "For refusing to let me wallow in a sea of self-pity."

"That's why we make a good pairing. We are both too stubborn to allow the other to indulge in self-indulgent whinging."

That drew a reluctant laugh.

They stood for an interlude in companionable silence. Somewhere in the garden, a nightingale's song rose above the rustling of the leaves. Charlotte watched the pale flickers of moonlight play hide-and-seek within the dark silhouettes.

Hide-and-seek. What if they never found Greeley's murderer? Could Wrexford make his peace with that?

"Tell me what happened," she said.

"We had better sit," replied Wrexford. He then told her about Griffin's revelation.

For an instant, Charlotte, was too shocked to speak. "Good God," she finally whispered. "Greeley's murder, a British traitor from six years ago, the arsonist responsible for the fire at Maudslay's laboratory . . ."

She frowned. "How can they possibly be connected?" The lamp flame seemed to shiver at her words. "And yet, how can they possibly not be?"

The anguish in Wrexford's eyes told her that he was thinking much the same thing. Shifting her gaze downward, Charlotte noticed the austere angles of his features, chiseled to a sharpness that she had never seen. *Grief, guilt, pain*—a volatile mix of emotions had pulled the flesh tight over his bones.

Forcing aside her own fears, she reached over to put her hand on his thigh. "What we've just learned about the ex-soldier being attached to Greeley's regiment gives Griffin another lead to follow," she said. "A tenuous one, perhaps, but nonetheless it may turn up a key clue that will explain what is going on."

"Our thoughts align," replied Wrexford. "It occurs to me that the fancy gentleman may have been an officer in the regiment—and if so, perhaps we have found our traitor."

He paused. "It's worth having a meeting with my friend at Horse Guards and going over past records to make a list of possibilities. Through his connections here in Town, Tyler can arrange for us to learn whether any of the possible suspects are residing close to London."

"And I shall think about another drawing concerning the fire," said Charlotte, "and how I can stir up just enough questions about the death of the arsonist while under lock and key at Newgate Prison to make the unknown fancy gentleman uncomfortable."

"You must do it very carefully, my dear," counseled Wrexford.

"Whatever the dangers, we shall meet them," she said.

"I'm sorry, Charlotte, but I can't let this go." He closed his eyes for just an instant. "It's now far too personal."

"I expected no less, Wrex." Charlotte smiled. "Perhaps it's a curse, but neither one of us is ever willing to shy away from the truth."

He hesitated, but then smiled back at her.

She allowed herself to savor the moment before revealing her own news. "You aren't the only one who made a discovery today."

"The manuscript?"

She nodded. "Yes, but I can't say that it sheds any light on the mystery of Greeley's murder."

Suddenly recalling Hawk's comment from earlier in the evening, she added, "This may mean nothing, but along with examining the manuscript, I also began to look through the pile of papers that you brought back from Greeley's desk. Do you perchance recall your brother and Greeley having a friend or acquaintance they called Eel?"

He shook his head. "Why do you ask?"

Charlotte explained Hawk's observation concerning the strange sketches on the scribbled notes. "But as I said, it's simply grasping at straws floating in the wind."

The statement drew a weary sigh. "I need to look at the manuscript."

"It can wait until morning." She took his hand and rose, drawing him to his feet. "You need some sleep."

Wrexford brushed back an errant lock of hair from her brow. "You're right," he murmured, slowly curling the strands around his finger. "Let us retire for the night. And hope that the light of day will bring us some much needed illumination."

CHAPTER 17

Roused by the rosy hues of dawn teasing through the window-panes, Wrexford headed down to his workroom, determined to find a way to piece together the disparate pieces of the maddening puzzle.

The manuscript lay on his desk, its title—*Nihil Est Quod Hominum Efficere Non Possit*—a taunting challenge that seemed to mock his efforts at solving Greeley's murder.

"There is nothing that man can't accomplish," he muttered, translating the Latin words as he opened the cover. "I damn well hope that is true."

Wrexford soon found himself lost in the intricate drawings and handwritten text. He pored over the pages, turning back and forth to study the images and notations. But try as he might, he couldn't find any clue that might point to a motive for the murder. Still, the earl couldn't help but be fascinated by da Vinci's scientific thinking.

"What a remarkable mind," mused Wrexford as he admired the polymath's amazing range of ideas for technological innovations. The numerous drawings of water in motion—swirling eddies, rushing streams, whirling currents—also caught his eye.

Sitting back, Wrexford pursed his lips in thought.

Tyler came into the room with the morning's newspapers and set them on the desk. "Is that the missing manuscript?" he inquired, edging around for a closer look.

"Yes," answered the earl as his gaze drifted back to a deftly drawn image of a river's turbulence. "I just recalled that Reginald Maitland, the Taviot consortium's chief engineer, mentioned there was a famous Swiss scientific thinker and mathematician whose work involved water—"

"Ah, yes, Daniel Bernoulli," said the valet. "He wrote a famous book on how fluids behave when they are in motion called *Hydrodynamica*." A grimace. "But don't ask me to explain anything about it. I once took a look at it and gave up after the first chapter. Like you, I've never had an interest in that area of science." A pause. "Perhaps Lady Cordelia would know if any of Bernoulli's findings could possibly relate to marine propulsion."

"I shall make a point of asking her," replied Wrexford. "I can't afford to overlook any clue, however far-fetched."

Tyler studied the drawing of swirling water for a moment longer, then shrugged and left the room.

After yet another round of leafing through the manuscript, the earl conceded that he could wrest no further information from its pages and turned his attention to the task of identifying what current or former officers from Greeley's old regiment might be residing in the area.

"Wrex." Charlotte paused in the doorway.

The earl looked up from penning a note to an acquaintance who served as a senior administrator of the army archives at Horse Guards.

"Forgive me for interrupting, but . . ." She made a face before approaching his desk. "It may mean nothing, but I just found this stuck in among the papers you brought back from Greeley's office."

A flicker of color caught his eye as she unfolded a piece of art.

"Why, that's—"

"Yes, it's one of my prints," she interjected. "An old one, and strangely enough, it looks to have been crumpled and discarded at some point."

"Perhaps Greeley changed his mind and decided to save it because of its satirical edge," mused the earl. "A great many people collect your art for its sharp-eyed view of the world and all its foibles."

Charlotte slapped it down on his blotter. "Take a close look at it and its captions."

After studying it for several moments, he let out a low oath.

"Damnation, indeed," responded Charlotte. "I had completely forgotten about this drawing. It was part of the series I did on Progress some months ago but was more of an afterthought."

She tucked a loosened lock of hair behind her ear. "I only included it because you had mentioned that some of the leading nautical engineers were holding a symposium on steam power and ships at the Royal Institution, which I decided to attend. However, they had little of interest to say, so it seemed that nautical innovations were stuck in the doldrums." A frown. "Still, I made a few sketches of their faces while they spoke, deciding that a series on Progress ought to include a failure as well as successes."

She looked again at the drawing. "It's no wonder that when I took the boys to visit the King's Dockyard I had the sense that I had seen Peregrine's friend Samuel Tilden before."

"I can see why you forgot about the drawing," replied Wrexford, after re-reading the captions. "Your point was that the engineers on land, with their experimental locomotives, were coming up with far more exciting innovations than the seagoing men of science."

"So I thought at the time," said Charlotte.

His gaze had moved from the captions to the caricatures. "However, I assume that the reason you're showing this print to me is because of *them* . . ." He tapped a finger to the two gentlemen in the foreground of the drawing. "Reginald Maitland and Samuel Tilden were the main speakers at the lecture."

"There were no other A. J. Quill prints among Greeley's papers. So the fact that he saved this particular one can't help but raise disturbing questions," reasoned Charlotte. "Given the fire at Maudslay's laboratory and its significance to the race to invent the technology for ocean travel, how can this discovery not connect in some way to Greeley's death?"

"But how?" Wrexford clenched his hands in exasperation. "As far as I can see, the da Vinci manuscript has nothing to do with modern technology."

"Save for the drawings of water," Charlotte pointed out.

They both darted a look at the manuscript lying at the corner of his desk. To the earl's eye, the open pages seemed to quiver with silent laughter.

Charlotte seemed to read his thoughts. "I know, I know—it's an absurd idea. And yet . . ." Her words trailed off in a frustrated sigh.

But after a moment, she looked up at him through her lashes. "There is another possibility, though it pains me to say it."

Wrexford nodded. "I know what you are thinking. Perhaps Greeley got involved with a radical group of returning soldiers who believe that technology is stealing their chances of finding work. Which might mean his murder is the result of a quarrel between factions."

She expelled a sigh. "But that still doesn't explain why the manuscript was taken."

"Or perhaps he saved the print because it showed Maitland—or Tilden."

Their eyes met.

"So let us decide our next move."

Wrexford rose abruptly. "We need to send word to Cordelia and ask her to come by as soon as she can. I was just telling Tyler that I remembered something from Maitland's recent lecture at the Royal Institution. He mentioned a book on mathematics and fluid dynamics. Perhaps she is familiar with it and can help us discern whether any of these seemingly unconnected clues might fit together."

"I'll have Riche dispatch one of the footmen immediately," replied Charlotte. But as she turned for the door, she hesitated. "I think it's only right that we also summon Kit, despite the fact that things are fraught between him and Cordelia. He wouldn't thank us for leaving him in the dark about our discovery and its possible connection to Taviot's consortium."

"Very well," conceded Wrexford, though he couldn't help but add, "Our friends will likely think we are mad as March hares."

"I daresay we are." A glimmer of humor flickered in her eyes. "Allowing an uncontrollable passion for justice to overwhelm all reason and restraint is clearly the sign of an addled brain." She made a face. "I apologize. I think you caught the malady from me."

Funny how she could make him smile, even under the darkest of circumstances. But as she hurried into the corridor, the light moment was quickly sucked under by the vortex of unanswered questions.

"Bloody hell," he muttered. "I feel like we're drowning in a sea of hidden secrets and lies."

Wrexford took another look at the A. J. Quill print before folding it up and taking a deep breath. Logic had always been his lodestone, yet no matter how meticulously he analyzed the facts, nothing was making any sense. By piecing together a set of hard-won clues, he had come to believe that Greeley's murder was linked in some way to a British traitor who had sold out his comrades during the Peninsular War.

But this new evidence seemed to say it was linked to the current technological race for mastery of the oceans.

There was another possibility . . .

"No. Impossible," he growled. *For it would mean—*

"Sorry to interrupt, milord, but this missive just arrived," announced Tyler as he rushed into the room and held out a letter. "It was delivered by a messenger from the French envoy's office, so I thought you would wish to see it right away."

Steady, steady. Wrexford slowly reached out and took it from the valet's fingers.

Tyler's face, he noted, had turned ashen. The valet knew the significance of a communication from a Frenchman.

The blood-red wax seal broke with an audible *crack*, allowing the single sheet of paper to unfold.

Four words, stark black on white, were scrawled in the center of the page.

The traitor's name.

"Oh, you bloody, bloody bastard," whispered Wrexford, his blood turning to ice—and then to fire.

"But, by God, I've finally got you."

CHAPTER 18

The earl dropped the letter onto the desktop and moved to the window.

Tyler hesitated, then picked it up.

"Ye gods." He blew out his breath and then read the name aloud.

"*The Earl of Taviot.*"

"Charlotte has already sent word asking Cordelia and Kit to come here," said the earl without turning around. "Dispatch a second message to Kit and ask him to bring Taviot's letter and the contracts from the consortium." Having another few samples of the miscreant's handwriting should confirm Taviot's guilt beyond a shadow of a doubt.

"Should we also summon Henning?" suggested the valet. "We'll need to decide how to bring Lord Taviot to justice, and given that the dastard is not without power or influence within the highest circles of Society, we ought to assemble our trusted inner circle for a council of war."

"That— " began Wrexford.

"That means you need to include Aunt Alison," came a muffled voice from the adjoining library. Raven pushed the door all the way open. "And *us*."

Hawk and Peregrine, who were standing just behind him, nodded in solemn agreement.

"Bloody hell, you imps of Satan know damn well that eavesdropping is against the house rules," snapped Wrexford.

"It's *not* breaking the rules if it wasn't intentional," countered Raven. "The door was half open. We couldn't help overhearing the conversation."

Wrexford swore again on realizing that it was he who had failed to click the latch shut after fetching a book earlier in the morning.

Taking the oath as a signal to press his point, Raven added, "M'lady says that keeping each other in the dark about what dangers are threatening our family and friends can lead to disaster. So we need to know what's going on."

His chin angled to a defiant tilt. "Surely you can't deny that we've been of help in catching other bloody, bloody bastards?"

"Don't swear." Charlotte came to an abrupt halt in the doorway and angled a wary look at Wrexford. "Why are you and the boys talking about catching bloody, bloody bastards?"

Tyler wordlessly handed her the note.

Her face turned as pale as the paper. "Is this—"

"Yes," answered Wrexford. "It's from von Münch's French contact. We have found our traitor—and likely the man behind the murders of both Greeley and the former soldier who set the fire at Maudslay's laboratory."

"Merciful heavens." Charlotte crossed the carpet and sat down rather heavily in one of the leather armchairs after reading the name.

"Tyler just said that we should call for a council of war," explained Raven. "And I told Wrex that it must include us and Aunt Alison." A note of challenge gave his words a sharp edge.

"She doesn't like it any better than we do when the two of you try to wrap her in cotton wool because of her age."

Charlotte stared at him in mute shock. And then surrendered with a sigh. "I—I suppose that I have been over-protective. I'm worried that the recent investigations may have put our family in danger—"

"Our family is used to danger," piped up Hawk. "We've all learned from you and Wrex that Evil mustn't be allowed to triumph over Good. And that sometimes means we have to take risks."

"Oiy," agreed Raven. "It's who we are."

"Out of the mouths of babes," said Wrexford. "Ours is not a conventional family." His gaze found hers. "Would you have it any other way?"

Her mouth quivered for an instant before slowly curling into a wry smile.

"Never. Which means . . ."

Without any further hesitation, she rose and addressed the boys. "Hawk and Falcon, you two fly off and fetch Aunt Alison. Raven, find Cordelia and Kit and convey the urgency of my previous messages." A quick pivot. "As for you, Tyler, take the carriage and bring Baz back here." She glanced at the clock on the mantel. "Mac has gone to purchase some new brushes and watercolor pigments for me, but she should be home shortly. Let us plan on convening our council of war in an hour's time."

Their marching orders received, the four messengers wasted not a moment in racing off to perform their duties.

"Speaking of family," began Wrexford. "I have a confession to make—"

Before he could go on, Charlotte turned and wrapped her arms around him. Warmth pierced through wool and linen to prickle against his fear-cold flesh.

"I fear that I'm not very good at being part of a family," he went on in a rush, before he lost the courage to reveal the less than admirable side of his soul. "Greeley's murder has reopened the old wounds surrounding my brother's death, and I've come to realize that I failed my father when he most needed me."

Remorse lodged like a stone in his throat, forcing him to pause for a moment before he could continue. "I thought only of myself . . ." Wrexford explained about his avoidance of his grieving father. "I'm too introspective." A huff. "Too impatient. Too sharp-tongued." He made a face. "I fear that I won't be a good husband or a good surrogate father to the Weasels—"

Charlotte pressed a kiss to his lips to silence his fears. She held him close for a moment longer before leaning back. "God knows, I, of all people, am aware of the complexities and conflicts that can tear families apart." Her eyes pooled with sympathy. "They appear deceptively sturdy, but in truth families are achingly fragile. However—"

"I should have bothered to look closer and see his pain," he said, determined to forge ahead. "Instead I withdrew into myself and focused my gaze on my own interests. It's a flaw—"

"Good heavens, Wrex! None of us are without flaws," interjected Charlotte. "Flaws are part of who we are," she continued. "But more importantly, they are often the core of our strengths."

"A frightening thought," he muttered.

"Oh, come," For just an instant, a glint of humor danced beneath her lashes. "Who would you be without your snaps and snarls?"

Slipping free, he perched a hip on the corner of his desk and folded his arms across his chest. "A better man?"

"On the contrary," she replied. "I won't make light of your fears, for they are very real to you. However, the boys and I see you through the prism of our own perceptions, which paint a very different portrait from the one you have sketched."

Outside the leaded windows, the scudding clouds momentarily allowed the sun to peek through, sending a flickering of gold-flecked light through the shadows.

"You are the most thoughtful individual I have ever met. You observe, you analyze, and you are open to seeing things that don't fit your preconceptions. You listen carefully and are willing to admit when you may be wrong. Yes, you have sharp edges, but you only use them to deflate the hubris of puffed-up popinjays."

She allowed a moment of silence. "The Weasels will watch, listen, and learn from you how to grow up to be men of honor and integrity. They could not have a better guardian."

"You give me too much credit," said Wrexford. "But—"

"But enough recriminations for now." Charlotte smiled. "Much as it's important for us to talk about the doubts that lurk in our hearts, let us put these very personal matters aside for the present."

Her gaze moved to where the note lay open on his desk. "We now know the identity of the villain behind the heinous crimes. And it's time to bring him to justice."

All at once, the shadows haunting his thoughts seemed to lighten.

"Indeed." He waggled a booted foot. "Let us go kick the Earl of Taviot into the deepest pit of Hell."

Charlotte moved closer and touched a palm to his cheek. "Don't be so harsh on yourself, Wrex," she murmured. "We all go through black moments in our lives. They are painful but also help make us wiser and stronger."

"Amen to that." He cracked his knuckles. "Taviot had better start saying his prayers."

"Ah, I hear Alison and the boys approaching." Charlotte took a seat by the hearth. She had fetched a notebook from her workroom and opened it to a fresh page.

"How could you not? A mounted regiment of Royal Hussars would make less clatter in the corridor," observed Wrexford as he busied himself with cleaning his pistols. "Speaking of the dowager, I assume that she is to be allowed unfettered freedom in the investigation."

"Alison has proved extremely helpful in the past, so it would be unfair to impose any strictures," replied Charlotte. "However, the fact that she isn't as mobile as she used to be should keep her out any of real trouble."

"A fair point," he acknowledged.

"Just don't repeat that within striking range of her stick."

"I may be reckless at times, but I do possess some sense of self-preservation." Wrexford wiped the oil from his fingers with a gunpowder-flecked rag. "We'll need to address how to handle Peregrine."

"Yes, he can't follow the same rules as the Weasels," replied Charlotte. "But I think all three of them know that already."

A loud *halloo* from the front of the townhouse announced that Raven had also returned. The echo of Cordelia's voice followed, which in the next instant was swallowed by Henning's rough-cut rumbling.

"Excellent, it appears that all our friends have arrived," said Charlotte. "I've sent Mac to bring several pots of coffee and a platter of ginger biscuits from the kitchen. Once everyone is settled, we'll tell them the news."

The messengers had been instructed to reveal nothing about the reason for the gathering, save to say it was a matter of great urgency. But Wrexford imagined that their friends could all guess why they had been summoned.

"So, who is the bloody bastard?" demanded Henning as he shuffled to the sideboard and poured himself a glass of whisky.

"Sit down, Baz," ordered the earl. "So we may get started."

"In that case, I will bring the bottle with me."

Cordelia looked flustered as she shrugged off her pelisse and tossed it on the back work counter. "I'm sorry, Wrex, but Kit hasn't returned from a meeting. Raven and I left word at his lodgings to join us here."

"A meeting with whom?" asked Wrexford.

"The note that he sent to me earlier this morning didn't say." However, the dangerous glitter in her eyes warned that she had her suspicions.

Damnation. He hoped Sheffield wasn't playing with fire. Making a deal with the devil without telling her would likely consign their engagement to the flames.

Poof—and then naught but a pile of ashes.

Not to speak of the other dangers to their friend if he had allied himself with Taviot.

Raven and Hawk, shadowed by Peregrine, took the opportunity to slip into the shadows by the library door and take a seat on the carpet as the others all settled themselves in the armchairs near the hearth.

McClellan trundled in with the coffee pot and biscuits. "Go ahead and begin, milord. I'll be back in a trice with some cups and saucers."

The earl rose. The room fell silent, and as he clicked the lid to his pistol case shut the sound reverberated like a gunshot off the wainscoting.

"As you all know, we've been struggling to untangle two conundrums and their ramifications. The first is, who murdered Neville Greeley and why?" He paused. "And the second is, who is responsible for skullduggery surrounding the race to create an oceangoing propulsion system?"

"Isn't there also a mysterious manuscript that has gone missing?" queried the dowager. "And aren't we wondering whether it is the thread that ties all these crimes together?"

Henning let out a rusty chuckle and raised his glass in salute. "Never let it be said that age inexorably steals all one's marbles."

"You're right, Alison," said Charlotte. "We know that a manuscript entitled *Nihil Est Quod Hominum Efficere Non Possit* was stolen from Greeley on the night of the murder. As for whether it ties into marine propulsion, we're hoping that Cordelia can help discern the answer—"

"You've found it?" exclaimed Cordelia.

"We have," answered Wrexford. He stepped back as McClellan returned with a tray of china and smoothly plucked it from her grasp. After carrying it to the counter, he circled back to his desk and resumed where he had left off.

"As Charlotte said, we hope that Cordelia can enlighten us on whether the manuscript holds any keys to unlocking the secrets of ocean travel. However, momentous though that answer may be, it now may be a moot point. The investigation into Greeley's murder uncovered evidence of another terrible crime, one from the past that provides a strong motive for wanting Greeley dead . . ."

Wrexford could feel all eyes on him. "We now have reason to believe that all the misdeeds of our two separate investigations are the work of one monstrous villain. And I now know who that villain is."

The name stuck for an instant in his throat. "The Earl of Taviot—"

A sudden *crack* cut him off as a pile of saucers slipped through McClellan's fingers and fell to the countertop, shattering into a myriad pieces.

"F-Forgive me." The maid began gathering up the shards but let them fall for a second time as Charlotte swept in and took hold of her arm.

"Enough shilly-shallying, Mac!" Charlotte led her to one of the armchairs and ordered her to sit. "Whatever dark secret you are keeping from us, the time has come to share it."

CHAPTER 19

Shoulders slumping, McClellan gave a reluctant nod. "Aye."

"Before you do so . . ." interjected Charlotte. The boys had flattened their backs against the dark wainscoting and gone very still—hoping, no doubt, that their presence would be forgotten. But despite them being worldly beyond their years, Charlotte decided that the coming confession was not something they ought to hear. Following Wrexford's lead, she had never inquired as to why McClellan had left Scotland. But one didn't require much imagination to suspect that it wasn't because of a minor transgression.

The earl shifted his gaze to the shadowed corner of the room. "Weasels—and that includes you, Peregrine," he intoned. "We have matters to discuss in private."

It was said softly, but Raven rose without argument, wise enough to hear its underlying note of steel, and marched for the door, his brother and Peregrine right on his heels.

At the last moment, however, Hawk wavered and came to a halt by Charlotte. "A-Are you going to send Mac away because . . ." His voice hitched. "Because she did something bad?"

Charlotte crouched down and pulled him into a fierce hug. "Of course not, sweeting. Mac is family. We simply need to hear what the problem is so that we can help."

The quivering of his mouth stilled, the corners curling up ever so slightly as he turned to McClellan. "Don't worry, Mac. We will help, too."

The maid swallowed a watery sniff. "Well, then, I know I have nothing to fear if the Weasels are on my side."

He flashed a gap-toothed grin before hurrying away.

Maintaining a sympathetic silence, Wrexford fished a handkerchief from his pocket and handed to McClellan. The maid was by nature a stoic—in that they were kindred souls—so he sensed how painful the moment must be for her.

The maid wiped the tears from her cheeks and blew her nose before carefully refolding the damp silk and setting it on her lap. "My apologies, everyone. I shall endeavor to spare you any further theatrics. As for confessing my crime, you're right. It's time you all know."

"I assume it has to do with Lord Taviot," guessed Charlotte. "He must have been one of the gentlemen who strolled past us on Bond Street."

McClellan nodded.

"So, did you purloin his priceless family jewels?" drawled the earl.

A mirthless laugh. "No, I picked up a poker and smashed in the skull of his younger brother, then pushed the miscreant's dead body over the stone ledge of his bedchamber window."

The dowager slowly raised her quizzing glass, the lens magnifying the brilliant blue glitter of her sapphirine eye. "Well, I daresay the miscreant deserved it. I've done a bit more delving into the family and its doings, and by all accounts, the youngest of the Taviot siblings was a thoroughly despicable fellow."

"True," agreed McClellan. "Though I am under no illusion

that the laws of the land gave me the right to be his judge and executioner." She shrugged. "Nonetheless, I did so."

"With good reason, I imagine," murmured Charlotte. "My guess is, he was trying to rape a servant?"

"A newly hired Highland lass, who had not yet been warned never to stray to that part of the castle," answered McClellan. "I had heard from other servants when I arrived to take the post that the miscreant was particularly vicious about forcing himself on women after he had consumed several bottles of whisky."

"You deserve a medal," muttered Cordelia.

"Scotland would more likely be of the opinion that I deserve a noose around the neck." A pause. "However, I decided not to stay in my position as mistress of the female staff long enough to find out for sure."

"Taking a life is a grave thing," said Wrexford after several long moments of silence.

"It is, milord," agreed McClellan. "I have blood on my hands, and if you wish to call Griffin, I shall willingly go with him to answer for my crimes."

All eyes were now focused on the earl.

"The laws of the land are the laws of the land," began Wrexford.

Tyler bowed his head, hiding his expression.

"But as we hold no official mandate to enforce them, I suggest we leave the matter for the proper authorities to settle." He looked around. "Are we all agreed?"

Everyone voiced a heartfelt assent.

"Then we need not speak of this again."

McClellan tightened her grip on the earl's handkerchief. "Words can't express my gratitude to all of you for your faith in me."

"Auch, we've come to be family," said Henning. "We know there's not a speck of blackness in your heart."

The maid looked to Charlotte. "I'm so sorry I didn't confess my sin sooner. Lord Taviot occasionally comes to Town for periods of time when Parliament is in session, and I take care to avoid the areas where he might seek entertainment. But it was a shock to see him here now."

She drew in a ragged breath. "Then I read in the gossip column of a newspaper that he and his sister were making the rounds in Mayfair to talk about their consortium, and I wasn't sure what to do. Tyler alerted me to Mr. Sheffield's interest in the investment opportunity, and I saw A. J. Quill's pen begin to poke into the race to build an oceangoing steamship."

"Sorry," mumbled Tyler. "Mac asked me to keep mum about her dilemma, and I felt beholden to respect her wishes."

"I know it was wrong of me to remain silent." McClellan lifted her shoulders in apology. "But I feared that I might somehow make trouble for you and His Lordship."

"Would Taviot recognize you?" asked Wrexford.

"I—I don't think so."

"What about Lady Kirkwall?" asked Charlotte.

"Perhaps," answered McClellan.

"It seems they have no reason to connect you to our household," mused Wrexford. "So the real threat is that either of them might spot you on the street and alert Bow Street to take you into custody as a fugitive from justice."

"I agree," responded Charlotte. "So we will take precautions. The two of us will avoid being seen in public together, and you must continue to be circumspect in your own outings. That should ensure your safety."

"Especially as Taviot will soon be worrying about a hangman's noose tightening around his own neck." Wrexford reopened his pistol case. "Speaking of which, let us return to the matter of bringing him to justice."

* * *

Charlotte couldn't help but flinch. She had never seen such a murderous gleam in her husband's eyes.

"You don't think that merely showing the letters you were given by the Frenchman to the minister of state security, along with samples of Taviot's handwriting, will be enough for Grentham to arrest him for treason?" asked the dowager.

"I would rather have more conclusive evidence," answered Wrexford. "So that the snake can't wriggle out of answering for his misdeeds."

"Like what?" inquired Tyler. He eyed the earl's dueling weapons. "A signed confession?"

The answering show of teeth was clearly not meant to be a smile.

"Do we know why Taviot was on the Peninsula six years ago?" asked Charlotte. "That may help us discern how to look for other incriminating evidence."

"He wasn't in the military, so I assume he was involved in one of the delegations dispatched by the Foreign Office to assess the progress of the war and deal with the local civilian authorities," answered Wrexford. "I'll have that information by the end of the day."

"And we ought not forget about his likely involvement in the clandestine attacks on Maudslay's laboratory and the naval research facilities at the King's Dockyard," offered Alison. "The consortium's coming reception is being held at its fancy laboratory near Hampton Palace, which will offer us the opportunity to do some sleuthing."

A chill teased down Charlotte's spine at the word *us*. "As for the skullduggery, I have an idea of where to look for additional proof of Taviot's misdeeds come nightfall. There may be a chance of discovering who hired the arsonist who set the fire at Maudslay's laboratory—and I suspect it may be Taviot," she said. "In the meantime, I shall think of how my pen can help prod him into making a mistake."

"Enough words for now. It's time for action," said Wrexford. "Tyler, take Cordelia and show her Bernoulli's book to see if she can discern whether he offers any mathematical insight into the sketches in da Vinci's manuscript. Charlotte and I have our objectives. The rest of you—"

"I can do some asking around among the returning soldiers who come to my clinic for medical help," offered Henning. "They may know something about the fancy gentleman who hired the poor murdered fellow who set the fire."

"And I can continue making inquiries into Taviot's private life," said the dowager. "As Charlotte is so fond of saying, very few secrets elude curious eyes or ears."

"Do it carefully, Alison," warned Charlotte. "Taviot has shown that he kills without compunction."

"We all need to exercise caution," advised the earl. "Let us—" He suddenly fell silent and cocked an ear.

Footsteps, growing louder by the moment.

Charlotte saw him pick up one of his pistols.

"Wrex!" It was Sheffield who called from the corridor, sounding a bit breathless.

The earl uncocked the weapon's hammer.

"Sorry to be late," added their friend as he rushed into the room. "I have something to tell you—" The sight of the deadly serious faces that turned his way brought him to a skidding halt. "Has there been another murder?"

Before anyone reacted, Cordelia shot back with an answer. "The only thing that has gone to the grave is the notion that Lord Taviot isn't rotten to the core."

Sheffield appeared shaken. "W-What have you discovered?"

"That Taviot is a treacherous snake who betrayed his country six years ago, during the retreat of General Sir John Moore's army in Spain." Wrexford went on to explain about the missive from the former French intelligence officer confirming that Taviot was guilty of passing him British military information.

"Good God," whispered Sheffield. "That would mean . . ."

"Yes, that would mean that he's responsible for my brother's death," finished the earl.

"However," added Charlotte, "Wrex feels we don't yet have enough solid evidence to prove him guilty."

Henning put down his empty glass. "Actually, Grentham and his lackeys couldn't give a damn about solid evidence. Pass on what you have to the minister, and if he feels it's credible, Taviot will simply suffer an unfortunate accident." A shrug. "Or fatal heart spasm."

"You're likely right," said Wrexford. "Still, I intend to gather the proper evidence and present it to the authorities. Otherwise, it's vengeance, not justice."

"As to evidence . . ." Sheffield cleared his throat. "I was in a rush to get here because I, too, have discovered some information about Taviot." He shot a guilty look at Cordelia. "I was an arse to ignore your warnings, but I wanted so much to believe that the consortium's grandiose promises were true."

"And you now have reason to believe their promises *are* lies?" demanded Wrexford.

"Not exactly. But given what I recently overheard, I have my suspicions that something devious is going on."

Sheffield angled another glance at Cordelia, whose sphinx-like expression was impossible to decipher. "I was invited to a meeting this morning with Taviot and several of his most prominent charter investors in one of the private upstairs salons at White's. I knew that they were going to press me to put money into the business, and, well, a part of me was flattered to be asked to join such an elite group of entrepreneurs."

Wrexford noted that Cordelia refused to meet Sheffield's eyes. *Not a good sign*. He could only hope that Sheffield's unflinching show of loyalty during Cordelia's blackest moment would remind her that while her fiancé's judgment was not perfect, his heart was always in the right place.

"And indeed, they were quite aggressive about asking me for a decision," continued Sheffield. "Taviot sent the others away and made a final personal appeal, which I put off by promising him an answer by the day of the gala reception. But as I headed down the stairs, I passed Maitland going up. The fellow looked agitated, and on impulse I waited until I heard him enter Taviot's meeting room, then crept back up to the adjoining salon."

"Where you pressed your ear to the connecting door?" guessed Charlotte.

"Yes," admitted their friend. "Ungentlemanly perhaps, but sometimes one must slither with the surrounding snakes."

"Get to the point, Kit, and tell us what you heard," urged the earl.

"Maitland sounded awfully rattled. I couldn't catch everything, but he seemed to be very worried that the distraction they had planned as their momentous announcement for the gala reception wasn't going to be enough to satisfy the increasing number of questions about the progress on a prototype for their oceangoing ship," explained Sheffield.

"The *distraction*," repeated Wrexford.

"That is the exact word Maitland used," confirmed Sheffield. "Taviot calmed him by saying that there was no need to worry. He said that he and their other partner had come up with an idea that would buy more time."

"What other partner?" asked Charlotte.

"I don't know," answered Sheffield.

"And he didn't elaborate on what he meant by the distraction?" inquired Wrexford.

"No." Sheffield cut off any further questions with an impatient wave. "But that wasn't the most important discovery. I also learned that they have another laboratory, one that seems to be where Maitland does his real experimental work. And before you ask about its location, Taviot mentioned that a new shipment of coal was being delivered to Dowgate Wharf so that Maitland could begin his testing of the new condensers. Which means the laboratory has to be in one of the buildings surrounding the wharf."

The earl took a moment to consider the news. "It might behoove us to have a look—" he began, only to stop short when a flutter of movement in the corridor caught his attention.

"Weasels!" he barked, though there was no bite to his voice. "You can stop skulking in the shadows."

"We weren't skulking," said Raven.

"And we weren't slithering," chimed in Hawk. "We followed Mr. Sheffield to see if you had finished your private meeting with Mac." He craned his neck to look through the door and gave the maid a beatific smile.

Mac blinked a tear from her lashes and smiled back.

"M'lady said we could be part of the council of war," reminded Raven.

"Oiy," added his brother. "There are things that guttersnipes can see and do that won't attract attention."

Wrexford doubted that Charlotte would find that unsettling thought a point in their favor. For now, however, he forced his thoughts back to the moment.

"The current council of war is over," he replied. "Once I finish making some initial inquiries, we'll decide on our next moves." To Sheffield, he added, "Which for us should include making a visit to the docklands tonight—to see what dark mischief Taviot and his cohorts have hidden there."

CHAPTER 20

Charlotte put down her pen and leaned back to study her drawing. It might be more provocative than Wrexford would like. However, she felt that she had erred on the side of caution, saying just enough to raise questions about who would profit from winning the race to build a revolutionary oceangoing nautical propulsion system without stirring overly lurid speculation.

If the government found that uncomfortable, so be it.

"Perhaps they will even thank me for it," she whispered as she picked up a brush and began to add colored washes to the inked lines. Assuming the attack on their own Royal Navy laboratory had not been a cunning ruse.

With Lord Grentham and his cadre of clandestine operatives, one could never be certain.

Cat and mouse. Though in this case the cat was no mere tabby but a shadowy panther with razor-sharp teeth and claws.

A shiver touched her spine, but Charlotte shook it off.

"Perhaps I've been too careful of late," she said, "allowing all my concerns—Wrex's pain, Mac's silence, Peregrine's imminent departure—to make me tread with too tentative a step."

I need to slip out of a lady's confining layers of silk and don unfettered urchin rags.

She quickly finished painting in the last of the highlights on her drawing, then rose and headed to her bedchamber. Wrexford had returned earlier in the evening, armed with the information that Taviot had indeed been part of a diplomatic delegation to the Peninsula. A friend within the Foreign Office had given him a dossier filled with the specifics of the group's duties and travels, but that had been set aside for later. They had both agreed that tonight was a time for action. Wrexford and Sheffield were headed to Dowgate Wharf. While she had proposed her own mission.

A tug loosened the ties of her gown, and a sinuous shrug had her skirts pooled on the carpet. *A mission that fits me like a kidskin glove.*

After pulling on a pair of threadbare breeches and tattered boots, Charlotte paused to pick up a package wrapped in oilskin, then hurried down the corridor to fetch Raven and Hawk for a foray into the slums of Seven Dials. She had already informed Peregrine that she couldn't allow him to be part of the mission. The boy had taken the announcement with his usual quiet good grace. But Charlotte knew that it had cut him to the quick.

Perhaps the package of newly arrived scientific books that Tyler had ordered from Hatchards would help assuage his disappointment.

She quickened her steps. Wishful thinking, perhaps. But it couldn't be helped.

Wrexford rapped on the trap of the hackney, bringing it to a halt in an unlit side street near London Bridge. "It's best that we get out here and go the rest of the way by foot," he said to Sheffield.

As he climbed down, a fug of unpleasant odors assaulted his nostrils, the stink of low tide twining with the earthy smells of rotting garbage and open cesspools.

"The laboratory is located in a cul-de-sac off the northeast corner of Dowgate Wharf," he added. After some argument about the dangers, the Weasels had been allowed to reconnoiter the area just before dusk—that section of the docklands was rife with urchins and day laborers looking for any way to earn a crust of bread—and discovering the exact location of the consortium's clandestine workspace had proved easy.

The earl looked around at the aged warehouses sagging cheek to jowl against each other. "Stay alert," he cautioned as they started forward into the gloom.

"Are you expecting trouble?" His friend was also checking the surroundings, though the weak dribble of moonlight did little to penetrate the shadows. "The consortium has no reason to suspect that we are aware of this location."

"Any number of things can go wrong when attempting an illegal search." Wrexford stopped to peer into a black-on-black sliver of space between two buildings. "You ought to know that by now."

He pulled a pair of black knitted toques from his pockets. "Leave your hat here and put this on. Pull it low on your brow to hide your hair. The thick cuff will shadow your features."

"But I'm very fond of this hat."

"You'll have no need of it for quite some time if we're spotted by the night watchmen and hauled off to Newgate Prison." He switched his own head covering and signaled for them to resume walking.

A breeze pulled at a rusted sign hanging above a padlocked door, setting off a fitful groaning that amplified the aura of tension in the air.

Wrexford fingered the pocket pistol tucked in his coat. "Have your weapon ready. As someone seems overly fond of using a knife, it's best not to be caught by surprise."

"Getting shot several weeks ago earned me a great deal of sympathy from Cordelia," drawled Sheffield. "Perhaps another injury will help soften her current anger." It was said lightly but couldn't quite mask the fear behind his words.

"Let us survive this current investigation, and then we shall see what we can do about winning back her heart."

"You think she will— "

"Sshhh," hissed Wrexford as they approached the end of the alleyway. "The laboratory is there," he said, pointing down the sloping footpath to a large soot-dark brick building which sat behind the high perimeter wall that surrounded the wharf area. A wrought-iron gate guarding an archway in the chiseled stones gave access to the cul-de-sac.

As they crept closer, Wrexford saw that it looked to be chained shut with a fancy German puzzle lock.

"Is that a problem?" whispered Sheffield.

"None whatsoever," answered the earl. He pulled a steel probe from his boot and crouched down. "These mechanisms are quite ingenious." *Click-click*. "They simply require patience and a good sense of touch."

The night was turning chilly as a gusty breeze swirled up from the river. Sheffield blew on his hands, his breath turning into a puff of silvery mist. "I imagine the night watchman makes regular rounds."

"Quiet," growled Wrexford. "I need to hear what the lock is saying to me." He twisted his probe several more times, earning a subtle *snick*. "Ha, we've come to a meeting of minds."

After unwrapping the chain, he eased the gate open just wide enough for him and Sheffield to slip through.

"Any idea where we should attempt to enter the building?"

asked his friend as the earl rearranged the gate and chain to disguise any signs of tampering.

There was a large, cobbled loading area fronting the wharves within the walled area, the rhythmic *whoosh* and gurgle of dark water among the wooden pilings rippling the stillness of the night. On the opposite side rose the silhouette of the laboratory building, unlit save for a scudding of moonlight.

"The main door is set beneath a shallow portico at the near end of the building," replied Wrexford. "The windows are all barred, and the portals for loading the supply wagons are forged of iron and fastened shut from the inside with chains. However, there's a recessed door around back, by the chimney for the forge and foundry, that will give us access directly to the laboratory workspace."

"How the devil do you know all that?"

"The Weasels have their ways of wheedling out information." A pause. "I prefer not to ask for the details." The earl peered into the gloom, checking for any movement around the docks. "Follow me."

He made quick work of opening the foundry door, allowing them to step inside.

The air was thick with the acrid smells of burnt coal and sooty smoke. Wrexford took a moment to light the small folding candle lantern he had brought with him. As the wick flared to life, the beam illuminated a massive anvil and a work counter filled with the usual assortment of blacksmithing hammers, chisels, and tongs.

A cursory inspection revealed nothing of interest.

The earl turned, the lantern's glow revealing an iron-banded oak door on the other side of the forge. A hurried check on what lay behind it showed a huge cauldron for melting iron and a collection of molds for casting engine parts.

"Let's move on," said Wrexford, retracing his steps. "But quietly, Kit. The place looks to be deserted, however it's best to err on the side of caution."

He moved stealthily through the gloom to a corridor leading deeper into the bowels of the building. As they came to the next workshop, a pungent fug of odors made him pause and take a few experimental sniffs.

"Chemicals," he muttered, as he signaled for them to enter. "Be careful not to knock into anything. Some of the substances being used here are highly volatile."

Holding the lantern high above the stone counter that ran the length of the side wall, Wrexford angled the beam to light up the array of laboratory beakers and bottles. Colors refracted off the beveled glass, pale yellows flickering with sparks of gold and amber. Lurking in the shadows at the far end of the counter sat a selection of blue liquids ranging from cerulean to an ominous shade of cobalt. He studied the entire collection for a long moment before summoning Sheffield to hold the lantern.

"For God's sake, don't drop it," he warned, then moved slowly along the orderly procession of glassware, examining the individual labels. Halfway down the row, he paused to remove the glass stopper from a bottle of greenish liquid and waved it under his nose.

A burning sensation bit at his nostrils.

Sheffield repressed a gagging cough as the noxious smell wafted his way. "Double, double toil and trouble . . . fire burn and cauldron bubble," he mumbled.

"Ye heavens, you've actually read Shakespeare's *Macbeth*," quipped Wrexford as he plucked a small vial from a shelf and carefully transferred a sample of the chemical compound into it.

"Only the ghoulish parts," replied his friend. "What unholy mischief are they brewing in here?"

"Chemicals are frequently used to test metals or temper formulas, so most of the bottles contain standard mixtures," came the reply. "But this . . ." Wrexford corked the vial, and as he held it up to the light, the liquid seemed to shimmer with a darker glow. "This is a highly potent—and highly flammable—accelerant, designed to turn a tiny flame into a conflagration within the blink of an eye."

Sheffield watched as the earl carefully sealed the cork tightly into the vial with a wad of soft wax and wrapped it in a protective layer of cotton wool. "You think it might be what was used to start the fire at Maudslay's laboratory?"

"Tyler has analyzed the traces of the accelerant that the Weasels found in the wreckage. It's a complex mixture, so if this is a match, it gives us actual proof that the source of the fire originated here."

"Science is a wondrous force in and of itself," mused Sheffield. "What a shame that it can be used for Evil as well as Good."

"The forces of the cosmos depend on us to define the morality of their astounding powers." Wrexford pocketed the sample. "Alas, human nature is the weak link in the chain of events."

"Are we done here, now that we've found telltale evidence?"

"Not yet," answered the earl. "I wish to find Maitland's workroom and see whether we can discover what his damnable secret design is."

In answer to her coded knock, Charlotte heard the iron bar slide out of its brackets and the bolts unlock, allowing the hidden back door of the tavern to inch open.

"Well, well, ain't seen ye around here fer a dog's age." The words were accompanied by the pungent scent of onions and garlic. "Where ye been, Magpie?"

"Living in a mansion on Berkeley Square," answered Charlotte.

A wheezing laugh. "Oiy—and I've bin invited te take up rooms at Kensington Palace."

"Then ye and the Duke o' Sussex ought te come by some afternoon and have tea wiv me," she replied, provoking another rumbling of mirth.

The door opened wider, revealing a beefy man with greasy hair and hands as big as ham hocks. He took hold of her sleeve and tugged her inside the small private office, then shut the door. "Oiy've missed yer sense o' humor, Magpie."

"And my purse."

He scratched his chin. "Well, I won't lie . . ."

"Good," interjected Charlotte. "Because ye know ye'll never get another ha'penny from me if your information isn't accurate."

A speculative gleam lit in his eyes. "Whacha lookin' fer?"

After leaving Berkeley Square, she and the Weasels had visited one of the rookeries in St. Giles known as a gathering place for out-of-work former soldiers. Armed with a handful of coins, the Weasels had made some inquiries as to where they might find any friends of the murdered arsonist who had been hired to set the fire at Maudslay's laboratory. And the information gathered by Raven and Hawk had led them here, to a seedy tavern not far from Cockpit Yard.

"Someone who knew Joshua Wooster, the former soldier arrested for setting the recent blaze that burned down a building near here."

"Wot for?"

"I don't waste my breath answering questions," retorted Charlotte, backing up a step. "Iffen ye got nothing to tell me, I'll go find the answers elsewhere."

"Wait!" Greasy Hair hesitated. "If I do as ye ask, do I still get my full share of blunt fer giving ye valuable information?"

"Ye know I'm always fair." She jingled her pocket. "Bring me someone who can give me wot I want, and I'll even pay you extra."

He disappeared through the door behind him, the brief opening and closing allowing a rumbling of voices from the taproom to waft in, along with a skein of oily smoke.

Charlotte shallowed her breathing. The odor of onions and unwashed bodies was growing more pronounced. As the moments ticked by, she edged over to the outer door and slid back the bolt, just in case Greasy Hair got any grand ideas about returning with several of his cronies and trying to take her purse by force. He wasn't one of her regular informants, and although word on the streets warned that it wasn't wise to diddle with Magpie, some people didn't get the message until push came to shove.

She grasped the pocket pistol in her jacket and eased the hammer to half cock.

A ham-fisted thud opened the taproom door halfway, and Greasy Hair slipped in with a ferret-faced companion in tow. The new fellow was dressed in a faded military coat that had once been red.

"Wot's ye wanna know about Joshua?" asked Ferret Face without preamble, his voice bristling with suspicion.

"Who hired him to set the fire?" answered Charlotte. "Your friend here will assure you that I pay well—but only for accurate information." A pause. "Diddle me at your own risk."

Ferret Face spat on the floor. "If I knew his name and where te find him, he would be a dead man by now."

"I know that Joshua claimed a fancy cove hired him," replied Charlotte. "Did he say what he looked like? Or describe any detail that might identify him?"

The ex-soldier narrowed his rheumy eyes. "Why are ye asking?"

"Because I work fer someone who wants to see that justice is done."

A mirthless laugh. "As if anyone gives a rat's arse whether people like me and Joshua ever get a whiff o' justice."

Charlotte eyed him with an unblinking stare.

"Wot's ye got te lose?" whispered Greasy Hair. "Magpie's money can at least buy ye a mug o' ale te raise in salute te your dead friend."

Ferret Face dropped his gaze. "The varlet didn't see me in the shadows—my feet were aching, and so I wuz sitting wrapped in a blanket wiv my back up against the wall. But oiy got a look at him as he left the alleyway after making his devil-cursed deal with Joshua."

"Describe him," said Charlotte.

"Tall. Broad-shouldered. A fancy pair o' boots that looked soft as a doxy's bum . . ."

That fits Taviot, she thought, feeling a flutter of excitement stir inside her rib cage.

A shrug. "Can't say I noticed anything else."

"What about the color of his hair?" she pressed.

The ex-soldier scrunched his face in thought. "Brown," he answered. "A reddish shade, like strong tea."

Damnation. "Not black, with threads of silver?"

He shook his head. "Naw. As he turned te leave, he passed through a blade o' moonlight." A grimace. "Brown hair . . . and Satan-dark eyes that made my blood run cold." His mouth thinned. "I warned Joshua that no good would come of dealing with such an evil-looking cove."

"Thank you." Charlotte passed over payment to both men and slipped away into the night while they were still eyeing their good fortune. She had been generous despite her disappointment. It had, she supposed, been naïve to expect that Taviot would have sullied his hands with wielding the actual knife that helped put gobs of filthy money in his pocket.

In some ways, that made him even more despicable.

"You may have had your co-conspirator perform the recent murders. But you are guilty as sin for both the past and present litany of deaths," Charlotte whispered to herself.

"And it's only a matter of time before Wrexford and I make you pay for your perfidy."

CHAPTER 21

"Not so fast, Wrex," whispered Sheffield. They had entered a cavernous space, and the earl was leading the way, the blade of lantern light flickering over the intricate mechanisms of the machines flanking the center walkway.

"These are precision lathes," explained Sheffield. "Whatever technical innovations Maitland is crafting here, these machines must be making the components. So it stands to reason that there might be some diagrams left out on the worktables, showing what the devil they are doing."

"Good thinking, Kit." Wrexford gave himself a mental kick for missing the connection, reminding himself not to let emotion cloud his judgment. He stopped and allowed the light to probe into the shadows between the lathes.

Sheffield let out a grunt of satisfaction on spotting a trestle table and stool set against the wall. Their hopes, however, proved short-lived. It appeared that Maitland and his supervisors ran a tight ship—none of the worktables yielded anything more substantial than a few errant crumbs of bread.

"The villains are being careful," observed Wrexford. "I take that as a good sign. Let's keep looking for Maitland's office."

A corridor led from the lathes to the rear of the building. They passed several more work areas—a carpentry shop, a storage room for rope and pulleys—before a last turn brought them face to face with two closed doors. Wrexford tried the one on the right.

Its latch lifted without protest.

"Nothing but lading bills and lists of deliveries," he muttered after searching through the papers atop the bare-bones wooden desk. Its drawers were empty, and save for a straight-back chair and pair of open wooden crates shoved up against the wall beneath the lone window, there was nothing else in the room.

Nothing.

And yet he could smell it. Malevolence tainted the air, its sour, sulfurous odor swirling up from the bowels of Hell. Some clue to its source was here, and by God, he was going to find it.

"Sorry if I've brought us on a wild goose chase," apologized Sheffield. "I was sure that we would find—"

"Let's try the other door." The candle flame sputtered as Wrexford grabbed the lantern, then flared into a red-gold blaze. He watched it sway, its color deepening as the shadows flitted across the room. "Have faith, Kit. Taviot is clever, but we're tenacious." The earl turned for the corridor. "He'll make a mistake, and then we'll have him."

The door didn't yield to his touch, which drew a smile. "As A. J. Quill is wont to say, no secret, however well-guarded, is truly safe." After passing the light to Sheffield, he crouched down and set to work.

"You need to teach me how to pick a lock," said his friend, observing the subtle probing of the earl's metal probe.

"The Weasels have been pestering me about that as well," he replied. "Heaven forfend that I unleash such mayhem and mischief on my own head."

Sheffield raised his brows. "Are you implying that I would be so childish as to misuse such a skill?" A pause. "Though the thought of gaining access to your wine cellar would be tempting. Riche has been surprisingly stuffy about revealing where he keeps the key."

A grunt . . . and then a click. "Forget about my brandy. We have more sobering matters to occupy our efforts."

Like the adjoining room, this one had a small window on the rear wall, and the faint glow of starlight filtering in revealed that they may have found Maitland's private lair.

Wrexford paused in the doorway to study the room before rushing in. *Scientific detachment*, he reminded himself. Tiny details mattered.

An oak desk and chair dominated the center of the space. Several stacks of books surrounded an inkwell and a jar of pens, while a ghostlike glimmer of white atop the dark leather blotter drew his eye to a disorderly sheaf of papers. A bookcase made from rough-sawn planks was set against the right wall, its shelves filled with an assortment of scientific journals. To the left was a fireplace, a tiny tendril of smoke curling up from the ashes in the grate.

"Someone was here not long ago," observed Sheffield. Shifting his stance, he darted a look back into the corridor.

The earl was already moving. "Close the door behind you, then have a look at the bookcase while I examine the desk and its contents." He took a seat in the chair and started with the books. The first group was technical treatises on steam engines. A number of torn scraps of paper protruded from the pages, clearly serving as placeholders. The second pile was much the same, with a few mathematical texts mixed in.

"What am I looking for?" asked Sheffield as he crouched down to look through the lower shelf.

"I'm not sure. But you'll know it when you see it," answered Wrexford. He didn't bother to check any of the bookmarked pages, sensing that the key to unlocking whatever grand secret lay at the heart of the mysteries within mysteries lay elsewhere.

He hurriedly skimmed the rest of the spines. *Nothing out of the ordinary.*

Muttering an oath, the earl pulled the lantern closer and started shuffling through the papers. They were all blank. He was about to move to the drawers when he noticed the small trash pail beneath the desk. Inside were several crumpled papers, which he fished out and smoothed on the blotter. At first the sheets appeared to be covered with disjointed scribblings—a few sentences, which were then scratched out and a new thought begun. But as the scattering of words sunk in, he realized that it was the rough draft of a speech.

Today I shall share a momentous moment in human progress, lost for centuries until now. That was crossed out with a black slash of the pen. *Today I shall reveal a momentous intellectual achievement, a highlight of human ingenuity in the form of a manuscript, hidden for centuries but now rediscovered by our consortium. . . .*

He stared in puzzled silence. Did the manuscript really hold some momentous secret? Or were Maitland and Taviot using it as the distraction that Sheffield had heard them mention—a puff of smoke with which to blind potential investors to the fact that the consortium was merely a clever scheme to defraud them of their money?

"Hell and damnation," he whispered, after reading the next sentence.

Sheffield shot to his feet. "What?"

Wrexford read it aloud. "*With the invaluable insight of the great Renaissance genius Leonardo da Vinci at our fingertips, we have picked up the torch of his brilliant thinking and used it to make another giant step forward in mastering the world around us.*"

"But . . ." Sheffield made a face. "But according to Cordelia, da Vinci's manuscript shows no great revelation."

Like Tyler, Cordelia had given up on trying to understand

Bernoulli's book on fluid dynamics after the first few chapters, as she was unfamiliar with that area of science. And while she and the valet agreed that da Vinci and Bernoulli seemed to have shared a keen interest in moving water, neither of them could see how that translated into a momentous engineering innovation.

"So it would seem," answered Wrexford. "It's still unclear whether the consortium is a fraud." He carefully folded the paper. "Be that as it may, this draft of a speech proves that Taviot and his co-conspirators stole the da Vinci manuscript, which directly links them to Greeley's murder. In the past, Taviot may have been clever enough to elude justice, but this time he's going to discover that his evil has grave consequences."

"Sorry." Raven shrugged in apology as he finished peeling off his filthy jacket and letting it fall to the floor. "We were hoping not to wake you."

"Pffft—surely you don't think I was sleeping." Peregrine pushed the door of his adjoining bedchamber all the way open. "In fact, I was . . ." He slipped into the room. "But never mind that for the moment. Did you and m'lady discover anything?"

"Yes and no," answered Raven. A muck-encrusted boot thumped onto the rug, followed by its mate. "We tracked down a friend of the murdered arsonist, and it turns out that he got a glimpse of the man who paid for the fire to be set. However, he couldn't give m'lady much of a description."

"Save for the fact that the varlet had reddish-brown hair with no trace of silver. So it couldn't have been Lord Taviot," added Hawk.

"The arsonist's friend also said the fancy cove who paid for the crime had Satan-dark eyes that made his blood run cold," mused Raven.

Peregrine's expression pinched in thought. "I know what he means. There are some people whose gaze feels as though it's trying to slice through sinew and bone and suck out your soul."

"Oiy," agreed Hawk. "When we lived in the slums, we learned to recognize that look and fly away from it like a bat out of Hell."

The Weasels had confided the truth of their origins to Peregrine—the three of them had sworn an oath of brotherhood, sealed with a knife prick to their fingers and a mingling of their lifeblood. There was only one family secret that Peregrine didn't know, and that was because Wrexford and Charlotte had decided that the dangerous truth about her *nom de plume* was too great a burden to put on the boy.

Peregrine nodded in understanding. "Right. If you watch carefully, you quickly discern how to spot evil and stay away from it."

"Speaking of evil, we need to have our own council of war." Now garbed in his nightshirt, Raven kicked his discarded clothing under the bed and sat down on the rug, gesturing for the others to join him.

The single candle flickered as Hawk put its pewter holder down between the three of them. The flame dimmed and then flared back to life, casting a fluttering of light and dark across their faces.

"Do you think m'lady can scare Satan Eyes into making a mis . . ." began Peregrine, and then stopped abruptly.

"What do you mean?" demanded Hawk.

"N-Never mind." Peregrine picked at a loose thread on his sleeve, refusing to look up. "It was a stupid thought."

"What were you about to say?" pressed Raven. "Remember our oath—there are no secrets between blood brothers."

"Yes, there are," came the whispered reply.

Trust. A fraught silence shuddered between them.

Hawk blinked in dismay. "S-Some secrets are complicated. They aren't ours to share."

"I understand that," replied Peregrine.

Raven expelled a reluctant sigh. "How did you guess about her art?"

Peregrine hesitated. "I wasn't spying—I swear it. My Uncle Jeremiah taught me to have a good eye for detail. M'lady showed me some sketches that she had done of us fencing, and I was fairly certain that I recognized her style of drawing."

Seeing their dismayed expressions, he hastily added, "This is my real family in every way that matters. I would never betray any of you."

"I don't doubt that for an instant, Falcon," said Raven. "Still, we need to inform Wrex and m'lady that you now know our most closely guarded family secret." A fleeting grin. "I doubt that they'll be surprised. And while Wrex grumbles that we're too damn clever for our own good, I think he's actually quite pleased that we possess sharp wits and know how to use them."

"Does that mean we are starting our council of war now?" inquired Hawk.

"Yes— " began his brother.

"Excellent," interjected Peregrine, "because you need to hear what I discovered earlier this evening."

"You weren't supposed to be sleuthing," pointed out Raven.

"I assure you, I didn't break any house rules. I was merely reading one of the new scientific books that m'lady gave to me earlier this evening," replied Peregrine. He got up and rushed into his room for a moment. "It is quite astounding what remarkable discoveries one can make within the pages of a book," he continued as he returned to his spot on the rug and held up a slim volume bound in nondescript blue cloth.

Hawk squinted at the title embossed on the cover. "What's a Yale?"

"In my history class at Eton, we learned that it's a mythical beast in medieval lore," answered Peregrine. "Like a unicorn, only with two long horns that can rotate around its head to ward off danger coming from any direction."

"Fascinating," muttered Raven. "But what does a Yale have to do with our investigations?"

"Actually, it has a great deal to do with finding the truths we seek. You see, it's also the name of a small, provincial college in America." Peregrine opened the book and started thumbing through the pages. "And this is an engineering treatise written by an undergraduate student who studied there during the time of our war with the former colonies."

Raven stopped fidgeting.

"His name was David Bushnell, and he invented an underwater warship—a submarine!"

Hawk's eyes widened in wonder. "Did it work?"

"It did, though there were technical difficulties with detonating the explosive that he planned to attach on the hulls of our war frigates. But that's not what is important about his invention."

Peregrine held up the book which was opened to display a large diagram that ran across both pages. "Look closely at what he used to propel his submarine."

"Holy hell." Raven's eyes widened. "We need to show this to Wrex and m'lady."

"Finish searching the shelves for any other piece of incriminating evidence, Kit," said Wrexford, "while I go through the desk drawers. Every little bit will help tighten the noose around Taviot's neck and ensure that he and his co-conspirators are punished for their crimes."

The methodical rustling of paper resumed as they went back to work.

Sheffield finished checking through the books and moved to the hearth as the earl riffled through the drawers.

"Nothing more of interest," muttered Wrexford.

"Come have a look at this." His friend was crouched down,

his fingers black from poking around in the coals. "Bring the lantern."

The beam picked up the fragments of paper that Sheffield had fished out from the still-warm ashes. Though badly singed, there was enough left to show that the scraps were part of a technical drawing. The earl could make out part of a mathematical equation scribbled beside part of an undulating curve.

"Those damnably odd shapes again," growled Sheffield. "What the devil do they signify?"

Wrexford fetched a small book from the shelf and carefully slipped the fragments between the pages. "It looks as though Maitland was being very careful to keep his actual work a secret. However, he made a critical mistake in consigning this sketch to the fire. It left us more pieces of the puzzle."

He slipped the book into his pocket next to the rough draft of the speech. "Which bring us closer to fitting together the whole picture."

Sheffield gave a grim nod and wiped his hands on his trousers. "So, it appears that Cordelia was right to have a bad feeling about Taviot and his consortium." A look of self-disgust flitted over his features. "How could I have been so bloody, bloody blind to the evil behind their promises?"

"They've pulled the wool over the eyes of a great many intelligent and influential people. It is a curse of human nature that we are inclined to believe things that we wish to be true. Evildoers have exploited that weakness since the Garden of Eden," replied the earl. "Give yourself some credit. You were wise enough to take your time to assess the investment opportunity and make the necessary inquiries."

"Only because Cordelia smelled a rat from the beginning."

"Which shows that the two of you make a good pairing."

"Assuming she'll still have me." His friend gave an uncertain grimace. "A husband ought not make mistakes—"

"Ye gods, what fustian! Stop being so terrified of matrimony. Perfection is the last thing Cordelia expects, or wants," growled Wrexford. "For some absurd reason she loves you as you are . . ."

Hope chased away the worst of shadows hovering beneath his friend's lashes.

"Whatever bumps lie ahead, trust that you will smooth them out together." Wrexford gave a last look around the dimly lit room. "Besides, the sins at the root of all these crimes lie with Taviot. However, what we've found here tonight will help ensure that he answers for them."

He turned for the door. "We've seen enough. Let's return to Berkeley Square."

They slipped out to the corridor, and after relocking the door the earl took the lead in retracing their steps. Moving swiftly but silently, they crossed through the chemical laboratory and were about to turn into the foundry area when the sound of steps scuffed through the stillness.

Wrexford blew out his candle and grabbed his friend's arm.

Sheffield signaled that he, too, had heard the sounds.

"Stay here," whispered the earl. Keeping close to the wall, he crept to the corner.

A moment later came the telltale rasp of hinges as the door to one of the connecting workrooms opened and closed.

He waited.

A moment later, a piercing beam of light speared into the corridor, probing, probing . . .

Wrexford uttered a silent oath as it grew brighter. A man stepped out from the gloom, making no effort at stealth.

"Maitland?" Raising his lantern higher, the man moved toward the foundry and took his time in illuminating the nooks and crannies.

One of the conspirators, concluded the earl, rather than a night watchman. The man was wearing a dark cloak over his coat and had a broad-brimmed hat pulled low on his brow. A dark length of cloth—the sheen indicated silk—was wrapped around the lower part of his face.

However, further speculation was cut short as the conspirator turned and started toward the chemical laboratory.

Retreating as quickly as he dared, Wrexford motioned for Sheffield to follow him. He had noticed an archway set within one of the laboratory's alcoves, and it appeared to lead back to the room holding the lathes, allowing them to escape notice.

Choices, choices. The earl decided that he didn't have the moral right to draw his weapon. To shoot the man would be murder. And that would make him no better than men like Taviot, who thought themselves entitled to play God in order to achieve their own ends.

Quickening his steps, he slipped into the murky shadows. Up ahead, a faint glow of moonlight flitted over the silent machinery. Making a split-second decision, Wrexford cut between two massive lathes—only to find a wall looming straight ahead and the way blocked on either side by the rods and pistons of the steam-powered behemoths.

"Keep low and creep back to the opening," he whispered to Sheffield. "My guess is he's headed to Maitland's private office, and we should be able to slip free once he's passed through the laboratory. However, if he comes this way, wait for my signal and then bolt for the exit while I knock him down."

"Two against one would provide better odds," replied his friend.

"Absolutely not," he shot back. "In any case, you're forbidden to do anything foolhardy. Otherwise, Cordelia would have my guts for garters."

"Don't worry," responded Sheffield. "You know me—I haven't got a heroic bone in my body."

Ignoring the quip, Wrexford cocked an ear. The ensuing silence was a good omen. A second ticked by, followed by another, and another.

Wrexford edged forward, deciding that after several more silent ticks it would be safe to move—

A pebble skittered over the stone floor. Then a dark-on-dark shadow fell over the opening.

Damnation. For a big man, the conspirator was awfully light on his feet when he so chose.

The earl glanced around, but he already knew that there was only one option.

"Go!" he cried to Sheffield as he sprang to his feet and launched himself at the masked conspirator.

The man turned just as the earl reached him and lashed out a vicious kick. Twisting away, Wrexford sent the lantern flying and grabbed for the fellow's coat collar. His fingers fisted in the fabric, but a glancing punch knocked him off balance.

His feet skidded out from under him, but he kept his grip and managed to land a fist to the man's jaw . . .

And then, with an audible *rip*, the wool tore away. His handhold gone, Wrexford crashed to his knees. A boot struck his midriff, the blow smashing the wind from his lungs and knocking him to the floor. As he fell, a flare from the burning lamp oil showed the conspirator had pulled a pistol just as Sheffield slid to a halt halfway down the center aisle.

Run, you bloody fool! Wrexford tried to bellow out a warning, but the words wouldn't come.

With a primal growl, Sheffield pivoted and charged.

The conspirator raised his weapon and took dead aim.

A thunderous *bang* rent the air.

Ears ringing, Wrexford watched in stunned disbelief as the conspirator hit the floor, knocked off his feet by the iron canister that had come hurling down from atop one of the lathes. His pistol skidded harmlessly off into the gloom as several more canisters crashed in rapid-fire succession onto the flagging and bounced away.

Another momentary burst of light sparked from the pool of

flames, and for an instant he caught a shadowy movement behind the massive gears and levers atop the lathe.

Then it was gone.

Rousing himself, Wrexford scrabbled to his feet. Sheffield had fallen in the melee but was up as well—and rubbing at the fast-purpling bruise on his cheekbone.

"Bloody hell," bellowed his friend, "the dastard is getting away!"

The clatter of fleeing footsteps echoed from deep in the bowels of the building.

"Let him go, Kit." The earl blenched and flexed his shoulders. "We have what we came for, so if he's more than a hired lackey, he'll get his just punishment." He began to pat his pockets to check that the vial was still intact and the papers hadn't disappeared, only to realize that he still had the scrap of wool torn from the conspirator's coat collar in his hand. Without thinking about it, he left it stashed in his pocket.

Sheffield made a face but didn't argue. "Yes, but it would have felt supremely satisfying to punch him in the nose."

"What a bloodthirsty fellow you have become." Wrexford stamped out the lingering flames licking up from the spilled lamp oil.

"Speaking of bloodthirsty . . ." Sheffield gazed up at the lathe. "We were extraordinarily lucky that those canisters fell when they did. In another instant—"

"In another instant, you might have been lying dead." He took a moment to choke down a spurt of raw fear. "What the devil were you thinking?"

Sheffield shrugged. "That only a craven coward runs and leaves a friend in mortal peril."

Unable to summon a retort, Wrexford changed the subject. Looking up, he studied the top of the lathe. "It defies reason to imagine that the canisters fell at exactly the right moment," he muttered. "I thought I saw a flutter of movement."

"A guardian angel?" Sheffield pursed his lips. "Who?"

"Haven't a clue," answered Wrexford. He had been asking himself the same question and couldn't begin to conjure up a logical answer.

"Ye heavens, do you think that the Weasels could have followed us?"

The earl froze for an instant as a chill took hold of his heart. But then he recalled the plans for the night. "No, Raven and Hawk accompanied Charlotte. And despite their ungodly cleverness, even they can't manage to be in two places at once."

An odd sound rumbled in Sheffield's throat. "That's assuming they are actually human, and not two afreets who used their sorcery to slip free from the pages of *The Arabian Nights*."

"Whatever black magic is swirling through the night," responded Wrexford, "let us take our leave of it and return home."

CHAPTER 22

"Good heavens." Charlotte winced in sympathy on seeing Sheffield's face as he limped into the earl's workroom and gingerly lowered himself into one of the armchairs. The nicks and bruises had his features looking distinctly lopsided. "Are you sure you should be up and about?"

Despite arriving home just a few hours before dawn, Wrexford had insisted on summoning both Sheffield and Cordelia first thing in the morning once he had heard about Peregrine's discovery.

Sheffield blew out a martyred sigh. "You're right, I *should* still be sleeping, but Wrex apparently thinks otherwise." He eyed the empty tea table. "I hope you are serving breakfast."

"McClellan will be here shortly with shirred eggs and toast," she answered. Noting the deep shadows beneath his eyes, she added, "And plenty of coffee."

"Excellent," called Cordelia from just outside the doorway. She had already unfastened her cloak and shrugged it off as she entered. Catching sight of Sheffield, she went very still. "What happened to you?"

"We're about to explain that," said Charlotte. "As well as inform the two of you about another critical discovery."

Sheffield looked surprised on spotting the three boys sitting cross-legged on the carpet, half in shadow by the storage cabinets. "In front of the Weasels?"

"I'm not a Weasel," pointed out Peregrine.

"You're an honorary one," countered Sheffield. "We all know you are capable of creating just as much havoc as they do."

That seemed to please Peregrine greatly.

"Yes, in front of the Weasels," answered Wrexford, as he came into the room from the adjoining library, a stack of books in his arms. "It was they who found the clue that has finally made all the pieces of the puzzle fit together."

"Actually, it was Peregrine who figured it out all by himself," said Raven.

"That must mean he deserves *all* the ginger biscuits," announced McClellan as she and one of the parlor maids brought in breakfast trays.

"Oiy, he does." Hawk gave Peregrine an admiring grin. "He's really clever and observant, especially with mechanical devices."

"I might have brought an extra plate of biscuits for you and your brother," responded McClellan, a smile tugging at the corners of her mouth. "Loyalty is just as deserving as cleverness."

"Perhaps more," murmured Charlotte. Despite the many challenges and threats that still lay ahead, she felt her heart swell as she looked around at her family and dear friends.

"Indeed," agreed Cordelia, darting a glance at Sheffield through her lashes. "I daresay that is why we're here."

"Sentiment is all very well," said Wrexford. "However, it's imperative to set emotions aside for now. We have a dangerous killer to bring to justice, as well as a financial fraud to expose." He poured himself a cup of coffee. "That is, unless by some miracle Taviot's consortium has actually succeeded in making its revolutionary propulsion system work."

"Revolutionary—ha, ha, ha," chortled Raven. He extended his forefinger and spun it round and round in a tight circle, causing Hawk and Peregrine to fall into a fit of giggling.

Cordelia stared at the boys, utterly mystified.

"Stifle your hilarity, Weasels," said Wrexford as he opened several of the books and arranged them on his desk. To Cordelia and Sheffield he added, "Come have a look at these illustrations, and I shall explain. Once we knew what we were looking for, Tyler found some relevant information and examples in my scientific library." He shook his head in self-disgust. "To think they were lying right under my nose."

Heads bent low, the two of them studied the various images.

"Why, it looks to be some sort of . . ." Cordelia looked up. "Some sort of screw?"

"Yes, it is based on some of the same basic principles," replied the earl. "But it's called a *propeller*." He made a face. "And I feel like a complete lackwit for not having thought of the possibility before now. The concept has been around for quite a while."

"Mechanical devices aren't your specialty," observed Charlotte. "But I'm surprised that the possibility didn't occur to Hedley."

"That's the challenge with new ideas—until some brilliant inventor makes a sudden momentous connection and proves them to be of practical use, they float around outside the parameters of conventional thinking." Wrexford blew out his breath. "Hedley's focus is on steam engines and how they can propel a traditional wheel, which has existed for millennia. It simply never occurred to him to imagine a new type of engine combined with a propeller to create a propulsion system capable of moving a ship through water."

Charlotte, too, was carefully examining the illustrations.

"Good heavens!" She pointed to the sketch of a flying machine powered by a screw-shaped device. "So it looks as though the stolen da Vinci manuscript may have some relevance to the concept of nautical propulsion!"

"Yes, there is some theoretical relevance," agreed Wrexford. "I'm no expert, but having skimmed through some of the explanations in these books, it appears that a number of thinkers throughout history have experimented with the scientific principles behind a screw mechanism like the propeller and how its spinning could be used to force fluid—such as water or air—in one direction and thereby create thrust in the opposite direction."

He opened another book and displayed an engraving of a primitive device. "One of the earliest examples of a practical screw mechanism was designed by Archimedes, one of the great scientific minds of ancient Greece. He designed a revolving device—known as the Archimedes screw—that moved water from one level of elevation to a higher one." He snapped the pages shut. "There's da Vinci, of course, who was clearly studying turbulence in water and in air with the idea that it was a force that could propel objects. And then our own Robert Hooke, who in 1680 observed that the vanes of a windmill were capable of moving water."

"Bernoulli—" began Cordelia.

"Bernoulli suggested using vanes—or blades—as a means of propelling boats through water, and even did some calculations on the optimal angles of the vanes for creating maximum thrust," interjected Wrexford. "He was mainly interested in the theory and mathematics of fluid motion rather than any practical application. However, he did realize the ramifications."

The earl then tapped a finger to the open book showing a primitive submarine. "Then we come to the journal that Peregrine discovered among the bundle of new scientific books sent from Hatchards. It shows an ingenious nautical invention created by an American student named David Bushnell in 1776, which used a propeller to move his underwater craft through the water."

Charlotte crouched down for a closer look. "It truly does look like an ordinary screw, magnified many times."

"Maudslay's lathes revolutionized the production of screws, making it possible to mill very precise threads in metal," said Sheffield.

"Which makes me wonder whether his work on a nautical propulsion system involved the idea of a propeller," said Wrexford.

"By God, you might be right. Maudslay never actually told me anything about the details of his work." Sheffield's jaw clenched for an instant. "So you think this proves that Taviot's consortium was behind the fire at Maudslay's laboratory so they could steal his idea?"

"Or it's possible that the government stole Maudslay's technical drawings first," suggested Charlotte. "And that Taviot's consortium then stole them from the naval laboratory at the King's Dockyard."

"That's pure speculation," replied the earl.

"Remember, I did notice strange curves—which now make perfect sense—on the technical documents I saw at the King's Dockyard," pointed out Charlotte. "So however Tilden and his fellow engineers came up with the idea, I am sure they were working on designs for a propeller."

She frowned in thought. "Their steam engine prototype looked radically different . . ."

"That's because it needs to power a crankshaft in order to turn a propeller," said the earl. "Never mind the detailed mechanics right now, but in a nutshell, you need to redesign the traditional steam engine for nautical use."

Cordelia was looking at one of the other open books. "It says here that the American inventor Robert Fulton was also experimenting with propellers in America. It stands to reason that Maitland was aware of this and may even have worked with Fulton on the idea."

"That makes sense," agreed Wrexford. "I'll also point out that James Watt experimented with a propeller design featuring four angled blades rather than a screw-type device when he began exploring the idea of steam-powered boats. But he abandoned the idea and stuck with paddle wheels." He held up yet another book. "And a man by the name of Stevens built a prototype steamboat with a propeller in 1804. It fared well in test runs, but interest in the technology never seemed to gain momentum."

"An idea ahead of its time?" mused Sheffield.

"Some entrepreneur will likely make a fortune when the moment is right," replied the earl.

"That brings us back to our two fundamental questions," said Charlotte. "We now feel certain that we can prove Taviot is responsible for a past betrayal of our country during wartime, a terrible act that led to the death of Wrex's brother and countless other fine men, as well as the recent murder of Neville Greeley. But as for whether the consortium is, in fact, a fraud . . ."

She looked to Wrexford. "That now seems less clear."

"Perhaps," he answered. "It does seem strange that Maitland would choose to wax poetic about the da Vinci manuscript when there are other more practical examples to use."

"But a genius like da Vinci and the story of a long-lost manuscript is most likely to capture the imagination of potential investors," observed Sheffield. "My involvement in business has given me an opportunity to observe people who wish to sell their goods or services to others. The best of them are skilled showmen. They appeal to emotion as well as practicality."

"You mean that they create an aura of desirability about a product?" mused the earl.

"Look at Josiah Wedgwood," responded Sheffield. "His genius lay in doing just that. In fact, it was he who thought of the idea of giving his pottery to influential people to create an aura of exclusivity and build demand."

"Interesting," said the earl.

Cordelia—who prided herself on practicality—tapped her fingertips together. "So, how do we discern the truth about the consortium? Do we simply wait for their gala reception, which takes place in two days, and see what they say?"

For a long moment, the only sounds were the clink of cutlery as Sheffield helped himself to eggs and gammon.

And then Wrexford cleared his throat. "I confess, my first instinct is to confront Taviot, now that we have material evidence proving his crime." A pause. "However, last night's encounter with one of Taviot's conspirators makes me realize the danger of allowing my emotions to get the better of me. We have the rule of law to deal with criminals."

Clasping his hands behind his back, the earl moved to the windows overlooking the back gardens. "So I intend to send word to Griffin and arrange a private meeting with him to explain what I have learned and pass over the evidence."

Charlotte couldn't hold back a hiss of relief. "I think that is extremely wise, Wrex." She shot him a look of gratitude. "Passions don't make for good life-and-death decisions."

Before the earl could react, a discreet knock interrupted the exchange. "Forgive me, milord and milady," intoned their butler, "but Herr von Münch is requesting to see you. He apologizes for the early hour but says it's quite urgent."

Wrexford glanced around at the others.

"I assumed that you would wish for him to wait in the main drawing room," added Riche, "rather than have me bring him here."

"Thank you. M'lady and I will join him there in a moment."

He met Charlotte's gaze. "Much as I like the fellow, there is no need for him to know about our inner circle."

"My apologies for intruding at such an ungodly hour," said von Münch as he turned from studying a watercolor painting of a stormy seascape and inclined a polite nod. "What a very interesting work of art. The nuances of light and the illusion of motion are remarkable, allowing the artist to capture the raw power of Nature."

"Mr. Turner possesses extraordinary talents," said Charlotte. "He helps one to see the very essence of his subject."

"Indeed," responded von Münch, his eyes crinkling in thought. "Rather like your gadfly satirical artist A. J. Quill. The fellow makes you think—and feel." A wry smile. "No matter if it's uncomfortable at times."

The remark caught Wrexford's attention. Since his recent involvement with Pierson, who was one of the government's top intelligence operatives, he couldn't help feeling suspicious when a relative stranger mentioned Charlotte's pen name.

"Art is meant to challenge one's preconceptions," Charlotte replied. "You have a perceptive eye, Herr von Münch." A smile. "But I daresay you haven't come here to talk about art."

"I would greatly enjoy such an exchange, milady," he said. "Regretfully, you are right. We have more pressing matters to discuss." His lips thinned for a moment. "I took a rather hurried leave from you last time I was here because the glass of wine you kindly offered suddenly reminded me of something I had overheard recently."

He turned to the earl. "A current member of King Frederick's personal staff was stationed in the wine region of Portugal during the Peninsular War to ensure that the flow of the country's famous ports to Württemberg suffered no interruptions." He cleared his throat with a cough. "As you know, my king has a prodigious appetite for sumptuous food and drink."

"And precious little conscience about what he must do to possess them," observed Wrexford.

"You will get no argument from me on that. However, let's put aside the king's peccadilloes for now."

Wrexford heard a note of rising excitement in the librarian's voice.

"I'm here because I am all but certain that I have discovered the name of your elusive traitor!"

The announcement seemed to hang suspended, sending ripples through the air.

"Let me guess," he replied. "You're going to tell us that it's Lord Taviot."

Surprise flitted across von Münch's face.

"We just learned of it ourselves," interjected Charlotte, with an apologetic shrug. "We were going to send word to you this morning."

"It turned that your French friend Dalambert's comrade decided to be forthcoming with the traitor's name," added Wrexford in explanation. "But how did you uncover it?"

"One of the king's wine stewards lived in the city of Oporto, the heart of Portugal's famous vineyard area, where he was part of the wine merchant fraternity," answered von Münch. "Naturally, gossip flowed among its members, along with a surfeit of spirits, and he heard of a profitable illegal enterprise that was smuggling shipments of port into Britain without paying the excise tax. It was a very clever system. A diplomat in Lisbon would keep track of the British navy convoys moving military men and supplies back and forth between Britain and the Peninsula, then send word when it was safe for the smugglers' ships to make the passage to the Cornish coast."

"And I take it the diplomat was Lord Taviot," said the earl.

"Yes. I pressed my Württemberg colleague, and he was able to remember that the British consul in Oporto had once let the name slip out when he was drunk and boasting of his cut of the profits."

"So, we have yet another nail with which to hammer home the miscreant's guilt," announced Charlotte with quiet satisfaction.

Wrexford watched the breeze ruffle through the twines of ivy framing the windows. He wasn't quite as convinced.

She read his expression and took a moment to interpret his silence. "What's wrong?"

"It's just that something isn't quite adding up for me," he said softly.

Von Münch appeared confused. "B-But surely there couldn't have been *two* traitors within the British diplomatic delegation?"

"And yet why risk getting caught in a smuggling operation when that would likely expose his far more serious crime?" said Wrexford. "We know he's ruthlessly clever . . . and the only reason he would do so is for money."

A frown. "But it makes no sense financially. He would have been making far more money betraying his country than from being a partner in a smuggling ring."

"Greed often overpowers reason," pointed out Charlotte.

Wrexford shifted abruptly and caught the librarian studying him with a searching stare. Charlotte was right—he had a perceptive eye.

What are you trying to see, Herr von Münch?

For a moment, the earl found himself wondering whether the librarian's steadfast help should be viewed in a darker light. It suddenly struck him that von Münch had been the one who had been passing them the most important clues. . . .

But he shook off such suspicious thoughts. "You're right. Money can poison one's mind. Be that as it may, we have solid evidence that Taviot is guilty of the greater crime."

"What are you going to do about it?" ventured von Münch.

"Vengeance is not the same as justice. I am going to hand over the incriminating information to the authorities. It will be up to the law of the land to judge him and decide his punishment."

The librarian gave a brusque nod. "I am not a ghoulish soul, but I shall not shed a tear when the Earl of Taviot is dancing the hangman's jig."

"May I offer you some tea? Or a stronger libation, Herr von Münch?" asked Charlotte.

"Thank you, but I won't impose upon your time any longer." A polite bow. "I'm sure you have a great many things on your mind."

"I'll see you out," said Wrexford, hoping his conflicted thoughts weren't too obvious to the librarian. Charlotte, he knew, would have sensed the change in his mood.

Sure enough, she was waiting in the corridor when he returned. "Is there something I don't know that has turned you against von Münch?"

"From the very beginning, he's expressed a remarkable commitment to helping us ensure that justice is done for Greeley," said the earl carefully. "And through his diligence we have made a number of important discoveries."

Charlotte raised her brows. "And you hold that against him?"

Put that way, it sounded absurd.

"Let's just say that there are some strange coincidences," he replied. "Through von Münch's connections, we find a copy of the missing manuscript—"

"Wasn't it Greeley's assistant who first learned that a copy might be at Buckingham House?" she interrupted. "You could have easily gained access to the King's Library without his help."

The earl didn't argue. "And then the fellow just happens to have contacts that result in us meeting the French intelligence officer who could identify a British traitor. A traitor, I might add, who has eluded our head of state security and his operatives." He frowned. "Grentham's reputation for ruthlessness is well earned. He's extremely good at what he does."

Charlotte's eyes took on a challenging gleam. "But he doesn't know every secret."

Wrexford wasn't entirely sure about that, but he decided not to spit in Lady Luck's eye by saying so.

"As for von Münch's ability to track down the French officers, his explanation rings true to my ears," she added. "The king of Württemberg was Napoleon's ally, and his troops were working with the French during the Peninsular War."

"In this case, it is you who are being the voice of reason," he admitted. "You're an excellent judge of people, and what you say makes rational sense. I like von Münch, too." A wry grimace pinched at his mouth. "Which is why I'm taking pains to look at him from all perspectives."

She allowed a ghost of a smile. "Put in artistic terms like that, I can hardly disagree. Let us exercise caution in what we reveal to him as we seek to take the final steps in bringing the miscreants to justice." The smile grew more pronounced. "But let us also not let vague suspicions color our thinking."

"Fair enough." Wrexford gestured toward the back of the townhouse. "And now we ought to return to the others. Kit needs to get some sleep before he nods off into his plate of shirred eggs. But after that, I'd like for him to arrange a meeting with his friend Maudslay and find out whether the fellow was experimenting with propellers."

He rubbed at his chin. "As for Cordelia, I'd like for her to visit Hedley and see if there are some mathematical calculations that can be made to predict how much power a steam engine would need to generate in order for a propeller to move a ship through stormy ocean waters."

He made a face. "Granted, I have no emotional investment in whether Taviot's consortium is legitimate or a fraud. But as a matter of principle, I dislike seeing anyone being cheated out of their money."

"And I shall think about what sort of provocative drawing I can do about a propeller that will grab the public's attention," mused Charlotte. "The fact that an American designed a warship using propeller technology may make some waves here in Britain, especially if I hint that advances in steam-driven propellers are on the cusp of changing how we navigate the world around us."

Wrexford didn't demur. It was time to put a stop to the evil emanating from Taviot—in all its guises.

CHAPTER 23

On returning to their inner circle, Wrexford lost no time in explaining the assignments he wished them to undertake. Cordelia hurried away to Hedley's laboratory at the Royal Institution, while Sheffield set out to find Maudslay. As for Charlotte, she headed upstairs to her pens and watercolors after asking McClellan to ensure that the boys were not late to their fencing lesson.

As Tyler retreated to the laboratory to analyze the chemical sample brought back from the consortium's secret lair, Wrexford leaned back in his chair, savoring a moment of quiet solitude in which to clear his thoughts before writing to Griffin and assembling his collection of evidence to pass on to the authorities—

A tentative knock on the adjoining library door was followed by a soft hail. "Wrex?"

"Come in, lad." He felt a pinch of guilt as Raven approached, realizing how little time he had spent with the boys of late. Death shouldn't overshadow Life, and yet he had allowed it to cast a pall over his family.

"I'm sorry to disturb you, but . . ." The boy swallowed hard, then let his gaze slide away.

"But what?" he encouraged. "I would hope that you're not afraid to speak to me about anything." Unlike Hawk, Raven was wary about revealing his feelings.

Raven's mouth quivered for an instant. "D-Do you remember when we first met—you know, when the name *Weasels* wasn't meant very nicely—and you told Hawk and me about your brother?"

"Yes, I remember," said Wrexford softly. "M'lady didn't like it. She thought that mentioning the fact that my brother had been killed would frighten the two of you."

"Ha!" Raven blinked. "As if we didn't know about the Grim Reaper and his blade."

Uncertain of where the boy was headed, he said nothing, waiting for him to take the lead.

"Then, when Hawk got snatched by that smarmy villain from the Royal Institution, you p-promised me that you wouldn't let anything happen to him. And you didn't."

Wrexford nodded, still mystified.

Raven swallowed hard. "So when you had us pick an official name for the legal documents that m'lady needed to make us her wards, I chose T-Thomas in honor of your b-b-brother . . ."

His voice cracked, forcing him to draw a ragged breath before he could continue. "I just want to know if you think we have enough evidence to make sure that muckworm Taviot will swing for his sins."

"Yes," answered Wrexford. "I believe we have enough to ensure that he is punished for his crimes." He took a moment to compose his thoughts. "As for hanging, that is a decision for a judge to make."

"But don't you want to see Taviot suffer? Won't that bring you some measure of satisfaction?"

"Vengeance doesn't soothe the soul, lad." Wrexford reached

out to touch Raven's shoulder—and then pulled him into a fierce hug. "It's forces like love and family which bring the light that helps banish the darkness."

His arms tightened. "That you carry Thomas's name forward with the same spirit of steadfast honor and integrity that he possessed is a source of true joy and comfort to me," he said. "My brother would be very proud of you."

"W-Would he?"

"Without question." Wrexford smiled. "Thomas would have loved your curiosity, your courage, and your compassion for others."

He ruffled Raven's hair. "As I said, justice will soon be done, and that should satisfy both of us. Indeed, by tomorrow, this should all be over."

"*Deo volente*," said the boy.

The aphorism—*God willing*—surprised a chuckle from Wrexford. Charlotte, a scholar of Latin in her youth, had clearly been tutoring the boy in the ancient language.

"*Nemo est supra legem*," he replied. *Nobody is above the law.*

Wrexford hesitated, then opened his desk drawer and took out a small silver picture case. He put it down on the blotter and clicked it open to reveal the miniature painting.

Raven leaned in to study the three faces.

"That is Thomas in the middle. To his right is Neville Greeley, and to his left is their friend Harry Baldwin, who lost his life at the Battle of Talavera."

"Thomas looks like you," observed Raven without lifting his gaze.

"No, he doesn't—he's smiling," said Wrexford, unable to keep his voice from catching in his throat.

That drew a laugh from Raven.

"Everyone loved Thomas's sunny smile," added the earl.

"It's a nice smile," said the boy after subjecting the portrait to further scrutiny. "But I like your scowls better. They're more interesting."

Raven moved closer, and Wrexford felt the warmth of the boy's closeness loosen the knot in his chest.

"Hawk smiles more than me. I dunno why—I guess it's just my nature. But m'lady says that it's not the smiles and scowls that are important. It's what lies in your heart that matters."

"M'lady is not only profoundly wise," he replied. "She is also profoundly compassionate and sees the best in us despite our flaws."

"She says the same about you." Raven ventured a shy grin. "I guess we're all lucky that we found each other."

"Indeed we are, lad." He pulled the boy into another hug, feeling himself blessed beyond words. Though Raven wasn't always comfortable with physical closeness, he made no move to pull away.

It was McClellan's call that drew them apart.

"Raven! Stop lollygagging! You mustn't be late for your fencing lesson. Harry Angelo is doing you boys a great honor. He's not to be kept waiting."

Raven was about to fly away when he noticed a crumpled scrap of cloth wedged between the books stacked on the corner of the desk.

"What's that?" he asked, eyeing the bits of gold and red embroidery threaded on the dark wool.

"A piece of my assailant's coat collar that tore off when I grabbed at him last night."

"May I have a look?"

"You're welcome to take it. I've examined it and can't see that it will be of any help in identifying the culprit." Wrexford shrugged. "Not that it matters. Griffin will see that all the underlings are also apprehended and made to pay for whatever transgressions they have committed."

McClellan called again.

"Now go! You need to get ready for your lesson." He carefully closed the miniature portrait's case and put it away. "And I need to plot out the last moves for bringing a black-hearted killer to justice."

CHAPTER 24

After rinsing out her brushes and putting away her paints, Charlotte gathered up the reference books she had brought up from Wrexford's library and set them aside. Though forced to take some artistic license in drawing a propeller—having never seen one, she had to guess at some of the nuances—she was satisfied with the finished artwork.

More importantly, her conscience was at peace.

"The issues it raises are important for the public to understand," she told herself. "Assuming the concept actually works, propeller technology would revolutionize ocean travel and thus greatly affect our nation."

As for the personal ramifications . . .

Now that they had evidence of Taviot's guilt, she hoped that the authorities would move without delay to apprehend him and bring the investigation into Greeley's death to an end.

And put Wrexford's old ghosts to rest.

Strangely enough, Charlotte found that the question of whether Taviot's consortium was a fraud had also come to matter to her, despite having no personal connection to the outcome. At first, she had seen it as merely an all-too-common story of business competitors resorting to skullduggery to reap great financial rewards. However, she now realized that given far-reaching economic and military consequences, it would be dangerous for the new technology to end up in such unscrupulous hands.

A discreet cough from Riche, who was standing in the open doorway, drew her out of her musing.

"A note just arrived from Lady Peake," he announced.

"Thank you." Charlotte rose and went to take it. "Ah," she murmured. A smile blossomed on her lips as she read it. "Would you kindly go to the kitchen and warn McClellan that she had better bake an extra batch of ginger biscuits? Aunt Alison is bringing her young relative, Midshipman Horatio Porter, to visit with the boys." Their fencing lesson done, the Weasels and Peregrine had returned to their eyrie.

"Very good, milady."

As he withdrew, she pondered the other information contained in the note. Alison had just received an invitation from Lady Kirkwall to attend a soiree this coming evening—a small and exclusive gathering for potential investors in advance of the gala reception—at the Taviot townhouse in Mayfair, and asked if Charlotte would like to accompany her.

At first it seemed a simple question—with an equally simple answer. Charlotte's first reaction was an emphatic *no*. It seemed at cross-purposes to have any contact with the family.

But on second thought, she considered the ramifications. Wrexford had not yet met with Griffin, and given his concerns about how the government might choose to deal with Taviot, perhaps it was wiser to attend. Wrexford and Sheffield had been wearing knitted toques and scarves that hid their features during the break-in at the secret laboratory, so it was likely that they would be thought mere thieves. However, it was imperative not to give the miscreant any reason to suspect that his misdeeds had been discovered.

If cornered, a desperate man was wont to do desperate things.

But of course, she told herself, it wouldn't come to that.

After dropping the note on her worktable, Charlotte turned and headed for the stairs to inform the boys of Horatio's impending arrival.

As she approached the half-open schoolroom door, the clack and whir of spinning metal, punctuated by hoots of laughter, announced that the boys were working on Peregrine's mechanical hound.

Thank heavens. Charlotte paused to savor the sounds of playful exuberance. Of late, she had found herself worrying that the investigations were putting too much responsibility on their youthful shoulders. Granted, Raven and Hawk were no strangers to the dark side of human nature, but . . .

Peregrine's sudden shout of mirth made her heart lurch. She had come to think of him as part of their family, but circumstances demanded that he leave soon for the Michaelmas term at Eton.

Change is an inexorable part of Life.

"Whether we want it to be or not," Charlotte whispered.

More laughter.

"*Carpe diem,*" she added, reminding herself that fretting over the future did no good. *Seize the day*—and every precious moment it offered in the here and now. In that instant, she vowed that when the current troubles were over, she and Wrexford would take Raven and Hawk to their country estate near Cambridge for some peace and quiet. An imperfect plan, as Peregrine would likely have naught but a few days to spend with them before school started. But one must bend with the prevailing winds rather than snap.

Forcing her thoughts back to the present, Charlotte rapped

lightly on the door. Taking a happy *woof* from Harper as permission to enter, she stepped into the room, a smile chasing away her fretting as she surveyed the chaos. Screws and levers of various sizes were scattered helter-pelter over the rug. Raven had just released the spring mechanism which moved the mechanical hound's legs while Peregrine lay sprawled on the floor, his nose perilously close to fast-moving pieces of metal as he watched the assembly of spinning gears.

"They are deciding whether to put in smaller gears to make the hound go faster," explained Hawk, pitching his voice to be heard over the noise. He was sitting above the fray, his chair angled close to one of the school desks.

Sidestepping the jumble of metal parts, Charlotte went to join him. "What are you drawing?" she asked, seeing he had a colored pencil in hand and several others lying beside his paper.

"Wrex gave us the scrap of fabric that he tore from his assailant's coat last night." Hawk's eyes narrowed in concentration as he contemplated his sketch. "I'm copying the bits of embroidery. My guess is the colored threads were part of an insignia, so I'm trying to see if I can spot a clue that might help me figure out what it might be."

"What a clever idea," she exclaimed. The thought hadn't occurred to her, and for a long moment, she, too, studied the bits of gold and red.

Alas, the flecks of thread refused to stitch into any coherent image.

The whirring slowed and then stopped. Raven scrambled to his feet and went to fetch a tiny tool from the wooden box beside Peregrine. "Would you like to see it walk again?" he asked her. "Falcon figured out a very clever way to install a spring mechanism, based on a sketch that Mr. Hedley gave him."

Charlotte repressed a wince on seeing him scrub his hands on the seat of his pants. However, compared to the hideous substances that usually clung to his fingers, whale oil was fairly harmless. "It's quite marvelous," she answered. "But why don't you save further displays for when Horatio arrives. Aunt Alison is on her way here, and she's bringing him for a visit."

She smiled. "Alison and I have a soiree to attend this evening, so I will suggest to her that it would be a nice treat for him to spend the night here with you boys."

"Hooray!" crowed Raven. "We've told him all about Peregrine's hound, and now he will have a chance to see it for himself."

"Hooray!" echoed Hawk. He put down his pencil and made a face. "I'm not very good at mechanics, but as I'm not making any progress with my pencil, I might as well pass you the gears and hold the turnscrew while you work."

"You can keep trying later," said his brother. "You never know when inspiration will strike."

"Don't be hard on yourself, sweeting," she counseled. "I don't see any clues in the fabric, either."

Raven returned to fiddling with the gears attached to the underbelly of the mechanical hound. "Perhaps Osprey will have some ideas on how to make the hound walk faster."

Peregrine nodded. "Right. He mentioned that Mr. Tilden is teaching him about engineering."

"I'm sure your fellow students at Eton will be very impressed with your creation when you and your hound return to school," observed Charlotte.

"I think they'll be even more impressed with your left jab and right upper cut," chortled Raven. "Any bully who looks to prey on you this term will find himself with a bloodied beak."

"Or black-and blue cods," sniggered Hawk.

Charlotte maintained a stoic silence. She didn't condone such gleeful savagery, but she accepted it as a necessary evil. Whether dressed in finespun wool or filthy rags, human nature was the same. The elite school for the rich and privileged ran on the same primitive wolf-eat-wolf rules as the London slums.

Peregrine had suffered nasty taunts and beatings the previous spring. However, he was now quite skilled in defending himself, which would earn him the respect of his peers.

Thanks to the Weasels, who had taught him all manner of kicks and punches that no proper little gentleman was supposed to know.

"I hate Eton." Expelling a sigh, Peregrine looked up at her with a beseeching look. "Can't I stay here and be tutored by Mr. Lynsley, like Raven and Hawk?"

If the decision was up to her, she would say "yes" in a heartbeat. "I fear not, Falcon. To us, you are family, but Wrex and I must respect that your cousin is your legal guardian until you reach your majority, and so we must—"

"Defer to his wishes, whether I like it or not," intoned the boy. "Would that I could snap my fingers and in the next instant turn twenty-one."

Charlotte felt a knife-like stab in her chest as she regarded the boys, thinking that the three of them would grow up way too quickly.

And then she felt a chill snake down her spine. Life was so fragile, and as her husband knew all too well, love was a wondrous power, but it couldn't work miracles.

Ha, just let the Grim Reaper try to swing his scythe at any of my loved ones—he will find himself in for a rude surprise.

Such morbid thoughts were chased away by McClellan's hail from downstairs, announcing that the dowager and her young relative had arrived.

"Come, let us all go down and greet Alison and Horatio. I am looking forward to meeting the young man."

Harper took the invitation to include him and shook off his nap with a gusty yawn.

"Mac has been busy in the kitchen," added Charlotte as they all trooped toward the stairs. "Do try not to make yourselves sick with freshly baked ginger biscuits."

The hound flashed his teeth in a canine grin, which swiftly gave way to an injured *woof* as Hawk wagged a finger and said, "That means you. Sweets are very bad for dogs."

Horatio was introduced to Charlotte, who welcomed him with open arms as the boys exchanged exuberant hugs with Alison.

"You may add these to the platter of biscuits," drawled the dowager, handing Raven a bag of Pontefract cakes. "However, don't—"

"Make ourselves sick!" chorused the Weasels and Peregrine.

"Precisely," she said with a laugh. "Now take Horatio up to your eyrie while m'lady and I enjoy a quiet cup of tea."

Charlotte, however, had spotted the expectant gleam in Alison's eyes. "Mac will fetch refreshments," she said as the boys hurried off. "While we—"

"Begin our plotting," finished Alison.

"Before we discuss that," replied Charlotte, leading the way into the parlor, "you need to hear about the latest developments."

The dowager listened in rapt silence as Charlotte recounted the details of Wrexford and Sheffield's clandestine visit to the secret laboratory and the momentous discovery concerning the propeller.

"Hmmph." Alison sat back as McClellan entered with the tea tray and then took a seat to join the discussion. "So, assuming Tyler's chemical analysis goes as Wrex suspects it will, we now have proof that Taviot's consortium caused the fire at Maudslay's laboratory?"

"Correct," confirmed Charlotte, accepting a cup of fragrant Oolong from the maid. "And the drafts of Maitland's upcoming speech for the gala reception wax poetic about the momentous discovery within the da Vinci manuscript—which, by the by, proves that someone within the consortium murdered Greeley—and yet we don't think there is any such revelation in its pages. So we have good reason to suspect that despite their experiments with a propeller, they haven't succeeded in building a workable prototype for an oceangoing steamship."

"Which would mean that the consortium is deliberately defrauding its investors," said McClellan.

"So it would seem," she agreed.

Alison looked a trifle disappointed. "Are you saying that there is no reason for us to attend tonight's soiree at Taviot's townhouse? If Wrex has all the evidence he needs of their skullduggery to pass on to the authorities, then there is nothing left for us to do."

"On the contrary, after thinking it over, I think it imperative that we make an appearance." Charlotte blew away the plume of vapor rising from her cup. "I've sent word to Wrex at the Royal Institution informing him of our plan. But I think he'll agree that we should be sociable and act as if nothing is amiss to avoid setting off any alarm bells."

"I dislike the idea of you two walking into the wolf's den," said McClellan. "But your reasoning makes sense."

"I confess, I'm also curious to observe Lady Kirkwall, now that we know the truth about her brother," admitted Charlotte. "I have found much to admire in her. It disturbs me to think that she is aware of the blackness of his heart as well as the crookedness of the consortium—and yet can promote the venture with such calm confidence." A shiver skated down her spine. "Do you think she knows?"

"I am the wrong person to ask," answered the maid. "There's no question in my mind that she and Taviot knew of their younger half-brother's depravity. So I can't help but think that the whole family is rotten to the core."

"Lady Kirkwall's late husband was also enmeshed in scandal," mused the dowager. "It does raise unsettling questions."

"Either she's very, very naïve," replied Charlotte. "Or very, very evil."

The spark rekindled in Alison's eyes. "Well then, another reason to keep a close watch on her and her brother and see if we can discern which of the two possibilities is the truth."

Wrexford made a second visit to the magistrate's office on Bow Street, only to meet with another apologetic shrug. It was, he knew, unreasonable to be so impatient. Griffin had apparently been sent by the magistrate to oversee the murder investigation of a night watchman in St. Giles, and God only knew when the earl's hastily scribbled message would catch up with him.

"If you hear from Griffin, send word immediately to my townhouse on Berkeley Square."

"Yes, milord," The clerk gave a pained sigh. "Be assured that I haven't forgotten your request."

Knowing that he was too unsettled to wait in his workroom for the Runner to respond, the earl sent word to Tyler of his intended destination and then headed to the Royal Institution to have a chat with Hedley about propellers.

The inventor hadn't been able to offer any help to Cordelia concerning the amount of steam power necessary for propeller-driven ocean travel, but Hedley was fascinated by the question and had begun to think about the possibiites. So the ensuing conversation was a welcome distraction from fretting over Griffin's whereabouts.

Charlotte's message informing him of Taviot's soiree also required his attention. But after thinking through the ramifications, he agreed with her that it was a prudent move for her and Alison to attend.

Afternoon was fading into night when a messenger from Griffin tracked the earl down at Hedley's laboratory with a note arranging a rendezvous at an out-of-the-way tavern in the slums of St. Giles.

Wrexford gathered up his portfolio of evidence and thanked

the inventor for his time. "As always," he said, "talking about the complex challenges of Progress with a man of your intellect is illuminating."

Hedley gave a wry chuckle. "Though not always of practical use to you, milord."

Once out on the street, Wrexford flagged down a hackney and headed east toward Soho Square, the glitter of Mayfair rapidly fading into the squalid shadows of the ramshackle rookeries. As he descended from the vehicle—the narrow lanes demanded that he go the rest of the way on foot—Wrexford couldn't help but wonder why Griffin had chosen the spot. Given his seniority and sleuthing skills, the Runner wouldn't be assigned to solving a crime in this area unless there was a good reason.

The reason soon became evident when Wrexford entered the seedy tavern. Through the fug of smoke and guttering lantern light he saw that Griffin wasn't alone. And the man with him was unpleasantly familiar.

"Sorry," apologized the Runner on catching the earl's expression. "This wasn't my idea."

"Indeed, your friend is way too principled to have betrayed your current activities," said Griffin's companion. "Do sit, Wrexford, before you draw attention to us."

There was little risk of that, thought the earl. The men who frequented this sort of place would make a point of seeing and hearing nothing. Still, he did as suggested.

"What are *you* doing here, Pierson?" he demanded.

At their first meeting, which had occurred earlier in the summer during the investigation into the murder of Peregrine's uncle, the man had introduced himself as a mere dogsbody. But Wrexford had since learned his name was George Pierson and that he was a top operative for Lord Grentham, the head of state security.

"I assume that you've finally learned that Taviot's consortium was responsible for the fire at Maudslay's laboratory," Wrexford continued, "and likely behind the clandestine attack on the Royal Navy's research facilities at the King's Dockyard."

"How do you know about the skullduggery at the King's Dockyard?" countered Pierson.

A mirthless laugh. "Surely it's not a state secret that Lord Lampson and my two wards were invited by Samuel Tilden to visit the naval laboratory. They happened to be there when it was discovered."

He placed his portfolio on the tabletop. "However, let us not waste time talking about the intrigue among the competitors trying to build the first oceangoing steamship. I've more important crimes to discuss."

"Ugh."

The clacking and whirring of metal had given way to a queasy silence.

Raven, who was lying spread-eagled on the rug, squeezed his eyes shut. "I think . . ."

"I think we have made ourselves sick," mumbled Peregrine. He, too, was flat on his back.

Harper eyed the empty platter and gave an indignant *woof*.

"I warned you," said Hawk primly. He had returned to his school desk and was studying the scrap of fabric that Wrexford had ripped from his assailant's coat collar. "I saved my share of Pontefract cakes for later."

"As did I," volunteered Horatio. "Sweets are a special treat, so I wish to make them last." He grimaced. "The food served by the Royal Navy is horrible."

"It can't be worse than the swill they give us at Eton," said Peregrine.

Horatio rolled his eyes. "Ha! Try salt pork and rock-hard biscuits teeming with weevils."

"Ugh," Raven clutched his belly and choked back a retching sound.

"Even more of a treat is to have so many wonderful books to peruse," marveled Horatio. He was looking through a volume of colored engravings on moving mechanical devices that the earl had purchased for Peregrine, the pages angled to catch the lamplight from Hawk's desk.

"I have an illustrated book on steamboats that recently arrived from America," offered Hawk, indicating the pile of books beside his sketch paper. "Would you like to see it?"

"Oh, very much so!" Horatio scrambled to his feet.

"Here." Hawk held it out, but as Horatio rose to take it, he froze, the air leaching from his lungs in an audible gasp.

The lamplight wavered while he fought to regain his voice.

"W-Where did you get *that*?" he demanded, pointing at the scrap of fabric that Hawk had been sketching.

"Save your breath, milord," growled Pierson.

Wrexford glanced at Griffin, whose face was unreadable in the flickering of light and shadow, then drew his gaze back to the government operative and remained silent.

Shouts, laughter, the thump of pewter tankards punctuating the rough-cut curses of the tattered crowd clustered by the barman's counter—the place was alive with all the little noises of downtrodden men drowning their sorrows, at least for the moment.

While at their smoke-shrouded table, Wrexford and Pierson were playing a waiting game.

It was Griffin who decided to end the stalemate. "Lord Wrexford, your note said that in addition to possessing evidence of other crimes, you also had proof that Lord Taviot was guilty of betraying our country during the Peninsular War."

In answer, Wrexford opened his portfolio case and slid out the letter samples given to him by the Frenchman.

Pierson didn't grace them with so much as a glance. "Forget those. You've got it all wrong."

For an instant the earl felt a stab of uncertainty, but he quickly shook it off. "The traitor's handwriting matches that of Taviot, and the dates of the diplomatic mission for the Foreign Office corroborate his presence in Lisbon," he retorted.

"I don't dispute any of that, but as I said, you've got it all wrong."

"What are you saying?' demanded Wrexford.

Pierson leaned forward and brushed the incriminating letters aside. "I'm saying that Taviot isn't the real traitor."

CHAPTER 25

No—it cannot be.

Wrexford felt a little light-headed. All at once, the humid heat and smells from the unwashed bodies seemed to have thickened the air, making it hard to breathe. Leaning back, he swallowed hard, aware of the beads of sweat slithering down between his shoulder blades.

His eyes pooled with concern, Griffin nudged his tankard of ale across the table. "Drink," he said softly.

The earl took a grateful gulp, the sharp, sour taste of the cheap brew loosening the knot in his throat. "Explain yourself, Pierson. Tell me why I can't believe the evidence that I see clearly with my own eyes."

"Because," answered the government operative, "the plot was conceived by a ruthlessly clever fiend who manipulated Taviot into appearing the villain, when in fact he was merely a pawn."

Yet another sordid game within a game? Pierson lived in a netherworld whose lifeblood was duplicity and deception. To its denizens, morality was a pitifully naïve concept.

"How?" asked Wrexford, though he was aware that the answer might not be anything close to the truth. "And I suggest that you try to be convincing. I'm in no mood to be manipulated by government lies."

"I only lie when it's efficient. With you, I know that doing so is more trouble than it's worth."

In the uncertain light, Wrexford wasn't sure whether the operative's expression was a smirk or a grudging acknowledgment of respect. And he didn't much care.

"Stubble the clever retorts before I shove your teeth down your gullet," he responded. "All I want out of your mouth is a credible explanation of what is going on."

"I have every intention of providing one if you'll give me a chance."

Wrexford signaled for Pierson to continue.

"Taviot has always been pressed to keep up appearances. The family coffers have never been as puffed up as his own sense of self-worth," began Pierson. "He has expensive tastes, and like many aristocrats, he has used his position of power and privilege for financial gain. He was willing to take bribes or sell his support for a business project or a bill in Parliament."

A half-mocking smile. "I'm sure you know what I mean."

"Have a care as to what you are implying," warned the earl softly. "I don't take kindly to being called a muckworm."

Wrexford's ire seemed to amuse Pierson. "No need to challenge me to pistols at dawn, milord. My superior and I are aware that you are one of those rare men whose soul is not for sale."

"The state of *my* soul isn't the issue," snapped Wrexford. "Let us return to Taviot. If the government knew of his flaws, then why did he gain a senior position in the Foreign Office?"

"Taviot possesses intelligence, complemented by cunning. He's also articulate and a good negotiator, all useful traits for a diplomat," came the answer. "Let us just say that it was decided that his strengths outweighed his weaknesses."

"And yet I have proof that says he betrayed our country."

Pierson heaved a long-suffering sigh. "In fact, you don't. What you have are coded notes for a wine smuggling scheme—at least, that is what Taviot believed he was writing, for a cut of the wine profits, of course. But in truth, he was humbugged into passing our military secrets to the French, which resulted in the outmaneuvering of General Moore's army, forcing its bloody retreat to the coast."

This information answered the question Wrexford had raised with von Münch about why Taviot would risk exposing his betrayal of his country just to share in the profits of a wine smuggling enterprise. Apparently he hadn't.

And yet it still didn't feel right.

"Codes within codes?" said Wrexford. "You expect me to believe that balderdash? It's more ridiculous than one of Ann Radcliffe's horrid novels!"

"Truth is sometimes stranger than fiction," responded Pierson.

"Enough word games," snapped the earl. "If what you say is true, then who is the real culprit?"

Pierson's supercilious smile wavered for an instant. He hesitated, taking the time to flick an imaginary mote of dust off his coat cuff before replying. "Actually, we are hoping that you might be able to help us uncover the man's identity."

"If that's a jest, it's not remotely funny."

"Like you, I'm not laughing, milord." A pause—and an actual flicker of humanity in the depths of Pierson's eyes. "I've been working to piece together the full story, so I'm aware of your brother's death in a French ambush, and how the murder of Neville Greeley drew you into this tangled intrigue."

A groan of wood against wood sounded as the operative slid

forward in his chair. "Our department suspected someone was feeding information to the French six years ago during the retreat of our army toward Corunna. But the trail was so well hidden that we couldn't manage to track down the culprit. It was put aside after the war, but when we heard recent whisperings that Herr von Münch—the personal librarian to our sovereign's son-in-law, King Frederick of Württemberg—was making inquiries among former French intelligence officers on your behalf, it occurred to Lord Grentham that you might have picked up the old scent."

Wrexford considered what he had just heard. "So what are you suggesting?"

"That we pool our information," answered Pierson. "That way, we both have a good chance of getting what we want."

"That's asking a lot." He locked eyes with the operative. "It means I will need to trust what you tell me."

Pierson didn't blink. "You're a man of logic, Wrexford. What reason would I have for giving you false information?"

A laugh rumbled in the earl's throat. "I don't pretend to understand the way your mind works. However . . ." He tapped his fingertips together. "In this case, I find myself inclined to take you at your word." *Tap, tap*. "You must have compiled a list of possible suspects."

"Yes, several members of Taviot's diplomatic delegation to Portugal had some skeletons in their cupboards that indicated they might be open to bribery if the price was right," replied Pierson. "But we could never uncover any real evidence on any of them." He gave the earl three names. "Perhaps your informants are better at digging up dirt than mine."

Wrexford made a mental note of the names. "As to my recent endeavors, I've been looking at the possibility that the traitor was a fellow officer in my brother's regiment." A pause. "And by the by, the arsonist who was hired to set the fire at Maudslay's laboratory was also attached to the same brigade."

Pierson's subtle change of expression indicated that he wasn't aware of that fact.

"But so far, I've found no connection between Taviot and any of the regiment's officers," continued the earl. "A friend at Horse Guards is continuing to examine the military records to see if any suspects come to light."

"Now that there appears to be a military connection, I'll ask Grentham to have his adjutants take a look at who was serving on General Moore's staff. Perhaps one of those officers had a connection to Taviot."

"Anything else you can tell me?" asked Wrexford.

Pierson's silence was eloquent enough.

"You might also consider putting pressure on the former French intelligence officers who are now serving their restored king here in London," said Wrexford. "One of them may know the identity of the real traitor."

There was no response from Pierson, but he didn't expect one. Without looking up, Wrexford continued to gather the letters he had brought to the meeting and put them away. "One last thing. I suspect that Taviot's consortium is a fraud, and that they have made no headway in inventing a nautical propulsion system for oceangoing steamships."

"We have reason to believe the same thing," said Pierson.

The earl went very still. "Did you, perchance, have an operative in their secret laboratory the other night?"

A shrug. "We didn't need to bother with such cat-and-mouse games. Our naval research lab has been experimenting with propellers for some time. In addition, we've had the finest minds at Oxford and Cambridge working on both the theoretical and practical aspects involving the mathematics and science of making an efficient steam engine that is powerful enough to cross oceans. Given their work, our government has recently concluded that for now, the current technology is not capable of building one."

"And yet Taviot and his consortium are raising a great deal of money from some very prominent members of the beau monde."

"We are aware of that issue, too. It will be dealt with." Pierson's smile—or was it a sneer—was back. "Discreetly, of course."

Deciding that he had heard all the useful information that Pierson was willing to give, Wrexford did up the fastenings of his portfolio. "Are you ready to leave, Griffin?" he snapped. "Or are you really drinking what's in that pisspot?" He slid back his chair. "At least I fork over the blunt for decent refreshments."

The Runner rose. "Now that you mention it, milord, I haven't yet had my supper."

As the carriage clattered past Clarges Street and slowed to turn into Curzon Street, Charlotte felt compelled to remind the dowager that the upcoming visit was neither the time nor the place for any sleuthing.

"Remember, we are here merely to be seen," she counseled. "We shall imbibe a glass of champagne, make polite conversation with the other guests, and then take our leave."

"My wits haven't gone wandering," replied Alison tartly. "I fully comprehend our marching orders." The steel tip of her cane tapped a martial tattoo upon the floorboards. "However, a thought occurred to me."

"I would rather not hear it," said Charlotte.

The dowager ignored the comment. "What if the government doesn't think that the rough draft of the speech is strong enough evidence to prove Taviot or a co-conspirator murdered

Greeley? I've asked around and know that Maitland went to Oxford. He could simply claim that he had seen the da Vinci manuscript in the Balliol College Library and remembered the details."

In truth, the same worry had been needling Charlotte's peace of mind.

"So what are you suggesting?" she reluctantly asked.

"Wrex and Kit didn't find the manuscript at the secret laboratory," said Alison. "Don't you think that there's a good chance Taviot is keeping it hidden in his townhouse library, rather than trusting it to be safe in the main laboratory up by Hampton Palace?"

Charlotte did, but she was loath to admit it. "Even if the manuscript is here, there is no way we can contrive to search for it, assuming that is what you are suggesting."

The wheels slowed to a halt, and they climbed down from the carriage.

After offering Alison her arm, she looked up at the blaze of diamond-bright light illuminating the drawing room windows. "Tonight's soiree is an intimate gathering for influential members of the ton," she continued. "The absence of either one of us, even for a brief interlude, will be noticed."

Seeing the dowager's disappointment, Charlotte hastened to add, "But it's a very astute observation. And one which sparks an alternate idea." Her mind began to race as they came closer to the ornate marble entranceway. "Once we are inside, I'll make note of where one might enter the townhouse unobserved. When we return to Berkeley Square, we can make plans for a break-in. If the Weasels set up a surveillance of the townhouse and alert Wrex when the family goes out for the evening, he and Kit can make a clandestine search."

"An excellent idea," murmured Alison just as the dark-painted portal swung open and Taviot's butler greeted them with a formal bow.

"Welcome, miladies. Please follow me."

He led the way across the black and white checkered tiles of the entrance foyer and up a curved staircase to the grand drawing room.

It was Lady Kirkwall who stepped away from a cluster of other guests by the doorway to greet them. "How nice of you to come on such short notice, Lady Peake." A flicker of surprise—or was it irritation?—lit in her eyes as she saw Charlotte behind the dowager. "And Lady Wrexford."

Assuming a false smile, Charlotte replied without hesitation. "My great-aunt's health has been a bit delicate of late." *Liars deserve naught but lies.* "But as she dearly wished to attend, I offered to come along, in case she found herself in need of any assistance."

"How thoughtful of you," responded Lady Kirkwall with perfect politeness, and then extended her hand to the dowager. "Allow me to help you to the sofa. I'm sure you would rather sit than be subjected to the rigors of standing."

"Oh, please—let us not make a fuss over my infirmities," said Alison. "I do not wish my friends here to think that I am at death's door." Gripping her cane, she looked around, the light from the myriad candle flames reflecting off her spectacles. "I shall circulate for a bit and make my greetings before I take a seat," she added as several members of Lady Thirkell's Bluestockings salon gestured for her to join them.

"Apparently the dowager is stronger than you thought," said Lady Kirkwall as Alison moved off to join them.

"One can't be too careful," replied Charlotte.

"A wise strategy." A pause. "In so many aspects of life." Before Charlotte could react, Lady Kirkwall turned in a swirl of silken skirts. "Allow me to fetch you a glass of champagne from the refreshment table."

Cat and mouse? Charlotte wished she could believe that

Taviot's sister was unaware of the rot that lay beneath her brother's patrician veneer. However, it seemed highly unlikely. The lady was too perceptive to be bamboozled. Which meant . . .

The room was warm, but Charlotte felt an icy chill flit down her spine.

Which meant the alternative wasn't pleasant to contemplate.

And yet, against her will, she sensed that in many ways, the two of them were kindred souls—women who had dared carve out a niche for themselves in a man's world. And as Charlotte knew well, it required far more than knowing how to wield a hammer and chisel. The real skills were far more subtle. Courage, strength, cleverness . . . all were far more effective when gloved in ladylike velvet.

Her conflicted thoughts, however, were interrupted by the approach of Taviot himself.

He was all smiles and well-oiled charm. "How kind of you to accompany your great-aunt. She is a paragon of wit, intelligence, and grace. A grande dame who serves as an inspiration to us all."

Loathsome, fork-tongued snake. For him, Charlotte had not a whit of doubt concerning her feelings.

She batted her lashes to blur the look of utter disgust that she feared was pooled in her eyes. "Indeed. And as you see, the dowager has taken a great interest in your project. She cares deeply about Progress and making the world a better place."

"As we all should," said Taviot smoothly.

As he raised his glass to sip his wine, she caught a glimpse of his gold signet ring. His crest featured a lion rampant.

It should be a cold-blooded serpent.

"I believe that our grand innovation will greatly contribute to moving forward with progress." Taviot chuckled softly at his own witticism. "I see my sister returning with your champagne, so if you will excuse me, I shall go have a word with Lady Peake about the opportunity to be part of our worthy endeavor. There are still several charter investor spots available, and their special benefits—including the prospect of an Act of Parliament favorable to business—ensure that the purchase price will guarantee a handsome profit."

Charlotte merely nodded, not trusting her voice. Her skin felt afire from the proximity of pure evil. Because of his traitorous actions, Wrexford's beloved younger brother was dead—

She caught herself, aware that she must not let her fury show. Drawing a deep breath, she steeled her spine and turned to meet Lady Kirkwall with a composed smile.

Several other guests drifted over to join them. Charlotte had noted that most of the select group were wealthy widows or ladies known to wield great influence with their rich husbands. Indeed, as her gaze surreptitiously followed Taviot, she saw two packets—investment funds, no doubt—discreetly passed to him.

As for the smattering of gentlemen, there was a trio of distinguished guests present—an admiral, a well-known member of Parliament, and a governor of the British Scientific Society—their black evening clothes standing out in stark contrast to the colorful gowns of the ladies. It was, mused Charlotte, a clever strategy on the part of the consortium to use its charter investors to encourage others to buy shares. Ladies of the ton were naturally inclined to give a prominent gentleman's words of advice great gravitas. The evening would likely be a very profitable one for Taviot.

But not for long . . .

"Forgive me for being slow to return with your champagne," apologized Lady Kirkwall. "I was obliged to stop and chat with several acquaintances about the consortium."

The lady next to Charlotte raised a question, and the conversation turned to all the ways Britain would benefit from having oceangoing steamships. The talk continued for an interlude, and Charlotte found her attention wandering as she considered how to get a look at the rear of the house. Were there a garden and a back terrace that would allow access to the outer doors of the kitchen and scullery?

"I take it that you don't have as keen an interest in science as your husband." Lady Kirkwall's pointed comment pulled her back to the present moment and the fact that the other ladies had moved away.

"No, it is not a passion," answered Charlotte.

"Oh?" Her companion eyed her with an inscrutable look and allowed several moments of silence to slide by. "And what does stir your passions?"

"I find art more compelling than machinery."

The answer elicited a strange smile. "Then we have something in common, Lady Wrexford. I, too, am passionate about art, and painting in particular."

Charlotte took a sip of champagne, the effervescence prickling like dagger points against her tongue. "Our tastes align."

"Do you prefer landscapes or a focus on the human form?" inquired Lady Kirkwall.

"I admire Turner and Bonington's depiction of the natural world," she answered. "But portraits are my primary interest."

"Indeed? I, too, find myself fascinated by faces." A hesitation. "They tell us so much about human nature."

Had a ripple of emotion stirred beneath Lady Kirkwall's lowered lashes? Charlotte wasn't sure.

"It so happens that we have a rather fine collection of painted portraits by Van Dyke and Hans Holbein the Younger in the picture gallery downstairs. Would you care to see them?"

"Very much so," replied Charlotte, seizing the chance to reconnoiter the rest of the townhouse. Besides, she was curious about this sudden peek beneath the mask of impenetrable reserve. In every previous interaction, Lady Kirkwall had given no hint of her personal interests or feelings.

"Excellent." Lady Kirkwall glanced around. "Give me a moment while I inform my brother of our intentions."

While she moved off to confer with Taviot, Charlotte looked over to where the dowager was sitting on the sofa, deep in conversation with two of her Bluestocking friends.

There was no need to disturb her, decided Charlotte.

"Please follow me," said Lady Kirkwall on her return. She led the way through a side salon out to the corridor, where two sharp turns brought them to a rear staircase.

"Actually, I'm not surprised to hear that art is your passion, milady," she continued as they began to descend. "I've heard that you were married to an artist and spent time in Italy before becoming the Countess of Wrexford." A pause. "Word is there's a touch of scandal lurking in your past."

Charlotte hesitated. Few people knew anything about her past. Her family had taken pains to cover up the truth about her elopement, and she herself was very guarded about the details of her marriage to Anthony Sloane. If anyone looked too closely at his activities on returning to London, they might uncover more than she wanted to reveal.

Which raised the question of how Lady Kirkwall appeared to know more than she should.

However, Charlotte chose to disguise her unease by responding with her own challenge. "As there is in yours."

"True," agreed Lady Kirkwall. "Any intelligent female who has the audacity to flaunt her cleverness and imagination is considered scandalous. Women are expected to submit to a life of dull and dutiful drudgery. Those who refuse to be corseted in rules threaten the hierarchy that men have created."

A throaty laugh. "We frighten them."

The lady's sentiments echoed her own. And once again, Charlotte sensed a quicksilver flicker of elemental connection between the two of them. Such sardonic wisdom about women and the world had not been won without a number of battles. And the scars that went with them.

"Rather than frighten the gentlemen," replied Charlotte, "I would prefer to change their thinking."

"Good Heavens, what an optimist you are." Lady Kirkwall's voice held a note of mockery.

"I like to think of Hope as a strength, not a weakness."

Lady Kirkwall shrugged, and yet a flicker of uncertainty seemed to belie her cynicism. "Then perhaps you're not only an optimist but also naïve." She gave a brusque gesture as they reached the landing, but her show of steel-sharp toughness didn't quite ring true. "This way."

The portrait gallery was an airy space located behind stately double doors. On the far wall, noted Charlotte, a bank of windows would allow a soft natural light to illuminate the room in the daytime. Even now, with night having settled over the townhouse, a mellow glow from the oil wall sconces brought the paintings to life.

"Your collection is impressive. This portrait of Sir Thomas More is one of Holbein's most renowned works," remarked Charlotte as Lady Kirkwall led her to a gilt-framed canvas to their right.

"Yes. Magnificent, isn't it?"

"Indeed. The brushwork and attention to detail are superb," answered Charlotte. "But what makes Holbein truly special is how he captures the intensity of his subject." She studied it for a moment longer. "That is what lies at the heart of being a great portrait painter—the artist must see straight into the sitter's soul."

Lady Kirkwall looked away. "And here I thought an artist's biggest challenge was to create a flattering likeness."

"That depends." Charlotte deliberately added nothing more, which seemed to discomfit her hostess. She then moved on to the next painting.

They moved slowly around the perimeter of the galley without further verbal sparring. Lady Kirkwall was knowledgeable about art, and they exchanged polite comments on technique and style.

"I see you have several lovely works by Gainsborough," exclaimed Charlotte after they had passed the windows and came to the next set of portraits. "*Lady in Blue* is quite a tour de force. He used his palette of pigments to create such a subtle range of the color."

She moved slowly down the row. "Ah—what a striking portrait by Thomas Lawrence, for whom I have a great admiration." After carefully scrutinizing the details, Charlotte added, "He captured your likeness quite well, Lady Kirkwall. I doubt that he had to resort to any of his tricks of the trade in order to make it flattering."

A faint flush seemed to tinge her hostess's face, though it might only have been a glimmer of red from the nearby sconce's flame. "Lawrence likes ladies. I think he's more interested in smiles and cleavage than in searching for the sitter's soul."

"I think he studies his subjects more than you might realize," replied Charlotte. "Lawrence is known for his double dot technique, which helps capture the emotion in his subject's eyes." She turned to face Lady Kirkwall. "Most people might miss it, but it seems to me that he's caught that subtle look of vulnerability that occasionally sneaks into your gaze."

The comment sparked a flare of anger—no, it was fear, Charlotte realized—but it was gone in the blink of an eye.

"You have a *very* vivid imagination, Lady Wrexford—" Lady Kirkwall bit off her words as a footman appeared in the doorway.

"If you will excuse me for a moment," she snapped, and moved away before Charlotte could reply.

Shifting her stance, Charlotte managed a peek into the shadowed corridor. The servant looked troubled as he bobbed his head and began to speak, but the hushed tones of the tête-à-tête made it impossible for her to make out what was being said.

The exchange didn't last long, and Lady Taviot returned with a hurried step that set her ruffled skirts to swirling around her legs.

"Please come with me, Lady Wrexford," she said, a sense of urgency underlying her tone as she indicated a connecting door to the left of the Lawrence painting. "We need to wait in the library."

"Is something wrong?" demanded Charlotte once they had passed into the adjoining room.

"There is no reason to be alarmed," answered her hostess. "Lady Peake is feeling a trifle dizzy—"

"I must go to her!" exclaimed Charlotte.

Lady Kirkwall caught her arm. "Come, calm yourself. You heard the dowager say she didn't wish to stir any gossip about her infirmities. My brother is handling it discreetly, by simply announcing that you wish for Lady Peake to join you in viewing the portraits. He will escort her downstairs without anyone suspecting any trouble."

Trouble.

At that instant, Charlotte heard the whisper of steps on the carpet behind her. She tried to whirl around, but Lady Kirkwall's grip on her arm was surprisingly strong. It took a second tug to pull free.

Too late.

The cudgel hit her skull with a sickening thud.

Knees buckling, Charlotte sank toward the floor. The room was spinning, spinning, spinning like a whirling dervish.

"Ye gods, what have you done!" Lady Kirkwall's voice sounded very far away. "The plan wasn't to harm her!"

"Plans have changed," answered a voice that sounded oddly familiar.

Blackness was closing in. Charlotte tried to claw her way back to consciousness, but everything had turned hazy and all she could hear was a loud buzzing, like the sound of angry bees.

And then there was naught but silence.

CHAPTER 26

"Where did you get that?" repeated Horatio when he received no answer to his first query.

Hawk hastily moved his sketchbook to cover the scrap of fabric. "I—I don't remember," he stammered, glancing at his brother for help. "W-Why do you ask?"

"Because it's important." Horatio moved a step closer. "It may be a matter of Royal Navy security."

"In what way?" demanded Raven. "If you know anything about the bit of cloth, you need to tell us."

"I'm sorry, but my oath as a midshipman—an officer in His Majesty's service—prevents me from revealing that information to you." Horatio turned back to Hawk. "Please—try to think harder about where you found that piece of cloth."

"I'm sorry, but his oath to Wrexford and our family prevents him from revealing that information to you," interjected Raven. "And it does for me as well."

"And me," added Peregrine from his spot on the floor.

A fraught silence held the four of them in thrall.

Peregrine slowly sat up. "Do you play chess, Osprey?"

"A little," said Horatio warily.

"Then you know what a stalemate is."

"I think so," came the answer. "A stalemate is when it's a player's turn to move, but his only choice is to put his king into check, which is forbidden by the rules."

"Correct. So the game can't continue," said Peregrine. "There can be no win as well as no loss."

"Unless the players agree to bend the rules?" said Raven.

A smile. "Correct."

Horatio frowned. "What are you suggesting?"

"Perhaps there's a compromise," pointed out Peregrine. "Lord Wrexford is a former military officer and has recently performed some important investigations for the Crown."

"I . . ." The warring of emotions was writ plain on the midshipman's face as his gaze moved in turn to each of his three new friends. "I cannot risk saying something that might inadvertently betray my country."

At the word *betray*, Raven shifted uncomfortably. "Oiy, betrayal is the worst sort of sin. We would never ask you to do that."

"Oiy," agreed Peregrine. "But given that we are all trying to do the right thing, perhaps there's another way to work together."

"Go on," said Raven.

"Osprey is Aunt Alison's relative—" Glancing at Horatio, he added, "I may not be part of this family by blood, but Lady Peake is of the opinion that friendship and love are even stronger bonds, so she insists that I call her Aunt Alison."

Horatio shuffled his feet, the flickering lamplight making it impossible to read his expression.

Peregrine cleared his throat and moved his gaze back to Raven. "As I was saying, given that Osprey is Aunt Alison's relative, that makes him part of our family, too. Which means that you could explain just enough about the fabric for him to decide whether his oath as a naval officer permits him to share what he knows."

Raven thought for a moment, then stepped back a few paces and beckoned Hawk and Peregrine to join him.

Horatio waited with stoic patience as a back-and-forth flurry of whispers took place.

"Oiy, that could work." Raven's announcement signaled that the private conference was over.

Harper raised his shaggy head and thumped his tail on seeing the boys come back together.

"Peregrine thinks we should trust you," continued Raven. "I'm willing to take the risk because if he's right, then we will have a good chance at apprehending an evil miscreant who has done great harm to both our family and our country."

The midshipman acknowledged the statement with a solemn nod.

"Go on," urged Peregrine.

"Wrexford encountered a man while looking for proof of skullduggery at a laboratory involved in work on an ocean-going propulsion system," said Raven carefully. "I can't tell you where Wrexford was, but he had obtained some critical evidence that would help identify the criminals."

He hesitated. "However, the man—who was clearly up to no good—attacked Wrexford before he could leave. In the course of the hand-to-hand fight, Wrexford ripped the piece of cloth from the man's coat collar, but alas, he got away before Wrexford could identify him."

"I've been looking at the pattern of colored threads on the scrap," offered Hawk, "trying to see if I can discern what the design might be. That might help us narrow down the possible suspects."

"We have reason to believe the man and his co-conspirators

are not only responsible for arson and murder but may also have been involved in selling British military secrets to the French during the Peninsular War," added Raven.

Shoulders squared, Horatio stood at rigid attention . . . and then let himself slump. "Damnation, I—I feared that something was terribly wrong," he said in a tight voice, "but I didn't wish to believe it."

The midshipman closed his eyes for an instant. "In the course of performing my regular duties in the storage areas of the King's Dockyard, I overheard several conversations that stirred some frightening suspicions. I tried to tell myself that I must have misunderstood, and that the man whose voice I recognized all too well—my superior!—was authorized to pass on such sensitive information. But then, there was some talk about the past that made my blood run cold."

He shook his head in disbelief. "I was so confused . . . my superior was being called Eel by the other man—"

"Eel!" exclaimed Hawk. "That ties your superior to a recent murder in Oxford."

"Osprey, you need to tell us the man's name," pressed Raven. "I swear, he's a dangerous traitor."

Horatio slid his hand across the desktop and pulled the piece of fabric from beneath the book. "I know what this is. And to whom it belongs." He hesitated. "You're right. I am convinced that he deserves no loyalty."

Tightening his hold on the scrap of fabric, he uttered a name.

"Holy hell," intoned Raven. "We need to tell Wrex and m'lady just as soon as they return home."

Pain knifed through her head, cutting into every nook and crevice.

A good thing, Charlotte told herself. For perhaps it meant she was still alive.

Then the pain came again, even sharper this time.

On second thought, death might be preferable.

However, as the vague sounds around her shaped themselves into words, Charlotte realized that she was still in the here and now.

"The servants have all been sent to the other establishment. The house is now empty and ready to be locked up."

How long have I been unconscious? She had no idea. An hour? Two? Her wits were still fuzzy.

"Seizing Lady Wrexford wasn't part of the plan." It was Lady Kirkwall, and her usual sangfroid sounded badly shaken.

"We had to improvise," came the reply. "Her husband left us no choice. He's getting too close."

Charlotte racked her brain to recall where she had heard that voice before. And nearly moaned from the agony of the effort.

"She's coming to," said the same voice. "We all need to move."

"Good Lord," intoned Lady Kirkwall "W-What are you going to do with her?"

"That's not your concern," snarled the voice. "Taviot, take your sister to the carriage. We'll meet at the appointed rendezvous."

"But— " began Taviot.

"Or would you rather stay and face Lord Wrexford's wrath?"

"You promised that I was protected— "

"And you will be, but only if you do exactly as I say."

Charlotte heard hurried footsteps moving away.

A pair of gloved hands seized her shoulders and lifted her up from the sofa. "Move." Her captor hustled her through the French doors leading out to a terrace and then down several shallow stairs to a garden walkway.

He let out a low whistle, and a moment later the crunch of gravel announced that someone was approaching.

"Take her to the carriage hidden behind the mews," said her captor as a shadowed figure came close. "Once you are out of Town and come to a secluded spot, you know what to do."

As the newcomer grabbed her roughly, Charlotte forced her eyes open and saw the silhouette of her captor—a broad-shouldered man—retreating into the night mist.

"Stop!" she ordered, though the word came out as a pitiful croak.

The effort earned her a hard slap from the man who now held her prisoner. "Shut your mouth."

Deciding that she was likely going to die anyway, Charlotte began to struggle. Tears—mingling fear and rage—wet her cheeks as she thought about all the reasons she had for living.

I will not go without a fight.

Another blow from the man stunned her, allowing him to muscle her past the mews and into the hidden carriage.

He rapped on the trap, signaling the driver to crack his whip, and sank back to the seat just as Charlotte recovered enough to renew her attack.

Punch, scratch, poke—fired on by desperate fury, Charlotte flailed at him, hoping to seize an instant in which she could fling open the door.

Wishful thinking.

The man easily caught her hands and used his superior weight and strength to pin her back against the squabs. Leaning in close—so close that his hot-as-Hades breath tickled against her cheek—he growled an oath and punctuated it with a teeth-rattling shake.

"Sheath your claws, Lady Wrexford. I'm trying to help you, but you must be still."

Head bowed, deep in thought, Wrexford followed the curve of the wrought-iron fence that circled the lush garden centered in Berkeley Square. The clatter of a late-night reveler's curricle racing over the cobbles made him pause before crossing the carriageway to his townhouse. He looked up and felt his spirits lift, despite the tangled worries weighing on his mind.

Home. It was now so much more than an elegant building filled with tasteful furnishings and pleasing art. The mellow light warming the windows was a beacon of . . .

How to describe its glow? He was not a poet. His eloquence was in observing and analyzing things that one could see and measure. Emotions were more elusive. But as he stared up at the limestone and granite façade of his residence, Wrexford felt a surge of wordless wonder at the joy of having Charlotte and his family as part of his very being.

He couldn't imagine his world without them.

"I have," Wrexford whispered, "become a sentimental fool."

The thought made him smile, but after spending another moment savoring the light through the scrim of flitting shadows, he crossed the cobblestones and let himself in through the front door.

It was late. He lit a candle from the entrance table and headed for his workroom, wishing to finish sorting his thoughts before heading upstairs to Charlotte, who was likely asleep by now. As he turned down the corridor leading to the rear of the townhouse, a flutter of lamplight through the half-open door caught his eye.

He quickened his steps. Perhaps Tyler had discovered some further clue in the chemical sample found at Taviot's secret laboratory. However, as he entered the room, he stopped short.

The work counters, usually a scene of cheerful disarray, had been neatly organized, the unruly piles of paper on his desk shuffled into order, the curio cabinet dusted—

"Ye heavens, what prompted this burst of activity, Mac?" he asked wryly, seeing the maid crouched in front of the hearth, stirring the coals to life.

She rose and slowly turned to face him . . .

And Wrexford's heart leapt into his throat.

"What's happened?" he rasped.

"I—I am not sure, milord," she replied. "P-Perhaps nothing—"

"You're not making any sense." Wrexford fought to keep his voice calm.

"As you know, m'lady and Lady Peake attended a soiree for potential investors at Taviot's townhouse this evening. However, they have not yet returned."

Wrexford felt his heart skip a beat.

"Tyler and Raven have gone to reconnoiter around Taviot's house, Hawk has run to see whether they have gone to Lady Peake's home, and Peregrine . . ." She lowered her voice and glanced at the door to the adjoining room. "Peregrine and Lady Peake's young relative, Midshipman Horatio Porter, are waiting in your library. It seems that Horatio was able to identify the scrap of cloth that you tore from the man who attacked you in Taviot's secret laboratory."

Feeling a little dizzy, Wrexford pressed his fingertips to his temples, hoping to stop his head from spinning. "Are you saying that he knows the name of the man?"

McClellan hurried to pour a glass of whisky from the decanter on the sideboard and made the earl take it before answering. "Yes."

He took a long swallow, its liquid fire finally burning through the haze of his initial shock.

As he stared into the whisky, Wrexford suddenly recalled von Münch's remark about it being hard to believe that *two* British traitors had been active during the Peninsular War.

But what if it were true?

He had assumed that Taviot was the evil mind behind the treachery. But a pair of villains working together would be the answer to a great many baffling questions.

As to Pierson's assertion that the government believed that Taviot was merely a pawn, Wrexford was inclined to disagree. After all, Pierson had made a point of Taviot's intelligence and cleverness, which meant he wasn't a man easily duped.

Setting aside his half-empty glass, the earl drew in a measured breath. "Mac, please summon Peregrine and Midshipman Porter."

The maid rushed to fetch the boys from the adjoining library.

"Sir!" exclaimed Peregrine. "Is there—"

"There is no news yet, lad. But never fear, we will soon have m'lady and Aunt Alison home." Wrexford made himself sound confident. He refused to consider an alternative. Turning his gaze on Peregrine's companion, he gave a friendly nod. "You must be Midshipman Porter."

"Y-Yes, milord." Horatio snapped to attention and gave a salute.

"At ease, Horatio." He gave the boy an encouraging smile. "I understand that you've identified the man to whom the torn fabric belongs."

"Yes, milord," repeated Horatio. "You see, I know who owns the coat, and I spotted the damage this morning."

He hesitated, then said a name.

The villain is trying to help me? Charlotte wondered whether she was now hallucinating. His words made no sense.

Still, she ceased her struggling. "W-Why?"

No answer, though his grip on her wrists relaxed ever so slightly.

Squinting through the gloom, she tried to make out any identifying features. But he was no fool. Only his eyes showed above the length of black linen wound snugly around his face, which also served to muffle his voice.

Those eyes. Charlotte was sure that she had seen them before.

Her captor—or savior—kept darting frequent looks out the carriage window. Charlotte decided to obey his orders for the moment, using the interlude to marshal her strength. She knew that she would never be able to muster the effort for more than one escape attempt, so she decided to be patient and wait for the right moment.

The road was getting rougher, and the buildings were giving way to a muddled darkness that seemed to indicate they were reaching the outskirts of Town. She felt her captor shift, his muscles tensing.

"Start to make a ruckus," he said. "Though I would prefer that you smack the seat rather than me."

It startled her to think he might have a sense of humor.

"I'm going to shout at the driver to stop and help me get you out of the carriage, as you're about to be sick," he explained. "Stay slumped, and for God's sake, don't get in my way."

The question of whether to trust him flashed through her still-aching head. But as he seemed the lesser of two evils, she decided to play along. Pounding her fists against the leather seat, she filled her lungs and began to wail.

Flinging open the door, her captor jumped down and reached back to grasp her arm.

"Damnation! Come help me with this hellbitch," he called.

"Hell's teeth, she's a bloody nuisance." The driver, a big bear of a man, lumbered over to join the fray. "Shouldn't we just twist her neck and be done with it?" He looked around at the scrubby hedgerows and glade of trees. "It's deserted enough—"

Before the driver could finish, her captor smashed the butt of a pistol against the man's skull. Quick as a cobra, he then wrapped an arm around the driver's throat and then tightened his hold.

A gurgle gave way to silence . . . followed by a thud as the body hit the hardscrabble road.

"Is he dead?" queried Charlotte.

"He'll awake in an hour or two, though he won't be feeling terribly well," answered her captor. "How is your head?"

"It feels as though a regiment of the Royal Household Cavalry has ridden roughshod over it." Charlotte winced as she fingered the lump above her right temple. "But I daresay I'll survive."

He reached into his coat and extracted a flask. "Perhaps a nip of brandy would help?"

"Bless you," she murmured. "Are you going to remove that rag around your face so that I may thank you properly, sir?"

A chuckle. "It would be ungentlemanly of me to refuse."

Charlotte watched in growing dismay as the man's face was revealed. "You!"

She expelled a grudging sigh. "Much as it pains me to say it, I owe you a debt of gratitude, Mr. Kurlansky." A pause. "Though I can't help but wonder whether you staged all this just to annoy me."

'Even *I* am not that devious, milady." His smile thinned to a grim line. "It was pure luck that I happened to be watching Taviot's house."

"Which begs the question of why you were there."

"Explanations can wait. Right now, I would rather return you to your home before your husband comes looking for you." Kurlansky grimaced. "And cuts my liver into mincemeat before I have a chance to convince him that I'm not the enemy."

The brandy had helped clear the cobwebs from Charlotte's head, and at the mention of the word *enemy* a spurt of panic suddenly rose in her throat. "Alison!" she cried.

Kurlansky appeared nonplussed. "The dowager was attending the soiree?"

"Y-Yes!"

"I saw no sign of her being a captive," he said. "I think it likely that she simply left the gathering along with the other guests and went home."

"No, no," protested Charlotte. "Alison would never have taken her leave without me." Steadying herself against the side of the carriage, she sucked in a breath and began to climb back in.

"I hope you are a dab hand at driving, sir. Because we need to fly like a bat out of hell to Berkeley Square."

CHAPTER 27

"Wrex!" called Tyler as he and Raven rushed into the earl's workroom.

Wrexford pushed aside the notes he had been scribbling and shot up from his desk chair.

"Thank God you have returned," continued the valet. "We had a look at Taviot's townhouse and—"

"And it's deserted!" exclaimed Raven. "One of the urchins who lives in the area told me that the servants all left in a flurry—in two coaches, headed east."

"The knocker was also taken down," added Tyler. For the beau monde, that was a signal that the family had departed town.

"What are we going to do, Wrex?" Raven tried to appear calm, but the earl saw the rippling of raw fear in the boy's eyes.

"If necessary, we are going to make a plan—and then we are going rescue m'lady and Alison," he answered without hesitation.

Raven swallowed hard and gave a fierce nod. "Oiy, of course we are."

"Horatio's new information has proved to be the missing piece of the puzzle," said Wrexford. "It finally explained why the whole picture of this mystery within mysteries has been so difficult to discern."

"You mean because there are—" began Tyler.

"Two master villains," finished the earl. "Yes, it's why the trail of evil deeds has been doubly hard to follow. But now that we have discovered the truth, we're no longer just flailing at shadows."

Wrexford glanced down at his notes. "I have been thinking... Given the identity of Taviot's partner in crime, I am certain that they know their perfidy has been discovered, so it stands to reason that they have seized Charlotte and Alison," he reasoned. "Which also means that our loved ones will be used as bargaining chips, so are not in any imminent danger."

Not yet.

He began to pace in a circle around his desk. "The villains will use them to negotiate—most likely for a deal that will allow them to escape from England." His steps slowed as he parsed various possibilities. "My guess is that they originally planned to take Alison hostage. Charlotte is a complication. And when one is forced to improvise, the chances of making a mistake are greater."

Clenching his hands, Wrexford tapped his knuckles together. "In any case, we must move quickly to put ourselves in a position to seize the advantage."

"How do we start?" demanded McClellan.

The earl's answer was delayed by the return of a breathless Hawk, who needed several moments to regain the power of speech. "Aunt Alison hasn't returned home!"

"S'all right," piped up Raven. "Wrex has a plan."

All eyes turned to him.

"First we need to marshal our forces," announced Wrexford. "Tyler, you fetch Henning. Raven, you must get Kit and then go to Lady Cordelia's residence and have her roused. Bring them both back here as soon as possible." To the maid, he said, "Mac, you and Peregrine take Horatio upstairs and see that he is settled for the night."

The maid nodded in agreement. The ensuing discussion was going to involve secrets that an outsider could not be permitted to hear.

"Come along, boys," she said as Tyler and Raven raced off to perform their tasks.

"What about me?" asked Hawk in a small voice once they were alone.

Wrexford sat back down in his chair and gestured for the boy to join him. Hawk was not only younger than his brother, but he also had a more sensitive nature. The earl knew that worries weighed more heavily on his small shoulders.

"I—I want to h-help," added Hawk, blinking back tears.

"It would be a great help if you would keep me company." Wrexford pulled the boy into his lap and wrapped his arms around him. He had meant the gesture to be of comfort to Hawk, but the weight and warmth of his dear little Weasel—a physical reminder of love and family—turned the faint spark of hope in his own heart into a blazing flame.

"Don't worry, lad. The devil himself wouldn't dare harm our loved ones. First of all, Alison would smack him with her stick."

Hawk looked up, his trembling mouth quirking to a tiny smile. "And m'lady would poke her pen in his arse."

"Quite right, lad," replied Wrexford, smoothing the tangled curls back from the boy's brow. "And then—"

His words were cut off by a sudden flurry of steps and a blessedly familiar voice rising from the shadows of the corridor.

"Halloo! Halloo! Where is everyone?"

* * *

Wrexford shot up from his chair so fast that he sent Hawk tumbling to the carpet. Charlotte would have chuckled, but the earl seized her in such a fierce hug that it squeezed the breath from her lungs.

"You might wish to be a trifle more gentle, milord." Kurlansky sauntered into the room as he peeled off his gloves. "Your wife has taken a nasty blow to the head."

"Then I shall put her down," growled Wrexford, "and proceed to thrash you to a pulp."

"Might I first pour myself a glass of spirits?" replied the Russian on spotting the tray of decanters on the sideboard. "I don't suppose you have vodka?"

"*Nyet*," said the earl.

"Wrex!" Charlotte caught his fist and uncurled his fingers. "Mr. Kurlansky deserves our thanks, not a bloody beak. He rescued me from a very unpleasant situation."

Wrexford quickly stepped aside as Hawk flung himself at Charlotte. "Then I suppose that I should offer you a drink after all." He gestured for Kurlansky to help himself.

After glancing around, Charlotte gave Hawk another hard hug and pressed a kiss to his brow. "Sweeting, please go up find the others and inform them I have arrived home safely while Wrex and I have a private discussion with Mr. Kurlansky."

The boy looked reluctant to let her out of his sight, but a warning cough from the earl made him turn for the door. However, he hesitated after a few steps and then hurried to Wrexford, who crouched down and exchanged a few hurried whispers with the boy before sending him on his way.

"Alison—I fear Alison has been—" began Charlotte.

"Yes, we're aware that she is missing," interjected Wrexford. "Raven and Tyler are fetching our inner circle of friends so that we may start planning a rescue." He caressed her cheek. "Sit down, my love. Let me pour you a wee dram of whisky, and then tell me what happened while we wait."

"You have a very fine wine cellar, milord," said the Russian after taking an appreciative sip of his brandy.

"Apparently you deserve more than pig swill," came the grudging reply.

Charlotte held back a chiding comment. She didn't blame the earl for being angry and upset. "He does," she responded, and proceeded to explain the events of the evening.

"But how did you come to be there, Mr. Kurlansky?" she added after finishing her account.

"As luck would have it, I've also been interested in the activities of Taviot and his consortium," replied the Russian. "I was spying on the soiree tonight and happened to notice that you were in trouble."

She frowned. "But how did you come to be the one who dragged me into the carriage?"

Kurlansky took the liberty of refilling his glass before answering. "I had noticed a nasty-looking ruffian skulking in the shadows by the carriage. Having witnessed the attack on you through the library's windows, I put two and two together and decided to insert myself in his place."

"I imagine he didn't take kindly to that," observed Wrexford.

"He did not." A shrug. "Be that as it may, the fellow is no longer a threat—to anyone."

"*Qui gladio vivit, gladio moritu*," intoned Charlotte. "He who lives by the sword dies by the sword."

Wrexford quickly moved on. "What's your interest in Taviot and his consortium?"

"Oh, come, milord." The Russian arched his brows. "A man of your intellectual prowess does not have to think very hard to realize that the tsar of Russia would be very interested in any new technological innovations involving sea travel."

"In other words, he sent you to steal the plans," muttered the earl.

"So your wife assumed." Kurlansky winked at Charlotte. "I did not miss your daggered looks, milady. And I confess that purloining the technical plans for an oceangoing marine propulsion system might have been my assignment . . ."

A pause. "Assuming they had a chance of working."

"What makes you think that the Royal Navy or Henry Maudslay have not been successful?" countered Wrexford.

"The fact that, like you, I'm very good at what I do."

Tired of the verbal sparring, Charlotte shifted against the soft leather cushions of her armchair. "Enough thrusts and parries." She closed her eyes for an instant as the movement sent a fresh stab of pain through her skull. "Mr. Kurlansky, are you saying that you think none of the inventors have come up with a workable system for an oceangoing steamship?"

The Russian inclined an exaggerated bow. "That is precisely what I am saying, milady."

"Which makes me want to assume the exact opposite is true," quipped Wrexford. "However, in this case, my own investigations have led me to the same conclusion."

"Using a propeller is moving in the right direction," mused Kurlansky. "It solves the propulsion part of the problem, as there is no doubt among marine engineers that it is a more efficient and reliable design than a paddle wheel. It's the steam engine that is the weak link."

"There are too many practical problems," agreed the earl. "Our current precision milling capabilities aren't sophisticated enough to create an engine powerful enough for sea travel. Efficiency is also a factor. Ships simply can't carry enough fuel for an ocean voyage."

"True, milord," said the Russian. "Though I have no doubt that sometime in the future—perhaps the near future—someone will build on the current designs and succeed in creating a breakthrough engine that will revolutionize seagoing ships."

"As our friend Mr. Sheffield recently remarked," observed Charlotte, "it's the right idea but has the misfortune of being conceived ahead of its time."

"That is the nature of innovations," said Wrexford. "For the few momentous successes, there are countless failures which for any number of reasons lie buried in the shadows."

Scientific breakthroughs require both genius and *luck*, reflected Charlotte.

"I assume you managed to open the complicated lock on Maitland's private office in the consortium's secret laboratory and that is how you confirmed your suspicions that he hadn't come up with any scientific breakthrough," said Kurlansky.

"Ah," Wrexford made a face. "So it was *you* who was shadowing Sheffield and me in Taviot's secret laboratory at Dowgate Wharf."

"*Da*," replied the Russian.

"Much as it pains me to say it, I, too, apparently owe you a debt of thanks for saving my friend's life."

Kurlansky smiled. "I have a good deal of respect for Mr. Sheffield. He's far more interesting than most people realize."

Charlotte's head was beginning to throb. Enough parsing through questions surrounding the marine propulsion system. Alison was in mortal danger.

"Now that we have ascertained you are not the enemy, Mr. Kurlansky—at least not in this endeavor—might I ask . . ." She was forced to stop and steady her voice. "Might I ask whether you have any idea of where Taviot and his co-conspirators might be holding the dowager?"

The supercilious curl of the Russian's smile gave way to a more enigmatic expression. Dare she hope it was concern? He didn't strike her as a man who gave a fig for sentiment.

Kurlansky hesitated in answering.

Not a good sign. He was likely spinning some skein of half truths and misdirections that she and Wrexford could ill afford.

"I confess, I did not witness your arrival and was not aware that Lady Peake was present," admitted the Russian. "I am truly sorry that the dowager has become entangled in this spider's web of intrigue." A grimace. "She must be terrified."

Charlotte wasn't sure whether to laugh or cry. "She's probably finding it a grand adventure. But . . ."

Wrexford came to stand by her chair. After tucking a loose strand of hair behind her ear, he placed a comforting hand on her shoulder and wordlessly passed her his handkerchief.

She hadn't realized that there were tears trickling down her cheeks.

Kurlansky was gentlemanly enough not to remark on it. He looked away, his knife-sharp eyes settling on the hearth, where a fluttering of tiny flames was rising from the coal. "I couldn't identify the man who hit you—"

"I know who he is," said Wrexford. To Charlotte he explained, "We have identified the piece of cloth I tore from my assailant's coat collar—don't ask how—and it belongs to Colonel Jarvis, head of military security at the King's Dockyard. I suspect that he and Taviot have been working together from the start."

"Jarvis! I knew the voice was familiar." Charlotte expelled a sharp breath. "So, Jarvis was not only spying on the Royal Navy's research but likely also responsible for the skullduggery in the naval laboratory."

"Yes," agreed Wrexford.

After blotting her cheeks, Charlotte squeezed her hand around the damp linen. "Thank you for all your assistance, Mr. Kurlansky. But if you will excuse us, we need to start planning—"

The Russian abruptly interrupted her. "There's one possibility that may help narrow the search for their hiding place. I had mentioned to Taviot that there is a Russian frigate waiting at anchor in Gravesend, where it can hoist sail and quickly put out to sea."

"Arranged by you, no doubt, to ensure a swift departure from England should you need it," commented the earl.

"Of course. In my profession, it's wise not to leave anything to chance," answered Kurlansky.

"And I take it you told Taviot about the ship as an incentive to share his secrets with you?" pressed Wrexford.

"I always believe in keeping all my options open. So, yes, I've been negotiating a deal with Taviot to relocate to Russia at the same time as I was taking a clandestine look into his business activities. As I said, I'm convinced that his consortium's current work is useless, but Maitland is a brilliant engineer and would be a great asset to Russia's naval research program."

He paused for a moment. "Knowing that Taviot will soon be facing scrutiny over his finances when it becomes clear his consortium is a failure, I assume that he's planning to take me up on the offer—without delay."

"Please don't lie to us," said Charlotte. "The dowager's life is at stake. Taviot is a scoundrel, but his partner in crime is an utterly ruthless murderer who won't bat an eye at killing an innocent lady."

"I'm aware of that, Lady Wrexford," answered Kurlansky.

The earl stepped away from Charlotte's chair. "Excuse me for a moment," he said abruptly and hurried into the adjoining library. He reappeared shortly carrying a handful of maps and spread them out on one of the work counters.

"Will you show us exactly where your ship is? By looking at the roads and the quickest routes to reach it, we may be able to identify the most likely hiding places." He looked to Charlotte. "It may be grasping at straws, but it will give us some idea of where to start."

Kurlansky was already studying the map of the River Thames and its estuaries opening into the North Sea. "Here," he said, tapping a finger to a spot by one of the coves. "My ship is here."

"Thank you," said Charlotte, suddenly feeling too fatigued to risk rising from her chair.

"*Pozhaluysta*," replied the Russian. He took a moment to tug at his cuff, his gaze still on the map. "If I were you . . ." *Tap, tap*. "I would start my hunt in these two spots." He indicated the island jutting down into the bend of river opposite the King's Dockyard and the nearby Bugsby's Marsh. "They are both convenient to his barracks and his escape route to my ship."

"That makes some sense," allowed Wrexford.

The two of them continued to study the map in silence.

"Might I ask a question, milord?" asked the Russian after several long moments had slipped by.

A brusque nod signaled for Kurlansky to continue.

"I can't help but wonder what drew you into this investigation," said the Russian. "It appears that Taviot and his consortium have no connection to you or your interests. And yet I get the feeling that there is some very personal motive driving your quest to expose their misdeeds."

Wrexford didn't look up from the map. "You are right. It *is* personal. And just so we understand each other, Kurlansky, I have no objection to you taking Maitland with you when you leave England. Investing is a risky business, and those looking to make a fortune ought to do their due diligence to make sure the project is legitimate before handing over their money."

He placed his palms on the counter. "However, I won't allow Taviot or Jarvis to leave the country—and that's not open to negotiation."

"I don't suppose you'll tell me why?" countered the Russian.

Charlotte waited, and when the earl didn't reply, she had to make a difficult decision. She was under no illusion that Kurlansky was now their friend. But he had put himself at some risk to save her neck—and that of Sheffield—so at the very least he deserved an answer.

"In addition to his current crimes, we have reason to believe that Taviot betrayed British military secrets to the French during the Peninsular War," she said.

Wrexford made no sign for her to halt her revelation.

"His acts of treason," she continued, "resulted in the deaths of a great many brave soldiers—"

"Including my younger brother," finished the earl, his voice barely more than a whisper.

The Russian lowered his lashes, but not before Charlotte saw a very un-Kurlansky-like flicker of emotion. "I see."

Rather to her surprise, Charlotte found she believed that the announcement had affected him. And his next words seemed to confirm it.

"You have my word that nobody but Maitland, assuming he chooses to leave these shores, will find refuge on the Russian ship."

"It seems I owe you another debt of thanks," replied Charlotte.

That drew a sardonic smile. "Have no fear, milady, I am sure that I shall find an opportunity for you to repay me."

Wrexford scowled but refrained from comment.

Voices suddenly came alive in the corridor—it was Raven returning with Sheffield and Cordelia.

"I shall leave you to discuss strategies with your friends," said Kurlansky, withdrawing to the doorway and stepping aside to allow the new arrivals to rush in. "I wish you good luck, Lady Wrexford."

He nodded to the earl. "And good hunting."

CHAPTER 28

"Charlotte!" cried Cordelia as Sheffield, too, stopped short on seeing her rise from her chair. "Oh, thank God you are safe!"

"M'lady!" Raven dashed past both of them.

In the first burst of excitement, Kurlansky slipped away without being noticed.

Raven nearly tripped as he tangled in Charlotte's skirts while trying to catch her in a hug. Wrexford kept both of them upright and raised his voice to be heard above the shouts and questions as everyone began talking at once.

"If you will all quiet down, I will endeavor to explain."

The noise immediately subsided, though Raven remained glued to Charlotte's side. She gathered him close and ruffled his hair. "Before you begin, Wrex, please pour yourself a brandy." A glance showed that Sheffield was also looking distressed. "And one for Kit as well."

The earl didn't argue. Fear and fatigue had deepened the lines of worry and hollows on their friend's face.

"Sorry it took me so long to return," piped up Raven. "Mr.

Sheffield wasn't home, so I decided to check with the porter at White's to see if he was there."

Sheffield cleared his throat with a cough. "M'lady doesn't need a long-winded explanation—"

Raven, however, went on in a rush. "But as he wasn't there I decided to give up and go on to Lady Cordelia's residence. And by a stroke of good fortune, it turned out that he was there, too."

A flush rose to Cordelia's cheeks. "We had some important matters to discuss."

"At midnight? In your night-rail?" replied Raven.

Sheffield was suddenly looking a little green around the gills. "I—I," he stammered, then simply fell silent.

"It's time for you to head up to the eyrie and join the others, sweeting," said Charlotte. "Wrex and I need to have a private discussion with our friends."

"But—"

"We have determined that Aunt Alison is being held hostage," she continued. "We need to confer with Kit and Cordelia before we make final plans."

Raven surrendered with an unhappy sigh and grudgingly left the room.

Charlotte smiled at the embarrassed couple once the boy was out of earshot. "Good heavens, did you really think that I, of all people, would be shocked at the idea of you two anticipating your marriage vows?"

Wrexford hastened to pour two brandies and brought them over to his flustered friends. "It's about time the two of you stopped shilly-shallying over pledging your troth. Bloody hell, if you are waiting for the perfect moment—the stars and the planets aligning, a chorus of angels singing assurances that a problem will never shadow the glow of nuptial bliss—then you are perfect idiots."

"I might have phrased it a little more diplomatically," said Charlotte. "But the essence of what Wrex said is true."

"But I've been such an arse," mumbled Sheffield. "We argued about something serious, and I was too stubborn to listen." He stared into his drink. "How can I now ask Cordelia to trust my judgment?"

"Kit—" began Cordelia.

"Ye heavens, arguments are natural—and both of you will take turns being the arse," replied Charlotte. "You will sort them out, because your strengths are far greater than your weaknesses." At that moment, all the fears squeezing at her heart gave way to a smile. "And because you love each other."

Wrexford fetched a glass of brandy for Charlotte and himself before adding, "I suggest that you don't argue with Charlotte over the power of Love. It's a dispute you will never win."

Cordelia took hold of Sheffield's hand. Their eyes met as their fingers twined together.

"Though only the devil knows why Cordelia is completely blinded by Love," drawled the earl on seeing the look that passed between them.

"Arse," shot back Sheffield.

Somehow the music of their ensuing laughter helped steel Charlotte's resolve. "You know, Alison has been very disappointed that there have been no wedding plans in which to meddle," she announced. "When we rescue her—"

When. Not if.

"I say we make a pact to celebrate the love and friendship that ties us all together by having you two finally set a date for your wedding."

"I agree," chorused Cordelia and Sheffield at the same time.

Wrexford took a long swallow of his brandy. "Now that we've resolved one of our challenges, let us turn our attention to the other."

The others went very still.

"We were fortunate beyond words tonight," he began. "Let

us hope our luck will hold." Charlotte was trying to keep a brave face, but Wrexford could see her strength was flagging, so he made himself hurry in explaining about Jarvis to Cordelia and Sheffield.

"Merciful heavens," whispered Cordelia.

Charlotte clasped her hands together and shot to her feet, a spark of fire lighting her eyes. "I need to fetch something from my workroom," she called as she hurried into the corridor.

The arrival of Tyler and Henning demanded a repeated account of Charlotte's rescue, along with the surmise that the villains were holding Alison as a bargaining chip.

"They have taken the Dragon prisoner?" growled the surgeon. "God help them," he added after a rusty laugh.

"Much as I admire the dowager's fearsome abilities," replied the earl, "I would rather that we get her home as soon as possible. I don't believe she is in any imminent danger—"

But before he could continue, McClellan appeared right behind them with a platter of food. "Sustenance is important to keep our strength up."

"So is whisky." Henning's voice was more gravelly than usual, betraying his fatigue. "When do we leave to rescue the dowager?"

"Not so fast," said Wrexford over the clink of crystal against crystal. "It's too dark to search the most likely areas, so we really have no choice but to wait until dawn to begin."

Tyler spied the maps on the work counter. "It looks as though you have some idea of where they may be holding her."

"Yes, Kurlansky—"

"Kurlansky?" exclaimed Henning. "And you believe a word that conniving rascal has to say?"

"In this case, yes. It was he who rescued Charlotte from Jarvis's clutches."

Before the surgeon could reply, Charlotte came rushing back into the room, a much wrinkled and folded piece of paper clutched in her hands.

"Everyone, gather around," she called, after moving to the earl's desk and opening it atop the leather blotter.

It was, saw Wrexford, the satirical print by A. J. Quill that he had brought back from Greeley's office—the commentary Charlotte had created after hearing the leading nautical engineers in Britain give a symposium on steam power and ships at the Royal Institution.

"Look." She pointed to one of the figures positioned behind the two gentlemen in the foreground of the artwork. "Maitland and Tilden were the main speakers at the symposium. So they were the pair that Wrex and I were focused on, wondering whether Greeley saved the print because he knew one of them. However, I drew in other participants—I didn't mention the names in the captions, but I now realize that one of them was Colonel Jarvis!"

"A military man, who is probably skilled with a weapon," said Wrexford. "You're thinking he is the one responsible for Greeley's murder, as well as that of the arsonist?"

"It seems a strong possibility. The witness I met at the tavern said the man who hired the arsonist had hair the color of strong tea," replied Charlotte. "Jarvis has dark reddish-brown hair."

Which meant the man was a ruthless killer. Once the dowager became expendable . . .

Keeping such disturbing thoughts to himself, the earl nodded. "Kit and I saw that he had no compunction about attacking us to keep the consortium's secrets safe."

"I wonder how he came to be working with Taviot?" asked Sheffield.

"My guess is that he decided Taviot's consortium was ahead in the race to build an oceangoing steamship and saw the opportunity to make an obscene profit by selling out his country," answered Wrexford.

But it isn't the past that matters at this moment—it is the present, he reminded himself. "Let us put those questions aside for now. We need to concentrate our efforts on studying the maps and figuring out exactly where the dastards are most likely to have gone to ground."

After a surreptitious glance at Charlotte, Henning began to fix himself a plate of food. "Take my medical advice, laddie. We'll have a better chance of doing that if we all have some sustenance and then get a few hours of sleep."

"I agree, and it makes sense for everyone to stay here," said McClellan. "The guest rooms off the north staircase are always kept ready for visitors. I'll show you to your quarters when we're done."

Wrexford was surprised to realize he was ravenous and joined the others in partaking of the cold beef, cheddar, and crusty bread that the maid had brought from the kitchen.

Simple but hearty fare, feeding the body, which in turn would help sustain the spirit.

He caught Charlotte watching him and gave her a private smile of encouragement.

"Eat something, my love," Wrexford counseled, seeing that she was merely crumbling a bit of bread between her fingers. "And then let me take you up to bed."

"Sleep would be ambrosial," she admitted. "Though I fear what nightmares may come to haunt me."

"I will stand watch over you and keep them at bay," he said, touching her cheek.

She covered his hand with hers.

"Oiy, oiy!" Raven broke free from the shadows of the corridor and skidded to a halt just inside the doorway, the other three boys right behind him.

"You had better not be here to beg for ginger biscuits," began McClellan, as she wagged a warning finger.

"To the devil with biscuits!" sputtered Raven, fighting to catch his breath. "You need to hear what Osprey just told us!"

Wrexford rose from his chair. "Come in, lad," he said, gesturing for Horatio to step into the aureole of light cast by the Argand lamp on his desktop.

Squaring his shoulders, the boy obeyed and snapped a military salute as he came to attention.

"At ease," said Wrexford, "and let us hear what you have to say."

Raven couldn't contain his excitement. "He may know where the villains are holding Aunt Alison!"

An instant of silence followed the announcement, and then everyone began asking questions.

"Quiet!" bellowed the earl. "Let the lad speak!"

To his credit, Horatio appeared unrattled, and Wrexford was suddenly reminded that despite his tender years, the boy was an officer in the Royal Navy and used to commanding tough-as-nails sailors.

"Please, go on."

"Yes, sir," replied the boy. "As I told the Weasels and Peregrine, I happened to overhear some private conversations that made me fear Colonel Jarvis was up to no good. However, as I had no proof, I didn't dare approach any of my superiors and confide my suspicions." He made a face. "He's the commanding officer of security, and I'm a lowly midshipman."

"That's understandable," responded Wrexford. "So . . ."

"So I decided to keep a careful watch on his activities and see if I might gather more evidence. I noticed that he occasionally took one of the rowing skiffs and crossed the river to Isle of Dogs, which lies just opposite the King's Dockyard. One early morning, when the fog was swirling enough to provide cover, I decided to follow him."

Isle of Dogs was one of the places suggested by Kurlansky, thought the earl as Horatio drew a deep breath.

"You see, I had watched him on several previous sojourns through my spyglass and knew what footpath he took. It was, perhaps, ungentlemanly of me to do so. But I told myself that if he was betraying his oath to our country, then it was my duty to learn the truth."

Charlotte had inched to the edge of her seat. "Quite right. And did you . . ." She swallowed hard. "Did you—"

"Did I see where Colonel Jarvis went?" finished Horatio. "Yes, milady, I did."

He looked back to the earl. "The colonel tied up his skiff east of the Ferry House and took a footpath that skirts along the tall reed beds that grow along the shoreline. There is an old, isolated brick warehouse near the water that looks to have been abandoned years ago. The colonel entered it—I saw with my spyglass that he had a key, so it seemed to me that he used it regularly. I didn't dare get too close, but I made up my mind that I would return at some point when I knew Jarvis had other duties and see what was inside."

A sound rumbled in Sheffield's throat.

"Don't rush the lad," said Wrexford, mentally saluting Horatio for being so observant.

"The thing is, sir, I haven't had a chance to go back yet. But it occurred to me that it may be where the miscreants are holding Auntie Peake."

"By God," muttered Wrexford as once again, everyone began to talk all at once.

"Wait—here's one other key piece of information you should all know!" The note of command in the midshipman's voice caught everyone's attention.

The room quieted at once.

Horatio's gaze was once again focused on the earl. "Milord, I know that you're aware of the Royal Navy's experiments with propeller-driven steamboats. One of our prototypes is kept at Isle of Dogs, in a secluded stretch of the shoreline just where the river takes a sharp bend upward after Greenwich Reach. The opposite shore is deserted, so it's a place where we can make test runs without drawing attention."

He drew in a hurried breath. "If Colonel Jarvis and his co-conspirators are looking to escape from England, the steamboat gives them a distinct advantage over traditional boats in the unpredictable eddies and tidal currents of the river as it opens into the sea."

"I think you're exactly right, Midshipman Porter." Wrexford acknowledged Horatio with his official title, no longer thinking of him as a mere boy. "It stands to reason that Jarvis will see his secret lair and prototype steamboat as all but guaranteeing his escape."

"And he thinks himself fiendishly clever in having a hostage," muttered Henning, "just in case his brilliant plan goes awry."

"Well, we are going to prove him wrong on all counts," said Sheffield. He looked expectantly at the earl. "So, Wrex, what—"

"Enough talking for now, Kit." Wrexford held out his hand to help Charlotte rise from her chair. "It's late, and we all need to be sharp for the coming confrontation. We'll reconvene just before first light and head to Isle of Dogs."

He cracked his knuckles. "Where we will rescue Alison and finally put an end to the villains and their horrific litany of murder and betrayal."

CHAPTER 29

Alison's silvery hair gleamed for an instant against the dark-as-Hades waves before the swirling current dragged her under—

Charlotte awoke with a scream quivering on her lips. A glance out the window showed that it was still dark. Still, she sat up in bed and pressed her palms to her brow, trying to get her bearings.

"I was going to let you sleep a little longer," came Wrexford's voice from the gloom of his dressing room. He moved out of the shadows, the glimmer of the waning moonlight catching the white of his dress shirt as he knotted a cravat around his upturned collar.

"You are looking very . . . lordly," she observed.

"As I have no official credentials to flaunt if questioned by anyone from the Royal Navy, I may have to depend on appearing every inch the aristocrat in order to convince Tilden to do as I ask." His jaw tightened. "But don't worry, no amount of well-tailored finery will constrict my ability to beat the miscreants at their evil game."

He took a seat on the side of the bed and studied her face. "A blow to the head is not to be taken lightly. How are you feeling?"

Like hell, thought Charlotte. But she wasn't about to admit it.

"It's an irrelevant question," she answered. "Surely you don't really think I would consent to stay in bed while Alison is in mortal danger."

A sigh. "It was worth a try," he said. "I was hoping against hope that the cudgel might have knocked some sense into you."

Softening his words with another sigh, he lifted her hand and brushed a kiss to her fingers. "Just promise me you won't attempt any heroics that are beyond your current capabilities. That could put you—and all of our loved ones—at risk."

Charlotte conceded the wisdom of his words with a reluctant smile. "I may be bullheaded at times, but I'm not a reckless idiot. In this particular situation, my heart will listen to my head." A tiny wince. "Which in all candor is feeling a trifle sore."

Before he could respond—or change his mind about the coming confrontation—Charlotte threw back the bedcovers and sat up. And felt a wave of dizziness. Taking a moment to steady herself, she gingerly swung her legs over the side.

Wrexford didn't miss her tiny grimace, but refrained from comment.

"I had better begin dressing," she said, the thought of McClellan's strong coffee a strong incentive to shake off her lethargy. The question was, what persona to assume?

The earl was apparently thinking the same thing. "It seems to me that you have two choices—assuming the role of the Countess of Wrexford or that of a street urchin." He smoothed the tails of his cravat into place. "In this particular situation, neither is ideal."

"I'm aware of that." Charlotte considered the dilemma. "If I accompany you as your wife, it corsets both of us in too many conventional rules of Polite Society."

"It would be a distraction," he agreed. "The Royal Navy would think me mad."

"And I would find silk skirts a cursed encumbrance if called upon to chase after the villains." She frowned. "However, I'm not quite sure that your having several street urchins tagging at your heels doesn't create just as many problems for you."

"Yes, I have been thinking about that, and I have an idea," answered Wrexford. "Dress as an urchin." He plucked up his coat from the back of the dressing-table chair. "I'll explain when you come down to the breakfast room."

Charlotte hurriedly donned a set of her well-worn rags—thank heaven there was no need to make herself presentable to appear in Polite Society—and smeared her face with a special soot-and-grease concoction that McClellan had created for her.

She stared at the grimy face reflected in the looking glass and added a few more smudges under her eyes.

"Like Tyler," she said to herself, "Mac is required to perform a number of awfully unconventional duties in this household."

After lacing up her boots and grabbing up her floppy hat, Charlotte made her way down to the breakfast room, where their inner circle was already assembled and partaking of a hearty breakfast.

Wrexford called for order as soon as she had filled her plate from the chafing dishes and taken a seat at the table. The first dappling of dawn was just beginning to tinge the horizon.

Light overpowering dark. Charlotte hoped it was a metaphor for the coming day.

"You had better have a plan," called Henning through a mouthful of shirred eggs. "Otherwise, I shall not be pleased about being roused at this godawful hour, despite the excellent breakfast."

"Hold your water, Baz," growled the earl, which set the four boys to giggling among themselves. However, his basilisk stare quickly silenced their hilarity.

The clink of cutlery also ceased.

"It seems that we finally hold the advantage over the villains," said Wrexford, "and we must make full use of it to strike before they take to the river and try to make their escape."

"What if . . ." began Sheffield, only to let the question trail off without finishing.

"Then we'll improvise," answered the earl. "Three carriages are waiting outside. We shall divide our forces . . ."

As Charlotte listened to him explain his strategy, the knot in her chest loosened. In the darkest depth of her heart, she had secretly admitted to herself that the chances of rescuing the dowager were not good. Jarvis was a cold-blooded killer . . .

But the Eel—Horatio had told them that Jarvis was called Eel by one of his henchmen—was now up against Wrexford.

And as the earl continued speaking, the odds suddenly seemed to be shifting in their favor.

Wrexford turned in a slow circle, surveying the cobbled courtyard and wharves of the King's Dockyard, where naught but the night sentries were on duty, waiting in yawning impatience for the change of the watch to happen and the daily activities to begin.

He had sent Horatio to change into his uniform before seeking to wake Samuel Tilden, the head of the research laboratory, and explain about Jarvis's treachery. The midshipman would gain them access to Tilden without delay. Then it was up to him to be convincing.

The earl's gaze drifted to the river, where pale skeins of mist were floating up from the swirling waters. He tried not to let doubts cloud his mind. The plan wasn't ideal, but they had been forced to move quickly. With luck, all the pieces would fall into place.

Luck. Wrexford much preferred to trust logic. But there had not been a choice. Drawing a deep breath, he made himself review his decisions, looking for any flaw.

Tyler had been dispatched to find Griffin in order to inform him about Jarvis and pass on Wrexford's request that the Runner bring a band of his cohorts to Isle of Dogs as soon as possible. Once there, they would join forces with Sheffield and his gang of urchins—which numbered four with Charlotte and Peregrine added to the Weasels.

Thank heaven Griffin had experienced how useful a band of ragged guttersnipes could be in keeping an enemy under surveillance, reflected the earl. The Runner wouldn't question their presence.

McClellan and Henning were waiting in the carriage just outside the walls of the King's Dockyard in case Alison required any medical attention after her ordeal as a hostage.

As for his own part—

The sudden clatter of hooves on the cobbles echoed like gunfire off the surrounding stone building. Thrusting a hand into his coat pocket, Wrexford gripped his pistol and whirled around.

"Lord Wrexford!" A rider, his wind-snarled garments coated with dust from a hard gallop, slid down from the saddle of his lathered stallion. "*Danke Gott.*" He tilted back his hat and wiped the sweat from his brow. "I feared that I might arrive too late."

The earl kept his weapon hidden but quietly thumbed back the hammer. "Too late for what, Herr von Münch?"

"To warn you about Colonel Jarvis!"

"Indeed?" Wrexford narrowed his eyes. "And what nefarious news have you miraculously discovered about him?"

For an instant, the librarian looked completely confused by the earl's sarcasm, and then his expression segued into one of shock. "*Gott in Himmel*, you think . . ."

He paused to wipe the dirt from his spectacles and place them back on the bridge of his nose. "You think me in league with the blackguards?"

"You have an ungodly knack of being the one to find the key information that my wife and I are searching for, and at just the opportune moment," he replied. "Why do you think that is?"

"Because the skills required to be a good scholar and historian make me an excellent sleuth," answered von Münch, his usual mild manner edged with a touch of fire. "Part of my work involves searching for clues in old documents in order to piece together a true and accurate story of some event in the past. I'm patient and meticulous, milord. I've learned to look at things and see connections that others might miss."

Wrexford felt his jaw tighten. As a man of science, he knew it was unwise to jump to conclusions based on circumstantial evidence.

And yet . . .

"You had mentioned that you were looking into the military officers who served in the same regiment as Greeley and your brother but so far had uncovered no connection. That got me to thinking," continued von Münch. "Your reasoning was sound, so I decided to dig a little deeper. It occurred to me that as Taviot was part of a diplomatic mission to the Peninsula, the delegation might also have included an army officer to represent the military's interests in any negotiations. So I did some research, and as my connection to King Frederick—and therefore to the British royal family—allowed me access to the necessary records, I discovered that Colonel Jarvis was indeed part of Taviot's delegation."

The explanation forced Wrexford to concede that he had been guilty of assuming that librarians were naught but musty scholars who lived in an abstract world of ideas and spent all their time with their noses buried in books.

"But the key clue came when I noticed that he had requested to move from the Foreign Office to serve as head of security for the Royal Navy laboratories at the King's Dockyard. Given all the evidence, it seemed to me that he must be in league with Taviot."

The librarian lifted his chin and locked eyes with Wrexford. "So I wanted to warn you without delay of the danger."

"It seems that I owe you an apology," began the earl, pausing as Horatio came running to join them.

"Lord Wrexford!" The midshipman, now dressed in his uniform, came to a halt and bobbed a bow. "I have some bad news! Mr. Tilden received an urgent summons from a sick family member yesterday afternoon and immediately departed for Yorkshire."

"Damnation," muttered Wrexford. "That seems a rather suspicious coincidence."

"I agree, sir," answered Horatio. "The thing is, Commodore Mather, the commanding officer here at the Dockyard, is a bit rigid and a stickler for going by the rule book. Without official orders from Horse Guards or the Admiralty directing him to cooperate with you, I fear we will spend the day trying to work through the military bureaucracy."

Wrexford swore again.

"But if I may be so bold as to make a suggestion, milord . . ." ventured Horatio.

"Fire away, Midshipman Porter."

"Well, sir, I command a unit of thirty men. And, um, I believe I've earned a modicum of loyalty from them by standing up on occasion to my superiors and arguing against disciplinary action for some trivial offense." Horatio glanced around at the deserted courtyard. "As you see, the bell has not rung awakening the dockyard to its daily duties. I could summon my men for an urgent security mission, and I don't think they would question my authority to do so. I could open the armory for weapons and dispatch a group of them to take two of the longboats and row you to Isle of Dogs, while I fire up our other prototype steamboat and—"

"Do it," interrupted Wrexford. "And quickly."

Horatio pointed to one of the jetties. "Wait there, sir," he said, and then sprinted away toward the barracks.

"You know where the villains are hiding?" asked von Münch.

"Yes," answered the earl. He gave a rapid-fire account of what had happened the previous evening.

"Your wife was injured, and Lady Peake has been taken prisoner?" The librarian's expression hardened. "I'll come with you. You may need someone to watch your back."

"I appreciate your courage," replied Wrexford, "but have you ever actually handled a firearm?"

"It seems you are making another assumption about librarians and our practical skills, milord." A twinkle gleamed behind the lenses of von Münch's spectacles. "As a matter of fact, my father was a champion marksman and won many shooting competitions in Württemberg." He drew a pistol from his pocket. "I've been honing my skills since I was a boy and consider myself a decent shot."

Spotting an empty bottle perched atop one of the pilings at the river's edge, he pointed it out to the earl, then took dead aim and squeezed the trigger.

Wrexford watched the glass explode in a shower of shards and allowed a grim smile. "Reload your bloody pistol and come with me."

The sound of a muffled *bang* from the other side of the river made Charlotte flinch. "That sounded like a pistol shot," she whispered, shifting closer to Sheffield within their hiding place among the tall reeds.

They both held themselves very still. To Charlotte, the pounding of her heart sounded louder than cannon fire as they strained to hear anything more through the rustling of the breeze.

"It's a naval dockyard," reasoned Sheffield, after a lengthy interlude of quiet. "There are any number of reasons for loud noises—the crack of a mast, barrels falling from the storage racks." He gave a reassuring pat to her shoulder. "Let us not imagine trouble. We need to keep our focus on where they are holding Alison prisoner."

Charlotte nodded, knowing he was right. Drawing a calming breath, she turned to peer through the tall reeds at the isolated building, its dark brick half obscured by the scrim of ghostly mist drifting in from the unseen river. From this distance, it looked as if it had been deserted for years.

Despite Sheffield's encouragement, her doubts refused to settle.

What if we are wrong? The question made her stomach start to churn.

Sheffield seemed to sense her anxiety. "Don't worry. Both logic and intuition tell us that they are here," he said. "The Weasels are creeping close and will get a look through the windows."

Another spurt of fear. "I should have gone with them."

"That would not have been wise," he countered. "They are still small enough to look like harmless little mudlarks. Even if they are spotted, they won't stir any alarm. Children are often seen along the river's edge, searching for any flotsam and jetsam that can been sold."

Charlotte knew he was right, but that didn't settle her nerves. So much could go wrong.

Sheffield checked his pocket watch. "Wrexford should have

finished arrangements with Tilden to dispatch an armed contingent of sailors to surround the house and cut off any access to the prototype steamboat moored at the Royal Navy's secret shed." He turned to Peregrine, who was crouched behind them. "Make your way to the road, and meet them at the landing area described by Horatio."

The boy nodded.

"And guide Wrex back to us while Tilden and Horatio move their men into position."

As Peregrine crept away, Charlotte looked down and began picking at a thread on her sleeve.

Reaching out, Sheffield stilled her fingers. "I know you are worried—"

"I'm not worried," she interjected. "I'm terrified."

"We all are," he replied. "We will get her back because . . ." He stared at the brick building. "Because we all simply refuse to believe otherwise."

That drew a shadow of a smile from Charlotte. "And heaven forfend that the forces of the cosmos dare defy our wishes."

"Precisely." He exaggerated a grimace. "Because that would mean they would have to face Wrex when he's in a truly foul mood."

Charlotte wouldn't have thought it possible, but a whispery laugh rose up in her throat. "Thank you, Kit."

"Well, you have to admit, when push comes to shove, we do manage to pull each other's cods out of the fire."

"Amen to that," she responded.

A rustling in the reeds cut off any further banter. Like a shadow flitting through the gloom, Raven appeared a moment later, followed by Hawk.

"The villains are there," he confirmed. "They have Aunt Alison tied to a chair."

Charlotte released a sigh of relief.

"With *very* thick rope," added Hawk with a scowl.

"S'all right," muttered Raven. "We'll have her free in a trice once Wrex arrives."

"Does she appear to be holding up under such duress?' asked Charlotte. "Did she look frightened?'

Raven and Hawk exchanged sniggers. "Actually, she looked hopping mad," said Raven.

"She called Colonel Jarvis a very bad name," added Hawk. "But she said it in French, so he might not have understood the insult."

Charlotte considered that nugget of information, which prompted yet another question. "Since when do you know how to swear in French?"

"Aunt Alison has been teaching us," admitted Raven. "She says a gentleman of the world should be able to curse in at least a half a dozen languages."

"We are learning Italian next," offered Hawk.

After swallowing a cough—or perhaps it had been a laugh—Sheffield changed the subject. "How many enemies are in the building?"

"Colonel Jarvis, Lord Taviot, two nasty-looking ruffians, and a fancy lady who doesn't appear pleased with the situation," answered Raven.

"It has to be Lady Kirkwall," said Charlotte. "Clearly she is in league with her brother, as she helped orchestrate the attack on me." Still, despite all the evidence to the contrary, something rubbed her wrong about thinking of the lady as purely evil.

"Bloody hell, how did I not see the darkness of her heart?" muttered Sheffield.

"I don't think it's that black and white, Kit," she responded. "Though I can't explain why."

They lapsed into an uneasy silence as the sun slowly peeked through the early morning clouds. For Charlotte, the minutes seemed to slide by with agonizing slowness. But at last she heard the squelch of steps through the marshland and turned to see Peregrine and Wrexford approaching.

"Thank heavens," she whispered, only to realize that another hazy shape was right behind them.

Von Münch.

Recalling Wrexford's suspicions and the earlier *bang*, her split-second reaction was to reach for her pistol. But the earl's face betrayed no sense of alarm, so she moved to take cover behind Raven and Hawk. Whatever the reason for von Münch's presence, the less he saw of her, the better.

Sheffield gave voice to her own question. "What's the librarian doing here?" he asked tersely as Wrexford crouched down beside him.

"Reinforcements," came the answer as the earl surveyed the brick building and its surroundings. "It turns out Herr von Münch is a crack shot. As to why he's here, he discovered how Jarvis fit into this pernicious puzzle and came to warn us."

Charlotte received a second surprise as McClellan suddenly materialized from the lingering fog.

"Oh—and Mac convinced me that she ought to be part of the rescue party. Having another steady finger on the trigger is a prudent precaution."

"Baz would have insisted on coming, too, but he's not moving well these days," added McClellan. "And while he's an expert with a scalpel, he concedes that he's not very skilled with a firearm."

The librarian looked bemused. "Yours is a rather unusual household, Lord Wrexford."

"That is one way of putting it."

"I'm rather surprised your wife didn't come along," added von Münch.

"That would cause a great scandal in Society if word got out," replied the earl. "One must have a care about such things."

"Yes, of course."

Wrexford looked away from the building to the swath of reeds closer to the river's edge. "Getting back to the rescue plans, Horatio's men are moving into position and will cut off any access to the prototype steamboat. Once I get the signal, we shall approach the building and take the villains by surprise."

Charlotte saw von Münch glance at her and the Weasels. "I can't help but be curious, milord. Why the band of, er, . . ." He paused, as if searching for words.

"Urchins?" suggested Sheffield. "Wrex and I have, shall we say, established a working relationship with a trusted group of them. They make excellent scouts and messengers."

The librarian nodded thoughtfully. "Clever." His gaze seemed to linger on her for a heartbeat . . . and then another. "But how—"

"Never mind that now," growled Wrexford. He turned to Raven. "How many doors into the building? Where are they, and which one is the best way to gain entrance without being spotted?"

Raven responded with a detailed report.

"Hmmph." Sitting back on his haunches, the earl considered what he had just heard.

Charlotte reached up to adjust the tilt of her floppy hat, managing to catch his eye just for an instant. The connection, however fleeting, stirred an inward smile. It was, she knew, irrational to think he was invincible.

But her fears seemed to flutter off with the rising breeze.

Wrexford must have spied the signal from Horatio's men, for he drew his pistols. "Time for us to move. Raven, you go with Herr von Münch and cover the rear exit. But don't take any action unless you hear me give the hoot of a barn owl." He thought for an instant. "Or unless all hell breaks loose. Then you have permission to improvise."

Raven nodded in understanding.

"Sheffield, Hawk, Mac, and Magpie . . . You four come with me," he continued. To Peregrine he added, "You circle around to the sailors and inform them that we're heading for the building."

Snick, snick. He cocked his weapons. "Move quietly, everyone—and quickly."

A pause. "I daresay the dowager is yearning for a cup of Mac's excellent coffee and a decent breakfast."

CHAPTER 30

Taking the lead, the Weasels picked a path through the swaying reeds. Once they had covered half the distance to the building, Raven turned and indicated that von Münch should follow him in cutting around to the left.

Once the two of them had disappeared in the marshland growth, Wrexford moved around to Charlotte's side. Their hands clasped together, but only for a moment. He dared not risk any further distraction. "Let us give them a few minutes to get into place before continuing."

"Is there any problem?" she asked as they waited. "We thought we heard a gunshot."

"Our mild-manned librarian was simply proving his mettle," he replied. "It appears your instincts were right."

He checked the area before getting back to the task at hand. "Tilden was called away yesterday afternoon—quite likely a ruse by Jarvis to confuse the chain of command at the King's Dockyard. However, he underestimated Midshipman Porter." A wry smile. "Who, by the by, is already a very fine naval officer."

"So Horatio has led his men here—" she began.

"Not precisely," answered the earl. "Horatio put his bosun in charge of the sailors who will guard the boathouse where the villains have moored the steam-powered prototype. He and I decided that as a further precaution, he would take command of the second prototype steamboat, which is kept in the laboratory boathouse, and lie in wait near the top of the river's bend, just in case the villains manage to slip through our net."

Seeing Charlotte go white as a ghost, he hastily added, "But I don't expect it will come to that."

"Nor do I." She raised a brow at Mac. "And you? You didn't think we could handle this on our own?"

McClellan's lips twitched. "I figured that someone ought to stay and tend to the dowager in case you two went haring off after the villains." She turned to Wrexford with a challenging stare. "Whatever negotiations you are planning to make, milord, I don't imagine you are planning on letting them evade justice."

"Correct." Though said softly, the word had the ring of steel.

The mist was beginning to blow off, but the hazy sun had yet to warm the salty chill from the air.

"Time to move," he announced.

With Hawk showing them the way, they followed in single file and threaded through the shadows of a glade of scrubby trees to reach the side of the house.

"The anteroom opens into the main room through a doorway on the left," whispered Hawk. "That's where they are holding Aunt Alison."

"Stay out here, lad, and keep watch. Trill like a sparrow if anyone approaches." Wrexford pressed a finger to his lips, a signal for everyone to stay silent, and then motioned for Charlotte and the others to follow.

On reaching the outer door, he slowly eased the latch open. A furtive look inside showed the unlit anteroom was deserted and shrouded with shadows.

So far, their luck was holding.

Wrexford slipped inside and motioned for his companions to join him. A few terse gestures indicated how he wanted to array his forces. He and Sheffield would step out of the gloom together, with Charlotte and McClellan aligned behind them, guarding their flanks.

He could hear the buzz of voices from the main room.

An argument?

Discord among the miscreants would only work in his favor.

After another hand signal, indicating that he would reconnoiter on his own, Wrexford crept toward the far end of the anteroom and angled a look around the corner.

A flutter of white. With a trembling hand, Taviot blotted his forehead with a silk handkerchief.

"Why me?" he whined. "Why don't *you* stay here while *I* and our men move the cases of money and letters of credit to the boat? You're better with a knife than I am." Taviot glanced at Alison. "Why not just be done with it? We don't need a hostage anymore, and a blade to the throat will finally silence the infernal Dragon."

Alison replied with a word—in English—no highborn lady should know.

Jarvis laughed, a sound that made Wrexford's skin crawl. But with the two ruffians standing next to several overstuffed leather satchels and Taviot positioned just behind the chair to which the dowager was tied, he dared not twitch a muscle.

"You really do have a filthy mouth, Lady Peake," said the colonel. "Enjoy breathing fire while you can." To Taviot, he continued, "It behooves us to keep her alive a little longer. Once we reach the Russian frigate, she will have served her purpose."

Lady Kirkwall made a sound in her throat as she rose from the crate on which she was sitting. "For God's sake—"

"My dear Elizabeth, surely by now, you know that I don't believe in God," said Jarvis, and added another laugh that resonated with pure evil.

"Aye, I know all too well that the only thing you worship is your own self-interest," retorted Lady Kirkwall, her voice shaking.

"A little late to be getting a conscience, isn't it?" sneered Jarvis. "You're up to your lovely neck in all this." He gave a lazy wave of his hand. "So sit down and stay quiet."

Gritting her teeth, Taviot's sister did as she was told.

"As for you, Taviot, the reason you must stay here and keep guard over the dowager is because I'm the one who knows how to fire up the steamboat and make it ready for our escape. And I need our two men to get the boiler stoked. So unless you are skilled in how the boat runs, shut your mouth and keep a close watch on the Dragon."

He angled a look out one of the small windows. "Stay alert. It's getting light, and there's a chance that officious little midshipman will take it upon himself to make an extra patrol of the isle."

"You were careless to let him spot your skullduggery with the steam engine," muttered Taviot.

Still, he grudgingly moved even closer to Alison's chair. A blade of sunlight flashed off steel as he raised his knife and waggled it near the dowager's throat. "Not another word or movement, you meddlesome bitch. I don't know how they came to know of it, but your niece and her damnable husband have cost me a fortune with their probing into ancient history. So if you give me the tiniest provocation—"

"Hold your nerve," warned Jarvis. "Give us a half hour to make things ready, and then follow along with the three of them."

It was only then that Wrexford saw Maitland sitting apart from the others, barely visible within the gloom of the storage alcove.

"I—I don't want to go to Russia," muttered the inventor.

"You would rather rot in Newgate Prison for the rest of your life?" asked Jarvis. "We've left papers in Taviot's townhouse that make you appear the ringleader of the consortium's fraudulent scheme." A pause. "As well as the murderer of poor Neville Greeley, so that you could obtain the da Vinci manuscript and convince your investors that you had discovered some momentous mechanical secret that would change the world."

"I knew nothing about your nefarious plan!"

"I doubt that the authorities will think that your protests ring true."

Shoulders slumping, Maitland made no reply.

Jarvis looked around with a supremely smug smile. "Well, now that you all understand the situation clearly, let us prepare to take our leave of jolly old England. There are plenty of Russian pigeons waiting to be plucked."

With that, Jarvis and his two cohorts hefted the satchels and headed for the rear exit, where a footpath led down to the river.

Wrexford had heard enough to formulate his next moves. He retreated to where Charlotte and the others were waiting.

"Jarvis and his two henchmen are heading to the boat, where I assume the sailors will apprehend him," he whispered. "We'll move in shortly to negotiate with Taviot. Hawk, go tell Raven and von Münch to be alert. Taviot can't be allowed to abscond with Alison—and I don't care whether that means blowing his brains out."

The boy dashed away.

Wrexford silently counted off five minutes, then motioned for them to move.

* * *

Wrapping her fingers around the pocket pistol hidden in her tattered jacket, Charlotte took up her appointed position behind the earl and Sheffield. Every fiber of her being was crying for action, but she knew that one errant step could prove fatal.

Patience, she reminded herself. A quality that she usually possessed in spades. And yet it was her fault that Alison was in danger—be damned with Wrexford's argument to the contrary—and until the dowager was safe . . .

Wrexford slowed and lightened his already soundless tread as he approached the doorway, snapping her attention back to the present moment.

A flicker of sunlight after the darkness made her blink, but in the next instant the main room came into focus.

Taviot had already grown restless with his guard duties. Shuffling from foot to foot, he kept glancing at the passageway to the rear door. "I don't see why we can't wait at the boathouse while they get the engine's boiler heated up," he groused. "What if they are double-crossing us and mean to flee on their own?"

Lady Kirkwall heaved an exasperated sigh. "They aren't. The same thought occurred to me, my dear brother. But it did so early enough for me to negotiate with Jarvis. He left Maitland here—and as he is the key reason Russia is willing to offer sanctuary, the colonel won't leave without us."

"Actually, none of you will be leaving unless you agree to free the dowager," announced Wrexford as he and Sheffield suddenly moved out of the doorway, weapons at full cock.

Quick as a snake, Taviot reacted by cowering behind Alison's chair and angling his blade a mere hairsbreadth from her neck. "Don't move another step, or I swear I'll slit her throat."

"And at the first spurt of blood you'll be a dead man," replied the earl calmly. "As you see, you have more than one pistol pointed at your worthless carcass, and more than one finger just itching for a reason to pull the trigger."

He allowed a pause. "However, I'm willing to negotiate."

Taviot wet his lips. "What do you have in mind?"

"Simply release her, and you have my word as a gentleman that we won't stop you from leaving."

"Ha! The word of a gentleman isn't worth any more than the spit and breath that forms it."

"Not everyone is a soulless reptile who gladly slithers through the blood of others if it will bring him some profit," replied Wrexford.

"Take the deal, Fenwick," Lady Kirkwall counseled her brother. She sounded weary beyond words. "Enough violence has been done. I trust Lord Wrexford to keep his oath."

"You've gone soft in the head," snarled Taviot. "I need a better guarantee than that."

"Very well," answered the earl. "I'll allow you to retreat with the dowager to the rear door. Leave her there, and you are free to make your escape." To Lady Kirkwall and Maitland, he added, "I don't give a rat's arse about you two. Go or stay as you choose."

Taviot hesitated.

"Otherwise, we are at a standoff," said Wrexford, turning his attention back to Alison's captor. "And I doubt Jarvis will wait very long for you to appear before steaming away to safety."

Sweat was now beading on Taviot's brow. "H-How do I know that you won't come after me if I do what you ask?"

"Because," said the earl, "you're not worth the bit of lead it would take to put a period to your existence." He let silence linger between them before adding, "If I were you, I would listen to your sister. The longer you stay here, the greater the chances of the authorities arriving. And I doubt they will be as generous as I am in offering you a chance to escape."

The knife blade, noted Charlotte, quivered as Taviot's nerves began to fray. In contrast, Alison was sitting very still with an air of unruffled composure.

"Get up, Lady Peake."

"To do so, I shall need the aid of my cane," replied Alison, her voice a bit faint. "My legs aren't as steady as they used to be, and this ordeal has taken a toll on my strength."

"Give it to her, Elizabeth," ordered Taviot.

Lady Kirkwall picked up the cane from atop a pile of crates and brought it over.

"T-Thank you," said the dowager, twisting the stick between her tied hands as she cleared her throat with a cough.

Charlotte tensed as she thought that she heard a tiny metallic click. Wrexford's expression remained unchanged, so perhaps she had been mistaken. Still, she kept her eyes riveted on Taviot. *What mischief is he planning?*

"Now, on your feet, Lady Peake." Taviot punctuated his order with a shake to Alison's shoulder.

"Undo her bonds, Fenwick!" snapped Lady Kirkwall. "You have her tied to the chair."

Taviot sucked in a nervous breath. "Lower your weapon, Wrexford—and you, too, Sheffield." His hand was shaking as he changed the angle of his blade. "I need to use my knife to cut away the ropes."

"Let us all remain calm," replied Wrexford as he complied and signaled for Sheffield to do the same.

Gulping in a ragged breath, Taviot sliced through the dowager's bonds, careful to keep her as a shield so that the earl had no chance of taking a shot at him.

A craven coward as well as a traitor and swindler, thought Charlotte in disgust. She had encountered some truly evil people in the course of her previous investigations, but Taviot's crimes touched a raw nerve. Thoughts of violence were normally abhorrent to her, but she found herself gripped by a sudden visceral desire to see his blood spilled.

"I'll need you to untie my hands so I can use my cane," said Alison.

"Ye gods, I'll do it." Lady Kirkwall was still standing beside the chair. Leaning down, she worked the knots free, allowing the rope to drop to the stone flaggings, and helped the dowager stand. But rather than step away, she fixed her brother with an implacable stare.

"Enough, Fenwick." As the whisper slipped from her lips, she tried to seize the hand holding the knife.

Taviot recoiled and managed to push her away. But the move had him off-balance for an instant—

A flash of steel! Charlotte eyes widened in shock as Alison twisted the knob of her cane and drew a thin steel sword from its ebony sheath.

Merciful heavens!

But before she could react, the dowager deftly executed a fencing two-step and evaded Taviot's attempt to grab her.

Panicked, he lunged again.

Scooting back, Alison calmly stabbed him in the thigh and watched him fall to the floor, howling like a stuck pig.

For the next few moments, everything was a blur. Charlotte rushed to pull Alison to safety, Wrexford hurried to kick the fallen knife away from Taviot's grasp, while Sheffield and McClellan raised their weapons to cover Lady Kirkwall and Maitland.

"Do something, Elizabeth!" screamed Taviot.

Lady Kirkwall slowly shook her head, her expression one of grim resolve. "No. It's time to put an end to this madness, Fenwick. No more lies and prevarications. I intend to confess everything about what you and I have done."

She closed her eyes for an instant. "I have sold my soul to protect the family name from scandal, only to find that the road to perdition is indeed a slippery slope. We have committed great evil and must pay—"

A gunshot rent the air, followed a fraction later by a second one.

Lady Kirkwall crumpled to the floor, shot by her brother.

"Damnation—I saw Taviot draw his pocket pistol, but he fired at his sister before I could react," exclaimed McClellan, as she tossed aside her smoking weapon—she had, Charlotte noted, been the one to shoot Taviot—and rushed to tend to Lady Kirkwall.

Charlotte kept tight hold of Alison. "Is she . . ."

"She's taken a bullet to the belly," answered McClellan. She tugged off her shawl and pillowed it under the wounded lady's head. "We need to send for Baz—immediately!"

"I'll go," volunteered von Münch. He and the Weasels had rushed into the room at the sound of gunfire. "The sailors will be more likely to take orders from me than from your urchins."

"Make haste," replied Wrexford, crouching down beside Taviot. "Kit, you had better go with him and explain to the officer in charge of the King's Dockyard what is going on."

As Sheffield and the librarian hurried away to recross the river, Charlotte settled Alison back in the chair, and the Weasels rushed to form a protective ring around her.

With myriad questions colliding inside her head, Charlotte hardly knew where to begin. *First things first*, she decided. "Is the miscreant dead?" she asked, keeping her voice pitched too low for Maitland to hear her.

"Yes." Wrexford looked up from examining Taviot's body. "The bullet pierced his sin-black heart."

"One fewer devil treading this earth," murmured Charlotte. A harsh sentiment perhaps, but she couldn't muster a grain of sympathy for such a thoroughly despicable man.

Wrexford rose. "But an even worse one is still at large."

Charlotte knew what he was going to say. And though it frightened her to death, she could not—she would not try to—stop him.

"And you're going after him."

"I am," he replied.

She nodded, not trusting her voice.

He rose and went to take hold of Maitland. "For now, I feel beholden to lock you in the storage alcove until the authorities arrive."

The inventor uttered no protest as Wrexford marched him to the far end of the room, where a door with a sturdy lock stood half-open. Head bowed, Maitland entered the darkened space. The earl turned the key and tossed it to Charlotte.

She pocketed it and followed him out the back door.

"I—I could come with you," she stammered, catching him in a fierce hug.

"You need to stay here with Alison," he replied. "And I think you know in your heart that this is something I must do on my own."

"Be careful," Charlotte whispered.

"Have no fear, my love." He brushed a kiss to her brow before turning for the river. "Lucifer and all his legions couldn't stop me from catching Jarvis and seeing that he's finally made to answer for all his crimes."

CHAPTER 31

"Oiy!" called Raven as the earl edged out the doorway. "I should come with you—in case you need me to run messages."

Wrexford halted. With luck, Horatio's band of sailors had already apprehended Jarvis, and it would simply be a matter of escorting the prisoner back to the King's Dockyard and turning him over to the proper authorities. However, he didn't underestimate the colonel. Jarvis had proved himself to be awfully cunning in the past, and a predator was always at its most dangerous when cornered.

"Very well," he said, deciding there was some merit to the suggestion.

Raven raced past him and had reached the reeds before the earl could have any second thoughts.

Once they were on the footpath leading to the river, Wrexford quickened his steps to catch up with the boy.

"Not so fast, Weasel. We need to make a few things clear between us."

Raven released a harried sigh. "I know what you're going to tell me, sir."

"You're right, it should go without saying. Nonetheless, I shall do so anyway."

Up ahead, a glint of sunlight reflected off the dark water, the rush of incoming tide stirring a swirling pattern of whitecaps and currents.

"You must do exactly as I say, without hesitation," he continued. "Give me your promise on that, or else turn around and return to the others."

A flicker of rebellion in the boy's eyes gave way to a grudging nod. "I understand, Wrex." He made a face. "Though I damn well don't like it."

The earl repressed a smile. "I don't expect you to like it. But I do expect you to obey my orders."

"Oiy."

"Thank you." Catching sight of a blue naval coat among the reeds, Wrexford veered off the path and called a soft hail to the sailor.

"Lord Wrexford!" The sailor snapped a salute. "The prototype steamboat wasn't in the boathouse when we arrived. It must have been moved to a different mooring place. Bosun White has us guarding the perimeter while he has gone to signal Midshipman Porter that it is missing."

As he feared, Jarvis had been clever enough to take precautions so the Royal Navy would not be able to interfere with his escape.

"We thought we heard an engine firing up in the next cove," added the sailor. "But we didn't dare make a move without orders from Midshipman Porter."

"You did the right thing," replied the earl. "Now, take me to Bosun White."

"Aye, sir." The sailor slung his musket over his shoulder and set off at fast clip.

As he followed, Wrexford began to calculate how big a head start Jarvis had. It was a complex equation of factors. *The river currents, the competing engines, navigational skills* . . . it would all come down to which boat possessed the right combination of power and an experienced hand on the helm.

The path broke free of the reeds and brought them to the river's edge. Raven let out a shrill whistle on seeing Horatio standing in the stern of a low-slung boat with a smokestack in its middle belching clouds of pale vapor.

The thump of pistons floated across the water, as the engine idled and a set of hemp ropes held by sailors on the shore kept the vessel moored close to shore.

Horatio waved for Wrexford and Raven to approach. "Jarvis has perhaps a ten-minute head start," he called. "I saw with my spyglass that he didn't have Auntie Peake as his prisoner, so I decided to wait for you and your orders. Is she—"

"The dowager is safe and unharmed," replied Wrexford as he shaded his eyes, and surveyed the river. "Have we any hope of catching him?"

Because of Kurlansky's promise, he wasn't worried about Jarvis receiving sanctuary on the Russian frigate. However, smuggling and all manner of illicit activities were rife along this stretch of the river. There were any number of ways for someone to lose himself among the harbors and wharves.

And Jarvis had proved himself slippery as an eel at evading capture for his many sins.

The question drew a small smile from Horatio. "I've been running test trials in these waters for weeks with this prototype, and Mr. Tilden and I have been tinkering with the engine and recently installed a larger propeller. So yes, we'll catch him." He gave a fond pat to the hull of his boat. "And that's a promise, milord. So hurry and climb aboard."

Wrexford began pulling off his boots. "Find Griffin and his men." He gave Raven directions to the spot chosen for the rendezvous. "Have them go to the King's Dockyard and wait there for my return."

Raven cast a longing look at the steamboat but then turned and darted off, a quicksilver blur that was soon lost in the shadows of the reeds.

"Prepare to cast off!" called Horatio to the sailors holding the ropes that tethered them to their comrades on shore.

Holding his pistols high overhead, Wrexford waded into the water and was pulled on board by a host of willing hands.

"Now stoke the boilers!" ordered Horatio, taking charge of the ship's wheel. "The hunt is on!"

Charlotte returned to the others, fighting to keep her emotions in check. Jarvis was a cunning and merciless killer.

But Wrexford is Wrexford, she reminded herself.

Somehow the thought was comforting enough to let her push aside her fears and deal with the drama unfolding inside the abandoned storage building.

"Are you sure that you are not hurt?" Crouching down, she pulled Alison into a gentle hug, as there was no longer any need to maintain her masquerade as a street-tough urchin employed by the earl. She sensed that Lady Taviot was not a threat . . .

"No need to fuss," assured the dowager. "I am quite well."

"Excellent—then I won't hesitate to ring a peal over your head for taking such an awful risk," said Charlotte. "But that must wait for a moment—as must a great many questions." She cast a glance behind her. "I had better help Mac."

"Go," whispered Alison. "What a terrible thing to happen," she added with a compassionate sigh. "But Evil begets evil."

Lady Kirkwall had indeed chosen a dark path, but it seemed that a glimmer of right versus wrong had still remained alight in her heart.

After a quick squeeze to the dowager's hands, Charlotte joined McClellan, who was kneeling beside Lady Kirkwall.

The maid had fetched Taviot's fallen knife and used it to cut away the clothing around the gunshot wound. She had also used it to slice some of her underskirts into strips of cloth to stanch the bleeding, but as Charlotte leaned closer and peeked beneath the padding, it was clear that the situation was not good.

Looking up, she saw McClellan's eyes reflecting the same grim assessment.

"I-Is there perchance any water?" Lady Kirkwall's breathing was growing more labored. "I—I find myself thirsty."

"There's a flask of brandy in my cloak pocket," murmured McClellan, nodding to where her garment lay atop one of the crates.

Charlotte rushed to fetch it. Brandy was even better than water, as it would dull the pain.

"Thank you," whispered Lady Kirkwall, after Charlotte had gently lifted her head and helped her swallow a sip. "I don't deserve your kindness, Lady Wrexford." Catching Charlotte's flicker of surprise, she managed a wry smile. "My appreciation of painted portraits has made me skilled at looking at faces."

Charlotte helped Lady Kirkwall take another sip.

"My sins . . ." A cough wracked her chest.

"None of us are without sin," said Charlotte, keeping Lady Kirkwall's shoulders cradled in her lap. "You have repented, so allow your soul to take solace in that." Small comfort, perhaps. But Lady Kirkwall was not a monster, and her last lonely moments on this earth should not be ones of utter despair.

"Again, your kindness . . ." She gestured for another sip of brandy. "Lean closer," she whispered. "I—I wish to explain some things. I am aware that Wrexford has suffered greatly from the actions of my family—"

"Don't try to talk now," counseled Charlotte. "You must save your strength. A surgeon will be here shortly."

Lady Kirkwall twitched her lips in a cynical smile. "We both know my strength will soon be gone. A confession may do us both some good."

"We are listening, milady," said McClellan as she changed the blood-soaked pads and resumed putting pressure on the wound.

A flutter of lashes. The lady winced and narrowed her eyes. "You—you look familiar. Do I know you?"

"Yes, I was once mistress of the female servants at Taviot Castle," replied the maid.

"The one who disappeared the night of my half-brother's death?"

McClellan nodded.

"We all assumed you killed him. The wound to his head could not have been caused by the fall."

"I did, milady."

Silence. And then a sigh. "With good reason. I am not unaware of his depravity." She swallowed hard. "Indeed, it lies at the root of all the ensuing evil. If I had not been so proud of our family reputation . . ."

Lady Kirkwall gave a weak wave. "My younger brother had run up enormous debts, and to save the family name from scandal, I embezzled money from my husband's business interests—I am quite skilled in finance—to cover the debts. I intended to replace the money, but his partners became suspicious before I could do so. I made the mistake of telling Jarvis and my brother of it—"

"How did you come to be involved with Jarvis?" asked Charlotte.

"He and Fenwick—that is, Taviot—had become fast friends at one of those hideously sadistic boarding schools where the aristocracy sends its sons to make them men." A cough. "It makes some of them monsters."

McClellan took the lady's hand and began to chafe some warmth into her flesh.

"With my brother's aristocratic connections and Jarvis's genius for scheming, they formed a lucrative partnership." She made a face. "For a time, I became besotted with Jarvis. My marriage was loveless, and his aura of danger was seductive. We became . . ."

"Romantically involved?" suggested Charlotte.

A wry laugh. "That is putting it politely. But yes, and so I confided my predicament to him and my brother. Jarvis said he would solve it." The memory seemed to send a spasm of pain through her body. "He murdered my husband and contrived to make it look like suicide. It saved me and the Taviot name from ruin." A grimace. "Oh, but at what a cost!"

Tears beaded on Lady Kirkwall's lashes. "You see, he had the evidence of my wrongdoing. And from then on, my brother and I were in thrall to all his evil plans." A pause. "Not that my brother needed much coercion. He loved money more than honor."

Wanting very much to learn the truth for Wrexford, Charlotte seized the opportunity to press for answers. "We have discovered that your brother and Jarvis saw an opportunity to make a fortune betraying Britain when Taviot was appointed to a diplomatic delegation tasked with assessing our country's military situation in the Peninsula," she explained. "Though our sources say the plan was Jarvis's alone, and that he duped your brother into sending coded messages containing British military information."

"I wish that were so," responded Lady Kirkwall, her voice growing fainter. "But no, Jarvis and Fenwick were clever enough to create enough smoke screens, as it were, to obscure their evil doings. They were both equally guilty."

Charlotte felt both relief and disgust at finally knowing the truth about the past. As for the present . . .

"I'm going to fetch Maitland," she said. "I know Wrexford has some questions concerning recent events, so I would like to ask the two of you about the consortium. However, as I don't wish to reveal my real identity to him, I shall disguise my voice—"

"Your secret is safe with me," assured Lady Kirkwall.

Charlotte fetched the inventor, and Hawk moved a barrel from the shadows to serve as a seat for him.

"Wrexford wishes to know the details of how the consortium's sophisticated plan for defrauding investors of their money came into being," she announced in a low, raspy voice.

"The irony is . . ." A rattling cough cut short Lady Kirkwall's reply.

McClellan's gaze turned grim. Time appeared to be fast slipping away.

But, rallying her strength, Taviot's sister managed to continue. "The irony is, this scheme was actually started as a legitimate venture. Jarvis had some training in steam engine technology and had been following the development of steamboats in America. When he heard that Maitland—a leading innovator in the field—had returned to England, he saw the opportunity to make a fortune by developing an oceangoing propulsion system and selling it to the government for its navy."

As the lady gasped for breath, Maitland ventured to speak up. "I—I never intended there to be any fraud. I truly believed I had made great innovations with a propeller design and could build a workable system. When Jarvis and Taviot came to me and offered to fund my research, as well as give me shares in the company that would make me a very rich man, I jumped at the chance."

"So what happened?" asked McClellan.

"The propeller prototype works," answered Maitland. "But I haven't yet figured out the optimum size and precise curves needed to propel a large ship through rough ocean waters." A sigh. "And I still haven't hit upon the right design for a steam engine capable of crossing vast oceans. Firstly, it had to be powerful enough to propel a ship through bad weather. And even more importantly, it needed to be efficient enough for a ship to be able to carry enough fuel for long voyages."

Maitland made a face. "I kept telling myself that the answer was there, just out of reach, and that I simply needed to think harder—and be given more time and money—in order to grab it." He fisted his hands in his lap. "And so I let myself be seduced by Jarvis's suggestion that we keep pretending that we were making great progress. I—I suppose that I came to believe my own lies."

"Jarvis can be very seductive," rasped Lady Kirkwall.

"We know the da Vinci manuscript was going to be a grand revelation at your gala reception. It's a rare and arcane item—how did the consortium come to know about it—and then to steal it?" growled Charlotte.

"I knew of it from my Oxford days, as I was a student in Balliol College. I thought it a clever idea . . ." Maitland's expression turned to one of self-loathing. "Until Jarvis calmly announced that he had stolen it and made sure that Neville Greeley would never tell a soul about the theft." He pressed his palms to his brow. "You must believe me, I had no inkling of the depths of his depravity until then. I swore to myself that I would somehow free myself from his clutches." A shuddering sigh. "But I was too cowardly to act."

"You are not the only one," whispered Lady Kirkwall. "But you may make amends by working for the good of mankind in the future."

"I swear that I will, milady," answered Maitland.

A smile touched Lady Kirkwall's lips. Releasing a breath, she closed her eyes.

A moment later, she was gone.

"Gibbs! Bowers!" called Horatio above the noise of the steam engine. "Bring up the two-pounder and bolt it into the brass mount on the bow!"

Wrexford leaned over the larboard railing and squinted through the swirls of vapor and ash spewing from the smokestack. The hull of the boat was cutting through the currents of the incoming tide at a fast clip, throwing up splashes of foam-flecked water.

Was he merely imagining it, or was there really a pale cloud of steam visible up ahead, indicating that they were indeed gaining ground on Jarvis's vessel?

"Milord!"

The earl turned to see Horatio turn the wheel over to one of his men and come to join him.

"We're catching up to them, sir."

"Are we?" Wrexford still couldn't make out any distinct shape through the haze.

Horatio grinned. "See for yourself." He clicked open his spyglass and passed it over.

Once the earl steadied the instrument and rotated the lenses, the stern and the smokestack of a steamboat up ahead sharpened into clear focus. He watched for another moment, taking satisfaction in seeing it grow slightly bigger, then snapped the spyglass shut.

"Jarvis is in the rear of the boat, manning the tiller, and his two cohorts are stoking the boiler," said Horatio. "But we are faster. Another quarter hour and we'll be in range."

"In range for what?"

"Blowing his propeller to kingdom come," answered the midshipman. "Colonel Jarvis doesn't know it, but Mr. Tilden and I decided to experiment with mounting a small bow chaser on our boat, as it might prove very useful when patrolling the river for pirates and thieves."

"Clever," said Wrexford.

In answer, Horatio turned on his heel. "Gunners!" he bellowed. "To the bow with the powder and shot." To the earl, he added, "I've had my men practicing their marksmanship. And they know just where to aim in order to disable the colonel's boat."

Wrexford fell in step behind the burly sailors carrying the bags of gunpowder and small cannonballs, while Horatio gathered a half dozen sailors from the starboard side and sent them to fetch muskets from the weapons box. Their quarry was now easily visible with the naked eye.

Closer, closer. He moved to the railing, tapping his palms impatiently against the varnished oak.

"We'll get him, milord," said the midshipman as he came to stand beside the earl. "My men are crack shots."

"I don't want him dead, Mr. Porter. I intend to take him alive."

"That may not be possible— "

"Just get me close. I'll take care of the rest."

"Sir!" called one of the gun crew. "We're in range."

Horatio hurried to take charge of the attack on the enemy. "Aim low at the stern, lads. We're looking to disable the boat, not destroy it." A pause. "We've put too much blood, sweat, and toil into crafting the hull and engine to let that miserable piece of filth wreck them."

A cheer went up from the sailors around them.

"Jarvis isn't liked by the men," confided Horatio. "He's a bully and a tyrant." He took a moment to gauge the wind. "Elevate the barrel another two degrees and then fire at will, Gibbs."

In the next instant sparks exploded from the brass snout of the bow chaser, followed by a crackling roar. The shot was a trifle short, the cannonball skipping over the water to land just behind the fleeing steamboat.

"That'll be a kick up his arse," shouted one of the sailors, drawing a chorus of laughter.

"Concentrate on the task at hand, lads," called Horatio. "Make the next one count."

But before they could reload and fire again, a sudden lick of flames shot up from the other boat, followed by a dull boom.

"Damnation," muttered Horatio. "I was afraid that might happen."

"What?" demanded Wrexford, as black smoke began to cloud the boat.

"Jarvis isn't experienced in actually operating a steamboat. He likely had his henchmen feed excess fuel into the boiler, thinking the hotter, the better. But too much pressure causes the boiler door to blow off its hinges," explained the midshipman. "Those two varlets will have been killed by the blast . . ."

With the other craft now helplessly disabled, their steamboat was fast approaching it. Wrexford saw Jarvis look back at them, then climb up on the stern and dive into the water.

"Sir, I'm afraid we have no choice but to shoot the traitor," said Horatio, "unless you wish to let him get away."

Wrexford was already peeling off his coat. "Keep your boat close, and be ready to throw me a rope."

"But milord—"

The rest of the midshipman's words were drowned by the sound of rushing water in his ears. The river was cold as the devil's heart, and for an instant the earl's limbs went numb with the shock of it.

But the fire of righteous resolve melted the ice. An excellent swimmer, Wrexford rose to the surface and, on spotting Jarvis thrashing toward shore, drew a deep breath and dove back under the waves.

It was midnight-dark beneath the surface, the tidal flow stirring a dangerous vortex of crosscurrents that could easily draw a man down to his death. Fighting their pull, the earl kicked like a dolphin through the underwater gloom, relentlessly pursuing the colonel. Coming up for air, he found he was nearly within arm's reach.

Jarvis snarled an oath on seeing him and redoubled his efforts to swim to shore. But the cold and the roughness of the river were fast draining his strength.

Wrexford laughed. "There's no escaping me."

Two swift strokes brought him abreast of the colonel, and with a grunt of savage satisfaction, he grabbed the man by the scruff of his coat. Kicking, punching, Jarvis tried to break free, but the earl's fist was like an iron vise, holding him prisoner.

Fear rippled across Jarvis's face as a wave slammed into him. Sputtering, he ducked under the swirling foam, emerging a moment later with a knife in his hand.

Anticipating the attack, Wrexford was ready for the strike of steel. Twisting away from the first strike, he grabbed Jarvis's wrist.

And the fight turned into a battle of wills as the waves buffeted their bodies. Jarvis was strong, but mere muscle was no match for Wrexford's unforgiving fury. He squeezed harder, feeling the other man's bones shudder beneath his grip.

With a feral scream, Jarvis slumped, his fingers spasming and releasing the knife. He tried to lash out a punch with his other hand, but Wrexford sucked in a breath and dove, dragging the colonel down with him.

One, two, three . . .

Jarvis was now thrashing in blind panic. The earl could feel the visceral fear pumping through the other man's veins—the knowledge that death was within spitting distance and all but certain to reach out and squeeze the life from his heart.

This is for you, Tommy, and for Neville Greeley, thought Wrexford. *And for all the other brave men who died because of Jarvis's lust for money*. However, he wasn't about to let the colonel escape so lightly.

A quick death was too good for him. Wrexford intended for him to go through a public trial and have his perfidy known to the world. Then, when the sentence of death for treason was handed down, he would take quiet satisfaction from watching Jarvis be taken to the gallows and hung by the neck until he was dead.

Faber est suae quisque fortunae. As one of Charlotte's Latin aphorisms said, *Every man is the artisan of his own fortune.*

The earl kept his prisoner submerged until all the fight died in his limbs. With a hard kick, he shot to the surface and drew in a gulp of air. "Mr. Porter," he shouted. "Throw me a line!"

A thick manila rope splashed down beside him. After looping it beneath Jarvis's armpits and tying a knot, he grabbed hold of the tail and gave a tug.

"Haul us in!"

A bevy of sailors was waiting to lift them into the steamboat. Half drowned, Jarvis lay sprawled on the floorboards, retching and wheezing for breath. "B-By God, I'll have you court-martialed for this and sentenced to five hundred lashes, you miserable little boy," he screamed at Horatio.

"Don't call me *boy*." The midshipman squared his shoulders, the sunlight winking off the polished brass buttons of his tunic. "I am an officer in His Majesty's Royal Navy, and you are a slithering muckworm who will soon be standing trial for a litany of crimes, including the betrayal of his country."

Horatio turned to his crew. "Clap him in irons, Bowers."

"With pleasure, sir!" The sailor fastened the manacles on Jarvis's wrists and stepped back, adding a kick that bloodied the miscreant's nose.

"Avast there," ordered Horatio. "The Royal Navy does not dishonor itself by abusing its prisoners." He met the colonel's malevolent glare with an unflinching stare. "However, I shall order an extra tot of rum for every man here at supper tonight so that we may raise a toast to the prospect of seeing this spawn of Satan hanging by his neck from the gallows."

A raucous chorus of cheers rose up from the men.

Sputtering invectives, Jarvis turned his head to snarl at the earl. "I shall see you in Hell, Wrexford."

"Perhaps," he responded. "But in the meantime, do keep my

seat warm for me." A flash of teeth. "I don't intend on joining you anytime soon."

More cursing, which fell on deaf ears. Wrexford turned away, feeling a strange mixture of emotions. The pain of personal grief was no less sharp—he knew it would be lodged in his heart for the rest of his days. But having brought the killers of his brother and Greeley to justice brought some measure of solace.

Far more than an act of revenge would have achieved.

I have Charlotte to thank for that, he reflected. A smile ghosted over his lips. Somehow, she made him a better man than he had ever thought possible.

He lifted his face to the freshening breeze and dancing sunlight. "Turn your boat around once you've finished fixing the tow ropes to the disabled prototype, Mr. Porter, and let us head for home port."

CHAPTER 32

Sunlight had warmed the early morning mist from the air. Birdsong twined through the plantings, the only sounds stirring through the townhouse gardens as no breeze had yet begun to stir the foliage from slumber.

"You should be sleeping." Wrexford came up behind Charlotte and touched her shoulder as she stood with her palms pressed against the windowpanes, gazing out at the oasis of tranquility.

"So should you." She turned and drew him close.

The scent of her—verbena edged with some earthier fragrance that he could only describe as essence of Charlotte—teased at his nostrils, making his pulse quicken.

"I feel more rested than I have in ages," he replied, curling a strand of her hair around his fingers.

"It is truly over?" she asked.

"It is, my love," answered Wrexford. "The devils are no longer a threat to us or our loved ones."

Charlotte smiled, but a question seemed to ripple in the depths of her gaze. "As to that—"

But before she could continue, a burst of exuberant laughter, punctuated by the rattle of china, echoed through the corridor.

"It seems that the Weasels and Peregrine are bringing Alison a cup of hot chocolate to begin the day," she said after hearing the door to one of the guest bedchambers bang open and shut. The boys had heartily approved of the decision that Alison should spend the night at Berkeley Square to ensure that she had recovered from her grueling ordeal.

"It's very sweet how protective they have been. They have barely let Alison out of their sight." Charlotte made a wry face. "Though I daresay that they are hoping to distract us from asking some uncomfortable questions about the sword cane."

"Indeed, all four of them have answering to do," said Wrexford. Hearing McClellan call a warning that the hour set for the gala breakfast was fast approaching, he added, "We had better dress and proceed downstairs." There were a number of explanations to be made in order to bring closure to an evil whose tentacles had proved frighteningly long. "The others will be arriving shortly."

"Hmmph . . ." Alison leaned back in her chair as McClellan and Charlotte brought over more savory selections from the chafing dishes on the breakfast-room sideboard and placed them in front of her. "Perhaps I should consider getting abducted more often."

"Heaven forfend," replied Charlotte, thinking of all the other dangers that had nearly ensnared them in a lethal web of lies and deceptions. "We were prodigiously lucky to have come through this investigation unscathed."

She looked around the table at their close-knit circle of family and friends—alas, Horatio's naval duties had prevented him from being present—who were finally all assembled in one place . . . and felt the prickle of tears. The previous day and evening had passed in a frenzy of activity. Dealing with the authorities, taking on the somber task of seeing to the mortal remains of Taviot and his sister. . . .

And most of all, ensuring that the dowager and all their loved ones were truly safe.

"But Lady Luck is notoriously fickle," she added, her voice tight with emotion.

"Auch, this is the time for a toast, not tears, lassie," said Henning, breaking the serious moment with a rusty chuckle. "It is not pretty at times, but somehow we get the job done." He raised his glass—filled with Scottish malt despite the early hour—and gave it a swirl, setting off flickers of golden sparks. "To Good always kicking Evil in the arse."

"A rather crass way of phrasing it," drawled Wrexford. "But I think we all agree with the sentiment."

The clink of crystal punctuated his words.

"And besides, it is my understanding that there is further cause for celebration." He eyed Sheffield. "As I recall, you and Cordelia made a recent promise . . . so I believe you have an announcement to make to Alison."

The dowager put down her fork and regarded their friend with an owlish stare.

"Er . . . umm . . ." Sheffield cleared his throat. "Yes, well, seeing as everyone is gathered here, Cordelia and I thought we would add to the festivities by informing all of you that we have set a date for our nuptials."

As he named the day, a pretty shade of pink colored Cordelia's cheeks.

"In addition, I'm happy to announce that we now possess a country estate, allowing us to begin setting down real roots."

Seeing Charlotte's surprise, Sheffield smiled. "Last night I went to inform my father of the wedding. You all know how fraught our relationship has been, so when he started questioning me about how I was going to support a wife, I was so damnably tired of being treated like a wastrel that I revealed what Cordelia and I really do."

A shrug. "Not only that, I gave him a lecture about the absurdity of not allowing members of the aristocracy to run a business and proceeded to explain in excruciating detail how the future will belong to those who have the freedom to become entrepreneurs."

Sheffield's expression turned to one of bemusement. "I assumed he was going to toss me out on my arse, as usual—but to my astonishment, he responded by saying how impressed he was by my pluck and ingenuity."

His smile stretched wider. "And then he promptly gifted me with one of his minor estates near Bristol, the port which handles much of our shipping to America." He shook his head. "Who would have guessed?"

Fathers and sons, thought Charlotte wryly, slanting a sidelong glance at Wrexford. Families were indeed complicated.

"Hmmph," said Alison after all the clapping and cries of congratulations had died away. "That date doesn't leave me much time to organize the wedding." She tapped her fingertips together as she pondered the challenge. "But with a bit more luck and the help of the Weasels, I think it can be done."

"And help from Harper," added Hawk. "It's now a family tradition that he leads the procession down the aisle."

The hound, who was lying beneath the sideboard in case anyone dropped any bits of ham, opened one eye and thumped his tail before falling back to sleep.

Once the laughter died away, Charlotte decided to address the less happy topic that was weighing on her mind before the hilarity got out of hand.

"It's all very well to shrug off the horrors of this investigation now that everything has ended well," she began. "But I fear we are in danger of taking luck for granted."

Her gaze moved to Alison.

The dowager crumbled a piece of the sultana muffin between her fingers. "I expect you are now about to ring a peal over my head."

"I am," confirmed Charlotte. "What madness made you take the horribly dangerous risk of attempting to cross steel with a desperate villain? You could have been . . ." A sudden sob welled up in her throat, forcing her to pause.

A spark of remorse glimmered behind the lenses of Alison's spectacles. "It actually wasn't quite as mad as you think. I had been practicing—"

"Practicing?" interjected Wrexford.

Out of the corner of her eye, Charlotte saw the three boys exchange guilty glances.

Sheffield coughed, trying to smother a laugh. "Sorry," he apologized. "I know it's not remotely funny. But dash it all, you have to admit, it was quite a sight to see Alison wielding her blade with the consummate skill of a Death's Head Hussar."

"Indeed." Wrexford raised a brow at the boys. "One wonders precisely how she came to hone such skills."

"Don't blame the Weasels and Peregrine," said the dowager. "It occurred to me that it might be useful if I knew how to defend myself—"

"Useful for what?" interrupted Charlotte.

"Sleuthing," answered Alison without batting an eye. "You have to admit that we seem to be making a habit of it."

Honesty compelled her to remain silent.

"My late husband possessed a very handsome sword cane, and when I broached the idea to the boys about learning a few basic tricks to fend off an attack—"

"We thought it an excellent idea," finished Raven. "So we taught Aunt Alison a few fencing moves." He lifted his chin. "Haven't you often said that a lady ought to know how to defend herself?"

Charlotte heaved an inward sigh, ruing the boy's batlike hearing.

"Aunt Alison is stronger and more agile than you might think," added Hawk.

"Indeed, we all think of Alison as invincible, sweeting," replied Charlotte. She looked around, letting the words assume a certain gravitas. "But had her captor been Jarvis, rather than Taviot, things might have turned out differently."

"I am aware of that," said the dowager softly. She let out a sigh as she looked down at her hands, as if realizing how frail they looked upon the smoke-blue silk. "Charlotte is right to remind all of us that hubris is dangerous."

"Pride goeth before destruction, and a haughty spirit before a fall," intoned Henning.

"Ye gods, Baz, since when have you started spouting proverbs from the Bible?" drawled Wrexford.

Rather than respond with his usual sarcasm, the surgeon looked thoughtful. "As nearly all the seven deadly sins were involved in this investigation, it seemed appropriate. Pride, greed, lust, envy, gluttony for power—the three Taviot siblings lie dead because of them. As for Jarvis, his wickedness was of truly biblical proportions."

He took a swallow of whisky. "As Charlotte said, we were lucky."

It was Alison who broke the ensuing pensive silence with a muffled *tap-tap* of her cane—one that didn't contain a lethal weapon. "Now that we have all been cautioned about avoiding the danger of hubris, I say we put aside talk of darkness for brighter thoughts."

"Indeed." Charlotte rose and hurried to ring the silver bell on the sideboard. "Let us count our blessings, for we have much to celebrate."

The door flew open, and one of the footmen rolled in a trolley shimmering with crystal goblets filled with sparkling champagne from the adjoining salon. She plucked up a glass and raised it to catch the sunlight. "To Cordelia and Kit. And the myriad good things that lie ahead for them—and all of us."

In the blink of an eye, the room was fizzing with good cheer. *Laughter, hugs, good-natured teasing*—Charlotte looked around, the tears beading her lashes now ones of joy rather than fear.

Wrexford came up beside her and smiled. Their fingers twined together in a quick embrace, the fleeting touch far more eloquent than any words.

A discreet cough from Riche cut through the giggling of the boys as McClellan permitted them each to have a half glass of champagne. "Milord and milady, Mr. Griffin is here in the corridor. Shall I—"

"By all means, show him in," said Wrexford. To Charlotte, he added, "I thought it only right that we invite him to partake in the festivities."

"I'm glad that you did." Charlotte smiled and hurried to greet the Runner.

Her heartfelt hug seemed to fluster him. "Forgive me," he said. "I seem to be interrupting a private gathering."

"Not at all. We wanted you to share in the celebration. Your efforts were invaluable in helping to ensure that justice prevailed in this investigation," she responded. "Though I fear that you may not always approve of our unorthodox methods."

"If that were true, it would be very ungentlemanly of me to say so," said the Runner, a twinkle lighting his eyes.

"Besides, we make him smell like roses to his superiors," said Wrexford, handing Griffin a goblet of champagne.

The Runner chuckled. "The scent of success is all very well, milord. But it pains me that we didn't enjoy nearly enough suppers together during our quest to solve this particular tangle of crimes."

"I am more than making it up by serving you a very expensive champagne," responded Wrexford. His expression then turned serious. "I hope that in addition to availing yourself of my food and drink, you have also come here to tell us that Jarvis is locked up in a cell at Newgate."

"I have, milord." Griffin took an appreciative sip of the wine. "And just so you know, I've been assured by the highest authorities that the dastard won't be leaving his cell until the day that he makes his final walk to the gallows."

Wrexford gave a gruff nod, indicating that he understood the oblique message from Grentham and the government that the traitorous eel wouldn't wriggle out of paying the ultimate price for his crimes.

"So, justice has been done," finished the Runner. "I hope you feel some measure of . . ." He paused, searching for the right word. "Resolution, perhaps?"

The earl considered the question. "A malignant force has been excised from society. That is a good thing."

"I still do not quite understand all the circumstances that brought Taviot and his sister to such an ugly end," mused Griffin.

"It seems the family was cursed with bad blood," offered Charlotte. "Though he covered his tracks well, Taviot turned out to be guilty of helping Jarvis betray Britain. As for Lady Kirkwall, she made a series of wrong choices. There is no need to regale you with all the sordid details. I have some sympathy for her, but she was not an innocent victim of Fate."

Griffin took a moment to consider what he had just heard. "And what of Maitland? Surely he was in league with the evildoers."

"Actually, he wasn't," answered Wrexford. "He joined the consortium fully believing that he could achieve greatness. When the experiments failed to produce the desired results, he, like all too many men of science, kept telling himself that he was oh-so-close—that the next try would bring the momentous breakthrough."

"Henry Maudslay has, in fact, offered Maitland a position at his research laboratory once it is rebuilt," added Charlotte. "His genius is real, and he can now work with a man of conscience who cares about creating real progress rather than a fraudulent company intent on bilking its investors of their money."

Griffin downed the last swallow of his champagne. "Since we are parsing through Good and Evil, what about that havey-cavey Russian? Some of my sources were hinting that he was up to no good."

"We are quite certain that Mr. Kurlansky is innocent of any skullduggery." Charlotte pursed her lips in a rueful smile. "At least in this particular investigation."

"Speaking of Good," said Wrexford, "I've also invited von Münch to come by. Without his help—"

"As to that, milord . . ." The Runner cleared his throat with an uncomfortable cough. "I was just going to broach the subject of von Münch—"

"Why?" demanded the earl.

Griffin gave a wry grimace. "Because in the course of our interactions during the investigations, you had mentioned your misgivings about his motives. And so I took it upon myself to make some inquiries about him."

"But surely . . ." Charlotte paused, feeling a bit shaken to think that her instincts about the librarian might have been all wrong. "B-But surely you're not going to tell us we misjudged him." She shook her head. "I'm sorry, but I just can't accept that. Von Münch proved his mettle and his loyalty—"

"Actually *von Münch* didn't, milady," interrupted the Runner. Catching Wrexford's scowl, he hastened to add, "The *real*

Herr von Münch, librarian to King Frederick of Württemberg, is at present ensconced in his quarters at the Ludwigsburg Palace, working quietly on his biography of the current king. Given his age and infirmities—he's close to eighty and suffering from weak lungs—he never travels these days, especially abroad."

"You are sure of this—" began Wrexford, then expelled a sharp sigh. "My apologies, Griffin. Of course you are." A frown. "Which raises two questions—who the devil is the man calling himself von Münch? And what were his motives for the ruse?"

"I'm afraid that I don't have answers for either of those questions, milord." Griffin sighed. "Once you expressed your suspicions, I made some discreet inquiries among the diplomatic delegation from Württemberg and established that the king's librarian did not make the journey to Britain. And once I learned of the man's age, I was sure that the fellow who called himself von Münch was a fraud."

The Runner paused for breath. "So I set out to learn where he was lodging—and one of my associates brought me the address last night. However, when I went to apprehend him for questioning, I discovered the rooms were empty. Further search led me to the nearby livery stable, whose head ostler confirmed that the man he knew as von Münch had appeared an hour earlier with a full set of saddle bags and ridden away in what looked to be great haste." Griffin looked to Wrexford with an apologetic shrug. "I'm sorry, milord, but it does seem that you were right to smell a rat."

"Perhaps not a rat," mused Charlotte. "Even with these revelations I find it hard to believe the fellow who was masquerading as von Münch is evil."

"Perhaps he's just amoral," muttered the earl. "Bloody hell, perhaps he's one of Grentham's operatives. Or perhaps he works for Kurlansky. Either of those two master manipulators might have had their own unfathomable reasons for dispatching him to become part of our inner circle."

Charlotte couldn't think of any reasonable retort. "We can speculate all we want, but the truth is, we may never know his real identity, or his real purpose."

"Unless," intoned Wrexford, "our paths cross again."

McClellan looked into the breakfast room from the adjoining side salon and gave an impatient wave. "Chin-wagging can wait until later. You must all come partake of the confections I've made to celebrate the upcoming nuptials. There are cream pastries and my special Dundee cakes to go along with more champagne."

Griffin gladly accepted the invitation, but Charlotte held Wrexford back.

"A moment, Wrex." The sounds of celebration in the salon were already growing boisterous, but Charlotte was aware only of the whispery thud of two hearts beating as one as she pulled him close. "Let us put aside the question of von Münch. What matters is us." Her arms tightened. "A-Are you truly at peace?"

"I have achieved all that I could hope for," he answered.

"Is that enough?" she asked.

"Yes." Wrexford brushed a kiss to her lips. "It is. The pain of the past will never die. But I have you and my family, and our ever-growing circle of friends, so the future promises more happiness than any man deserves."

Charlotte tightened her hold. "And to begin that future, I swear that we are going to have a prolonged stay at our country estate after we host Cordelia and Kit's wedding. Think of it . . ." A sigh of longing. "An interlude of uninterrupted peace and quiet."

"*Deo volente*," quipped Wrexford. *God willing*.

She laughed at the Latin phrase. "Let us make a pact. No drama, no dead bodies. Just us and our family."

The earl's mouth twitched. "Be careful what you wish for."

"We'll deal with the future when it comes," replied Charlotte. The laughter in the other room was growing louder. "But for now, I say we simply savor the present moment."

A small sound—it may or may not have been a laugh—rumbled in Wrexford's throat. "And offer up a plea to Eris, the Greek goddess of Chaos, that no more mysterious friends or villains appear from nowhere to turn our peace and quiet upside down."

AUTHOR'S NOTE

Those of you familiar with my Wrexford & Sloane series know that at the heart of each book's plot lies a scientific innovation of the Regency era, which is generally defined as 1800–1838. Indeed, historians consider this time period to be the birth of the modern world because of the fundamental upheavals in thinking that were taking place in every aspect of society, especially science and technology.

However, in this book I've chosen to give a slight twist to my usual formula. As I've researched a number of specific developments to feature in my plots—a computing engine that was a precursor to the modern computer, electricity in the form of early voltaic batteries and multi-shot pistols, to name a few—I've been fascinated by how many failures, dead ends and clever prototypes that *almost* work result before the "ah-ha" moment when a breakthrough takes place. This pattern—innovation rarely moves in a straight line—is, of course, not unique to the Regency and remains common to this day.

So I decided to play with the idea of an innovative and technologically sound invention that was actually under development at the time in which this story is set—a propeller-based propulsion system for oceangoing ships—but which then proved unworkable until further scientific progress was made.

Generally speaking, a propeller is a mechanical device with two or more blades that turns and pushes or pulls an object in one direction by forcing a mass of water or air in the opposite direction. (Those of you who took basic physics will perhaps recognize this as Newton's Third Law of Motion—action and reaction.) Elements of the propeller concept have been understood for centuries. In 220 BC, Archimedes, the ancient Greek polymath, designed a turning screw to lift water from one level to another. (I will interject here that screws and propellers work on the same physical principle of converting rotational motion into linear force.) In the early 1500s, perhaps inspired by the genius of Archimedes, Leonardo da Vinci (more on da Vinci in a moment) sketched a "helicopter" powered by what we call today a screw propeller.

In 1738, the renowned Swiss mathematician Daniel Bernoulli deduced the basic principle underlying how the shape of propeller blades rotating through water or air currents create a pressure differential between the two surfaces of each blade, which produces the force pushing the fluid in one direction, and thereby creates thrust in the opposite direction. In 1752, Leonhard Euler, another Swiss mathematician who is considered one of the all-time greats in the field (more on illustrious Swiss individuals to follow) took Bernoulli's insight and derived the fundamental mathematical equation—known as Bernoulli's Equation—in the form used today.

Again, the physics geeks reading this will understand that Bernoulli's principle can be derived from Newton's Second Law of Motion—force equals mass times acceleration. For those of you who are turning green around the gills, I promise there will be no more Newton or physics lessons!

By the Regency era, a few prototype boats using propellers powered by steam engines were chugging along the canals of Britain. But the real challenge—a revolutionary innovation that would truly change the world—was inventing a marine propulsion system that could power ships across vast oceans. The engineers of the era understood in theory how it could be done. However, in 1814, the year in which this story is set, the technology of the era just wasn't yet capable of creating a behemoth engine with enough power and efficiency to move a large ship through rough seas. More work was also needed on the appropriate design of propeller blades.

As the story suggests, some of the villains in this story were genuinely convinced that given more time and money their ideas would actually be made to work. Others in the consortium were merely charlatans looking to make a huge profit from the initial investors before the project failed. Again it's a pattern that continues to this day.

It took years to make the final breakthrough in propeller propulsion. It wasn't until 1838 that a consortium led by Isambard Kingdom Brunel launched the *SS Grand Western*, a paddle-wheel steamship, and initiated regular transatlantic service using steam engines made by Henry Maudslay and his partners. (Brunel's insight was that larger-hulled ships were actually more fuel efficient—I will spare you the mathematical explanation for why!)

However, even at the time of this story it was clear that paddle wheels had inherent flaws for ocean travel as they performed best in shallow depths. Innovators understood the future lay with propellers, and there was an explosion of patents for propellers from 1816 through 1846 as inventors worked furiously to design the optimum combinations of blade curves and pitch, as well as better engine efficiency.

During the 1830s, both John Ericsson and Francis Pettit Smith were refining prototypes of screw propellers. In 1839, Pettit launched the *SS Archimedes*—note the nod to its scientific heritage—which was the world's first steamship powered by a screw propeller. (Ericsson went on to build *SS Princeton* for the U.S. Navy in 1843, the first-ever warship to use the same technology.) Inspired by the design of *SS Archimedes*, Brunel launched SS *Great Britain* in 1845, an iron-hulled giant that was the first screw-propeller steamship to cross the Atlantic. Its voyage marked the new age of maritime travel that the competing consortiums in this book were trying to achieve, one that revolutionized world trade and naval military power.

And now, enough on oceangoing marine propulsion history!

Moving on to some of the specific details in my story . . . the da Vinci manuscript stolen from the Merton Library is purely fictional, but the drawing of the "helicopter" described on one of its pages is based on the actual da Vinci drawing in his workbooks. And as von Münch notes to Charlotte, da Vinci invented many innovative mechanical devices, and his notebooks also show a lifelong interest in water currents and turbulence.

Henry Maudslay was a leading engineer in Regency England, and as described in these pages, his precision lathes helped the Industrial Revolution kick into high gear. He did turn his skills to marine steam engines, and became a leader in the technology. William Hedley, the inventor of "Puffing Billy," is also a real person, as is David Bushnell, the Yale student who invented a propeller-driven submarine used to attack a British warship in 1776. The other inventors and military men in the story are the creation of my own imagination.

Lord Taviot and his evil consortium are also fictional, but there was much real-life skullduggery going on as companies were forming to take advantage of new business opportunities. And as Sheffield points out in the story, the resulting wealth was going to a new class of entrepreneurs, not the aristocracy, who in many cases were done in by their traditional view that gentlemen didn't sully their hands in trade. The aristocracy was also poorly positioned to take advantage of investment opportunities because their wealth was tied up in land ownership, allowing for little liquid capital and thus making it hard to compete with the rising mercantile class and their superior cash flow. Together, these two factors would plunge many of the old families into financial ruin by the end of the century.

On a purely personal note, I had a little fun with the von Münch character. Researching background material for the Peninsular War and potential plot twists for the betrayal that led to the death of Wrexford's brother led me to read about King Frederick I of Württemberg. He did, in fact, side with the French during much of the Napoleonic wars, even though his father-in-law was King George III. As described, he was "Fickle Freddie," as he switched alliances in 1813 and sided with Britain and its allies.

But even more interesting for me was discovering that my Swiss maternal great-great-great-great grandfather (I may be off a "great" or two), Ernst Joseph von Münch, was librarian to the King of Württemberg! I knew from family history that Ernst was a well-respected political philosopher and professor of religious history, but this discovery was such fun. Now, in the spirit of full disclosure, he was librarian to Frederick's son, King William I, who was a much more enlightened monarch than his father. But I decided to take artistic liberty and make him a character in this book. (And in homage to my Swiss grandfather—also named Ernst—who won many medals and trophies for marksmanship, I made my fictional von Münch more than just a bookish scholar!)

On that note, I will put down my pen. I hope you've enjoyed these glimpses into the backstories of the book.

—Andrea Penrose

Don't miss the next in Andrea Penrose's enthralling Wrexford & Sloane mystery series

MURDER AT KING'S CROSSING

When the murder of a scientific genius on the verge of a momentous discovery upsets the wedding of their dear friends, Wrexford and Charlotte must risk all they hold dear to deconstruct a sinister conspiracy . . .

Celebration is in the air at Wrexford and Charlotte's country estate as they host the nuptials of their friends Christopher Sheffield and Lady Cordelia Mansfield. But on the afternoon of the wedding, the festivities are interrupted when the local authorities arrive with news that a murdered man has been discovered at the bridge over King's Crossing, his only identification an invitation to the wedding. Lady Cordelia is horrified when the victim is identified as Jasper Milton, her childhood friend and a brilliant engineer who is rumored to have discovered a revolutionary technological innovation in bridge design. That he had the invitation meant for her cousin Oliver, who never showed up for the wedding, stirs a number of unsettling questions.

Both men were involved in the Revolutions-Per-Minute Society, a scientific group dedicated to making radical improvements in the speed and cost of transportation throughout Britain. Is someone plotting to steal Milton's designs? And why has her cousin disappeared?

Wrexford and Charlotte were looking forward to spending a peaceful interlude in the country, but when Lady Cordelia resolves to solve the mystery, they—along with the Weasels and their unconventional inner circle of friends—offer their help. The investigation turns tangled and soon all of them are caught up in a treacherous web of greed, ambition, and dangerous secrets. And when the trail takes a shocking turn, Wrexford and Charlotte must decide what risks they are willing to take with their family in order to bring the villains to justice . . .

Read on for a preview . . .

PROLOGUE

"Damnation!" Hair spiking up in disarray, spectacles sliding down the slope of his beaky nose, the man glanced up from the work papers strewn across his desk and stared at the clock with a look of dawning horror. "What pernicious quirk of the cosmos has made six hours fly by in the space of one?"

It was, of course, an absurd question. He of all people knew that the laws of the universe were governed by a mathematical precision. *That was the beauty of the world and how it worked.* It was astounding how often one could understand so many elemental scientific truths if only one was skilled enough with numbers to figure out the complex equations that revealed the hidden secrets.

"Equations that can be put to practical use in bettering the lives of countless people," he whispered, his gaze returning for a moment to his scribblings.

But for now, the grand scheme of abstract problem-solving would have to wait. He was late—horribly late—for a very important engagement.

"I tend to lose myself in all the possibilities when I'm caught up in the excitement of discovery, but there is still time . . ."

The man gave a rueful grimace at the piece of paper pinned above his work table. The reminder, written in giant, bold-faced letters by his good friend, stared back in stern reproach.

"But even though the hour at which I should have departed has long since passed, if I ride hard through the night and take the shortcut of North Abbey Road to King's Crossing, I can make it to the junction of the Cambridgeshire Turnpike before dawn . . ."

He was already stuffing a notebook—he called it his scribbling book—into his coat and then added the handful of papers he'd been working on, which he placed into an oilskin portfolio, and which he then carefully slipped into the leather satchel lying beside the valise holding his clothing for the trip. "Which means that I can still arrive at close to the appointed time."

A smaller packet lay on his blotter. The man hesitated.

Choices, choices.

A recent unsettling incident had made him cautious. He knew that his fellow members of the Revolutions-Per-Minute Society—all fine fellows but limited in their imagination—were curious about his latest innovations. But they wouldn't comprehend his reasoning, even if he took the trouble to explain. Only Hapatia, his childhood comrade-in-exploration, understood that transcending the ordinary required a willingness to be bold, no matter the consequences. He couldn't wait to pay her a visit and explain all about his new calculations and what he intended to do with them.

But in the meantime . . .

The ticking of the mantel clock warned that there was no time left dithering. He squeezed his eyes shut and forced himself to focus. And then, as often happened when he put his mind to a conundrum, the solution flashed into his head with startling clarity.

Smiling, he picked up the packet and threw it into the banked coals of his tiny hearth, then picked up the poker and stirred up flames, watching in satisfaction as the packet was quickly reduced to ashes.

The man turned back to his work table for one last look. A good thing, for he spotted a sheet of folded stationery half hidden among his pens. "Thank God that I didn't forget this," he said, and shoved it in his pocket.

"Now, I *must* be off."

Grabbing up his bags, he hurried to the livery stable where he kept his horse and was soon galloping out of town in a cloud of dust.

At first luck was with him. But the wind soon kicked up, fitful gusts bringing a damp chill to the late-summer evening. The man looked up and muttered an oath. Iron-gray storm clouds were blowing in from the west, causing the light to fade quicker than he expected. A prick of his spurs urged his horse onward, hoping to outrace the rain. Though the North Abbey Road would shorten his journey considerably, it was a miserable excuse of a thoroughfare, unfit for man or beast when the weather turned foul.

As for the rickety wooden structure spanning the river gorge at King's Crossing . . .

"Bloody hell." Wincing in dismay as the first drops of rain spattered against his hat, he tugged his oilskin cloak from his saddlebags and put it on, hoping for the best.

But darkness soon swallowed the road, forcing him to slow his horse to a walk. Thunder rumbled, and before the echo died away the skies shuddered and suddenly released a torrential downpour. Shrieking like banshees, the accompanying high winds forced him to shelter for a time within a copse of pine trees.

The minutes ticked by with maddening slowness.

When at last the storm abated, allowing him to continue, he found the ruts in the road were growing deeper and deeper as water sluiced through the mud, creating a helter-pelter swirling of pebbles and rocks.

His horse stumbled as the footing turned treacherous. Swinging down from the saddle, the man grasped the reins and led the way up the winding road, anger making his blood boil. He had warned the authorities on numerous occasions that neglect of the region's roadways was not only foolhardy but short-sighted. The world was changing, and forward-thinking men understood the key to progress was—

A flicker of moonlight interrupted his thoughts.

"Thank heavens," muttered the man, gazing up at the night sky, where a twinkling of stars was beginning to show through the mist. The storm looked to be scudding off to the south.

As the wind settled, the roar of the river just over the crest of the hill further buoyed his spirits. Once he had traversed King's Crossing, the worst of the journey was over.

However, his optimism proved short-lived, for when he approached the primitive bridge—it was little more than rough-hewn planking laid across two massive oak-and-iron support beams that spanned the ravine—he saw that the heavy downpour and high winds had caused a section of rotting planking to fall away into the ravine, leaving a yawing hole across the entire middle of the bridge.

No, no, no—I must get across!

However, there was no choice but to turn back and give up his plans.

Still, he hesitated, eyeing the exposed section of the right-hand beam where the planking had fallen away. It looked undamaged, and while his horse could not cross such a narrow walkway, it was just wide enough for him to pick his way over the gap on foot.

Daunting, perhaps, and a trifle dangerous. But he had a great deal of experience around bridge construction sites and wasn't afraid of heights . . .

Mind made up, the man unslung his bags and tied his tired horse to a nearby tree.

"I can hire a post boy at the Three Crowns to take the long way around to fetch my mount," he muttered, "and once my business is done I can then ride on to pay a visit to Hepatia." The story of his absent-mindedness and the havoc it had wreaked with his travels would likely garner a good laugh when told in the comfort of a gracious drawing room with a glass of fine spirits in hand.

Warmed by the thought, he drew in a deep breath and shouldered his bags. Without hesitation, he stepped onto the bridge and started forward.

Unsure of the planking that still remained, he kept to the outer edge of the structure, taking care to center his steps over the beam. *Focus, focus*—he needed to keep himself balanced and alert to any shifting of the rain-soaked oak. The rush of the roiling water on the rocks below warned that the slightest mistake could prove fatal.

Halfway across, the gap forced him to walk along a width of wood that was barely more than eight inches. It looked even narrower in the gloom and swirling fog, and after swallowing hard, he forced himself to lock his gaze on the silhouette of a tree on the other side.

It felt like forever, but he finally inched across the gap and onto more solid footing. Quickening his steps, he hurried across what remained of the planking and reached the other side, his boots sinking into the mud of *terra firma* with a welcome squelch.

Despite the chill of the night, the man realized that his brow was beaded with sweat—

"Halloo?"

A tentative call suddenly floated out from the darkness up ahead.

"Is someone there?" added the disembodied voice.

"Yes, yes," answered the man, feeling unaccountably comforted that he wasn't the only one traveling on such a hellish night. "But if you are looking to cross the cursed bridge, you are out of luck—unless you are willing to risk a drop to your death." He drew in a quick breath. "The planking has fallen away in the middle."

"But you were daft enough to cross the wreckage on foot?" A blade of lanternlight cut through the fog. "I feared as much, Milton." The blade grew brighter. "Thank heavens you survived."

The man—his name was Jasper Milton—let out a relieved laugh on recognizing the voice. "I can't tell you how happy I am to see you, Axe!" Whatever the reason that had forced his friend—the moniker "Axe" was a private joke between them—to be on the road in this devil-damned weather, he was glad to encounter a kindred soul. "But how did you know I was traveling tonight?"

"Don't you remember me coming to your room early this morning?" interrupted Axe.

"I . . ." Milton scrubbed a hand over his face. "I sometimes get things jumbled in my head when I am concentrating on a scientific problem."

"I'm well aware of that. Which is why I decided to wait for you at the Three Crowns Inn, thinking that we could ride together for a while before parting ways for our final destinations. But when you didn't arrive at the time you should have— "

"I was late in leaving," explained Milton.

"Alas, why does that not surprise me?" replied Axe dryly. "When the inn got word earlier that the bridge at King's Crossing had been badly damaged in the maelstrom, I worried that you might have decided to take the shortcut in order to make up for a delay. And so I thought that I had better come look for you in case you had suffered some injury."

"Thankfully no," said Milton. "Though I'm soaked to the bone and my bags are damnably heavy." A wince. "But what are you doing here? I thought you were heading—"

"A last-minute change in plans, which appears a stroke of luck. My horse is tethered close by." Axe stepped free of the fog. "You're an idiot—you know that, don't you?" he added as he set the lantern down with a long-suffering sigh. "Here, let me give you a hand."

"You're a more thoughtful friend than I deserve—always acting as the steely support to keep me from spinning out of control! " exclaimed Milton as Axe grasped the straps of the valise and leather satchel and slipped them free of his aching shoulder. "I'm very much obliged to you."

"Since we are speaking of friendship . . ." Axe paused. "Allow me to make a last plea for you to change your mind about your plans for your latest innovation. Think of—"

"Absolutely not." Milton stiffened. "If that's why you've come to find me, you've suffered an uncomfortable trip to find me for naught. My mind is made up."

"Allow me to remind you that we made an agreement. A very lucrative one—"

"And I've explained to you why I've decided that I can no longer be part of it."

"But see here—"

"Enough!" he snapped. "You're an excellent fellow, Axe, but your vision is limited. You don't see the grand scheme or the far-reaching effects my contribution to history will have on mankind."

"You seemed to think that my vision was clear enough when I explained my idea and how we would both benefit—" began Axe, only to be cut off again.

"As I said, I've changed my mind, Axe."

"But it was *my* concept that led you to think of—"

"We both know that I am the only one who can actually make the grand scheme," said Milton.

"Because I'm not as clever as you are?"

A shrug. He shifted and made to step around his friend. "Come, I'm anxious to arrive at the Three Crowns—"

Whatever words were about to follow were swallowed in a gasp of pain as a razor-sharp length of steel cut between his ribs. An instant later it pieced his heart and all sensations dissolved into oblivion.

"I'm sorry." Axe pulled his knife free, allowing Milton's mortal remains to flop to the ground. "If you had only listened to reason, this wouldn't have been necessary." He put the valise satchel down beside the lantern, careful to avoid any puddles, and then crouched down to regard his friend's lifeless face.

"But no, you were too stubborn to see beyond your world of ideals and abstraction." Axe reached out and closed the unseeing eyes. "The Future will thank me for being more pragmatic."

Without further words, he searched the dead man's clothing and removed his purse and a notebook. A branch cracked close by, causing him to spin around in alarm. But the weak beam of light showed nothing but a ghostly swirl of fog, which quickly dissolved in a gust of wind.

He quickly rifled through the valise and satchel. A grunt of satisfaction sounded as he set the satchel aside and looped the valise over his shoulder. Then he set to work dragging the body back to the bridge. It had started to rain again—which was, he decided, all for the good as it would wash away all signs of what had just taken place. However, it took some muscle and awkward maneuvering to navigate the slippery planking. He didn't dare venture too far on the damaged bridge—just enough to ensure that his act of foul play would never come to light.

An unfortunate accident would be the verdict. The violence of the body's fall onto the rocks below would make the real cause of death impossible to discern.

The wind from the new squall swirled through the nearby trees, setting off a leafy moan from the shuddering branches. The rain stung his eyes, making it impossible to see anything more that an amorphous blur of shadows. But after another few steps the churning of the river below told him that he had gone far enough.

Axe hoisted the dead weight of the corpse upright. And then, with one last, mighty effort, he managed to lift the body and send it plummeting down into the blackness.

A clap of thunder, a flash of lightning.

Axe flung the valise into the void, and stepped back from the edge of the bridge.

"I promise you, Milton, this is all for the good," he said as and wiped his palms on the front of his coat. "You would have squandered your brilliance. While in my hands, your ideas will be developed to their fullest potential."